FIRST FATE

Book One in the Waves of Fate Series

KENDALL TALBOT

Copyright

Published 2021

First Fate

Book One in the Waves of Fate Series

© 2021 by Kendall Talbot

ISBN: 9798557295192

Except for use in any review, the reproduction or utilization of this work in whole or in part in any form by any electronic, mechanical or other means, now known or hereafter invented, including xerography, photocopying and recording, or in any information storage or retrieval system, is forbidden without the permission of the publisher.

This book is sold subject to the condition that it shall not, by way of trade or otherwise, be lent, resold, hired out or otherwise circulated without the prior consent of the publisher in any form of binding or cover other than that in which it is published and without a similar condition including this condition being imposed on the subsequent purchaser.

All rights reserved including the right of reproduction in whole or in part in any form.

This is a work of fiction. Names, characters, places, and incidents are either the product of the author's imagination or are used fictitiously, and any resemblance to actual persons, living or dead, business establishments, events, or locales is entirely coincidental.

Dear reader, the author has done extensive research regarding the consequences of an electromagnetic pulse, however, for the sake of a great story, she has also had a little fun with her creative license. Kendall hopes you love First Fate.

Kendall loves to chat with her readers. You can contact her at www.kendalltalbot.com

Edited by Lauren Clark at Creating Ink.
Proofread by Lisa Edward.
Cover design by Christian Bentulan.

v.2022.2

About the Author

Romantic Book of the Year author, Kendall Talbot, writes action-packed romantic suspense loaded with sizzling heat and intriguing mysteries set in exotic locations. She hates cheating, loves a good happily ever after, and thrives on exciting adventures with kick-ass heroines and heroes with rippling abs and broken hearts.

Kendall has sought thrills in all 46 countries she's visited. She's rappelled down freezing waterfalls, catapulted out of a white-water raft, jumped off a mountain with a man who spoke little English, and got way too close to a sixteen-foot shark.

She lives in Brisbane, Australia with her very own hero and a fluffy little dog who specializes in hijacking her writing time. When she isn't writing or reading, she's enjoying wine and cheese with her crazy friends and planning her next international escape.

She loves to hear from her readers!

Find her books and chat with her via any of the contacts below:

www.kendalltalbot.com
Email: kendall@universe.com.au

Or you can find her on any of the following channels:

Amazon
Bookbub
Goodreads

Books by Kendall Talbot

Maximum Exposure Series:

(These books are stand-alone and can be read in any order):

Extreme Limit

Deadly Twist (Finalist: Wilbur Smith Adventure Writing Prize 2021)

Zero Escape

Other Stand-Alone books:

Jagged Edge

Lost in Kakadu (Winner: Romantic Book of the year 2014)

Double Take

Waves of Fate Series

First Fate

Feral Fate

Final Fate

Treasure Hunter Series:

Treasured Secrets

Treasured Lies

Treasured Dreams

Treasured Whispers

Treasured Hopes

Treasured Tears

If you sign up to my newsletter you can help with fun things like naming characters and giving characters quirky traits and interesting jobs. You'll also get my book, Breathless Encounters which is exclusive to my newsletter followers only, for free.

Here's my newsletter signup link if you're interested:

http://www.kendalltalbot.com.au/newsletter.html

Dear reader, the author has done extensive research regarding the consequences of an electromagnetic pulse, (EMP) however, for the sake of a great story, she has also had a little fun with her creative license. Kendall hopes you love First Fate.

Kendall loves to chat with her readers. You can contact her at www.kendalltalbot.com

Edited by Lauren Clark at Creating Ink.
Proofread by Lisa Edward.
Cover design by Christian Bentulan.

Chapter One

GUNNER

Gunner McCrae scowled at the satellite image of the category-three storm cell. The damn thing had been chasing them since Rose of the Sea left Hawaii yesterday morning. If the hurricane continued to intensify like it was, the Captain would need to rethink the cruise ship's course ASAP.

Without warning, his monitor died. As did the nav system. And the radar.

"What the hell?" Gunner jolted back, scanning the bridge. Every single screen was blank. The lights were also out.

The Captain drove his hands through his thick hair. "Shit!"

Captain Nelson rarely swore. Never in front of women.

Gunner spun to his Captain, seeking clarification. Nelson's eyes were wide, darting from one screen to the next, his thick brows drilled together. "Sir?"

"The whole bridge is down." The Captain's gaze shot along blank consoles. "Everything's dead." He spoke with his usual composure. But his expression was that of trapped horror. "We're dead in the water!"

"What the hell?" Gunner held the utmost respect for Captain

Nelson. He was the father he'd never had. A pillar of strength. A man in control.

He didn't look it now. For the first time since Gunner had known him, Nelson was lacking in action. Gunner stood and strode alongside the center console, jabbing buttons, desperate for a flicker of life. Nothing. "But how?" Not even the indicator lights flared.

First Officer Cameron Sykes slapped the Electronic Chart Display joystick and shook his head. "I got nothing."

"No. No. No!" Nelson drove his hands through his hair again. "This can't be happening." When his eyes darted from Gunner to the dead equipment and back again, Gunner's neck hairs shot to attention. Nelson's expression was loaded with fear.

Second Officer Pauline Gennaro spun to the Captain, yanking off her headset. "Comms are down. I can't even get the engine room online."

"It's an electromagnetic pulse." Nelson's voice quivered, lacerated with anguish. "An EMP. It has to be."

"All the security monitors are down too." Deck Cadet Reynolds pushed back on his chair.

Sweat beaded Safety Officer Robert Hastings' forehead as he stared at the closed-circuit televisions. The monitors should display key aspects of the ship in rotation, providing multiple visuals of each deck. Every one of them was blank.

Even the exit sign over the door was out.

Darkness seeped into the bridge. It wasn't designed for blackouts. Day or night, Gunner could usually see every inch of the room. The banks of computers should be lit up like the party deck at the rear of the ship.

But with the sun hanging low on the western horizon, Gunner could barely see the length of the bridge. He turned to Nelson. The Captain's eyes were wide, his lips pale. "Are you sure it's an EMP, sir? It could be—"

"Look around." Nelson barked. He smacked his lips together as if wrestling with his words, or unable to voice what he needed to say. "The electronics are dead." His Adam's apple bobbed up and down and he cleared his throat. "Not just the computers.

Satnav. Lights. Comms." He sucked in a shaky breath. "They're all on different circuits, yet they all died in the same instant. If it was just one, maybe even two circuits, we could attribute it to mechanical or system failure. But the whole bridge . . ." Shaking his head, he glanced at his wrist. "Even my watch is dead. Yours?"

Gunner stared at the watch his wife had given him last month for their tenth wedding anniversary. The screen was blank. He blinked at it. Tapped the glass. Nothing. The hairs on his arms bristled, adding to the dread crawling up his back.

"It was an EMP. And it's happened exactly as they said it would when I was back in the navy. Everything fried in an instant." Nelson leaned his palms on the blank GPS console. He huffed out a breath. "It's the only explanation."

Scraping his thoughts together, Gunner glared at Nelson. The air in the bridge seemed to crackle, loaded with static. "But how can that be? The hull's solid metal. We're protected."

"Below decks maybe. But up here on the bridge . . ." Glancing to his left, Nelson's eyes bulged. "And look." He pointed at the exit. "The door was open . . ."

Sheryl, the middle-aged woman who'd been cleaning Rose of the Sea's bridge since its maiden voyage twenty-five years ago, was humming to herself and gliding a squeegee over the glass like it was the most important job on the cruise ship. The squeak of rubber was like nails scraping up Gunner's back.

Nelson's face washed with a gray tinge. He slowly shook his head. "We can't even sound an alarm." He jabbed the ship's horn button. The blast that usually blared from the loudspeakers could wake an entire island. Not this time. "If . . ." Nelson sucked a breath through clenched teeth. "If I'm right, the whole world is—" He clutched his chest. His eyes flared.

"Sir!" Gunner ran to his aid.

Nelson didn't just fall. He keeled sideways, smacked his head on a chair and hit the floor without so much as a hand to halt his impact.

"Sir! Captain!" Gunner dropped to his knees and turned Nelson over. His blue eyes were open. His mouth too. His protruding tongue was motionless.

Gunner pressed his finger to the clammy skin beneath Nelson's neck, praying for a pulse . . . nothing.

"Shit! Someone get the doctor." Gunner tilted the Captain's head back, opening his airway, but the crew failed to move. "Now!" He hadn't meant to yell, but the fury behind it must've shocked Miguel into action, because the ship's quartermaster gasped and raced out of the bridge like he'd been torpedoed from the room.

Gunner began compressions, pushing with all his weight behind his overlapping hands. "One, two, three." He'd only ever performed CPR on medical dummies. They'd never felt like this. This was too confronting. Too real. The Captain was a friend. They'd done their rookie cruise together nineteen years ago and they'd kept in touch ever since.

"Is he breathing?" Without pausing his compressions, Gunner stared at the Captain's lips, expecting them to move. They didn't. "Someone check. Quick. Thirteen. Fourteen. Fifteen."

Third Officer Jae-Ellen Rochford fell to her knees and leaned her ear to the Captain's lips. Easing back, she shook her head. Tears flooded her eyes.

Twenty-four. Twenty-five.

The bridge became silent—too silent. Like a funeral parlor. Gunner jolted. Something else had stopped.

The engines.

This can't be happening!

Gunner paused compressions and Jae-Ellen gave two breaths into the captain's mouth. The three remaining staff stared at him, their eyes wide, their mouths open. Shock or dismay or disbelief had them rooted to the floor.

But there was something else.

Gunner's heart thudded against his ribs. Realization slammed into him like a wrecking ball. With the Captain out of action, he was in charge of the ship.

Him . . . Gunner McCrae . . . Captain.

One. Two. Three.

He wasn't prepared. Far from it. This was his maiden voyage on Rose of the Sea.

I've only just been promoted to Staff Captain, for Christ's sake.

He worked damn hard. But it wasn't to rise up the ranks.

No. He worked hard to keep his mind off his guilt.

Sixteen. Seventeen.

He was not worthy of this captaincy. Of any captaincy.

It should be someone else. Someone smarter. Braver. Someone more trustworthy.

It should be Captain Nelson.

"Check again," he barked at Jae-Ellen.

She pushed her fingers under Nelson's chin and shook her head. "No, sir. Still no pulse."

"Where the hell's the doctor?"

"I'll go check." Safety Officer Hastings bolted past Sheryl who stood with her squeegee in one hand, her other hand over her mouth and her bulging eyes glued to Captain Nelson.

A vise clamped around Gunner's chest at what he saw over her shoulder. The sun was sinking. If an EMP strike *had* fried every electrical component on the ship, in less than one hour, they'd be in a total blackout.

Twenty-four. Twenty-five.

"Pauline, get the flashlights ready," he ordered.

She spun on her heel and raced to the back of the bridge. Sykes returned his attention to the computers. Reynolds did too.

Jae-Ellen gave Nelson two more breaths and as Gunner restarted compressions, he glanced at the consoles. Every one of them was blank, as if a giant harpoon had been shot through the entire bank of computers, obliterating their central cores.

Sykes shifted from one to the next, flicking switches, bashing the keyboards. The Global Maritime Distress and Safety System was dead. All the navigational instruments were dead. Even the switchboard was dead.

They were at the mercy of the ocean.

Sykes grunted, snapped up the binoculars and scanned the darkening sea.

Jae-Ellen checked the Captain's pulse again and shook her head.

"Come on, Stewart." Gunner spoke through clenched teeth. "Don't do this. Hang in there. We need you. *I* need you."

"Shit! Sir, the flashlights are dead." Pauline banged one on a table. "Every one of them." Shaking her head, she tossed it aside and grabbed another.

Pressing harder, Gunner restarted his compression count. "One. Two. Three." But with each push on the Captain's lifeless body, his brain shunted between the fact that he was actually trying to keep the Captain, his good friend, alive, and critical aspects of his years of disaster-management training.

Captain Nelson wasn't the only one who needed help. There were 922 passengers and 215 crew members aboard Rose of the Sea. His first responsibility was to the passengers, then the crew. Then himself.

He returned his gaze to Stewart. *Twenty-one. Twenty-two.* His unblinking eyes confirmed he was dead. Without the Captain, they were in trouble.

Without engines and satnav and depth gauges and collision warnings, they could hit a reef and there was absolutely nothing they could do about it. They weren't just in trouble; this was a critical emergency.

But he had no means to communicate with the passengers or crew, let alone the mainland.

He couldn't even contact his wife and daughter.

Twenty-four. Twenty-five. Twenty-six.

Acid churned in his gut as he pictured Adelle and his beautiful seven-year-old, Bella. Gunner's home in the seaside town of Rugged Shores was wedged between Los Angeles and Santa Barbara.

If this EMP strike was an act of terrorism, then either of those major cities could've been prime maximum-casualty targets.

His throat was bone dry. His heart banged in his chest.

Then again, an EMP detonation anywhere over the United States would decimate the entire country.

Are Adelle and Bella safe?

Are they together?

And my mother . . . is she okay?

Each thought sliced him like a switchblade, inflicting another slash of dread.

He had no answers. Based on the blank equipment around him, it would be a very long time before he did.

A sense of uselessness oozed into his brain like black ink, staining his sanity. Sweat dribbled down his back and without air-con, it was going to get hotter.

He paused for Jae-Ellen's breaths and continued again.

The eyes of the crew were heat-seeking missiles, burning into him. Every person aboard Rose of the Sea was counting on him to keep them safe. They were relying on him to know what the hell he was doing.

In the space of a heartbeat, his easy cruising life, where he hid his disgrace with a good day's work and fake laughter, had become a violent tempest with the potential to kill every soul on board. He needed to keep up his ruse, for everyone's sake.

For a long, agonizing moment, he was crippled with indecision.

A painful pulse thumped behind his eyes.

A high-pitched squeal resonated in his ears.

The compressions he was performing on Captain Nelson's lifeless body were his only constant. He'd lost count. He'd lost track of time. The crew glared at him, placing him on a stage with a million-watt light, demanding he perform. That's what he'd been doing since he was thirteen—performing. Pretending.

Acting like he was one of the good guys.

"Sir? What should we do?"

The fear lacing Jae-Ellen's words was the prick he needed to burst his panic bubble. It was time to get his A-game on. "Pauline, your turn on CPR."

"Yes, sir." Pauline pulled back her dark hair, tugged a band from her wrist to secure it, then fell to her knees at Captain Nelson's chest. Without missing a beat, Gunner removed his hands and Pauline slotted hers into position to start compressions. "One. Two. Three."

Gunner pushed up from his knees and turned to the First Officer. "Officer Sykes."

Sykes stepped his polished boots forward. "Yes, Captain."

Gunner did a double take. A lump of anxiety dropped in his stomach like a released anchor.

He was the Captain of Rose of the Sea.

A title he was not worthy of receiving.

Chapter Two

GUNNER

But every soul on board needed Gunner to act like the captain. So that was exactly what he had to do. "Sykes. Record in the logbook our last known location, heading and speed before we lost power. Then get those binoculars going. We're blind out here without radar. Every five minutes, send out a mayday call. I know it's not working, but you never know. Hopefully someone will hear it."

"Yes, sir." Sykes saluted and shifted away.

"Officer Reynolds."

The deck cadet jumped at his name and shuffled forward. "Sir?"

"Grab one of those two-ways." He eyeballed the row of handsets lined up on the shelf. "Run down to the engine room. I need a full status of what's going on down there."

"Yes, sir." As Reynolds picked out a two-way, Gunner stared at the Captain's unblinking eyes. What would Nelson have done next if their situations were switched?

"Ummm, Captain?" Reynolds' words wobbled off his tongue. "Sir, these are all dead, sir."

Gunner blinked at Reynolds, then at the dozen two-way radios lined up on the rack. Of course they weren't working. One electromagnetic pulse had reduced every one of them to nothing but paperweights. "Shit." The bolt of reality stung like a Band-Aid being ripped from an open wound. He turned his attention back to Nelson. "Any pulse?"

Jae-Ellen placed her fingers on the Captain's neck. "No, sir."

Gunner's brain was under attack as he tried to predict possible scenarios.

Drifting at sea without engines.

Unable to contact home.

None were good.

He stared at Nelson's unblinking eyes and his mind slammed to the last time he'd seen eyes like that. It'd been twenty-five years ago. He'd just turned thirteen, yet he could still recall his relief at witnessing the life slip out of those frosty blue irises.

This time was the exact opposite. Seeing Stewart's lifeless body had a lump swelling in Gunner's throat.

"Mayday. Mayday. Mayday. This is First Officer Cameron Sykes of Rose of the Sea. Mayday. Mayday. Mayday. This is First Officer Cameron Sykes of Rose of the Sea. We are seeking immediate help."

Sykes' mayday call lobbed another distressing thought grenade into Gunner's brain. It was impossible to know who was listening. Pirates were real. And they would love nothing more than to attack a crippled ship. Especially a cruise ship. Other than a few handguns, they had no way to protect themselves. He made a mental note to ensure the guns in the safe were loaded and ready. *The safe!* Everything inside it would've been protected from an EMP.

"Reynolds. The safe . . . there's a sat phone in the safe."

The cadet raced to the back wall of the bridge. After a pause, Reynolds cleared his throat. "Sir, it's locked, sir."

"Shit!" Gunner's blood drained. The safe had two combinations. Gunner had one. Captain Nelson had the other. "Who else has the Captain's safe combo? Sykes, is it you?"

Sykes lowered the binoculars. "No, sir, I have the same as you. It was Hastings, sir. He's gone to find the doc."

Gunner mentally tallied what else was in that safe. Along with the satellite phone, there were more two-ways, all the passengers' passports, six handguns and a supply of ammunition. The sat phone was their only way to contact the mainland to find out what the hell happened. And without the guns, they had no way to defend themselves. *Damn it!* They needed to get into that safe.

"Sir." Reynolds was back in view, awaiting instruction.

For the briefest of seconds, Gunner considered instructing Pauline to stop CPR. But when he looked at Captain Nelson, he blocked out the pale, pasty skin and the wide, unblinking eyes before him. Nelson was everything he wasn't. Charismatic. Courageous. Honorable. He couldn't stop. Not yet. "Come on, Captain. You fight this. Fight it with all you've got. You hear me?"

Out the corner of his eye the deck cadet's polished boots shifted into view. He was waiting for the Captain's instructions. *His* instructions. "Reynolds, run down to the engine room and bring me back a status report. Better yet, get the chief engineer up here. And tell Hastings to get his ass back up here too."

"Yes, sir." Reynolds' heavy footfalls sounded as he sprinted through the open door.

Sheryl was gone. The squeegee had been upended in her bucket.

"What shall I do, sir?" Second Officer Pauline Gennaro glanced up at him without stopping compressions.

Despite her bloodshot eyes, she was holding it together. She had a tiny frame, like his mother. Though, unlike his mother, Pauline's clenched jaw and fiery eyes portrayed both drive and determination. His mother had lost both of those the moment she'd been sentenced to twenty-five years in jail.

He knelt at the Captain's chest again and overlapped his hands. "Let me take over." Pauline eased back and Gunner began compressions. *One. Two.* But each push was pointless. Nelson was dead.

"Captain. What shall I do?" Pauline's eyes drilled into him.

Nine. Ten. Eleven. The hard sheen in her eyes displayed her turmoil, making it nearly impossible to reply. But he had to. Everyone was counting on him to keep his shit together. "I need the crew to know comms are down. Have them muster in the main meeting room. I'll make an announcement there as soon as I can. Get them to help you pass the word that this is top priority and I need them assembled ASAP."

"Yes, sir." Pauline scrambled to her feet. "What shall I tell the passengers?"

Twenty-eight. Twenty-nine. Thirty.

He stopped for Jae-Ellen to breathe into the captain's mouth again. "Tell them it's a routine test. Nothing else. Not yet. Not until we know exactly what's going on and how long it could last. We don't want to create panic."

"Are we going to abandon ship, sir?"

Pauline's question was a bolt of horror he hadn't considered. Abandoning ship was a drastic measure, only undertaken when all else was lost. They were not at that point. Not yet at least. "No, Pauline. We're not." He didn't even want to hint at that nightmare. "Now go!"

"Yes, sir." Pauline sprinted out the door.

"Mayday. Mayday. Mayday. This is First Officer Cameron Sykes from Rose of the Sea. Mayday. Mayday. Mayday. This is First Officer Cameron Sykes on Rose of the Sea. We are seeking immediate help."

Gunner admired Sykes' professionalism. Never in all his years of training did Gunner think he'd be involved in a major emergency. With more than three hundred cruise ships carrying more than half a million passengers on the water nearly every day of the year, cruising was considered to be one of the safest vacations available.

Gunner had a disaster on his hands that could blow that statistic well out of the water.

Outside the large bank of windows, the sky was an equal mix of orange from the setting sun and the blackness of night. Any minute now, they were going to be in absolute darkness. Gunner wiped sweat from his brow. "Any pulse?"

Jae-Ellen felt Captain Nelson's neck. "No, sir."

Gunner adjusted his position on his knees, and as he continued compressions again, he glanced at the digital clock at the front of the bridge. It was blank. "Shit!" He checked his watch. *Damn it.* He couldn't breathe, let alone think straight. Forcing his brain to focus, he inhaled, let it out in a huff, then glanced at Jae-Ellen. "Is your watch working?"

She flicked her wrist. "No, sir."

"My watch still works." Sykes' voice cut through the silence. "It's seventeen fifty, sir."

Gunner frowned at Sykes, unable to comprehend why his watch had been saved from the EMP.

"It's analog, sir." Sykes read his mind.

Gunner lost count of his compressions as he mentally listed everything he knew about EMP. Back when he'd taken the training, the concept of a nuclear warhead being detonated in the Earth's magnetic field had been bandied around as sensationalism.

But if the Captain was right and someone had detonated a nuclear weapon twenty or so miles up, then this ship wouldn't be the only one in trouble. In a flash, high-energy gamma rays would've reacted with air molecules to produce positive ions. Those ions caused a charge acceleration that radiated an instant electromagnetic pulse. That supercharged pulse would've fried every electronic gadget within line of sight of the blast zone.

But that was just the start.

The pulse would've then traveled along electronic cables and obliterated anything it came into contact with. Miles and miles of cables connected the computer monitors in the bridge to just about every other piece of equipment on the ship, meaning the electronics on the bridge wouldn't be all that were affected. Engines, propulsion, exhausts, water, sewerage, refrigeration, waste—the list went on and on.

His EMP training had been seven years ago, and back then the experts had been adamant that one nuclear explosion could take out the entire United States.

What could seven years of perfecting that bomb do? Take out two continents? Three? The whole world?

The experts had said that within the first twenty-four hours, hundreds of thousands of people would die. The elderly. Infants. The young. The sick. Those with electronic implants had no hope.

Gunner froze.

A chill raced up his spine.

If it was an EMP, then Captain Nelson's pacemaker would've taken a hit too. Even if Gunner did bring Stewart back to life, he would never stabilize.

"Any pulse, Jae-Ellen?"

Gunner tried not to look at the Captain's swollen tongue as Jae-Ellen checked his neck. "No, sir."

Gunner squeezed his eyes shut, then, with a breath trapped in his throat, he stopped compressions. "I'm sorry, Stewart." He opened his eyes and glanced at Jae-Ellen. A tear spilled over her lower eyelid and her chin dimpled. "Time, Sykes?"

"Eighteen oh six, sir."

"I'm calling Captain Stewart Nelson's time of death at eighteen oh six. Sykes, please make a note of that in the logbook."

"Sir." Sykes paused. "The logbook is electronic."

Gunner shoved his hands through his hair and groaned. "Grab paper and pen. Write it down.

Sykes nodded. "Yes, sir."

Gunner leaned forward and glided the Captain's eyes closed, then he sat back on his haunches and heaved a forceful sigh. Gunner had always been blessed with good health. His wife, however, had lost fourteen months to breast cancer. Thankfully, she'd been in remission for eight years now and was obsessed with keeping fit and healthy. He and their daughter benefitted from Adelle's obsession and none of them relied on medication.

Unlike hundreds of his passengers. The demographic of those onboard Rose of the Sea was typical of most cruise ships. More than sixty-five percent of the holiday-makers were more than sixty years old. Retirees had time and many also had money. Unfortunately, they also came with their share of health issues that required medical intervention.

His breath caught as another thought grenade lobbed in. Some passengers would've had pacemakers, or other forms of electronic medical devices.

Every one of them was probably dead now too.

A wave of nausea hit him so fast he had to grip onto a chair and swallow back the bitter bile in his throat.

It was a long moment before he shifted to stand, and every movement was robotic, as if he were weighed down with a chain-mail robe. Gunner turned his attention to the consoles lining the bridge. The three-quarter moon, low on the horizon and reflecting off the blank screens, was about to be their only light source.

He glanced down at the Captain, hardly able to believe what he was seeing. Captain Nelson had been an absolute stalwart. A man who truly commanded attention. He didn't deserve this fate. Gunner removed his jacket and draped it over Stewart's face and chest. There were body bags in the medical centre. When the doc showed up, he'd make him go back down and get one.

He dragged his eyes away from the lifeless body and looked out over the relatively calm ocean. Prior to the system failure, they'd been tracking a storm seven miles east of their location. Now they had no way to monitor it or adjust their heading.

Their nightmare was just beginning.

They didn't even have Morse code. The age-old encoding scheme had been replaced with modern technology and the equipment had been declared redundant many years ago. Yet, even if they'd had such a machine, other than SOS, he'd have no hope of communicating anything else. He hadn't so much as thought about it in over a decade.

"Shit! Sir!" The alarm in Sykes' voice had Gunner spinning to the First Officer. His wide, panicked eyes shot a new level of fear through Gunner's gut. "You better take a look at this, Captain."

Gunner strode to the front of the bridge, and Sykes shoved the binoculars into his hands, casting his wild eyes toward the sunset. "There, sir, at your nine o'clock."

Gunner raised the binoculars. His blood drained. His gut twisted.

A silent scream tortured his brain. "God help us all."

Chapter Three

MADELINE

The elevator jolted to a stop and was pitched into complete darkness.

A scream tore from Madeline Jewel's throat as she slammed her back against the wall and clutched the railing. "What was that?" Her voice was shrill, choked with fear.

"I don't know." A man was in there with her, but it was impossible to see him.

He banged on the elevator door and she just about burst out of her skin. "Hey, can anyone hear me? Help!"

Madeline's feet were frozen to the floor. Her heart thumped against her ribs. Her breaths shot in and out in short, sharp gasps.

The blackness was complete, like a monster had swallowed every light particle, offering no variation, no shadows. Not even a glimmer between the doors. Madeline had slipped into an alien vortex. A foreign land. An evil dark space.

Shocking aspects darted across her mind like wasps.

The enclosed area inching in on me.

The complete stranger in here with me.

A man. Bigger than me. Stronger than me.

She couldn't see.

She couldn't *breathe.*

Her mind slammed between the horror of now and her childhood nightmare. One second she was stuck in an elevator with a stranger, the next she was trapped in a windowless room with a monster.

Blackness reached out.

Invisible fingers crawled along her skin.

Spiders scurried up her neck.

She lurched forward. "Help!" She slammed her fists on the door alongside the man. "Help!" She had to get out. "Help!"

Together they pummeled the door and screamed for help.

Her chest squeezed, tightening around her lungs. "Help!" Her brain squeezed too, pushing out every ounce of sanity. "HELP!"

She couldn't believe this was happening. Madeline avoided elevators. Yet there she was, stuck in one. As the minutes ticked on, her panicked breathing sucked in the darkness. The emptiness threatened to suffocate her. The lump in her throat did too. "It's so dark in here."

"Oh, hang on, I've got a phone."

Her heart skipped at his words and when the phone sprung to life, she just about wept with relief.

He jabbed a few buttons on his cell, then huffed. "No signal."

"What?"

"No signal. But that's normal in an elevator. Don't panic."

"Don't panic? We've been in here too long. Something's wrong." Her stomach twisted into painful knots.

He shone the light on the side wall. "Okay, let's see. There must be an emergency phone in here."

His methodical manner was a thousand miles away from hers. As her gaze bounced from the closed elevator doors to his light illuminating the button panel, panic clawed at her throat. Her knees weakened, barely able to hold her upright.

He popped open a small panel beneath the buttons. "Ahhh, here we go." He held the handset to his ear. "Hello?"

An ounce of hope tickled her brain.

"Hello, is anyone there?" He frowned and leaned forward to

inspect the wall panel. "There must be a call button or something. Oh, here it is."

But after a moment of silence, he shook his head. "Hello? If anyone can hear me, we need help. We're stuck in an elevator. Ahhh . . ." He leaned in to study the panel. "Elevator number three hundred and four. Help. Please."

He turned to her, a frown rippling his forehead. "It's weird; I can't hear anything."

"Let me try." Madeline strangled the handset, holding it to her ear. "Hello, is anyone there? Hello!" The emptiness on the line was strange. Not even a crackle. "It's completely dead."

"I know. Weird, huh?"

He hung up the handset and snapped the compartment shut. Then he jabbed every button on the panel. Not one of them reacted.

"What could be wrong?" Her voice was shrill, unrecognizable.

"I don't know. I better turn this off, save the battery." The light blinked out, pitching them into utter blackness.

It was impossible to comprehend how it could be so completely dark. Like they'd fallen into a black hole in space. The silence, too, was foreign.

Sweat trickled beneath her arms, down her temples.

She shuddered. Her breaths shot in and out. Her head began to swim. She pressed her back against the cold metallic wall and clutched the railing to keep herself upright. "No. No. NO!"

"Hey, it's okay." The man's soothing voice cut through the screaming in her head.

"We're trapped." Her voice wobbled with emotion.

"Don't worry. Help will be here soon."

"You don't know that." Despite her pulse thumping in her ears, she heard him shuffle toward her and she braced herself. If he touched her, she wasn't sure she'd hold back the terrified scream clawing at her throat.

"It's all right. We'll be okay."

"But . . ." She sucked in a shaky breath. "Why's it so dark? Where's the emergency lighting?"

"Don't know. I wondered that too."

Their elevator was positioned at the rear of the ship, in the center, which meant the nearest windows were on the other side of the cabins. Although they didn't benefit from natural light, the halls were always illuminated. The extreme blackout meant that both the corridor lighting and the emergency lighting wasn't working.

Madeline thought back to her crew training, trying to recall a scenario that would explain their situation. She couldn't think of one.

Whatever was going on, it wasn't good.

"My name's Sterling, by the way. Sterling Rochford."

Sterling had stepped into the elevator on the fifth deck and seconds after the doors had shut, the lights had gone out. All she could recall of Sterling's appearance was that he had nicely styled blond hair and that he was taller than her. Which wasn't unusual. At just five foot four, Madeline found nearly everyone was taller than her.

"I . . . I'm Madeline." She didn't reveal her last name. It was something she'd learned the hard way. The media had used and abused her surname both during her childhood abduction and after her rescue.

Apparently, Jewel was perfect fodder for their attention-seeking headlines.

Help us find our precious jewel. Jewel is priceless.

And then, when she was rescued . . . *Our miracle jewel, a diamond found amongst the ashes.*

Even now, sixteen years later, people had odd reactions when they realized who she was. Some were left speechless, which made it awkward when they clearly wanted to ask or say something but didn't know how. Others said sorry, though why they did that was impossible to fathom. And then there were those who asked question after question, obsessed by some morbid quest to delve into the five and a half months of her life that defined her. One hundred and seventy-three days she'd been trapped in that dungeon.

It'd felt like years.

Madeline shuffled sideways and heard Sterling shift toward her again. She retreated farther, pressing herself against the wall, trying to make her body as small as possible. Praying he kept his distance.

In the silent metallic cube, every noise seemed amplified. Her own breathing. His breathing. A sharp ticking sound that created a hollow heartbeat to her new living hell. *Tick. Tick. Tick.*

She gasped. "Oh my God. The engines have stopped."

"What?"

"The engines. Listen. They've stopped."

"Hmmm. I think you're right."

The walls of the elevator groaned as if it were alive. She was trapped in a monster. Her heart beat faster—a machine gun tempo. The rabid pulse thumped in her ears, taking her panic to a whole new level.

A burst of laughter from somewhere outside had Madeline launching at the doors. "Help! Help us. Is anyone there?"

"Help us," Sterling yelled as he too thumped on the door.

"Hello." The woman's reply came from the very top of the elevator doors. *Shit! We're stuck between floors.* "Hello! Help us. Please!"

"Shhh, can you hear something?" The female voice was chirpy which was so, so wrong.

"In here. We're stuck in the elevator." Madeline banged her fists on the metal.

"Where's the elevator?" Someone—no, more than one. Two people giggled again. A man and a woman. Maybe more than two people. "Sorry, we can't see."

"We're in here." Sterling thumped on the doors.

"Please help us." Madeline looked up toward the sound of their voices, but still saw absolutely nothing.

"It's pitch-black out here. We can't see." They giggled some more.

Madeline wanted to scream her fury. "Neither can we!" They were acting like fumbling around in the dark was fun.

It was far from fun. It was a house of horrors, with no exit. A living volcano was building inside Madeline; rage was the red-hot lava. She was set to explode.

"What's going on?" Sterling yelled.

"We don't know," the woman said.

"Can you open the doors?"

"I don't know. Hang on," a man replied.

Their muffled voices drifted away and Madeline's fear hit a whole new level. "Are you there?" Panic burned her throat.

"We can't open them. We'll go get help."

"No! Don't leave us," Madeline shrieked.

"We can't get the doors open. We'll get help, I promise."

"Don't go." A sob burst from Madeline's throat.

"Hey, it's okay." Sterling touched her shoulder and gasping, she shot backward, slamming against the wall.

Her chin quivered and she couldn't fight the terror a second more.

She slipped to the floor, hugged her knees, and burst into tears.

Chapter Four

GABBY

"I can't do this anymore. I want a divorce!" Gabrielle Kinsella glared at her husband and saw both confusion and fury in his eyes. Her own fury came in waves. Waves that grew more powerful every time Max avoided the difficult discussions. In spite of that, or maybe because of it, their fights were becoming more frequent.

Twice before, Gabby had made that divorce statement. But each of those times she'd been a little tipsy and he'd laughed it off as the alcohol talking. This time was different. She'd only had three wines.

This time, she wanted him to know just how serious she was.

He reached for her hand but she snapped it away, and clenching her teeth, she stared out over the ship's railing. Another couple were standing barely four feet from them and when she turned toward them, their shameless ogling gave her a horrid feeling they'd overheard what she'd said.

Gabby glared at them until they shifted their gaze and silently prayed they hadn't recognized her. Last thing she needed was to be the subject of tabloid headlines tomorrow morning.

In an attempt to distance herself from prying eyes, she shuffled a few paces away, pressed her hips to the top rail, and gazed across the Pacific Ocean.

The horizon was a potpourri of citrus colors as the golden sun merged into the indigo water. Its final gasp of the day was postcard perfect—one that several couples on the top exercise deck around them seemed to be enjoying. Not her and Max though. Not with twelve days of bickering coming to a head.

Max had demanded they take this vacation, insisting they needed the time to patch their marriage together. He'd said it was a chance to put their ongoing turmoil behind them and start afresh, and he'd proposed it like the fourteen-day cruise was some kind of miracle potion designed to shed years of frustration and breathe new life into their marriage.

It hadn't.

Max let a group of joggers run past before easing into the railing beside her. "Come on, Gabby. You don't mean that." His gloomy nuisance was laced with dismay. Like he thought this fight was a mere bump in the road.

It wasn't just a bump. It was Mount Vesuvius, set to explode.

"Yes I do. You've changed."

The vein in his neck pulsed. "Changed? From when we first met. Is that what you mean? That was twenty years ago. Of course I've changed."

Gabby huffed. "I mean now . . . lately. Since. . ." She let the sentence hang. It was an argument that'd been plaguing them ever since he'd decided his days as a stay-at-home dad were over and that he wanted to start a personal training business.

But the kids still needed him. If anything, they needed supervision even more now that they were fifteen and thirteen. He needed to be home with them, not gallivanting around with women half his age.

"Go on . . . you can say it," he said. "Since I started Maximum Fitness. Is that when I changed?"

Although he'd been training for two years, Gabby had never thought he'd follow through with his ludicrous business plans. But he had, and it wasn't until he'd started securing clients that she'd realized just how serious he was. "Yes, exactly," she said. "And you know it. You're never home anymore."

"And?" Max had an infuriating way of remaining impossibly calm when they fought. While she wanted to scream at him till her throat hurt, he became more passive and composed. They were opposites like that. Too far opposite.

As usual, Max waited for her response with dogged silence that left her no choice but to answer.

"Just that," she snapped. "Before you started this . . . this thing, I'd come home and we'd all sit down to dinner together. Like a proper family. Now I never know *when* you'll be home."

"Do you realize how hypocritical you are?" He threw his hands out like he was catching a ball. "For ten years, the kids and I have been waiting for *you* to come home."

She spun to face him dead on; her teeth clenched so tight her jaw trembled. Gabby jabbed her long red nail at his chest. "Don't you put this on me!"

He made a show of inhaling a deep sigh and she wanted to slap him. "But it is on you. We made a decision that I'd stay home to raise the kids while you chased your career. I made sacrifices."

Frustration had her trembling. "*You* made sacrifices." Gabby had made the biggest sacrifice any woman could make. She'd given up everything to have Max's children.

She'd never imagined falling in love.

But she had. She'd never imagined getting married. But she'd done that too. But the one thing she never ever wanted was to have children. Not after her mother had obliterated her happy family fantasy with her deathbed confession.

Happy families were fictitious. A lie.

But as a woman, it was what she was supposed to do. To be a mom.

To prove her love and commitment to her husband.

Spinning toward the ocean, she inhaled the salty air in an attempt to stem the fury coursing through her.

The sound of sniggering had Gabby glaring at the couple along the railing. They were making amateur attempts at sneaking glances at her and Max. It took several infuriating seconds before the pair retreated from Gabby's dagger eyes.

"Gabby, we've talked about this." Max leaned into the railing at her side. "It's time for me to return to work. I want to do this. I like it. I'm helping people again."

"Exactly, and it's all you care about. Your clients." *Your young, beautiful clients.* She slapped that thought away before she blurted it out.

"You know that's not true. The kids are the world to me, just like you are."

She spun to him. "Last month, you were out ten weeknights. School nights, Max. When you should've been home with the kids."

Max lurched back, his eyes finally flaring with emotion. "You counted!"

"Of course. I needed a tally, because I don't think you understand."

"Wow. Your hypocrisy is appalling. You have no idea how much of your children's lives you've missed pursuing your stupid career."

She gasped. "You didn't mind my stupid career when you purchased that brand-new Mercedes. Or your stupid limited-edition Indian motorbike."

"It's not about the money, Gabby, and you know it."

"Oh my God, you're so frustrating." She turned to the ocean again and clutched the railing. Gabby let out a long, slow breath and her eyes snagged on a plane positioned low in the sky. Way too low.

A weird silence had engulfed the air.

She cocked her head. *Huh, the music has stopped.* Leaving the railing, she strode across the fake-grass running track and looked down to the pool deck below. Along with their instruments, the band's colorful flashing lights had stopped too.

The giant screen that'd been playing the annoying *Dumbo* movie was now blank.

Both above-ground spas had stopped bubbling and the kids' water park was no longer squirting streams of water into the air.

The lights over the bar were off and every light along the running track had gone out too.

A woman emitted a blood-curdling scream and Gabby searched the hundred or so people below for the source of the cries. She found the woman amongst the crowd, kneeling beside an elderly man who lay sprawled on the floor and looked to be unconscious.

"Look at that plane," someone called out behind her.

Gabby turned back toward the ocean and when she caught sight of the plane again her stomach sank. It was much lower than when she'd first seen it. It wasn't a huge plane—maybe one of the island hoppers she'd seen in Hawaii. But its angle was all wrong. The pilot should be pulling it up, aiming skyward. But the plane was doing the opposite.

A prickle of excitement teased her journalistic cravings. Her heartbeat upped a tempo. Her senses heightened as she tried to memorize every tiny aspect of what she was witnessing.

Identifying a drop of extraordinary in an ocean of boring was Gabby's expertise. She was good at her job. Better than good. Her numerous journalism awards proved that.

Her heart beat faster. *Something else is wrong. I can't hear the plane's engines.*

All she heard was the whistling wind as the wings cut through the air. It wasn't a massive jet airliner, but she'd flown in enough planes to know there would be about seventy passengers on that aircraft. Gabby could picture their panic-stricken faces. She imagined the pilot's frantic efforts to pull it up. She visualized people screaming. People crying. People praying.

A crowd had gathered at the ship's railing, looking out to the aircraft. Some had their phones out, but the way they were jabbing at the buttons, it seemed they weren't working.

The cockpit windshield glinted in the setting sun, creating an eerie beam of light that pointed right at her. Gabby's thumping heart skipped a beat. None of the plane's windows radiated any light. Those passengers were in the dark. Something was terribly wrong and she was about to have a front-row seat to a story that could launch her career to the next level.

Gabby plucked her phone from her pocket. Jabbed the buttons. It was dead. "Shit!"

She turned to Max. "Give me your phone."

He fumbled in his pocket, and shoved the phone at her.

She prodded the buttons. It too was dead.

Gabby handed it back to him, but his gaze remained glued to the horizon. The anger that'd been blazing in his eyes moments ago was gone, replaced instead with something else . . . fear.

She spun back to the plane. Alarm zipped up her spine. Her momentary excitement over a headlining story vanished. "Jesus! It's going to crash right into us."

"Shit!" Max clutched her wrist. "I think you're right."

As if choreographed, the surrounding crowd hit panic mode in the exact same instant. Women screamed. So did men. Many ran for their lives. Just as many bolted toward the railing.

The plane was barely half a mile out.

"Pull up. Pull up," Max shouted.

"It's a terrorist," someone yelled.

"Suicide bomber," another screamed.

Pandemonium broke out. People scattered in all directions. Some remained at the railing, either too shocked or too stupid to move.

A quarter mile out.

Max yanked her forward. "Run." They dodged other passengers as they sprinted along the running track. Unable to tear her eyes away, she willed the plane's nose to angle upward. It didn't.

Two hundred yards.

Things seemed to move in two speeds, all at once both lightning fast and at a crawl. Her gaze snapped from one point to another. She wanted to absorb it all. Every critical detail. But at the same time, she wanted to wish it all away.

One hundred yards.

Gabby liked being close to the action, but this was too close. Way too close. Every aspect was frightfully real.

Terrified passengers running and screaming.

Little kids being trampled by the frantic mob.

The white trail behind the plane's wings as it torpedoed right at them.

The fear in her husband's chocolate-brown eyes.

The plane's angle shifted slightly, the right wing lower, but it was still on a collision course with the ship. With them. Her mind skidded to those images of the 9/11 planes that'd been playing on the airwaves for over two decades.

She was about to be dead-center in the middle of the biggest news story of her career and her damn phone was dead.

"Run, Gabby! Run!"

The plane hit the ocean, right wing first. An explosion of water arced up over the aircraft. The plane cartwheeled. It spun in the air. It bounced off the water again; flipping upright so the nose was pointing at the sky.

Then it slammed into the ship.

The sound was horrendous—a freight train crashing into solid metal.

An engine sheared off, and Max tackled her to the ground as the spinning projectile took out the running deck behind them. It careened through the party area below, crushing dozens of people as it skidded across the dance floor and disappeared over the other side of the ship.

Chunks of wreckage crashed into the deck, some as big as cars, some the size of suitcases.

Some were suitcases.

A plane seat slammed into a deck chair barely two inches from Gabby's feet. The person still buckled in the seat was crushed with a sickening crunch. She snapped her eyes away, hoping that horror was the worst she was going to see.

Yet at the same time, she knew it was just the beginning.

An explosion erupted deep in the bowels of the ship, and the giant mirror behind the bar burst outward. The barmaid's bloody corpse hit the floorboards; hundreds of tiny shards of glass disfigured her pretty face.

It all happened so quickly. Nobody had time to move.

A moment of stunned silence settled on the party deck.

A heartbeat later, chaos broke out.

Max shifted sideways, and Gabby eased up onto her knees and stared at the carnage.

People screamed.

People were ran.

People froze, crippled with shock.

Gabby had seen bloody aftermaths before. But they'd been so different. They'd been five minutes, ten minutes, sometimes hours after the event. Never had she witnessed the initial impact. As her eyes bounced from one bloody body to the next, her mind bounced from the before to the after.

Beautiful young couples dancing. Mangled and broken limbs.

People laughing and sipping cocktails in the spa. Entire spa obliterated.

Family of five eating ice cream. One small girl remaining with her ice cream upended on the floor.

It was like flipping cards on a tarot deck, only every second card was Death.

Gabby spun her gaze ocean side. Through a giant hole in the railing, she watched a plane's wing disappear. A spout of water signified its demise and seconds later, two bodies floated to the surface. One was a child; no bigger than her son.

A thought hit her with brutal clarity. A beehive exploded in her stomach. She shot her eyes to Max.

Her heart thumped so thick in her throat she could barely speak. "Where are the kids?"

Chapter Five

ZON

Zon Woodrow had no idea what the fuck everyone was doin'. When the lights had gone out earlier, people had started screaming, like the darkness was out to get 'em or something. Then there was the huge bang. One second, the casino had been a buzz of glowin' lights and annoying music; next second, people were ducking for cover and screamin' even more.

Idiots had even started running, but they were on a ship. Not like there was anywhere to go. And with the poker hand he had, Zon wasn't goin' nowhere. The bang was probably a drinks cart fallin' over. Now that'd be a reason to scream.

Besides, if it was serious, there'd be sirens and stuff. People were so dramatic.

The card dealer was an Asian woman, and she was about the size of his loudmouthed twelve-year-old step-sister. Not that she was really his sister. His mom had nicked off when Zon was nine and returned seven years later with six-year-old Bitchface in tow. Zon had been forced to accept her as kin.

Like fuck. She weren't no sister to him. Never would be neither.

Now there was another Bitchface in front of him, and she'd stopped dealing right when he was about to be hit with his next card. She'd even put the fuckin' deck back in the card holder and was glancing around at the other dealers with a stupid look on her face.

"Oy." Zon thumped his fist onto the poker table, making the chips on the green felt jump. "What the fuck're ya doing?"

Bitchface slipped back another step. "Sir, I'm sorry, but we have to stop."

"Like hell. I was winnin', you bitch." Although he could barely see, he peeked at his cards again. Ace, king, jack and a ten. All in spades. For the first time in his life, he was one card away from a royal flush. All he needed was the queen of spades. He was about to win big time. It was his lucky fucking day.

And the stupid bitch had stopped dealin'.

He knew what this was about. They were watching. Them people behind them security monitors around the casino. They'd seen his hand. They'd seen the card she was about to deal him. They knew he was about to beat the bank.

Zon glared up at the black dome above the table and flipped the bird. "You getting this, asshole?"

"Steady on, mate." The guy at his side was all suit and tie, and looked down his nose at Zon. He'd met assholes like him before. Thinking their fancy suit and polished shoes made their dollar more valuable than his.

"Fuck you, *mate*. I was winnin'."

The asshole pretended to ignore Zon by looking around the dim casino.

All them annoying jingles coming from the hundreds of slot machines cramming the casino had stopped too. Other than the fools still screaming, it was mostly silent.

It sure was weird.

"Hey, come on, what's going on?" A dude as big as a hippo bashed the side of the machine, then erupted into a coughing fit until he was gasping for air.

"Mine's dead too," said the woman beside him. Her gray hair looked like she'd wrestled with a toilet brush. Reminded him of his grandmama, 'cept she wasn't as fat as this woman was. His grandmama had been real scrawny.

"Ladies and gentlemen."

Zon turned toward the voice. A guy dressed in white was standing at the front of the room. Behind him, the bar lights that usually lit all the booze were out. The only light they had was from the last of the sunset coming in from the open double doors and the giant windows on either side of the casino.

"There's no need to panic, but it seems we've had a minor power failure. Please sit tight, and we'll have this sorted as soon as possible."

Zon grabbed his poker chips and shoved them into his pockets. Then, when the dude and the chick standin' beside him turned toward the bar, Zon siphoned a tower of their chips his way too. They were both so drunk it wasn't like they'd even notice. He felt the dealer staring at him and turned to eyeball the bitch. The way she was lookin', she'd seen what he'd done.

He didn't give a fuck.

Zon leaned forward and sneered at her. Wasn't even a second before she backed away even farther.

He glanced up, and as he sneered at the black dome above the table, a thought gripped him like gator jaws. Without power, all the fuckin' security cameras coulda stopped workin' too.

It was a whole new kinda payday.

He waited till the dealer veered her eyes away before he stacked another hundred bucks worth of chips onto his original bid. "Hey, bitch. You gonna finish this hand or what?"

She jumped. Her hand went to her chest and she glanced over her shoulder, no doubt looking for security. But Zon had already seen the fat asshole waddle toward the bar.

"I'm sorry, sir, but all play has stopped temporarily." Her voice was high-pitched and freaky. Like she was stuck in a video game.

"I know what y'all doin'. Them fucking assholes don't want me winnin'." He eyeballed the security dome wonderin' if he was right about 'em not working.

"Sir, please . . . give the lady a break. She's just doing her job." The toffy-nosed shit sounded all fancy with his posh accent.

"Or what?" Zon barked.

The prick eased back, then after a pause, he climbed off his chair and reached for his chips next to his played cards.

"Hey, don't go touching 'em. Game's not over."

"I think you'll find it is." The English prick made a show of looking around the room.

Other gamblers were leaving tables. Some-a the ones on the slot machines, though, hadn't moved. They were just sittin' there, looking around, waitin' for someone to tell 'em what to do. Nobody knew what was goin' on. Even the staff.

The minutes ticked on, and the standoff between Zon and Bitchface continued. All this waitin' was makin' him thirsty. He snatched up his beer bottle, but he'd drained his Bud at least ten minutes ago.

"Oy." Zon pointed at Bitchface. "We oughta get free drinks. We bein' inconvenienced like this an' all."

Again, she glanced at the security guard. He was tinkerin' with somethin' behind the bar. Maybe tryin' to secure the cash. The chick behind the cashier's counter was in near-darkness but even in the limited light she looked like she was shittin' herself.

Hang on. What else has been affected by the blackout. *Fuck me.* It could be everythin'.

Are them pop-up security screens still workin'?

Years ago, back in his footy days, before he'd gone an' broke his ankle, he'd done a smash-and-grab at a convenience store. He'd been stupid back then though and drunk, and the cashier had got the jump on him. It was a miracle the cops had only given him a warnin'. Maybe 'cause they'd known what was coming for him when he got home.

His daddy had smashed the shit out of him. Teachin' him a lesson an' all. He'd lost a tooth and broken his nose in that beatin'. His fucking nose still whistled when he wasn't concentratin'.

"Listen. I betta get a drink in the next minute or I'm gonna get real cranky."

The fancy prick rolled his eyes.

Zon launched to his feet, sending his chair flying. "You got somethin' to say?"

The prick held up his hands. "I didn't say anything."

"No, but you were thinking."

A cocky smirk crawled across his lips. "I'm always thinking."

Zon jabbed his finger into the asshole's chest. "Don't you go gettin' all high and mighty on me."

"Sir. Do we have a problem?"

Zon spun to the guard. Despite his fat gut, he'd managed to sneak up on Zon. "Yeah, we got a fucking problem." Zon flicked his hand toward the dealer. "The bitch knows I'm winnin' so she's stopped dealin', and ain't nobody getting me a drink."

"We're sorry for the inconvenience, but we've had to close down the casino. Please can you make your way—"

"Like fuck. I ain't goin' no—"

The guard lashed out, grabbed Zon's wrist, and before Zon knew what was happenin' his hand was shoved up behind him, his chips had gone flying, and his face was squished into the green felt on the poker table.

"Get the fuck off me!"

"You need to calm down."

"Get off me, you fuck!" Zon wrestled against the guard. He couldn't believe the fat prick had gotten the jump on him.

"Calm down, sir."

"I know my rights."

Next second, Zon was flung from the table and hit the floor in a full-body slam. His arm was wrenched so far up his back he thought it was gonna snap. "Fuckin' hell! You're gonna break my arm."

"Correct. If you so much as move, I'll do exactly that."

"Jesus, what the hell're ya doin?" His nose whistled and it only made him more angry. "Fuck!"

"I'm putting you under arrest. What's your name?"

"None of your fuckin—" He howled as his other arm was yanked up behind his back.

"Your name!"

35

"Zon Woodrow." He didn't give his real name. Richard Nyxzon Woodrow. His stupid slut of a mother named him after a president or somethin'. That was bad enough. But spelling it the way she did made it a thousand times worse.

He'd spent his junior years being called Dick Nyx. Then he'd gotten smart and strong. And angry. That was when he'd fucked off the Richard part and the Nyx bit, and he'd been Zon ever since. No one questioned it. Especially not since he'd shaved his head and grown his beard. The red-tinged facial hair made him look like a rebel from one of them *Viking* movies.

Nobody questioned him about nothin' no more.

Except the fucking security guard. Zon'd get him though, when the time was right. That fat guard was gonna wish he'd never met Zon.

A metal clip was slapped onto his wrist. Handcuffs. He knew them well.

"Fuckin' hell. What'd I do? This is corruption. You knew I was winnin'."

The guard rolled him over and Zon looked up at the fat prick. Zon drew back and spat, but the fat globule came back down and splattered his own shirt. The guard kicked him in the gut. It didn't hurt though; Zon's daddy had kicked him enough times for him to know when it was meant to hurt. That didn't . . . confirmin' the guard was nothin' but a fat pussy.

"Get up."

Zon cursed and wriggled around on the floor, trying to stand. But with his hands behind his back it was impossible. "I can't."

"That's right. You're in my control now. You are going to show me some respect."

Zon spat again. This time it landed on the guard's shoe and when that boot slammed into his gut, Zon buckled up in pain. "Fuck! What'd ya do that for?"

"I asked if you were going to show me some respect."

"This's brutality." He turned and spied the English prick, all grinnin' and stuff. If he weren't tied up, Zon woulda punched that smirk right off his face.

The guard dragged Zon to his feet; the fuckin' handcuffs sliced into his flesh. "Jesus Christ. You're hurting me."

"I'm going to hurt you more if you don't comply."

"I am fuckin' complyin', you shit."

"Now walk."

"I ain't leavin' without my chips."

The guard shoved him in the back and Zon stumbled forward.

"You getting this? It's corruption," Zon shouted to no one in particular.

The guard pushed him again and as he staggered through the casino, Zon expected every bastard to be looking at him. But it was weird. A couple of oldies were on the ground, flat on their backs. Some looked dead. Some were even getting CPR. The woman in the cashier's booth was slumped over, and the chick beside her was crying.

Every single coin bandit was blank and heaps of people were thumping the sides of the machines, like that'd make 'em cough up their money.

The guard shoved him through the door and the second they stepped onto the promenade deck, Zon spied a huge cloud of smoke drifting across the ocean. It was coming from the back of the ship. "Shit. That don't look good."

"No." The guard frowned. "It doesn't."

A few people ran past them, lookin' like they'd shat their pants. A couple of old dudes were flat on their backs. One dude was as white as a ghost and an old woman was fallin' all over him, crying.

"Huh. He looks like a goner."

The guard slapped him across the back of his head, but said nothing.

An old guy, whose wooden cane was getting a workout, wobbled toward 'em.

"What's goin' on?" Zon shouted at him.

"A plane flew into the ship. Didn't you see it?"

"Shit, huh? Is it bad?"

The old guy silently shook his head, but his eyes said enough.

It was bad.

At the sound of footsteps running, Zon turned. One of the crew was sprinting toward them. Her tits bounced up and down with every step, making the show mighty pleasant.

"Oh, thank God. Willis," she said. "I need your help."

"What's going on?" The guard strode to her.

She glanced at Zon and her eyes bugged out so much she looked like some of 'em rabbits Zon chased for target practice. The guard stepped to the side. But they underestimated his excellent hearing, 'cause he still caught every word.

"A plane hit the back of the ship. It's a mess. And Captain Nelson had a heart attack. And . . ." She gasped for air. ". . . and he said it was an EMP." She spoke a million miles an hour, all hysterical like.

That last comment had the fat guard's eyes bulging. "EMP? Are you sure?"

"It was the last thing the Captain said before he passed."

"Jesus."

"I need your help. All our comms are out and Captain McCrae wants the crew down in the meeting room ASAP, so we have to get the message out verbally."

"Okay." The guard strode to Zon. "It's your lucky day."

"Yeah? Don't sound like it." He nodded toward the smoke. "What the fuck's an EMP?"

The handcuffs were released from his wrists and the guard shoved him in the shoulder. "I don't want to see your ugly face again. You hear me?"

"Yeah, well, I don't wanna—" Zon didn't even get to finish his sentence before the two of 'em raced into the casino.

He stepped to the railing and peered over the side.

"Faark." Half a plane was sticking out of the ship. Flames blazed up what was left of the red tail, and it looked like it'd taken a chunk outta the side. The hole was fucking huge.

He'd been nine years old when 'em planes had crashed into the World Trade Centre. His daddy had made him watch it all fucking day. He'd rambled on about al-Qaeda and Muslims and said how it was just like when them Japs did that kamikaze shit. His daddy had always blabbed on about the war.

But Zon knew how much bullshit dribbled outta his old man's fat mouth. Especially when it came to the war. His daddy was too dumb to have survived a real battle.

Zon leaned out over the railing. If that was a suicide bomber, then the asshole had done a fucking good job of killing his-self.

He turned to a bunch of voices as the guard, the chick with the nice tits, and what looked like all the casino staff raced past him. They was all headed toward the back of the ship where the smoke was so black ya couldn't even see through it.

They shouted at each other as they ran, talking about maydays and SOSes and shit. Zon's gaze fell on the row of lifeboats at the edge of the promenade deck. *Should I steal one now?* Before the shit really hits the fan.

Out of habit, he reached for his cigarettes. But they weren't there. What he did feel, though, was all them chips he'd shoved into his pockets.

It really was his lucky day.

With all them staff gone, that casino was ready for his pickin'.

Chapter Six

GABBY

Gabby darted her gaze to a child floating face-down in the pool and in one thumping heartbeat, her creative brain morphed the child's body into that of her daughter with her long dark hair wafting around her. Max must've seen Gabby's terror because he clutched her hand and squeezed for her attention. "The kids are okay. They're in the kids' club."

"We have to go to them." Horrifying thoughts whizzed across her brain.

His eyes glanced past her to the mangled body in the plane seat. "They're at the front of the ship. They'll be safe where they are."

Gabby shook her head. "You don't know that." She spoke through clenched teeth, furious that he didn't agree.

He squeezed her hand harder. "Trust me. You don't want them seeing this. The crew will look after them. These people need our help."

Gabby scanned the carnage. Bodies were everywhere, some writhing in agony, some deathly still. People were in all stages of shock. Crying. Screaming. Absolute stillness. Raw emotions were at the forefront for everyone, including the crew. Many seemed too stunned to move.

Max, however, jumped into action.

He squatted beside a woman in her swimsuit whose leg had been torn off below the knee. She was sitting up, looking at the wound as if admiring her tan. With the amount of blood she'd already lost, Gabby predicted she wouldn't survive. Max touched the woman's arm and she blinked at him. "Hey, help is coming soon, okay? You hang in there."

Gabby guessed the woman would be thirty-five, forty at the most. Despite her shocking injury, she still looked beautiful. A classic Audrey Hepburn semblance with flawless skin and striking eyes. With her beauty, and her apparent nonchalance over her injury, it would've been a confronting photo that would have had audiences around the world talking.

The woman looked up at Gabby, and her blank expression confirmed she was in shock. Gabby had seen varying degrees of shock dozens of times.

She'd lived through it once herself.

A thin smile formed on the woman's pale lips. "Can you find Daniel for me, my husband? Tell him where I am." The woman was so calm it was spooky.

"Of course we will, love," Max said. "Now close your eyes and rest."

She nodded but turned her gaze back to her leg and the growing blood pool beside her.

Max's firm grip on the woman's hand sparked a memory of the day Gabby had met him. He'd arrived at her car crash in the first ambulance and had held her hand as they'd cut her out of the upturned wreckage. While she'd transitioned from hysteria to unconsciousness, he whispered all the right things to keep her calm.

She would've died right there on the Blackwood Road Bridge if he hadn't been with her.

Her stomach twisted into tight knots. The injured woman would not be so lucky. Glancing away, Gabby stepped up to what was left of the mangled railing. The party deck below was utter bedlam.

Bloodied victims were strewn everywhere. The pool water was

no longer crystal blue. A bikini-clad body floating face-down, staining it crimson, was the reason.

It would've made a compelling photo.

Gabby checked her phone again. Dead. She couldn't believe it. This could be her once-in-a-lifetime opportunity to contend for the Pulitzer and her only recording device was useless.

When she'd started her career as a reporter, it'd been Gabby's job to be first at the scene of a tragedy. She'd seen her share of blood and gore. The majority of the incidents were just sad misfortune. Victims who'd died as a result of their driver wrapping the car around a pole. Or a tragic house fire that'd engulfed an entire family.

The most confronting had been a school bus that'd tumbled down a ravine. She'd been the first reporter at that one and had fought her emotions to capture some remarkable footage with just her iPhone.

Now, for the first time ever, she was at the forefront of a story that would make worldwide headlines, with only her own recall for reference. She tried to take it all in, mentally listing every aspect that would make the sensational story compelling reading. The world needed to know what had happened. What was still happening.

But blood and mangled bodies were no longer what fascinated people. Audiences had become immune to it. She'd become immune to it. What she needed was the X factor.

Max stood, and when he shook his head, the distress in his eyes confirmed the woman wasn't going to make it. He ran to the next victim, knelt down, and searched for a pulse. The man's chest injuries were so extensive several rib bones jutted from his bloody flesh like mangled fingers. He must've been dead, because Max was up again and moving onto the next person in a flash, who also looked to be dead.

Three dead passengers in a space of about twenty yards.

It took a certain person to remain calm when all hell was breaking loose. Max was one of them. Gabby was another. She was a great reporter. So good that her career projection had had some of her competitors making unfounded suggestions that she must have slept with her superiors to rise up the ranks so quickly. That had only driven her to work harder.

Even before the plane had hit, Gabby had known the bloodshed was going to be extensive. But glancing around and seeing the number of people who weren't moving confirmed she'd underestimated how bad the carnage would be. There was no telling how many fatalities there were in the decks below. Their deck had been hit with just an engine and other minor debris, but after it'd ricocheted off the water, the bulk of the plane had slammed into the decks below.

Two thoughts blazed through her like forked lightning.

Did the plane damage the hull?

Are we sinking?

She strode to the outer railing, leaned out and gasped. "Oh my God."

Although it would've been the photo of her career, it didn't offer the level of elation something like that usually would. The impact had carved a huge hole in the side of the ship. One dangling life raft was on fire and several others were gone altogether. Black smoke spewed from the wreckage, confirming that either the ship was on fire or the plane was. Or both.

Shit! Why isn't there a siren?

Surely the Captain would've sounded the horn.

Why aren't the staff commanding everyone to report to their muster stations?

"Max!" she yelled. He was kneeling before a little girl who was screaming for her mother. She was about six or seven years old and was wearing a pink polka-dotted swimsuit. A streak of blood stained her neck.

Gabby strode to him and touched his shoulder. "Max."

"What?" He leaned in to examine the little girl's wound.

"This is serious, Max."

"I know."

"No, you don't know. I think the ship will sink."

His gaze shot to her and with clenched teeth, he indicated to the girl with his eyes. "Jennifer can't find her mom, Gabrielle. I need you to stay with her while—"

"Oh no, no, no." Gabby shook her head. "You're not leaving me."

"People need me." He'd given up his paramedic career a decade ago, yet Max always jumped in when aid was needed.

"*I* need you." Gabby glared at the intensity in Max's eyes, pleading with him to make the right decision.

"Stop it, Gabrielle. People are dying."

"Max!" She spoke with forced calm. "A hell of a lot more people are going to die if this ship sinks."

"It's not sinking. The siren would've sounded." Max turned back to the little girl. "Where did you last see your mom?"

The girl glanced at her side. "She was right here." Tears streaked down Jennifer's cheeks. A sob burst from her throat. "Now she's gone."

"Okay. It's all right. Now tell me, what was your mom wearing?"

As the little girl described her mother's floral dress, Gabby wanted to scream. They didn't have time for this. They should be getting their kids. They should be putting on life jackets and racing to their muster station.

Everyone should be.

Max glared at Gabby. "Jennifer needs you." Max unclasped Jennifer's fingers and placed the small palm into Gabby's hand. "Look after her."

"Max. I mean it. Don't go."

He stood, pecked her cheek, and then raced down the stairs like an elite gymnast.

Chapter Seven

GABBY

As Max moved from one bloodied body to the next, Gabby's feet were glued to the artificial grass. The carnage on her level was nothing compared to on the party deck beneath theirs. Blood was everywhere. Mangled bodies were too.

A steady stream of people flooded into the area below via a set of double doors next to the bar. Every one of them had the same reaction. First was mild inquisitiveness. Next came gasps of horror. Gabby spied a teenager who seemed to be using her phone to take photos.

It was the impetus she needed to unroot her feet from the floor.

"Hey, Jennifer, let's see if we can find your mom." Clutching her tiny hand, Gabby led the girl down the stairs, and as Jennifer's wide-eyed gaze shot from one bloodied corpse to the next, and her complexion faded to deathly pale, Gabby conceded that Max was right. Their children did not need to see this.

But it wasn't just the graphic scene that was distressing. It was the agonized screams. A lot of people were in horrific pain and the unbearable cries around them had Gabby's stomach churning. It didn't matter how many times she'd heard it—the sound of a person screaming in absolute agony was the most sickening of all.

She tiptoed around rubble, careful not to step on any blood, or outstretched fingers, heading toward the teenager in the denim shorts. The girl must've sensed her approach because she spun her way, glanced up and down Gabby's body, but promptly looked away.

"Hey." Gabby noted the phone's screen was indeed illuminated. "Is your phone working?"

"No." She chomped on purple chewing gum as she spoke.

"I can see that it is."

"Only the camera." She bulged her heavily made-up eyes.

Gabby wanted to slap the cockiness right off her pretty young face. "Everyone else's phones have stopped."

"So?" The girl zoomed in on a bloody body and snapped a few photos.

"Where were you when the plane crashed?"

"In the toilet. Go figure, huh?" The girl shuffled toward another victim and Gabby scanned the bedlam for Max.

It'd been a long time since she'd seen him in this capacity. While she avoided the bodies, he dived in, not afraid to get his hands covered in a stranger's blood.

She glared at the staff who should be helping him. Several were still standing behind the bar and judging by their stunned expressions, and lack of action, they obviously had no idea what to do.

The bitter stench of blood filled the air.

Many were dead. Many more were critically injured, some beyond hope. Yet Max was the only person who was doing anything.

The two barmaids, whose only problem just ten minutes ago would've been running out of little cocktail umbrellas, were sobbing hysterically as they knelt beside the bloody corpse of their colleague who'd taken the full impact of that exploding mirror.

They would be in shock, but that was no excuse.

They should be taking control.

It was probably the same on the lower decks, especially the dining area, directly below. The buffet had opened just minutes before the plane had hit. One minute, passengers could've been deciding between Atlantic crab claws and caramelized beef cheeks. Next minute they could've been fighting for their lives. Or worse. Dead.

"You." Max pointed at a woman wearing a tiny white uniform. "Come help me."

Gabby recognized her. The young barmaid had made her children chocolate milkshakes a few nights ago. But the chirpy young crew member who'd babbled non-stop while she'd made the calorie-overloaded drinks was gone, replaced instead with a fragile woman who looked set to crumble to pieces at any second.

Max had a convincing way about him, and although the barmaid's eyes had her looking like she'd seen a zombie, she still ran to his side. "Place your hands over this wound. Keep the pressure." Max grabbed her hands and showed her what to do, and to Gabby's surprise, despite the horrific amount of blood, she did as instructed.

"Where's the Captain?" Max asked her.

"We don't know. We can't contact the bridge."

Gabby's mind skidded to what she'd noted earlier. Every single piece of electronic equipment on the deck had died. The lights. The music. The movie. Their phones.

The cruise ship had been in trouble before the plane even hit.

An escalation of voices caught her attention and Gabby turned as seven crew members and a security guard burst through the double swinging doors.

"Jesus Christ." The guard's bulging eyes scanned the carnage as he strode to the two crew members who were still demonstrating utter incompetence by sobbing hysterically.

Holding Jennifer's hand, Gabby coaxed the girl forward, aiming toward the new group's hasty huddle. Despite the surrounding bedlam, she still managed to catch snippets of their dialogue.

". . . Captain's dead."

"No . . . heart attack. . . . pacemaker. . ."

"EMP."

". . . stopped. . . engines. . . nothing."

"No coms . . ."

Gabby's mind snagged on the EMP acronym. Electro Magnetic

Pulse. Several years ago, she'd covered a story on a bunch of crazies who were preparing for the end of the world. The Preppers, as they'd called themselves, had garnered enough supplies in two shipping containers they'd buried beneath the ground to create a life-saving compound. They'd estimated they could live like that with a dozen personally selected friends for ten years.

Ten years! She couldn't even imagine why they'd want to.

They'd gone into extensive detail when explaining the Electro Magnetic Pulse phenomenon to her, and at the time, Gabby had believed they were completely nuts. But the story had rated well. Audiences loved the crazies.

Now, though, she wasn't so sure they had lost their minds.

An EMP strike would explain why everything had stopped. The lights, the music, their phones had all shut down at exactly the same time.

It would also explain why the plane had fallen from the sky. Even though its impact was some time after the power failed, it still made sense. Planes didn't just plummet straight down; they glided.

The most famous one was the A320 that Captain Sullenberger had landed in the Hudson River. If her recollection was correct, he'd had about four or five minutes after his engines failed to land that plane.

However, the difference there was that Sullenberger hadn't lost all power; he'd still had some control. The plane that hit the cruise ship would have been completely incapacitated after the EMP strike.

That pilot hadn't stood a chance. Nor had all those passengers.

The effects of an EMP attack would also explain why nobody had triggered the emergency sirens—there was no power to do so. Gabby recalled the Preppers keeping two-way radios and other critical electrical equipment in a contraption they'd titled a Faraday cage. Basically, it was a metal box that shielded the contents from a gamma blast.

It would explain why denim-shorts-girl still had a working phone. She'd been inside the ship, in a toilet, when the EMP had hit. Gabby's hopes were growing. The bulk of the ship was its own

Faraday cage. She may get her hands on a working phone after all. If so, she'd be able to find out what the hell was going on.

And she'd be able to relay her story directly to headquarters.

A young crew member staggered through the doors, launching Gabby from her burgeoning wave of hope. But the second she recognized the woman, fear whipped up Gabby's neck like a viper. It was Priscilla, the young crew member who was in charge of the kids' club. Tears streaked her flushed cheeks and her wide, darting eyes screamed her distress.

Gabby launched Jennifer up to her chest and as the little girl strangled Gabby's neck, Gabby ran to Pricilla. Each step was like she was wearing cement boots.

Gabby clutched Pricilla's arm, digging her nails in. "Where are the kids? My kids? Sally and Adam. Where are they?"

Pricilla's eyes bulged. Her lips trembled. "They . . . they were doing a Pokémon hunt?"

"What?" Gabby's heart exploded in her chest. "Where?"

"I don't know." Pricilla jammed her fist to her mouth as if stifling a scream. "I can't raise them on the walkie-talkies. They could be anywhere on the ship."

A strangled cry burst from Gabby's throat.

Chapter Eight

GUNNER

"Jesus Christ!" Gunner leaned over the port side rail in an attempt to assess the damage to the stern. Clutching the metal, his heart hit locomotive pace. His eyes snagged on every critical aspect.

The plane had punched an enormous crater into the mid-to-rear sections of the ship, and the tail jutted out the side like the end of an arrow. Black smoke spewed from the wreckage.

None of the runners he'd sent earlier had returned, and without comms, or closed-circuit television, he had no idea what the hell was going on. There would be fatalities—there was no doubt about that. It was his job to make sure there weren't any more.

Before the setting sun stole all visibility, he had to inspect the damage himself.

He strode back inside and eyeballed Sykes across the dimly lit room. "Sykes, you're in charge of the bridge. Continue with visual surveillance and mayday calls."

"Yes, sir." Sykes saluted and aimed his binoculars out to the blackness beyond the window. The waxing moon was about to be the only light. It was hardly enough. If a petrol tanker was right in front of them, they'd have no chance of avoiding it.

If pirates were to attack, they were all dead.

He turned to Jae-Ellen. Her wide eyes radiated fear. Or shock. Maybe both. Pauline's expression was exactly the same. Ignoring their distress, he did a curt nod, hoping to portray confidence. "Right. You two come with me. Let's go."

He led the way out the door and down the stairs to the eleventh deck. He had hoped the emergency lighting in the interior of the ship had been insulated from the EMP.

He was wrong. It was completely dark.

The urge to run full tilt toward the devastation was powerful but stupid. Instead, he maintained a hasty stride with his hands held forward to avoid colliding with anything. He was heading for Petals, the buffet restaurant at the stern.

His brain snagged on the timing of the crash. Mealtime. The buffet restaurant would've been heavily occupied. There could be dozens of fatalities.

His heart lurched. It could be hundreds.

But the damage to Petals wasn't his greatest problem. If the extent of that smoke was anything to go by, then he could have another emergency on his hands.

A fire on a ship was a catastrophe.

"Sir." Jae-Ellen cleared her throat. "Why didn't the emergency lighting come on? Aren't they on a separate system, designed to never extinguish?"

Her question was an intelligent one.

The answer was terrifying. The ship's wiring was its central nervous system.

And that made an EMP attack its worst enemy.

His brain scrambled for a way to put that into words that didn't terrify them any more than they already were but that also didn't insult their intelligence. "An Electro Magnetic Pulse is different to any other kind of nuclear explosion. It's unlikely to be seen or felt by humans. But it is hell on electronics. This ship is crammed with extensive wiring that connects every digital aspect to the bridge."

Gunner's hands hit a wall and he glided his way toward the stairwell he recalled was to his right. "An EMP strikes in two stages.

The first one is a super-strong radio wave that overloads and burns out any electronic devices it encounters. The second stage instigates cascading failure as the electromagnetic pulse shoots along every connecting electrical cable. Emergency lighting is all over the ship. It just needed one of those lights to be hit with that super-charged pulse for it to zap all the connecting wires. It's a domino effect. Take out one, take them all out. System-wide blackout."

"Jesus!" Jae-Ellen's breath hitched.

"So . . . so you *do* believe it was an EMP strike, sir?" Pauline's voice was barely audible, drowned out by crippling emotion.

As he launched up the stairs, the railing guiding his way, he considered her question. He'd been thirteen when he'd told a lie that'd ruined his family. Ever since then he'd committed to telling the truth. He just hoped his two senior crew members could handle it. "If *just* the ship had been affected, we could've attributed the blackout to some kind of system failure. But add in the demise of that plane and it puts the situation on a catastrophic level. One that the world has never experienced before. So yes, unfortunately, I do think it was an EMP."

Jae-Ellen made a noise like she'd been punched in the stomach. "Oh my God."

"What're we going to do?" Pauline's shrill voice bounced off the stairwell walls.

He wanted to look them in the eyes and portray the integrity he'd been faking for decades. But it was impossible in the blackened stairwell, so he kept going. At the top landing, he crossed the carpeted hall and headed for the exit doors. "We must do our best. That's all I ask. But we've got to keep it together. For the sake of the passengers. Understand?"

"Yes, sir."

Gunner had strolled the length of the ship at least a hundred times since he'd boarded twelve days ago. It usually took about ten minutes.

Now, he did it in three.

The second he pushed through the outer doors he was hit with a sound that had his gut contorting. People screaming. With the diminishing sun's waning light, he bolted along the deck, heading toward the cries with his heart in his throat. It would be bad. He just had to brace himself. Act cool. Calm. In control; like a Captain should be.

He failed.

His first sighting of a victim had his own silent screams blasting at his ears.

It was a passenger from the plane. The poor woman hadn't stood a chance. She'd been still strapped in her seat when she'd catapulted into the gelato stand. A shattered pane of glass had punctured through her chest, pinning her and the chair to the refrigerated counter.

When a drop of blood spilled from the glistening shard and splattered onto the deck, Gunner fought the instinct to whirl around and sprint away. His stomach was a ball of scorpions, twisting, turning, stinging. Bile shot to his throat. But he bit it back, determined to fake his bravado better than he'd ever done before.

For the first time in his career, he hated the sunlight. The remnants of the setting sun seemed to be ramping up his visibility, allowing him to see sickening sights with a heightened awareness that he wished would disappear.

If that woman's demise wasn't horrific enough, the next body he saw was. It was Sarah. The young crew member who'd worked at the gelato stand. Only yesterday, she'd served him up the daily delight with a smile to match.

She was sprawled on the floor. Her open eyes confirmed she was gone, as did the bloody gash that'd nearly decapitated her.

Jae-Ellen ran to the railing and Gunner clenched his jaw as he tried to block out the sounds of her throwing up.

"Hey, check that one out."

Gunner spun to the man's voice, and what he saw was nearly as sickening as the gruesome victims.

Two men, identical in appearance—one was taking photos.

Gunner strode to them and snatched his phone. "Give me that."

"Hey, that's mine."

"As Captain of this ship, I'm requisitioning this phone."

"Bullshit." One of the twins lunged at Gunner, and with his fury already at boiling point Gunner jumped sideways, snatched the man's arm, curled it up behind him, and shoved him face-first into a wall. "You two are despicable. Where were you when the plane hit?"

"None of your fucking—"

Gunner yanked his arm higher.

"Shit. Shit. Okay . . . we were in our cabin."

Gunner eased off a fraction. "What deck?"

"Deck six."

"Was there any damage?"

"How would we know? There's no lights. It's black as hell down there. Hey, stop it, you're hurting me."

Gunner let go and spun him around. "What did you see on your way up here?"

"Nothing." He rubbed his shoulder.

"There were those people in the elevator," the other man said.

Damn it, Gunner hadn't even considered the elevators.

"Hey guys, you should come see—" A young woman burst through Petals' double swinging doors, but she stopped short when she spied Gunner.

"Ma'am. I'm Gunner McCrae, the ship's Captain. I need your phone."

She glanced at her iPhone, then snapped it behind her back.

"Ma'am, I demand you hand over your phone."

The woman spun on her heel and took off. Pauline raced after her and the swinging door flung back and forth after they shot through it. A woman screamed and seconds later Pauline shoved the passenger back through the doors by a fistful of hair.

"Give him your phone." Pauline spoke into the woman's ear with surprising calm.

"Here." Her eyes blazed as she shoved the phone forward. "It doesn't work anyway."

"What's your pin code?"

"Nine, six, six, six." She glared at him.

Gunner jabbed the pin and the phone lit up, but no signal appeared. It made sense. The phone had been spared from the

EMP pulse because they were below decks, but the strike would've obliterated all the satellites. It was something else he hadn't considered. Even if he could get the satellite phone from the safe, it would be hopeless anyway.

The phones would be useful for lighting and the time, nothing else.

He put the phones into airplane mode to save battery and shoved them into his pockets. "You should be disgusted in yourselves. Show some respect. Now follow me. We need your help."

Gunner strode ahead and only half expected them to obey as he thrust through the doors to the dining hall. A barrage of noises had his stomach churning. People screaming. Wailing. Sobbing. People calling for help.

Yet there was something else—a strange empty static. A void that should've been filled with all sorts of sounds. Music, kitchen equipment, the ever-present electrical hum. Laughter.

It looked like a bomb had exploded. Tables, chairs, buffet counters, and giant slabs of marble had been blasted apart. An enormous section of the roof had caved in, revealing a mass of wires that dangled down like thousands of deadly jellyfish tentacles. Smoke clouded the room making it impossible to see to the other side. The air was tinged with opposing odors of enticing meals and toxic fumes. Crockery, cutlery, food, masses of debris, and bodies littered the floor.

A gory chunk of flesh slipped off the ceiling and splattered onto the patterned lino at his feet. The disgusting sight triggered a starter gun in Gunner's brain. He raced to an extremely obese man on the floor who had a nauseating mix of bloody flesh and the roast of the day across his chest. Gunner knelt at the passenger's side and felt for a pulse in the folds of his neck. The man was dead.

Gunner crawled to another passenger. A woman this time. She, too, was dead.

With each body he examined, he found it harder to breathe. His lungs burned as he struggled to inhale. He struggled to exhale too. He struggled to think . . . to comprehend what he was doing. What he should be doing. The situation was brutal. Sickening. Each additional body he confirmed as deceased was shocking. Young children. Middle-aged women. Elderly couples. It was a battlefield of blood and gore . . . and every single victim was innocent.

"They're all dead." Jae-Ellen's voice bordered on hysterical.

Gunner blocked out her distress and pushed onto the next victim. The situation was a ticking bomb.

He needed to examine the damage to the rest of the ship.

He needed to see if the hull had been compromised.

He needed to make a decision on whether or not to abandon ship.

Chapter Nine

GUNNER

For the sake of all souls on board, Gunner needed to leave the victims that were injured, dying or already dead in Petals restaurant and inspect the impact zone.

Gunner checked one more victim, and after confirming she had no pulse, he pushed to a standing position. A flood of heat washed through him, bathing his already clammy skin in a sickening veil and pushing him to the edge of consciousness. He clutched a chair, and sucked in heady gasps, determined to shove the wave of nausea down.

"Captain! This woman's alive." Pauline's comment was the reprieve he needed.

"Okay. That's good." His eyes skipped to the three passengers who'd followed them into the restaurant. They were standing aside, mouths and eyes wide, seemingly unable or incapable of moving.

"This one's alive too." Jae-Ellen was kneeling beside an injured woman, who was sitting up and holding a bloody hand to her forehead.

Two alive in a field of bodies. The ratio was terrifying.

Gunner scanned the dining room, doing a visual assessment of impending danger. Satisfied it was safe, he pointed at the identical men. "You two. What're your names?"

"Ken," said one.

"Colin . . . Col," said the other.

"Okay, clear this area. I want nothing but the bare floor."

The twins nodded and when they gathered an upturned table and lifted it upright, two bodies were revealed.

Gunner raced to the women who were both lying face-down in a mutual pool of blood. Before he'd even felt for a pulse, he knew they'd be dead.

They were.

He glanced up at the woman who'd been with Col and Ken. Tears streamed down her cheeks; finally, she was showing some compassion. "What's your name?"

"Brandi."

Gunner stood and stepped back from the blood. "Do you have family aboard?"

She pointed toward Col and Ken. "Just my twin brothers."

"Looks like you got lucky." Gunner used his eyes to indicate to the bodies at his feet.

She sucked her bottom lip into her mouth and her chin quivered.

He turned to his Third Officer. "Jae-Ellen."

Jae-Ellen glanced up from the injured woman who, other than the gash on her forehead, seemed to be okay. "Sir."

"There are first-aid stations in the kitchen; take Brandi with you and grab as many supplies as you can."

"Yes, sir." Jae-Ellen leaned in to speak to the injured woman. Once the woman nodded, Jae-Ellen stood and sprinted Gunner's way. Her eyes held his gaze, portraying both an inner strength and a fragile veneer. She was holding it together. . . for now.

"Here, take this phone; it'll be your only light." He placed his hand on her shoulder, and was surprised to feel her trembling. She was suffering more than she was letting on. But for the sake of both of them, he couldn't even ask if she was okay. It was a stupid question anyway; neither of them were okay. Not a single person on Rose of the Sea was okay.

Jae-Ellen nodded, and with the flashlight on, she sprinted toward the kitchen area with Brandi in tow.

"Also, grab whatever you can to cover the bodies. And find a notepad and pen," he hollered after them.

"Yes, sir."

The brothers were making a thunderous racket as they tossed chairs and tables aside. But in between each clatter, the stillness was disturbing. Deathly. Petals should be a hive of activity with hundreds of people enjoying their evening meal.

Instead, it'd become a morgue.

Gunner shoved that distinction aside and stepped toward the blast zone.

The explosion had created a hole in the side of the ship that was the size of a double-decker bus. He inched up to the edge, looked into the giant chasm and gasped. A young bearded man was dangling from a rod of metal reinforcing. Several poles had pierced his torso, pinning him to the shredded circumference like some kind of sick artistic homage to Jesus on the cross.

Gunner forced his eyes away and peered into the crater. The destruction was shocking. Five decks had been directly impacted by the collision. The blast zone from the resulting explosion looked like a prehistoric monster had taken a giant bite out of the ship.

He prayed the hull remained intact.

If not, he had a whole set of additional problems to deal with. And very little time.

Halfway down the hole, a dim light was filtering through, offering a slight visual. At the very bottom were the remains of the plane. A column of dirty smoke spewed from the plane's carcass and drifted out to sea. Movement in the plane caught his eye and he searched the smoke for clarification. A heartbeat later, his breath died. Flames! The air punched out of him so fast his ears stung. "Shit!" His stomach heaved a violent warning. Searing. Painful. Urgent.

Tongues of orange fire were licking up the side of the plane wreck creating a tornado of glowing embers that filled the air like thousands of deadly fireflies. It was impossible to tell if the sprinkler systems had triggered. And even if they had, it was impossible to know if the water pumps were working.

He had to get down there. And fast.

Out of the corner of his eye, he saw Jae-Ellen sprinting back with two first-aid kits and a handful of linen. He strode to her. "Jae-Ellen . . . Pauline . . . keep assessing the victims. Just do your best with the injured."

They nodded, grim-faced.

The light was draining away from the room, and with it went the light from Jae-Ellen's eyes. Gunner had to force her distressed look from his mind and keep moving.

"Brandi, use the passenger lanyards to make a list of the victim's names and check their pockets for phones. Keep them if they are working. Then cover the bodies. Okay?"

Her eyes bulged and when her face washed with gray, he thought she was going to throw up. Ignoring her reaction, he spun to her brothers. "Col and Ken, once you've finished clearing this area, move all the bodies over there." Gunner pointed at the largest seating area in the middle of the room.

"Sir?" Jae-Ellen's bottom lip quivered. "Where are you going, sir?"

"There's a fire down there. I need to extinguish it and assess the damage."

"Are we abandoning ship, sir?" The terror in her voice was brutal.

"I'll know more soon."

"Sir?"

"Yes?"

A tear trickled down her cheek, and she slapped it away as if annoyed by its presence. "Don't abandon me, sir."

He touched her trembling shoulder and waited until her gaze met his. "I promise you, every single person still alive right now will leave this ship before me." The second the sentence tumbled from his lips, he knew it was a lie. But it was just like the lies he and his mother had told. Once they'd been triggered, the landslide of consequences were unstoppable.

That was twenty-four years ago. Since then, his life had forever been carved into before that moment and after.

Now he was trapped in another life-defining moment.

Except there was one extreme difference. In his past, there had only been two lives at stake.

Now there were hundreds.

Gunner always knew his lifetime of lies would one day come back to haunt him.

But he'd never imagined it would be as catastrophic as this.

Chapter Ten

MADELINE

Madeline didn't mean to rock as she hugged her knees. But she couldn't help it. It was a trick she'd learned to help transport her mind from reality. Her concentration was on moving her body, back and forward, back and forward, not the blackness seeping into her brain. Nor the constant tick that echoed about the metallic cube, counting out the never-ending seconds of their entrapment. *Tick. Tick. Tick.*

"Hey, Madeline, don't worry. They're coming back. I'm here with you." Sterling was calm, way too calm.

"I hate the dark." The words blurted from her mouth, and she regretted them the instant they were uttered. Years of therapy had helped her grasp how foolish being afraid of the dark was, yet it had still failed to exterminate the grip that phobia had on her.

Flashbacks to the long dark hours she'd endured at the hands of her kidnapper were always there. Lurking like a predator. Preying on her weakness. Darkness served as their highway, giving the retched memories unfettered access to her conscious mind.

Darkness was her enemy.

She even slept with a small nightlight. And despite their initial objections, her cabin-mates had allowed her to keep it.

"Hey, mind if I sit with you?"

She jumped when he spoke, but there was something about his voice that she found soothing. Madeline latched onto the melody, begging for it to simmer her frantic thoughts. The extent of her indecision throbbed in her chest and it was a long, agonizing moment before she convinced herself that she was fine. That *he* was fine. She sniffed back her tears. "Okay."

He sidled in beside her and sat so close their shoulders touched. "I'm here for you, okay? We'll do this together."

She nodded and then, realizing Sterling couldn't see her, she said, "Okay."

He was nestled in beside her, close. Way too close. She'd never let a stranger sit with her like this before. Especially a man. And she was torn between staying frozen in position and shuffling sideways.

"There you go. Want me to put my light back on?"

"Yes please."

He did, and as he rested his phone facedown at his side so the light was shining upward, she wiped her fingers beneath her nose, and sniffed back her imbalance.

"So, you must be staff, huh?"

"What?" Her mind puzzled. "How did you know that?"

"I've got one of the cheapest cabins on the ship. On the bottom decks. You came up from a lower deck, so I figure you came from one of the staff cabins."

"Yeah, you're right. I usually take the stairs."

"Pfft. I bet you wish you had this time."

"Yeah. I'm trying to rest my ankle. I hurt it in last night's performance."

"Oh, are you a dancer?"

"Yes. Did you see the show?"

"I did. You were the best in your row." He chuckled.

She huffed out a shaky laugh. "Did you see the high-ropes act?"

"Yes. Oh my God. Was that you?"

"Sure was."

"Wow. So. . . no fear of heights then."

"Nope." She'd take climbing a mountain over tunneling beneath it any day. "Just the dark. What about you? What do you do?"

"I'm a teacher. Elementary school. I've been doing it for about six years now."

"Huh. I could never do that," she said. "Don't have the patience."

He huffed. "It can be trying, that's for sure."

They fell into silence. Each night on all of the eleven cruises she'd worked on, she'd found the repetitive beat of the engines therapeutic. She'd used that beat as her focal point to lull her to sleep. But with both the lights and the engine beat gone, the emptiness smothered her. Seeped in. Crawled up her spine. Tickled her neck.

The minutes ticked on and her mind slipped once again to her eight-year-old self. Nearly every waking moment during her entrapment, she'd dreamed of being rescued. But the days had become weeks and the weeks had become months.

And Madeline had lost the ability to hope anymore.

She'd been held captive for five months. She'd thought it was longer. Two years. Maybe three. Without a window to the outside world, there was no day. Only night. Tracking time had been impossible.

Exactly like now.

Had the sun already set?

The incessant noise was the only clock. *Tick. Tick. Tick.*

Desperate for another avenue of focus, she cleared her throat. "So, ummm, were you enjoying the cruise?"

He rumbled out a small groan. "Yes and no."

"I mean before this." She huffed.

"I meant before this."

"Oh, you weren't?" She glanced at him and saw what she thought was sadness in his expression.

"It was meant to be my honeymoon."

She scrambled for a suitable response. "Oh. That's ummm . . ."

"My lovely bride didn't show up at the church."

"Oh, wow. You poor thing."

"Yep. I spent our wedding night alone in our fancy hotel hoping she'd at least have the decency to explain herself in person. She never turned up. So, I figured we'd already paid for our honeymoon cruise; I might as well take it. Unfortunately, none of my friends could join me on such short notice. So it's just me. All alone."

"Oh, that's terrible." But it didn't sound that terrible. Not the alone bit anyway. Being alone sounded perfect. That was all Madeline wanted. To be alone. It was why she'd taken this job. So she could get a deposit together to buy her own little apartment. All by herself.

He huffed. "I've spent twelve days trying to figure out what went wrong."

Madeline knew the pain of a broken heart. "Did you get your answer?"

"No. The only answer I got was that it's time to move on."

She understood that plan. Working on cruise ships had been her new beginning. "How long were you together?"

"Eleven years. We met in high school."

"Wow." When Madeline had been dating Aiden, she'd thought he was the love of her life. He was the first man she'd let into her heart. The only man. She'd thought they'd get married. Have children.

She'd been wrong. Madeline smacked those thoughts away. Aiden didn't deserve even a second of her precious time.

"Yeah, you'd think you'd know someone after eleven years. Apparently not."

"I'm so sorry." Nothing she said would ease his pain. But his story proved what she already knew. . . it was impossible to ever really know someone.

He sighed. "I guess it's a good thing. Better for it to happen now than in a few years' time, or worse, when we had kids."

"That's true."

With each pause in their conversation, the silence somehow intensified. A trickle of sweat trailed down her temple and when she swiped it away, she realized what else was wrong. "Oh no."

"What?"

"The air-con has stopped too. It must be really bad."

"What would make everything shut down like that?"

She shook her head. "I have no idea."

"They haven't sounded any alarms or anything, so it can't be a total catastrophe, like hitting an iceberg."

She chuckled. "Not likely. We only left Hawaii yesterday."

"That's true. Now that you mention it, it is getting hot. How long do you think we've been here?"

"Too long."

"No, seriously. How long?"

She heaved out a sigh. "My guess is an hour at least. Check your phone. What time is it?"

"Oh." Sterling brought the phone's screen to life. "Shit, it's six-forty. We've been in here about forty-five minutes. Someone should've come for us by now." He frowned at the screen and moaned. "Bugger."

"What?" The screen glow highlighted his corrugated frown.

"My phone's nearly flat." He pushed up from the floor and banged on the door. "Hello! Can anyone hear us?"

She joined him, and together they screamed and hammered the door for help until her throat burned and her fists hurt. Giving up, she slinked back against the wall, slid down it, and hugged her knees. As the minutes ticked on, she tried to ignore the pressure in her bladder.

Tick. Tick. Tick.

The phone's light went out. Madeline gasped.

Thousands of gnarly fingers reached out to her in the blackness. They crawled along her skin, up her neck, through her hair.

Madeline curled into a ball and screamed.

Chapter Eleven

ZON

Zon had thought the day he'd won the cruise ticket in a poker game was the luckiest one of his life. He'd been wrong. Today, right now, was his luckiest day. He'd nearly got the whole fuckin' casino to his-self. There were just a couple of losers who were still sticking by their slot machines, waitin' for the stupid things to turn back on.

Then there was the old bird crying over the dude on the floor. He was dead. No amount of crying was gonna bring his sad ass back.

Zon had seen dead people before. Especially old ones. They turned so white their skin was practically see-through. And they always died with their mouths open, like they were about to start yabberin' again. When his grandmama had kicked the bucket, she'd been dead a long time before his mama noticed. Zon had seen when she'd taken her last breath; she'd gasped for air like she had a giant wad of wet pastry or somethin' stuck in her throat. But he didn't bother telling no one. He figured they'd learn it soon enough. His grandmama had been dead a full three hours before his mama started screaming. It would a been longer if them damn flies hadn't started buzzing around his grandmama's mouth.

His granddaddy, though—when he'd kicked it, he'd done it all dramatic-like, just like he did with everythin' in his life. He'd had a beer in one hand and a cigarette in the other when he fell face-first into the griddle they'd had over the fire, cookin' up some crawfish. Ruined the whole fuckin' meal. While his mama was screaming, Zon's daddy had been cussing over wasting his good beer on trying to put the old bastard out.

So yeah, Zon had no issues with seeing dead people.

First thing he'd done when the fat guard had nicked off was scope out the casino. It'd felt mighty fine striding through the shadows knowin' nobody could see him. Once he'd done a lap, he'd moved to the bar and waited a whole minute before he went around the other side and helped his-self to some whiskey. And not just any old liquor either. The one he'd picked needed the ladder. It had to be expensive when it was on the top shelf. When he saw the label, it was like it'd been sittin' there waiting just for him. Whistle Pig—The Boss Hog. Yep. Damn straight. He was the boss hog now.

Tasted sweet as honey too.

Especially with the packets of pork rinds he'd nicked.

He liked being behind the bar, knowing that he could take whatever he wanted. Years back, he'd considered workin' in a bar, but then he'd thought about all them pricks who'd be getting pissed and havin' a good ol' time while he'd be working his ass off for minimum wage. Fuck that. He'd rather be out gator hunting.

Zon took his time chompin' on the pork rinds and swigging the whiskey. All the while, he was waiting for them slot machine losers to leave. About a dozen or so had, but there were still six sitting in the dark. The woman had stopped crying and when she'd got up and left, she hadn't even looked in his direction.

It was like he was invisible. It felt so fucking good.

He was down half the bottle when he climbed up and grabbed the remaining three Boss Hog's from the top shelf. They were for later. He tugged the trash can out from under the counter and tipped all the fruit and shit into a corner. Then he started fillin' it up with the good stuff. Whiskey. Rum. Tequila. Nuts, and not them cheap beer nuts either—he grabbed the entire rack of cashews. He took the tip jar, a dozen cans of beer, and all the pork rinds. With the trash can nearly full, he put the lid back on, and stepped out from behind the bar.

He strode toward the nearest poker table and just about went ass over tit when he tripped over his own size-thirteen boot. It wasn't too often that alcohol messed him up. But either that expensive shit was more potent than he'd figured or the boat was startin' to do some serious rocking.

Zon was near on chuckling to himself as he wobbled across the room. "Whoa." He felt the need to put his hands out and laughed as he waddled around the dealer's side of the table. He'd seen her put the tray of chips into the compartment beside where she'd been standing. The key she'd used to lock it had been around her scrawny neck.

He bent down to look at the compartment. It was near impossible to see in the darkness. But one rap on it with his knuckles confirmed it was metal. Not much chance of kicking his way into that one.

When he stood, his fingers slid into the slot where the dealer shoved the money after changing it into chips. It was like the poker gods were showin' him the way. He felt around beneath the table and found where that money went. Beneath the money slot was a container about the size of a shoebox; it too was metal. But the stupid dipshits who'd designed it didn't account for what they'd screwed it into . . . the wooden tabletop. His lucky streak kept getting hotter and hotter. He reckoned a good ol' kick would dislodge that piggy bank just nicely.

He glanced around. Other than the dead dude on the floor, he couldn't find nobody. He checked again 'cause he didn't remember seein' 'em all leave. Yep, he really was alone. Zon lay on his back beneath the table and put his right boot up on the money box, testing the distance. After a couple of beats listenin' to hear if any of 'em fuckers came back, he gave the box a full-on kick. The table splintered like kindling, and with one more kick the whole thing came away.

Zon didn't bother countin' the money; he just shoved it in his pockets and moved onto the next table.

He repeated the process with all six poker tables, and the four blackjack tables. The one at the roulette wheel was chocka-block full a chips. He'd had to resist hollerin' for joy over that find. But he had a new dilemma. It was a mighty nice one though. He had so much money and chips that he needed a way to carry them.

He found a carton of Coke cans behind the bar. After tipping out the contents, he poured in the chips. The cash he shuffled into neat piles, folded over and shoved into all four pockets of his jeans. It wasn't ideal, but there weren't no way he was letting that loot outta his sight.

A woman ran past the doorway, and the way she was screaming he expected a zombie to be on her ass. He stared at the entrance, waiting for that miracle, but after a while he gave up. Deciding his looting had reached maximum capacity, he hefted the Coke box under one elbow and grabbed the trash can, but it didn't budge. Fuck it was heavy. All he could do was drag the damn thing across the carpet.

If he had to make a run for it, he was screwed. Especially as he couldn't really run no more. Not after his daddy had chopped off his little toe. Now that had been pain. Zon had come to accept punishment when it was deserved.

But choppin' off his toe. . . that had been fucked up.

It wasn't his fault the baby gator had bit off his sister's finger. If he'd known that was gonna happen, he'd a brought home a bigger gator in the hope it'd eat Bitchface's whole fuckin' hand.

It had been fucking funny when the gator did it though. Her own fault for trying to pat it. Who in their right mind patted a gator? Stupid shit deserved it. His daddy didn't see it like that though, and Bitchface had smirked through his punishment like she was the fuckin' queen.

The wound never did heal properly though, on account of 'em never getting him medical attention. From that day onward, he'd changed the way he walked. And runnin'. . . well, that was near on impossible.

He lugged the bin and the box to the double doors at the entrance to the casino and stashed them to the side. Zon strode out onto the promenade deck like he owned it and a huge blast beneath his feet had him tumbling forward. Every window exploded outward, showering him in glass.

He caught the railing just before his ass went overboard. If it wasn't for the life raft, he'd be swimming right now.

He turned to survey the deck. Glass and shit was all over the place. He checked his arms, his face, his shoulders expecting to see blood everywhere. But there was nothin'.

Zon roared with laughter. Damn it felt good.

Dumb luck sure was lookin' after him tonight.

Chapter Twelve

GUNNER

An explosion resonated deep in the ship, knocking Gunner sideways. His elbow cracked on a railing as his knees hit the decking. "Shit! What the hell was that?" He scrambled upright and scanned for danger, expecting to see the ceiling crashing down. His brain slammed between running back to Petals and confirming Jae-Ellen and Pauline were okay, and committing to his decision to inspect the damage.

Was the ship sinking?

A vision of water pouring into the lower decks flooded his brain.

It was the boot Gunner needed to get his act together.

The sliver of moon that had been providing the only natural light was useless once he passed through a set of fire safety doors. Using precious battery life on the phone he'd taken off one of the deceased was not ideal. But he had no choice. It was pitch-black in the internal passageway.

He turned on the light and out of the darkness, a man staggered toward him, blood pouring from a head wound and oozing through his fingers. Gunner raced to him. "Hey, you okay?" It was a stupid question. Of course he wasn't okay.

"Yeah." The man cringed. "Hit my head. I'll be fine. But what the fuck's going on?"

Dodging his question, Gunner said, "There's a triage set up in Petals. Use the outside deck and head to the back of the ship." He pointed at the doors and tapped the man's shoulder. "The crew will help you."

Gunner sprinted away, heading for the main stairwell that traversed from the running track on deck twelve right down to the lowest passenger cabin deck . . . deck four. Although he'd been on the ship for just a dozen days, he'd made it his mission to study the layout from day one and was confident he could make it to the lower levels without an elevator.

The elevator!

His heart lurched for those poor people stuck in there. They'd be trapped in complete blackness. Just like the injured passengers he'd left in the dining hall, Gunner had to block them from his mind and stay focused.

At the end of the corridor was a soft glow, and hoping it meant a light was working, he picked up his speed. But there was something else coming from that direction. A strange sound, like a pack of trapped animals, wild and forlorn.

He turned the corner and his heart thudded to a stop.

It was a scene from *The Walking Dead*.

The stairs were jam-packed with people scrambling upward, a couple of phones lighting their way. Some were injured with bloody flesh wounds. Some were covered in debris and what looked like plaster dust. Some of the women were crying. All of them looked terrified.

Their attire—men in dinner suits and women in expensive evening wear—indicated they'd come from the à la carte restaurant, Lily's.

Gunner should put his head down, push through them and continue onto priority one. But he couldn't do it. He leaned over the railing. "That's it, ladies and gentlemen. Keep coming up this way. Go to the buffet restaurant. We've set up an emergency room."

A burley man in a designer suit who stood at least a foot taller than the rest pushed past an elderly couple and clutched Gunner's arm. "Hey! What the hell's going on? Why are all the lights out?"

"Sir, we're having some technical difficulties. You need—"

"Technical? Bullshit!" he blurted.

"What about the explosions?" someone yelled.

"We saw that plane crash into the ship," a woman shouted out from the crowd. "Was it a terrorist?"

"No. It wasn't a terrorist." The crowd closed in around Gunner, trapping him on the landing.

"It's just like nine-eleven. We're under attack."

"Are we going to sink?"

"Should we go to the life rafts?"

"Okay. Okay!" Gunner held up his hands. "Listen up. I'm Captain Gunner McCrae."

"You're not the Captain." The big man loomed over Gunner. "We sat at Captain Nelson's table two nights ago. Who the fuck are you?" He leaned in, and Gunner reeled at the yeasty beer on his breath.

The crowd continued to multiply, circling him like hungry hyenas. Phone lights were aimed at him, thrusting him into the spotlight. He squinted against the glare. His brain flashed back to the police interrogation room he'd endured all those years ago, with one very bright light that had been aimed right at him. He'd been terrified then. He was close to that now.

His stomach twisted. A bitter taste flooded his tongue. Pain flared behind his eyes. He wanted to say he was just Gunner McCrae who, until a few hours ago, was the newly promoted staff Captain. He wanted to say he didn't deserve to be in charge.

He wanted their understanding.

But when his gaze fell on an impeccably dressed elderly woman who was dabbing tears from her eyes, he realized they didn't care about him. They didn't want a sob story; they wanted a man in charge. A man who knew what the fuck he was doing.

Swallowing back the self-pity, he planted his feet on the ground and raised his arms. "Quiet! Listen up." His heart thundered as he waited for their mumbling to settle. "I'm sorry to say Captain Stewart passed away, and I am now——"

"Jesus! What happened?"

"Was he murdered?"

"Are we under attack?"

A wave of agitation raced through the throng.

"Please!" Gunner raised his voice. "Please just listen." Although he had to yell over the crowd, he forced authoritative calm into his voice. "Listen to me, please." He waited a few beats and the crowd hushed. "Captain Stewart died from a suspected heart attack. Now remain calm, and make your way to the buffet restaurant. The crew are waiting for you there. Please! Please go. And keep calm."

The murmurs hit fever pitch. Some started moving. Most didn't. But he couldn't waste another second.

Gunner pushed through the crowd, forcing his way down the stairs. "Go to the buffet restaurant. Deck eleven. Remain calm." He repeated the orders over and over. "Go to Petals restaurant."

The crowd reached out to him, fired questions non-stop.

"What happened?"

"Are we sinking?"

"What was that explosion?"

But he ignored them all. He had questions of his own that needed answers.

Shining his phone light at each landing, he counted the decks as he went. *Eight. Seven.*

"Go to deck eleven."

Six.

"Remain calm."

The lower he went, the less people he encountered, which was understandable. The timing of the attack meant that the bulk of the passengers had been either in the restaurants or on the party decks.

Five. "Remain calm."

At the next landing he checked the wall schematic nestled between two sets of elevator doors. *Four.* The lowest deck with passenger cabins. He turned, strode to a door labeled 'No Access. Crew only,' and pushed through. Down another set of stairs, he entered the crew passage that traversed from bow to stern. It stretched black and ominous before him. To his relief, in the distance he spied a lit-up emergency exit sign. "Thank God," he mumbled. It was a good sign.

"Hey, there's someone."

Gunner spun to the voice and from the gloom, two people strode toward him. "Hello."

A middle-aged couple reached his side. "What's going on?" the man asked. "What's happened?"

"Sir, madam, I'm Captain Gunner McCrae. Do either of you require medical attention?"

"No, sir." Confusion drilled onto the man's face. "What happened to Captain Nelson?"

He bypassed their question by asking one of his own. "May I have your name's and ranks please?"

"I'm Quinn, bar staff, and this is my wife Cloe from catering."

It wasn't unusual for couples to work on cruise ships. It was how he'd met his wife. *Oh, God.* His heart clenched. *When will I see her and Bella again?*

His heart nearly stopped. *What if it was never?*

"An explosion woke us. Comms are down and the engines have stopped. Want to tell us what's going on? Sir?"

Quinn's question jolted Gunner from his horrifying thoughts. His clipped tone gave Gunner the impression he had a take-no-crap personality. If he did, then he was exactly the type of man Gunner needed. Gunner had intended to direct every person he encountered toward the top deck, but he made a snap decision to utilize Cloe and Quinn instead. "Do either of you have medical training?"

"Just basic first aid." They looked at each other.

"Sir? Where is Captain Stewart?" Cloe frowned.

"He had a heart attack."

"Oh my God." Cloe's eyes darted to her husband. "And the explosion? What was it?"

"A plane crashed into the ship."

He'd let that shocking detail sink in, but there wasn't time. He needed to keep moving. "Cloe, Quinn, I need to get to the lower decks to assess the damage from that plane crash. Can you help me?"

"Yes, sir." Quinn was quick to answer.

"Of course, sir." Cloe squeezed her husband's arm.

"Please, call me Gunner, and thank you." Gunner huffed out a sigh. "Let's move." He spun on his heel and made a beeline for the exit sign in the distance.

"How bad is it?" Quinn was right on Gunner's heel.

"It's bad. The explosion blasted a hole across five or six decks."

"Shiiit," Quinn said.

At the exit sign, Gunner pushed through a door labeled as an emergency exit and entered another stairwell. Next second, the lower door burst open and a huge crowd of people wearing blue uniforms flooded into the stairway. Laundry staff. Despite holding something over their mouths, every one of them seemed to be talking. Their garbled frantic speech was heightened by their language—Spanish.

"Ladies, are you okay? Is anyone injured?"

They carried on as if he wasn't there.

"Does anyone speak English?"

"*Si. Si.*" A woman in the middle of the crowd caught his attention by nodding at him, yet she continued walking. "What is happening? Smoke everywhere. Nobody say anything."

"Go to the top deck. And keep calm. Do you understand?"

Without a response, she merged into the crowd and continued trudging up the stairs. He had no idea if she'd understood.

His cruise ship company prided itself on its multicultural human resources. At a guess, seventy percent of the crew would've declared English as their second language. He himself knew three languages, but Spanish wasn't one of them. He'd never have thought the diversity of multicultural personnel as his impediment before. Now though, with comms and emergency sirens out of action, it was going to make communication even harder.

Once the women had stormed past, he continued to the next landing and with Quinn and Cloe at his side, he checked the wall schematic with the phone light. Second deck.

"There's something else going on, Captain, isn't there? Was this a suicide bomber?" Cloe's voice portrayed as much authority as Quinn's had.

Gunner turned to her. "No, I don't believe so."

"Captain McCrae." In the green emergency lighting, her eyes took on a dark almost unearthly appearance. "My brother died in the nine-eleven attacks in tower one. So don't bullshit me. Was it a terrorist attack?"

He heaved out a sigh and mentally slapped himself for treating them poorly. "I'm sorry. I should've given you the complete picture. I . . . *we* . . . believe our complete system failure, and the subsequent plane crash, was from an EMP attack."

Cloe's hand shot to her mouth. Her eyes darted to Quinn and back to Gunner. When she lowered her hand, her lips were drawn to a thin line. "What do you need us to do?"

Gunner let out a rushed breath. "Thank you." He turned, and as he raced down the last set of stairs, he voiced his plan. "When I looked down into the blast zone, I saw flames. Not sure of the extent of it. But first thing we need to do is put the damn fire out and assess the damage."

"What's an EMP?" Quinn asked.

"It's an Electro Magnetic Pulse," Cloe said, and as she explained the impact of such an attack to her husband, they raced down the corridor.

At the exit door, Gunner braced for a second, then pulled it open. Thick smoke smothered the corridor, making it impossible to see.

He slammed the door shut. "Shit!" Gunner's thundering heart hit a whole new level.

"What?" Quinn barked.

"Smoke. It's bad. We'll need something to cover our faces."

Buttons went flying as Quinn yanked open a plaid shirt he'd been wearing over a white T-shirt. "Will this do?"

"That'll do it," Gunner agreed.

"Show pony." Cloe rolled her eyes Gunner's way as Quinn used his teeth to tear the shirt into three portions.

With the fabric tied over their noses, Gunner pushed the door open again. The green emergency lighting filtered through the smoke creating a toxic-looking cloud. He glanced left and right, but unable to see three feet in front of him, let alone any flames, he stepped into the corridor. As they headed toward the engine room, the dense smoke was black and laced with a caustic odor that had his eyes stinging.

A man in gray overalls stumbled toward them.

Gunner raced forward and clutched the man's shoulders. "Are you okay?"

He shook his head. Tears streamed down his soot-smudged cheeks and blood oozed from a gash on his shoulder.

"What's your name?"

"Garcia. Garcia Lopez."

"Can you walk?"

"*Si. Si.*"

Gunner turned to Quinn. "Can you take him to the stairwell?"

"Yes, sir."

"Thank you. But come straight back."

Quinn stepped in behind Garcia and placed his hands around the man's waist. "Okay, let's go. You're going to be fine."

"Don't be too long," Cloe called to Quinn.

Gunner turned his gaze back to the corridor ahead. It was much wider than the passenger decks above as it catered to the trolleys that carted luggage for up to sixteen hundred passengers as they embarked and disembarked every fourteen days.

For the first time since he left Los Angeles, he was grateful the ship hadn't been at maximum capacity. February was the least-popular month to cruise to Hawaii. If it had been any other month of the year, then the death toll on Rose of the Sea would already be much higher.

Several more staff stumbled through the smoke and after assessing they were not severely injured, Gunner instructed each of them to get topside.

With each step, the smoke became thicker. More dense. More toxic. It reeked of burned rubber and charred meat. And there was only one explanation for that . . . burned bodies. The putrid air was like razor blades to his throat. Bile burned the back of his tongue.

His brain clanged with opposing commands.

I have to get out of here.

I have to do this.

Pain nipped behind his eyes, attacking his eyeballs.

Quinn returned with a rush of labored breathing, launching Gunner from his hijacked thoughts. While Cloe fussed over her husband, making sure he was okay, Gunner wiped stinging tears from his eyes and searched the smoky corridor for signs of life . . . or the source of the smoke.

A flash of red caught his eye. The fire equipment. Relief washed through him as he raced toward the compartment that was recessed into a wall to stop it from obstructing the corridor. With the dim visibility, it was lucky he hadn't walked right past it.

He lifted a portable fire extinguisher off the hook and handed it to Cloe. "Ever used one of these?"

"Only in practice; never for real," she said.

Quinn nodded. "Same here."

"That's good enough for me." He grabbed a third one for himself and the weight alone instilled a sense of hope that everything would be okay. But when he turned back to the smoke that was getting thicker by the second, he conceded just how inadequate the fire equipment was. He should send Cloe and Quinn upstairs to be with the rest of the crew, not lead them into hell.

He was about to voice exactly that when four men burst through a set of double doors and staggered forward, united with their terrified cries. Their bloodshot eyes were wild, disoriented.

"Are you okay?" Gunner tried to talk to them, but either they didn't speak English or they were too distressed to comprehend.

Every crew member had to pass an English language test. But throw in extreme stress and communication was near impossible.

He wasted too many precious seconds with the men before he conceded it was pointless. Gunner pointed down the corridor. "Exit that way. Go up." Using his hands, he tried to convey his meaning.

When the foursome scrambled off, Gunner's gaze snagged on Cloe. Her eyes were loaded with terror.

With his anxiety at tipping point, he clutched her shoulder. "If you want to return topside, I understand."

She glanced at her husband, and as if they possessed some kind of telepathic communication, they turned back to him and said in unison, "No thanks."

"We're right where we need to be, Captain," Quinn clarified.

The Captain designation was a punch to Gunner's gut.

It should be Captain Nelson down here with Gunner at *his* side. A sense of utter inadequacy smashed into him like a tidal wave. The pressure to make the right decisions, to know what he was doing, to save lives, thumped a painful beat behind his eyes.

Thump. Thump. Thump.

Forging through crippling doubt, he turned toward the double doors and forced his feet to move.

Five steps later, Gunner's boot sloshed into water.

Chapter Thirteen

MADELINE

Madeline shifted on the elevator floor, moving her foot from side to side, assessing her injured ankle. When she'd landed awkwardly on the stage last night, it was immediately obvious she'd done significant damage. But it wasn't until she woke this morning and saw the swelling around her ankle bone that she realized just how much.

She'd suffered worse. Much worse. Those wounds had been inflicted a long time ago though, and the pain associated with them had almost faded into oblivion.

Almost.

But in the tiny, blackened elevator, it was impossible to stop her childhood nightmares crawling into her brain. For sixteen years she'd been fighting them. Fighting them hard. But they were always there, waiting to be triggered by the smallest of things.

Or the biggest. Like now.

The darkened space launched her right back into that tiny windowless room.

The closed door reminded her of how many times she'd wished for the door, the only exit in that dungeon, to open. But each time it did, it brought recurring horror.

Professor Flint.

Her kidnapper had insisted she call him that. *Professor Flint.*

She'd found out later, when he'd died in the house fire, that his real name was John Smith. But his name wasn't the only insignificant thing about him. He wasn't a professor either. John Smith was an unmarried car park attendant who'd claimed to still live with his mother. He wasn't even on the police radar.

In the weeks following Madeline's miraculous rescue, after she'd been released from hospital, the police had told her they'd believed her abduction two streets from her own home had been an opportunistic one.

They were certain that she'd been John Smith's first and his last kidnap victim.

None of that information had helped.

It was ironic that the house fire had both lost a life and saved one. How long would she have remained captive if Professor Flint hadn't fallen asleep drunk with a cigarette in his hand?

It was a question that strangled her brain way too often.

She hugged her knees to her chest. But a visual of her sitting in that exact same position on the rotten mattress in his dungeon flashed into her mind, and she curled her feet to her side.

Smith's escape from conviction haunted her as much as what he'd done. He deserved to rot in a tiny cell for the rest of his life. Instead, he'd died of smoke inhalation in his sleep. It was too easy. He should have suffered. Like she had.

Sometimes her tumble down Memory Hell became so vivid that she had to vomit out the horror inside her.

Sometimes, she wished she'd died in that room.

Flashbacks invaded her brain when she least expected it.

A rainy day would have her smelling the dank concrete walls that had seeped with dirty water during each downpour.

Dripping sounds would have her blocking her ears. The smell of smoke would bring back brutal memories of the night she'd nearly died.

She could smell it now. Smoke. It invaded her nostrils like it was acid seeping in and corroding her brain. Fear crawled up her neck.

Invisible spiders inched up her hairline. She shuddered and squeezed her palms to her eyes until pretty colors darted across her eyelids.

"What's that?" Sterling's voice shot through the silence.

She flinched. "What?"

"Smoke. Can you smell it?"

"Shit!" *It wasn't my imagination.*

Sterling scrambled to his feet. "Help! Help!" He banged on the doors. "We're in here. Help!"

She launched at the door and thumped her fist on the metal with him. "Help!"

"We have to find a way out, Madeline." He touched her shoulder.

She recoiled. Hours and hours of therapy had failed to eradicate that involuntary reaction to surprise human contact. Fright was permanently pending at the forefront of her brain.

"We have to find a way out." Sterling's hands scraped across the doors.

Shoving her anxiety aside, she inched her fingers over the smooth metal. At the button panel she jabbed each one, desperate for a flicker of life. Nothing.

She lowered to her hands and knees. With every breath, rancid smoke clawed at her throat. Suddenly she was eight years old again, crawling on the dirty floor in complete darkness, searching for an escape from the smoke-filled hellhole. The memories smothered her. Engulfed her, along with the profound sense of looming death that'd oppressed her for years. Her chest squeezed. She couldn't breathe. She couldn't think. Tears stung her eyes. "We're gonna die. We're gonna die. We're gonna die."

"Hey, hey. No, we're not. Okay? We are not going to die." His hand brushed her shoulder again.

She cringed at his touch and a gasp tumbled from her throat as a tornado of terror twisted inside her, growing in size and power.

"Hey, come on. It's okay. We'll find a way out."

"We're trapped. I'm trapped." A sob burst from her throat. "I'm trapped again."

"Hey." His hands gripped her shoulders and he tugged her to his chest.

She wanted to both scream her lungs out and melt into his embrace. She did neither. Her body stiffened, useless against the raging emotions barreling through her. Flint had forced himself on her; the weight of his body had pinned her down.

"Madeline." Sterling's tone was a dose of warm chocolate, luring her back like a buoy, pulling her out of her nightmare. His hands were gentle, caring. His voice was calming.

She forced her brain to acknowledge the differences between her kidnapping nightmare and what was happening now.

Between her childhood self and her twenty-four-year-old self.

Between Sterling and Flint.

"Listen to me." Sterling clenched her shoulders and eased her away from his chest. "There must be an exit in the roof. Do you think you could climb up on my shoulders and have a look?"

Madeline flicked tears from her eyes. "Okay." She swayed toward him and he turned around. Surging way beyond her comfort zone, she placed her hands on his shoulders.

"That's it. Use the hand rail."

She didn't need the hand rail. Years of dance training kicked in and with ease, Madeline launched herself up his back and curled her legs across his shoulders. He wrapped his arms over her thighs to keep her in position, just like a little child sitting on their daddy's shoulders. She put her hands up and touched the ceiling. "Okay, I can reach. Walk around."

"I'll start in the corner."

"Oh my God, it's here. It's a panel." It'd been so easy. Too easy. Like it was some kind of sick joke.

"Can you open it?"

Madeline placed both palms on the panel and pushed upward. It moved an inch. But that was all. "It's stuck."

"Try again."

Gritting her teeth, she pushed again but it wouldn't budge. "It's not lifting. Something's stopping it." With the panel held ajar, she guided her fingers through the tiny gap, trying to work out what was obstructing it. Her hands closed around a circular metal object. Fury raged through her.

It *was* a sick joke.

Here's the escape hatch, little girl.

Your freedom is right here, baby Jewel.

But let's not make it that easy. Let's padlock the door shut. See how you handle this new challenge.

Madeline screamed her fury.

Sterling wobbled beneath her and she nearly toppled off his shoulders. "Jesus. What? What?"

"It's padlocked."

"What? Are you sure? Why would they do that?"

"I don't know."

"Hop down. I have to see."

Madeline scooped her legs off his shoulders and slid down his back.

"Do you think you can hold me?"

She tried to recall his size, but his appearance was already a forgotten memory. "Maybe. What do you weigh?"

"About a hundred and eighty pounds."

She groaned. "I don't think so. Sorry."

"Okay. Okay." He paused. A scratching sound had her trying to recall if he had a beard. "Are you sure it's a padlock?"

"Yes. I felt it."

"All right, we'll have to pick the lock. What've you got in your pockets? Anything?"

She had nothing. The only item she needed on the cruise ship was her door card, which acted as both her cabin key and a charge card if she wanted to buy something. And she never carried her phone. Nobody ever called her, and she didn't have anyone she wanted to phone either. She'd stopped carrying it around since she'd started working on the cruise ship. "No. Sorry. Nothing other than my lanyard and a card swipe."

"What about a hairpin or jewelry?"

Her hair was in a high ponytail and it was long enough that she didn't need clips. "No, I don't. But it won't help anyway. It's one of those padlocks with the numbers. Not a key one."

"Jesus Christ!" Sterling's booming voice echoed off the walls.

It was the first crack in his calm demeanor.

It scared the hell out of her.

Coughing had the acrid air stinging her throat. The smoke was like chalk on her tongue, bitter and wrong. This wasn't ordinary smoke. It was from burning rubber or fuel, dense and hostile. It hurt to breathe. Smoke stung her eyes. Panic barreled through her. Shoving backward, she crumbled to the floor.

She hugged her knees. "We're going to die."

Her heaving sobs had her gasping for breath. "We're going to die."

Chapter Fourteen

GABBY

Gabby clutched Jennifer's tiny body to her chest and raced to the crew huddled at the bar. "Please help me. I have to find my children. They were doing a Pokémon hunt. Do you know where they are?"

The chubby security guard looked down at her. Tiny spider veins across his nose flared red and the flush of pink invading his neck exaggerated his unfit appearance. His cheeks wobbled as he shook his head. "Sorry, ma'am. No, I don't."

Gabby peeled the little girl off her chest and thrust her at the guard. "Her name's Jennifer. Do something useful and find her mother." She spun around. Max ran toward her. Desperation flared in the whites of his eyes. *He knows the kids are missing.* Over his shoulder, was Pricilla, tears streaming down her face as she watched Max sprint away.

"Let's go." Max clutched Gabby's hand and as he lurched her forward, she tried to block out Jennifer crying out for her mommy.

But just as Gabby had done with numerous disaster scenes, she cast the harrowing wailing aside, along with the tangled emotions it provoked, and focused on her job. That job was finding Sally and

Adam. Max's vise-like grip around her hand and the determination on his face confirmed he was right there with her.

It was about time.

Hand in hand, they sprinted around the bar, past a miraculously intact hot tub and back up the stairs to the running track.

"How will we find them?" By the time she'd reached the top, she could barely breathe. The exertion was more physical exercise than she'd done in years.

"We'll start up here and work our way down," Max spoke without breaking stride.

The sun was gone. Low on the distant horizon was the three-quarter moon. Stars dotted the velvet blackness and without the dazzle of lights that usually lit the top deck, the Milky Way was as brilliant as it was dramatic.

She hoped like hell that the crew knew how to read the stars. If the high-tech navigation equipment on the ship *had* been obliterated by the EMP strike, even if they scrambled into life boats they'd be screwed if nobody knew how to navigate them home.

Her thundering heart slammed to a halt. They could be lost at sea forever.

That was a headlining story she did not want to be a part of.

Fighting a vision of drifting at sea for days on end, she scanned the deck below, searching for Sally and Adam.

The farther they ran from the wreckage, the less people they encountered. Once they reached the front of the boat, they were the only people on the running track. Max launched down the steps two at a time and Gabby scrambled to keep up with him.

"Sally! Adam!" They alternated turns in calling out their names.

Every silent response stacked another layer of dread in her heart.

The entire play area that was usually bustling with children of all ages and their cautious parents watching over them, was deserted. They raced past the bowling green, the crazy golf, the basketball court, the ping-pong tables, and through a set of doors to a video arcade that was eerie and quiet without the bright lights and thumping music that usually blared in the confined space.

They ran past the coffee shop and the beauty salon where just two days ago Gabby had taken advantage of a full treatment . . . eyelash extensions, brows waxed, fake tan intensified, and her nails done. It had been the best four hours of the cruise.

They passed the gymnasium. It, too, was dark and empty. Max had spent most of his cruising time inside those sweat-infused walls. It was where he'd met the two young women who apparently 'needed his help'. It was an annoying coincidence that they lived just one suburb over from their home, where Max had set up his fitness studio. The women had promised to become Max's tenth and eleventh clients. They would have no idea that they'd instigated Gabby and Max's latest argument.

That heated discussion already seemed like days ago.

Rowdy noises emanated somewhere up ahead and when they passed through yet another doorway, she groaned. The stairwell was packed with people charging upward.

Gabby paused at the railing to catch her breath.

The people were of all ages, young and old. Some were dressed for dinner; some were in their swimsuits. All looked petrified. In the minimal glow from their phones, their troubled appearances were just ghostly outlines.

Only a couple of them looked to be physically injured. Mentally, however, was no doubt another story. Dozens of women were crying. Some sobbed hysterically.

The ship swayed and her hip slammed into the railing. Wincing, she clutched the balustrade to steady herself and peered down the stairwell. It was dark. Very dark. It explained why everyone was coming upward.

All the lights were out. She had thought the ship's hull would've protected the lighting down below. It hadn't. And that meant things were much worse than she'd thought.

On a lower landing, a couple wearing cheesy souvenir T-shirts were using a phone light to guide their way.

Gabby's tiny flashlight was useless in comparison. She clutched Max's arm. "We need a phone."

Max frowned at her. "They don't work."

"For light they do. Phones that were inside the ship seem to have the flashlight working."

Max's eyebrows drilled together. Obviously, he still had no idea what was going on.

When the stranger with the phone reached the top landing, Gabby touched his shoulder. "Sir, may I borrow your phone please? I need to find my children."

He cocked his head and an inquisitive frown corrugated his brow. It was possible he recognized her. She decided to capitalize on that. "I'm Gabrielle Kinsella. You may have seen me on *America Today*? I'm the news anchor."

He nodded once, but shifting his phone aside, he shook his head and lowered his gaze. "Sorry. We need it too." They started to move away.

"Sir, please . . . my children are somewhere on the ship. I have to find them."

"Look, I sympathize." He eased in behind his wife and hustled her forward. "I really do. But my wife——"

"Forget it." Max snatched Gabby's hand. "I have an idea. Let's go." He led her down the stairs, pushing past more passengers.

"What idea?"

"That restaurant we went to, with the candles."

She'd scheduled that dinner to coincide with the ship's departure from Hawaii. The pretty lights of the port, the candles on the tables, and the fancy champagne were all meant to be romantic. But while Max had rambled on about jogging through Kaloko-Honokohau National Historical Park with a group of young fitness fanatics he'd hooked up with, she'd tried, but failed, to explain her fascination at flying in the helicopter over Kilauea Volcano. It wasn't their first conversation that highlighted just how detached they'd become. "Lily's?"

"Lily's. . . that's it." He clutched her hand, leading her around the turn in the stairwell. "We'll grab candles and matches. Come on." He leaned toward the plan of the ship positioned at the edge of the stairs and she shone her light there.

"We're here." Max pointed at the schematic. "We need to get

here. Deck seven." Lily's was three floors down, and at the rear end of the ship. He nodded at her and it took her a moment to realize he was seeking confirmation.

"Yes, that looks right." It was probably the first thing they'd agreed upon since they'd boarded the ship.

Back in the stairwell, darkness swiftly descended on them. When the floor shifted beneath her, Gabby stumbled sideways, clutching Max's hand for support. She hadn't noticed the ship swaying like this in the previous twelve days. Maybe the darkness was playing havoc with her equilibrium. She hoped that was all it was.

Max strangled her hand. "Maybe we should go back up to the running deck and approach Lily's from the steps at the rear of the ship. Agree?"

"I agree." Another joint decision. Things were looking up.

By the time they'd returned to the top deck, the crowd had tripled. The chaos had tripled with it. Voices were loud and riotous.

Gabby raced to the railing and searched the throng, desperate to see her children. "Do you see them? Are they down there?"

Sally was wearing a fuchsia-colored matching shorts suit Gabby had bought for her more than a year ago. It'd been too big for Sally at the time and her daughter had only just started to wear it. Gabby's mind snagged on the fight she'd had with Sally that morning. She'd wanted to wear the outfit again, but she'd already worn it four times on the cruise. Her daughter's lack of fashion sense was an ongoing battle. Thank God Max had intervened though. If he hadn't, Sally wouldn't be wearing the bright outfit, and therefore wouldn't stand out in the crowd.

There was sufficient light from numerous phones and the silvery moon, now high above them, but she still couldn't see her daughter.

Her eyes kept darting to the number of bodies lined up against the far railing. The quantity of deceased had accumulated significantly since she'd last been on that deck. Some of them had been draped with jackets or towels, and she was equally torn between racing down there and inspecting the bodies beneath the covers and refusing to believe that her daughter or son could be amongst them.

The passengers were like disturbed ants. Chaos reigned and

there were no clear leaders. Hundreds looked like complete fools standing around in bulky life jackets.

Nobody seemed to be in charge.

Gabby had witnessed her share of situations where a lack of leadership led to dreadful decisions. The distress of the burgeoning crowd confirmed it wouldn't be long before fractured groups began to form. Bedlam was about to take over.

Max's wide darting eyes flicked from one injured person to the next. His anxiety confirmed he was torn between helping the wounded and looking for their children.

Gabby's heart hit a maximum tempo as she prepared to give him an absolute mouthful.

He turned to her, maybe sensing her fury, and his eyes confirmed his turmoil. "We've got to keep moving."

Relief flooded through her as she squeezed his hand to hers. He led the way, pushing through the crowd, back past the bar, and in through the double doors.

People were still streaming up the stairs, all going the opposite way to them. Some looked petrified. But, in a disgusting contrast, several were sniggering, and looked to be enjoying themselves. Clearly, they were still oblivious to the disaster unfolding around them.

From what she'd learned from the Preppers about the predicted aftermath of an EMP strike, those idiots wouldn't be so amused come morning.

If they made it through the night, that was.

Chapter Fifteen

GABBY

Thankfully, there were enough phone lights amongst the crowd to give Gabby and Max sufficient light to see their way. Nearly every person they encountered fired a question at them.

What's going on?
What was that noise?
Why are the lights out?

Gabby ignored them. Max didn't. He wasted precious time by directing them to the top deck where everyone else was. When he stopped at an elderly couple, Gabby clamped her jaw and surged ahead. Hopefully her leading the way would be the impetus Max needed to keep focused.

Back at deck seven, she stepped through a set of double doors and entered a dark corridor. Using the walls to guide her, she edged along the passage.

"Gabby. Gabby, wait!" Max's feet pounded behind her.

"No, Max. We don't have time to waste." She pushed through yet another set of double doors and immediately felt an openness, like she'd entered a massive room.

She'd reached the atrium.

The giant stair-lined void was the centerpiece that linked four levels. She stepped up to the railing and looked down. A dim light filtered from somewhere below, but its eerie green hue made the area look as uninviting as a mass suicide.

Max pointed into the void. "Look, the emergency lighting is working down there."

"Oh, yes. You're right." She wanted to slap herself for not thinking of that.

"Maybe the kids went to our cabin?" Max said.

"Oh God, I hope so." At the sound of giggling, Gabby spun toward the avenue of shops that lined the atrium.

"Max. The shops!"

He spun to her, frowning.

"The souvenir shop has candles and lighters."

"Good idea."

Utilizing the broad, curved staircase, they raced down to the shops Gabby had strolled through way too many times out of sheer boredom. The creepy green glow gave the atrium a weird ethereal hue but thankfully, it provided sufficient light to allow her to see the way.

As they sprinted across the carpeted area, a couple of teenagers rummaged through the shelves in one of the tacky resort-wear shops. "Hey!" Gabby yelled out.

They both ducked down behind the counter.

"I know you're there." She scowled.

Gabby wasn't surprised to find no staff minding the shops. She also wasn't surprised to see people picking their way through the wares. She'd witnessed enough pillaging in her life to know it was inevitable. When things got tough, grubs went looting. That'd been the headline she'd wanted to put on her report during the riots that'd occurred as part of Occupy Oakland in 2011. Her boss had vetoed it.

Gabby strode into the souvenir shop. "Do you kids know the ship is sinking?"

"What?" A girl who was barely older than Sally stood up.

"Where are your parents?"

"None of your business." The girl's head wobbled and Gabby wanted to slap the immature indignation off her pimply face.

"Well, you need to find them. The ship's sinking. You should be on the top deck."

"Bullshit." Pink chewing gum danced across her tongue. "I don't believe you."

"Really? Do you see anyone? Any crew?"

"Oh, yeah?" A young man, probably just shy of eighteen, strode to the girl's side and in the glare of his cell phone, his enormous black afro made his white skin look deathly pale. "Why aren't there any warning sirens?"

Gabby flicked her hand to the surrounding darkness. "Look, genius. The power has gone out. They can't sound the alarm."

The pair looked at each other and without a word, they simultaneously spun around and bolted away. Seconds later, four other people much older than the first two popped out from behind cabinets and raced after the teenagers.

Gabby rolled her eyes to Max. His skin too looked pale.

"Do you really think the boat is sinking?" His shoulders rose with a deep breath, like he was steadying himself for her response.

"I don't know. But I do know the ship's in trouble." She strode to the wall of candles at the side of the shop. "And we need to find the kids."

Forcing the word *hypocrite* from her brain, Gabby grabbed the biggest candle she could hold with one hand and went to the front counter where a selection of tacky cigarette lighters plastered with Rose of the Sea emblems were displayed. She also shoved as many Snickers bars as she could fit into her pockets. Lord knows when they'll be eating again. And the kids will be hungry.

They set off down the atrium stairs. With each new level they descended, her heart pounded more and her brain swam with rotten thoughts and unfathomable questions.

They didn't encounter any more people and the silence was disturbing.

It was like the whole ship was deserted.

At the bottom landing, Max lit his fist-sized, coconut-scented candle and leaned over to light hers. Using the light, he studied the ship's deck plan. "We're here, deck six. We need to get to deck four." Using his finger, he pointed out the way. "We'll go along this corridor to these stairs. Come on, let's go." He raced off ahead, and shielding her candle with her hand, she scrambled to keep up.

The sway of the ship had intensified so much it was difficult not to bounce off the walls.

Since day one of the cruise, she'd been cursing about their cabins being on the lowest deck. The kids were too old to be sharing a cabin with them but Max had insisted they have adjoining rooms, so he'd booked the cheapest rooms available . . . on the lowest level, right in the middle of the ship. Their rooms didn't even have a window.

They entered a corridor that was pitch-black, and the flickering of her vanilla-scented candle created ghostly shadows that raised the hairs on her neck and had a shiver creeping up her spine. Gabby hated that she was spooked. She'd always prided herself on her level-headedness. That skill alone had allowed her to access many bloody massacres that'd stopped other reporters at the door.

Max called out the room numbers as they strode past the doors. "Four thousand and seventy-four . . . four thousand and seventy-six . . . four thousand and eighty-two. Stop!" He spun to her.

Her heart lurched at the fear in his eyes. "What?"

"Smoke! Do you smell it?"

She inhaled. "Shit. Yes I do. Oh my God." Her brain scrambled. Unexpected fire anywhere was not good. Fire on a ship was a major catastrophe. It made finding the kids even more urgent. "We have to keep going."

Max clenched and unclenched his jaw, his eyes darted left and right. His uncertainty was tangible.

She went to push past him, but he stopped her. "Why haven't the sprinklers triggered?"

"Must've been affected by the EMP."

"By what?"

She wanted to shake his shoulders, to yell at him, to get it through his head that they didn't have time for this shit. Instead, clenching her fist, she said, "I heard the crew say we were hit by an EMP strike. It's destroyed all the power." Confusion drilled across his face and she huffed. "Look, if you're scared, I'll go first."

His jaw dropped. His eyes bulged. "I'm not scared, Gabby. I'm cautious."

"We can be cautious once we have the kids." She pushed past him and as she strode along the corridor, shielding her candle, his feet stomped to catch up behind her. A glow ahead caught her eye and she increased her pace.

The smoke intensified. It stung her eyes. A foul taste lacerated her throat. Her foot fell into nothingness.

Screaming, she dropped into the void. Her candle went flying.

Max clutched her wrist, saving her fall.

Her body slammed against mangled walls, punching the wind out of her. The chocolates spilled from her pockets.

Shredded metal clawed at her legs.

"Gabby!" Max's voice was shrill, unhinged. "Gabby! Are you okay?"

Gasping for breath and dangling by just one hand, she stared wide-eyed at the giant chasm before her. It was a disaster zone—equal parts plane wreckage and destroyed cabins. Fires dotted the enormous cavern. A central column flickered with flames providing enough light that on the other side she could see a cross section of at least four decks.

An enormous area of their deck had caved in.

A horrifying thought shot through her like venom.

Their cabin could be gone.

Chapter Sixteen

GUNNER

As water lapped at Gunner's feet his mind skidded through all possible scenarios that could've caused the flooding. Burst water mains. Pierced holding tanks. Drinking fountains damaged.

Ruptured hull.

That last thought was horrific. None of his training had prepared him for a situation like this. Major catastrophes on cruise ships weren't unheard of. Costa Concordia. Titanic. But considering the thousands of cruise ships touring the world on any given day, incidents were extremely minimal.

Gunner was dead center in the middle of a cruise ship disaster that would make the history books. He just hoped that both he and his ship would fare well in the retelling of the Rose of the Sea disaster in the years to come.

He stepped through the double doors into a holding area that was stacked to roof height with cubes of recyclable rubbish. Cans. Bottles. Cardboard. Paper.

If the fire was in there, the whole place would've disintegrated in minutes. Confident it wasn't, Gunner sloshed through the water to another set of fire-safety doors.

Beyond this doorway was a small holding room that had the sole purpose of keeping the engine noise contained. He pushed through, stepping over the elevated threshold. Water streamed through the tiny gap in the next set of doors.

Thankfully, the pressurized spout was only knee high.

Out of nowhere an image of his daughter spilled into his mind. She was playing in knee-deep water in a blow-up pool. Her smile radiated in the sunshine. Starbursts of light glimmered off the rhinestones on her tiny bathing costume. He could still hear her giggling as she stomped around, splashing water over the sides. Gunner squeezed his eyes shut and his knees just about buckled beneath him. *I'm coming home to you, baby girl. You and your beautiful mamma. I promise.*

Swiping that image away, he forced bulletproof bravado into his voice. "Okay, this is it." He met Cloe's gaze, then Quinn's. Their jaws were set as if they were determined to do what had to be done, yet their wide eyes betrayed their semblance of courageousness. "It's not too late to change your minds."

"We know, sir," Quinn said. "If this all goes to shit, being next to you is exactly where we should be, right, love?"

Cloe gave her husband a lopsided grin and reached for his hand. "Exactly."

Gunner repositioned the fire extinguisher beneath his elbow and pulled the pin. Cloe and Quinn followed his lead. "Just aim the nozzle at the fire and squeeze here." He indicated to the trigger.

"Yes, Captain," they said in unison.

Gunner nudged the door open with his boot and a flood of water spilled into the holding space. It was too dark to see inside. But that was a good thing. It confirmed there was no fire immediately beyond the doorway. "Here we go."

He kicked the door open, stepped over the elevated threshold and sloshed through the knee-deep water. The stench was horrific. Gunner gagged and swallowed hard, forcing back bitter bile. Smoke, thick and black, filled the air. It reeked. Nasty and corrosive. Gunner cursed the strip lighting that illuminated the room with a green haze.

Water rained upon them and a wobbly sigh burst from his throat. "Thank God! The water's from the sprinkler system."

"And not the ocean, you mean?" Quinn's nervous grin was justified.

"Exactly." Gunner's eyes adjusted to the dimness and he got a visual of something that would haunt him forever.

A body slumped at a computer console with smoke wafting from his scorched orange overalls. The skin on his face and hands were a sickening combination of red raw, charred black, and peeling chunks.

Flames licked at the monitors and what looked like a series of clipboards. Gunner blasted them with the extinguisher.

With that done, Gunner cringed as he searched for a pulse on the man's neck. There wasn't one.

Barely four feet away was another body. "Jesus Christ!" Gunner searched his memory, trying to recall how many crew would be in this area. Best guess was twenty. He hoped it was less.

"What happened here?" The plaid mask failed to hide the horror stamped on Cloe's face.

"Looks like a flash fire." Gunner confirmed the second mechanic was dead too. "There must've been a gas leak. The superheated air would've killed them almost instantly."

He dashed to another small fire and extinguished it too. Continuing farther into the engine room, within a hundred feet he confirmed twelve dead and had to put out several small fires, each of which required just a short blast from his extinguisher.

These ships were built to withstand combustion. Humans, however, were not.

The blast zone was massive, carving a hole that spanned three decks in height and was big enough to swallow ten dump trucks.

A giant bank of tubular pipes that threaded from a deck below right up through to the ceiling had been ripped to shreds. Colorful wiring spewed from the pipes that fed the electricity into the ship. The EMP was like a million-volt lightning strike overloading the circuit, and the entire cabling system had exploded.

Every single piece of electronic equipment on the ship had been incapacitated in a nanosecond.

In 2013, an engine fire had rendered the Carnival Triumph cruise ship powerless and without propulsion, which had caused five days of havoc for more than four thousand passengers as the ship was towed to shore. After that incident, Blue Earth Cruise Lines, that owned twenty-two ships, including Rose of the Sea, declared that their fleet would each have an additional engine installed. But it wasn't that easy. A new engine required a large footprint, which on a cruise ship was a precious commodity. Then, once it was installed, it required duplicate wiring throughout the entire ship. All that required space, time, manpower, and billions of dollars.

Rose of the Sea wasn't slated for her additional engine though. In fact, she had never been scheduled to receive it at all. She'd served the company for twenty-five years and had served well, but her cruising life was nearly over. It was impossible to believe that her unblemished history was now obliterated.

Shaking his head, Gunner studied several giant pieces of equipment that were spewing thick black liquid from burst piping into the knee-deep water. "Careful you don't slip."

Gunner sloshed past a bank of computers. Every one of the charred and melted monitors were dead.

A flickering light in the distance caught his attention, and he headed for it.

Seconds later, he saw a visual that had his brain splitting in two.

The plane wreck.

It appeared like an apparition through the smoke.

The cockpit had taken the full brunt of the impact and had fully concertinaed upon itself. What remained of the plane's fuselage was upright, a streak of white against a charred black background. Every window was shattered. The plane's impact had been curtailed when it had somersaulted in the water before ploughing into the ship. If it had hit full-on, it would've been the equivalent to being hit by a loaded torpedo. He shook his head, trying to free that shocking thought from his brain.

His eyes whiplashed to one of the plane's shattered windows. A passenger was still there, slumped in the seat. "Oh, shit!" Gunner wanted to punch himself. He'd been so consumed with his ship's fatalities that he hadn't stopped to consider the aircraft's casualties.

As Gunner scrambled over charred wreckage and indistinguishable chunks that were once part of the well-maintained equipment of the engine room, he braced for another round of horrific carnage inside the plane.

The sounds of water pouring from the sprinklers and the odd hiss when it hit a hot surface added a strange staccato to the groans and creaks from both the plane wreck and Rose of the Sea.

He entered the fuselage through the gaping hole where the wing had been. Miraculously, some of the chairs were intact, but his brain screamed at him to be realistic.

No one could have survived that crash.

Hauling himself from one seat to the next was like climbing a mountain. The seats were all horizontal and some bodies were still strapped in, like a horror ride at a theme park. Except nobody got off at the end.

"Hello, is anyone alive? Hello?" His voice echoed about the eerie void as his phone light streamed through the smoke like an alien's eye, seeking life amongst the mounting death toll.

"Is anyone alive?" Quinn and Cloe joined the search and together, the three of them trawled what was left of the wreckage.

Each time Gunner checked for a pulse on a charred corpse, he held his breath and prayed he'd be able to wipe the sickening stench from his memory.

It seemed an eternity before he'd confirmed there were no plane survivors.

With that done, he exited the plane's carcass and, jumping onto a pile of debris, he turned his attention back to his ship.

Above the nose of the plane was a giant chasm. It was a couple of beats before he realized it was the crater he'd initially looked into from Petals restaurant. As he'd estimated, six decks had been impacted by either a direct hit from the plane or the resulting explosion.

Both Quinn and Cloe had black streaks of soot across their faces by the time he rejoined them against the wall. Their shoulders sagged as if bearing the weight of the horror around them. When they looked at him with pleading in their eyes, he felt the pressure to say something reassuring. To convince them they would be okay.

But he couldn't form words. His brain was as scrambled as the wiring dangling from the ceiling. He gazed across the catastrophic damage.

In the distance he spied the water holding reservoir. The entire side had ruptured, like a colossal monster had clawed its way out of the half-million-gallon tank.

Farther behind the reservoir, the mutilation to the desalination plant was brutal. Although the discoveries helped explain why there was so much water on this deck, any hope Gunner had of sourcing fresh water from the main water supply was gone.

Despite that major handicap, there was some good news. The hull seemed to be intact. That was a good thing. Maybe the only good thing.

But without the experienced crew, or power, or computers, or complete wiring, there was no hope of starting the engines again.

His empty stomach twisted as a wave of utter hopelessness curled through him.

Rose of the Sea was officially dead in the water.

Chapter Seventeen

MADELINE

Sterling eased in beside Madeline and squeezed her to his chest. His heart pounded in her ear, the beat equally terrifying and therapeutic. She fought the urge to shove him away. Fought it hard. Madeline didn't do embraces. Not with men. Not ever. And especially not with people she didn't know.

"Hey, it's okay. Don't cry. We're not going to die."

Her hands remained at her sides. Her fists curled into rigid balls. "I'm so scared."

"Me too." He glided his palms over her back.

Panic was a living, breathing thing, scurrying through her insides and brain like a million spiders. Her mind slammed from those cold days in the dungeon to the dark silence of the elevator. One second, she was with her kidnapper; the next, she was being hugged by a complete stranger.

Professor Flint stunk with a putrid odor. Decaying fish or rotten teeth. When he left the dungeon, the stench remained. It would invade her nostrils. Rot her tongue.

Sterling was nothing like that. His cologne was lovely . . . delicate hints of citrus and spice.

Focusing on his thumping heart, she forced her panic attack

down. Unfurling her fists, she did something she hadn't done in years—she curled her arms around a man. Despite the smoky air, she inhaled deep, breathing in Sterling's scent that was at once both manly and elegant.

It was the reality check she needed.

She was not alone.

History was not repeating itself.

The worst aspect of her childhood horror wasn't being imprisoned in a hideous dungeon. It wasn't the monster who abused her at will. No. The worst part was the endless solitude. Nobody to talk to. Nobody to share her grief or pain with. Nobody to hold.

Nobody.

Solitude had carved away at her sanity. Second by second. Minute by minute. Week by week.

It was why solitary confinement was considered barbaric. Being forced to be alone with nothing but your own thoughts for an extended period of time was the worst kind of hell.

Her current nightmare was very, very different to her last one. Sterling was there. And although he was a stranger, she already felt like he was a friend. She inhaled to the count of five, exhaled, and eased back from him. "Thank you. I'm sorry about that."

"There's no need to thank me or say sorry." He glided his hand down her arm, and when he squeezed his fingers around her palm she squeezed back. It was a brief connection between them, but just like the hug, it was more than she'd allowed any man to do in a very long time.

"Thank you." She wiped the tears from her eyes. "I'm just glad I'm not alone."

"Yeah, me too. We're in this together."

The ship groaned, reverberating around them. Deep and mournful, like they were trapped in a giant with a bellyache.

"Shit." Madeline blinked at the blackness around them. "What the hell was that?"

"I don't know, but we need to get out of here. There must be another way out."

Swallowing back the bitter taste of smoke, she reached out to touch the wall, and realized it was the door. She attacked the tiny groove between the doors, desperate to pry them apart with her fingers, but it was useless.

The ship groaned again, like it was warning them to stop. As Madeline glided her fingers inch by inch over the cold metal, her mind yanked back to Professor Flint. He'd told her she'd never escape. He'd told her to stop trying.

Flint had yielded total control over her existence.

Her food and water had been rationed by him. Sometimes she'd go for days without a meal. Her hunger pains had been crippling. But her thoughts that he'd abandoned her were worse.

Not once did she shower or bathe. When she was finally rescued, she was still wearing the same clothes she'd been abducted in.

Flint had also controlled her light. The room had a single bulb that hung from the ceiling like a pregnant spider dangling on a web. Each time he switched it on, the glare was so blinding she could barely open her eyes. But once her eyes did adjust, she was torn between squeezing them shut again and watching his every move.

Shoving that thought from her mind, Madeline shifted her searching from the side wall to the back wall. Nothing but cold metal.

Nothing but blackness.

One day, a mouse had appeared in her dungeon. It'd terrified her at first. But her squeak had been so sweet and delicate . . . the most beautiful sound Madeline had ever heard.

Despite being perpetually starving, she'd shared her food with Peanut. That was what she'd called her . . . Peanut. After her favorite food . . . peanut butter. It was a cruel joke though. Especially as she'd thought she'd never taste it again.

Peanut slept down her shirt, tucked in right next to her belly, sharing their warmth.

That little mouse had saved her in so many ways.

Sometimes Peanut would disappear for so long that Madeline feared Flint had killed her. Then she'd magically reappear.

Madeline had taken way too long to comprehend that Peanut had a way in and out of the room.

After that realization, each time Professor Flint visited Madeline she stopped using the light to watch him. Instead, she searched for Peanut's access point. It seemed like months before she saw it. It was a tiny pipe in the very corner where the foul carpet met the wall.

When she was alone again, plunged into pitch blackness, she'd crawled to that spot, got down onto her belly and peered into the pipe. There'd been nothing but a tiny breeze that had touched her lips like butterfly wings.

She'd lain there, breathing in that fresh air, and that was when she'd felt a bulge beneath the carpet. Scraping it back, she discovered a trap door. The construction had been rough. The timber splintered. She'd thought maybe a kid had made it. Her memory was so vivid she could still feel the adrenaline rush that had blazed through her when she'd thought she'd found a way out.

But it wasn't.

What she'd found in that hole still fed her nightmares.

It had taken her a while to work out what she was touching. But when she did, she'd screamed until her throat had burned.

It had been bones and a skull and shriveled up skin.

The light had come on and as Flint had dragged her from that pit, she'd seen two things that scarred her for life. One was a skeletal mummy with leathery skin that had barely held the bones together, and empty eye sockets that had stared at her like the devil. The other was that the trap door led to nothing but a grave pit.

Madeline's hope of escape had been shattered into a million pieces.

Here's your escape route, little girl. Ha ha ha ha ha.

You can spend the rest of your life in the ground, little girl. Ha ha ha ha ha.

Professor Flint had taught her a valuable lesson that day. When he'd punished her for trying to escape, she'd learned that handling pain was as easy as flicking a switch in her brain. She'd screamed the first time he'd driven the lit cigarette into her arm. She'd screamed the second time too. But not the third. Nor the fourth. She'd learned how to block out pain.

From that day forward, nothing he did hurt her.

As Madeline moved her exploration from the back wall to the other side of the elevator, she tried to shake the rotten memories free, but something was there, niggling at the edges of her thoughts. Telling her to keep digging.

Digging.

The escape hatch she'd thought she'd found.

Digging.

The mummified skeleton hidden beneath the carpet.

Digging.

The answer came to her out of nowhere. "The carpet! There might be a door under the carpet." She rolled to her hands and knees, feeling along the edges.

"What?"

"There could be a door beneath the carpet." Madeline dug her fingernails into the join where the carpet met the wall, desperate to get some purchase. "Help me."

Sterling crawled in next to her.

"We need to pull the carpet back."

"Okay. Okay."

The carpet was secured tight, making it impossible to get into the groove, let alone beneath it. "We need something to wedge in there."

"My swipe card." She unhooked her lanyard off her neck and shoved it into the gap between the carpet and the wall. "Come on!" she yelled into the blackness.

"How about my phone case?" Sterling shuffled about, no doubt fishing his phone from his shorts.

"Good idea." The smoke was becoming thicker and more pungent. More potent too. If they didn't get out of there soon, they'd likely pass out from smoke inhalation. When Flint's house had caught fire, and smoke had poured into her dungeon, she'd crawled beneath her rubber mattress. The fireman who'd saved her had called her a very clever girl.

It'd been the first nice thing anyone had said to her in five and a half months.

Sterling leaned forward. "Okay, let's see." His words were ironic, given that they couldn't see a thing.

Whatever he was doing made a squeaking noise. "It's working."

Madeline gripped the edge and together they tugged on the coarse matting. Sharp popping noises confirmed it was coming away from the clips securing it in place. Fighting against the stiff fabric, they curled it over and stood on top to stop it from flipping back.

On her hands and knees, Madeline examined the dirty floor. "Here it is!" Her heart leaped. "I knew it."

The rectangular panel was flush with the rest of the floor and she ran her fingers around the outer edge, seeking a latch, but there was nothing. Sterling was right there with her. His breathing was erratic and she couldn't decide if it was the smoke or his eagerness caused his panting.

"Oh, here we go. It's a ring pull," he said. "Get back."

She crawled aside and a loud bang confirmed he'd flipped it right back so it had hit the floor.

She leaned in, and shoulder to shoulder, they peered into the hole. A slight draft wafted over her face with a combination of smoke, fumes, and sea air. When her eyes finally adjusted to the gloom, a glimmer of light flickered below.

But a chill raced up her spine.

It was a very long way down.

Chapter Eighteen

ZON

Zon kicked a chunk of glass away, and leaning against the railing, he scanned up and down the outer deck. After that explosion, he was expectin' more people to come running. As long as they kept on runnin' that was fine with him.

But the minutes ticked on and nothin' happened.

Not a single person was around. Normally, this area would be full a people coming an' goin' between the fancy restaurants and the stupid dance shows. It was like all the fuckin' passengers had jumped overboard. Other than him, the only person around was the dead dude near the slot machine.

The lack of light was weird, but it was the quiet that gave him the creeps. Except for that explosion, he hadn't heard nothin' for ages.

His hankerin' for a cigarette was huge, but there weren't no way he'd waste time goin' to his cabin to get one. Not when he had a pile of loot to take care of.

He could take the stuff down to his cabin, grab a smoke while he was there. But he had so much, it'd be a bitch to haul it all that way. Besides, he needed to figure out what was goin' on. The boat swayed again, and he thumped his head on the life raft.

"Fuck yeah." He grinned. The life raft saved him before. It was gonna save him again. It was the perfect spot to hide everything.

With nobody around, he didn't need to go all covert. He undid a hook, and a ladder slid down and halted on the deck. Zon glanced left and right, confirmed he was still alone, and climbed up. The front and back covers of the raft were solid orange plastic. But the middle third had a soft canvas section. He flicked shards of glass off the cover, unhooked it, and peeled back a corner. It was too dark to see inside, but he didn't care.

Returning to the deck, he wedged the cardboard box beneath his arm, carried it up the ladder, and shoved it through the gap in the canvas. The box musta tumbled sideways as hundreds of them poker chips rattled around like bullets in a barrel.

The trash can full of booze was a different story. It was too heavy to carry up the ladder. Not the worst problem in the world. He solved it by cartin' the liquid gold up in three trips. It took way longer than he'd anticipated, yet not one person came along. He'd a liked to have hidden the stuff better in the life raft, but without light it was impossible.

He climbed back down, and when a burst of lightning sizzled across the sky, he scanned the deck again. The whole fucking thing was deserted.

Somethin' serious was goin' on. And for the first time since he came on board, he felt like he was missin' out. Riding the sway from side to side, he strolled the deserted deck, heading toward them fancy restaurants at the back of the ship. It was mighty quiet.

"Fuck me." The engines had stopped.

Maybe they'd all abandoned ship, and he was the only bastard left onboard.

The boat groaned and pitched him sideways toward the railing. He gripped it for support and as another streak of lightning blazed through the sky, it lit up dozens of white-crested waves beyond the railing. He'd seen nothin' but flat ocean since they'd left LA.

No wonder the boat was rocking all over the place.

He needed to take a piss and trying not to bang into the railing no more, he headed for the restrooms at the end of the deck. He pushed into the men's room and the stench hit him like a sonic boom. Vomit and shit. He backed the hell outta there, shaking his head, trying to rattle the stink free.

Givin' up on that idea, he carried on along the deck and finally spied a glow filtering through the viewing windows in the double doors ahead. He pushed through, and followed the light toward the Chinese restaurant.

When he heard voices, a weird rush of blood skipped through him, like he was relieved he wasn't alone. It was an odd feelin'. Zon would rather be alone any day; it was the only way to avoid bein' fucked over.

When he rounded the corner, his jaw dropped.

About fifty people were using cell phones for light as they stood around the Chinese buffet. Pickin' at the food with their hands, they were shoveling it into their mouths like they hadn't eaten for a month.

He swaggered over, acting all chilled.

A few glanced his way, but the majority just kept on going, shoving handfuls of fried rice or satay beef into their mouths. Nearly all of 'em were in Hawaiian shirts, like they were part of a dance group or somethin'. Although their fat guts indicated they were not.

Zon joined them at the buffet. "What's going on?" He scanned the food. It didn't look so appetizing since they'd scavenged through it and as no steam rose from the trays it'd have to be stone-cold. "Why's there no power?"

"Plane crash," the chick beside him said, her mouth full with what looked like chicken.

"Didn't you see it?"

"A plane crashed into the boat."

"An explosion killed the power."

They all answered at once, speaking over each other and shoving food into their mouths as they added bits to the conversation. Zon kept his mouth shut, sharing his gaze between who was talking and the grub.

"At least it's just the power, and not the start of a pandemic, like on that Ruby Princess ship in 2020."

"That's true. We figured we better eat before we get rationed like them poor people on that Carnival cruise ship."

"Yeah, the Carnival Triumph. Remember that? Four whole days without power. What a disaster."

"They sued, you know. Hey, maybe we could make some money."

Zon silently sniggered. He'd already made a shit load of money. He plucked a couple of pork ribs from the buffet and began nibbling as they carried on their yabberin'.

"Next they'll be telling us to shit into plastic bags."

"Oh yeah, they called that cruise disaster the poop cruise."

A few of them laughed. But Zon reckoned they'd stop laughing once they smelled that stench in them bathrooms. Or the dead bodies, like that old guy who'd keeled over in the casino. "So did many people die?"

About six people looked at him with bulging eyes.

"Where you been hiding, man?" A young chick with six earrings in her right ear glared at him like he was an alien. "A heap of people died. The plane took out about six decks. There are bodies everywhere."

"Huh. That don't sound good."

"Nope. Not good at all," said a skinny guy whose Hawaiian shirt featured a bikini babe on a giant surfboard.

A light blinked off and one of the chicks reached for her phone. "Ah shit, it's dead."

"Yeah, mine died ages ago."

"Maybe we should turn a couple of them off. Save them for later. Who knows when we'll be able to charge them again?"

"Good idea." A group of them reached for their phones and when they turned off the lights, the room grew even smaller.

Zon licked his fingers. "I heard the Captain was dead."

"Really? So who's running the ship?" Earring chick picked at something in her teeth.

Zon shrugged. "Don't know."

The chubby guy at the end who was just about to bust outta his shirt reached for a chicken leg. "I'm not worried. They have plans for stuff like this."

Zon scooped up another couple of ribs. He hadn't realized how hungry he was and even though the ribs were stone-cold, they still tasted mighty fine. The ship swayed and a few of them rode it out with a bit of a cheer, like they were on a roller coaster or somethin'. "You reckon they'll abandon ship?"

"Nah, the crew just keep telling us to remain calm."

"Yeah, just chill. I don't hear any sirens."

"Maybe they can't sound the siren without power?" Zon said.

A few of them looked at him, and he could tell they were thinkin' it through.

"Nah," the fat one said. "They'd have a back-up plan. Nobody's that dumb."

"Here. Want some prawn crackers?" Earring chick handed him a bowl and he took it.

"The navy will probably rescue us tomorrow."

"That'd be cool."

"We'll be on the news."

Zon remembered what that chick in the white uniform with the bouncing tits had said earlier. "I heard one of the crew say it was an EMP strike."

Several of them gasped and dropped their food. The conversation stopped.

"Are you for real?" The fat dude's eyes were enormous.

"Yeah." A whole bunch of 'em looked like they'd shat their pants. "What the fuck's an EMP strike?"

Chapter Nineteen

GABBY

Gabby screamed as jagged wires clawed at her dangling legs, tearing her flesh. Pain ripped up her shins, her thighs. Splintered wood and broken pipes stabbed into her back and neck. The agony was excruciating. Tears stung her eyes as she snapped her gaze from the destruction around her up to Max.

His jaw was clamped. His eyes flared. His knuckles bulged white, clutching desperately around her hand.

Her heart banged in her ribs, set to explode. "Pull me up, Max. Pull!" she screamed at him. Her voice was panic-driven, shrill.

"I'm trying." A growl released from his throat, like he was an angry beast, as he adjusted his grip.

Searing pain ripped through her shoulder. Her arm was being pulled from its socket. She shrieked at the agony. It sounded wrong, barbaric.

The ship swayed. Max tumbled sideways.

She scrambled to hold on, digging her nails into his wrist.

I'm going to die!

But her fury took over. Max spent half his life in the gym. He boasted non-stop about how strong he was, yet he couldn't pull her up. His eyes were wild with confusion. Like he too couldn't understand. "Jesus Christ, Max, what're you doing?"

"Kick, Gabby!"

"I am!" But each kick against the debris sliced another gash in her flesh. She clenched her teeth blocking out the torture. Using her other hand, she clawed at shredded metal and crumbling chipboard and mangled wires—anything that would give her purchase.

Inch by inch, he dragged her upward.

Inch by inch, her body came under attack.

Her gaze snapped from Max's bulging arm to the demolition around them. Her thoughts slammed from her blinding misery, to Sally and Adam. Her mind bounced from one brutal mental image to another.

Sally's bloody body, crippled and lifeless.
Adam, unconscious, surrounded by smoke.
Chunks of skin carved off her legs.

Max released an almighty groan and yanked her up over the final mangled edge. A tortured scream ripped from her throat at the vicious scraping of her legs. She flopped onto the ground, her emotions wobbling between relief and agony.

Max crawled to her and pulled her to his chest. "Oh, babe, are you okay?"

She forced back tears, determined not to cry. Determined not to look at her aching legs. Horrifying questions zapped across her brain. None of them had an answer.

Is our cabin destroyed?
Were the kids in there?
Are they injured? Her chin dimpled. *Are they dead?*

No! She refused to believe that. She'd seen dozens of accidents where people survived the impossible.

Max glided his hand down her back. "I told you we had to be careful."

"Jesus, Max." She shoved him back and thumped his thigh. "Why the hell did you have to say that?"

"What?" Max's candle provided the only light, creating equal shades of light and dark. But it was enough to see his irritation.

"I already feel like a fool. You don't need to rub it in."

"I'm not—" He huffed. "I'm sorry. Are you okay?" His eyes shifted to her legs. "Do you think you can walk?"

In the dim light, the rivers of blood threading up her shins made it look like she'd crawled through barbed wire. The cuts were deep. The scars would be unsightly. She'd never be able to wear a skirt again. Shutting down that ill-timed thought, she swallowed the lump in her throat. "Yes, I'm fine."

Anger and emotion swirled together, fighting for dominance. With each ragged breath, she sucked in the acrid smoke. It burned her tongue. Stung her eyes.

The surging adrenalin that'd been holding her upright evaporated in a flash, and her body melted into Max's embrace. "Do you think . . . the kids—" Her chin quivered. Tears blurred her vision. "Do you think our cabin—"

"I don't know."

"What if they went back there?"

"Honey . . ." He clutched her to his chest. "I don't know."

With each beat of his pounding heart, her emotions tipped the scales on her anger. Gabby hated crying. It showed weakness and instability. But the harder she fought it, the harder it was to breathe. The lump in her throat was enormous, blocking her airway. A wobbly inhalation had the smoke-filled air burning her lungs, and unable to fight anymore, she released a heaving sob.

Max clutched her to his chest. As she wrestled with her embarrassing meltdown, she tried to study the destruction zone through her blurry vision. The plane crash and following explosion had demolished several floors of cabins, destroying the access passage. She looked across the other side of the giant crater, to where the corridor to the cabins continued.

Blinking through the tears, she spied a green glow emanating from the left-hand side of the corridor. "Max! Look!" She pushed back from him, pointing across the void. "It could be okay. The emergency lights are on over there."

"You're right." Max nodded. "We'll have to go up a few floors and see if we can get there from the other side. Do you think you can walk?"

The worry in his chocolate-colored eyes confirmed his concern for her. It was absolute. But before she succumbed to his pity, she scraped herself together. She was a strong, independent woman. Wiping away her tears, she reminded herself she was Gabrielle Kinsella, anchorwoman for *America Today*. She was quite capable without a man's help. And she wasn't about to change that now.

Refusing to look at the bloody striations zig-zagging up her legs, she pushed to her feet, straightened her skirt, and dusted her hands on her thighs. "Let's go find Sally and Adam."

"Okay. Stay behind me this time." Without waiting for her response, Max gathered his candle from the floor and strode back along the dim corridor. "I bet the kids are fine. They're probably eating pizza or something and haven't even realized what's going on."

She wanted to say, *"Don't be ridiculous."* Sally and Adam were not stupid. If anything, they were most likely looking for them. But Max was probably just trying to ease her stress. "I hope you're right."

She'd taken a couple of steps, before she realized she was only wearing one shoe. The other one had torn off when she'd fallen. *Damn it.* They'd cost four hundred dollars *and* they were brand-new.

Their first two attempts at reaching their cabin failed, forcing them to go up three decks before they could get back down the other side. It took forever and with each frustrating minute, Gabby's erratic emotions spun like a roulette wheel.

Fury over not knowing where their kids were.

Worry over whether or not they were okay.

Dread that they weren't.

Guilt if they were.

Mild annoyance over the possibility that the kids were indeed eating ice cream somewhere.

And then fury would return.

The fact that neither she nor Max knew where their fifteen and thirteen-year-old children were highlighted just how fractured their family had become. Her mind flashed to that family that'd been eating ice cream on the pool deck just before the plane had hit. The next time she'd seen them, only the young girl had remained.

A paralyzing vise squeezed her heart as her mind slotted her family into the positions of those poor people. In the blink of an eye, nearly an entire family had been wiped out. Those were the stories Gabby lived for. It would be a ratings winner. Her stomach lurched at the irony of that horror.

The tang of blood confirmed she'd bitten her tongue.

Darkness heaved in around them. Blackness was complete, swallowing all shapes and angles.

The long, windowless corridors provided no light. Max's candle was almost futile, proving to be more of a hindrance than help. Each time it snuffed out she cursed him first and then herself for losing her candle when she tumbled into that crater.

The ship's sway had escalated so much that even with her hands out, it was impossible not to bump into walls.

Although the smoke seemed less dense, it still carried a caustic smell. Her tongue laced with the bitter taste and her thirst was unbearable.

Nobody was around. Normally, these corridors would have dozens of people strolling about. But it'd been forever since they'd encountered another person.

When they finally reached the end of deck four, a question blazed through her like a bolt of lightning.

Was the Captain abandoning ship?

The question drove both despair and determination through her.

Gritting her teeth and fighting her swirling thoughts, she sprinted behind Max, following the green emergency lighting to cabins 4274 and 4276.

Max banged on the first door. "Sally, Adam, are you in there?" He swiped his card, but it didn't work. "Shit." He bashed the door with his fist. "Sally! Adam!"

Gabby bashed on their cabin next door. The silence cut another slice from her heart.

A deafening explosion thundered below their feet. Gabby screamed. The walls shuddered. The doors rattled.

The green lights blinked out.

In the ensuing silence, the ship emitted an almighty groan.

"What the hell was that?" A wave of nausea ripped through her and a toxic smell as familiar as it was unwanted invaded her nostrils. Her knees buckled and she crumbled. Max caught her, tempering her fall, yet her hip hit the ground with enough force to bruise.

"Gabby! Gabby, stay with me babe."

His voice was distant, like he was talking through a tunnel. And although she thought her eyes were open, she saw nothing. Her breathing grew louder and she clamped her teeth so hard her jaw ached.

Max pulled her head onto his lap and stroked her hair. "It's okay, babe. I'm here, just ride it out, honey."

His voice was a million miles away, and lower in pitch, like in slow-motion replay. The smell was hideous and she bucked with a violent gag, trying to rid the stench from her body. It was in her mouth, in her veins. Invading her body. She bucked again; tremors rained through her.

Max clamped his arms around her body, pinning her down. "It's okay, Gabby. I'm here with you, honey. You're okay."

Her breathing was heavy. It hurt. Her chest hurt. As did her throat. A groan tumbled from her lips. Blood coursed through her veins in thick, forceful pulses making her fingers and legs spasm. *Oh God. It hurts too much.*

"There you go. It's over now." His warm palm rested on her cheek and he leaned in to kiss her forehead. "Hey, baby. You back with me now?"

Her words wouldn't form. Her tongue wouldn't move. All she could do was moan.

"Good girl. It's okay. You're nearly there."

She swallowed the violent bitterness and inhaled a hint of Max's tropical cologne. It was one of the things she loved about him—he always smelled so good.

A flickering light came into view—a flame. Her heart thudded.

Coarse carpet scraped at her legs. She squinted at her surroundings. *Why am I on the floor?* She tried to push up.

"Okay, take it easy."

She blinked at the voice. It was Max, but she could barely see him. "What happened?"

"You had a seizure, babe. That's all."

Her legs were stinging, foreign. Her tongue was a brick, barely able to move. She smacked her lips together. Peering through the darkness, she tried to make out shapes. Everything was rectangular. A door. A long passageway. She searched her brain, trying to piece things together, but the puzzle remained jumbled. "What happened? Where are we?"

Max touched her cheek, gentle and warm. "It's a long story. Give it a moment and you'll remember."

No sooner had he said it, than memories flooded back. The plane crash. The woman with no leg. The bloody body in the pool. The covered bodies. Sally and Adam. "The kids! We're trying to find them." A rod of fear scraped up her back.

"That's right. Are you okay?"

"Yes. We need to find them."

He touched her shoulder. "And we will; just give yourself a moment. Where's your medication?"

Her breath hitched.

Without my drugs, I won't survive.

She pointed a shaky finger at the locked cabin door. "In there."

Chapter Twenty

MADELINE

Madeline's stomach flipped as she looked down the elevator shaft. It was dark and uninviting. The bottom was a long way down. At least six decks. The glow far below provided enough light to see the walls. But only just.

Sterling was on his stomach beside her. His sharp breathing confirmed his mutual distress.

To the front of the shaft was the bottom half of an elevator door, confirming they had stopped between levels. She turned to Sterling and was surprised by his pale blue eyes; for some reason she'd thought they were brown. His hair was blond and wavy. He looked more like a professional surfer than an elementary school teacher. "Do you think we can open those doors?"

He groaned, but nodded. "It's worth a try."

She wriggled forward, lowering herself farther to get a better look. The walls on the left were a series of metal rungs like a giant ladder. Each rung was positioned a good four feet apart. On the other side of the shaft were a series of metal grills, like shelves on a bookcase, also about four feet apart. Beyond that was another large rectangular void. The other elevator! "Oh my God."

"What?" Sterling turned her way.

"What if there are other people stuck in an elevator? Maybe they're rescuing them first. It would explain the delay."

He scrunched up his forehead. "But why wouldn't they tell us? How many elevators are there?"

Blinking at him, she considered his reply. "You're right. It doesn't make sense. There are only eight elevators. They should have come to us by now."

The silence was so complete that the words *ghost ship* tumbled into her brain.

She shoved that shitty thought aside. "We have to get to those doors."

"Yeah. But how?"

Once they reached the wall, reaching the doors would be easy. Getting out of the elevator was the hard part. The trap door was positioned against the back wall, right in the middle. The back wall of the elevator shaft was a giant sheet of metal that ran straight down to the bottom. Down the middle of it were two parallel bars that were separated by about six inches. It wasn't exactly designed for climbing.

Weaving her hand through the trapdoor, she reached toward the bars on the back wall and groaned. "Damn it. They're covered in grease. They'll be no help . . . too slippery." She pulled her hand back in and wiped grease on the rolled over carpet.

The distance between the trap door and the side wall was about four feet. Madeline was five foot four. She had an idea. "If you hang onto my feet, I should be able to reach those grills."

"Jesus!" His eyes bulged. "Are you crazy?"

"You saw me on the high ropes. This is nothing."

"That's not a great comparison."

"We have to try. I can't stay in here any longer."

He huffed. "Me neither. Maybe *I* can reach the grills."

"Only if your arms are four feet long."

His groan confirmed he agreed.

Madeline was willing to give it a go. But she had one serious problem to address before she did anything. Clearing her throat, she cringed at what she was about to say. "Sterling?"

"Yeah?"

"I'm sorry, but I need to go to the bathroom."

"I am *so* with you on that." He chuckled. "You can go first."

She wriggled back from the hole, and because he was still on his stomach at the back of the elevator, looking down the hole, she moved to the front, near the door. Her choice of outfit today was a shorts jumpsuit. Which meant she had to strip right out of it to go to the bathroom. For the first time since she'd been trapped in the elevator, she was annoyed that there was some light.

With her breath trapped in her throat, and silently praying that Sterling didn't glance her way, and that the stupid lights didn't suddenly spring to life, she unzipped out of her clothing, stepped to the corner and squatted. The ship's sway forced her to put her hand on the wall to avoid toppling over.

"How long do you think we've been in here?" he asked.

Jesus. I'm practically naked and he's talking to me while I'm trying to pee.

Heat blazed up her neck. Dying on the inside, she was torn between answering and trying to get it over with. When the sound of her peeing on the carpet filled the silence, adding another layer to her humiliation, she cleared her throat. "It's got to be hours."

"Four? Five?"

"At least."

She finished and redressed quicker than any dress changes she'd ever done for her stage performances. "Your turn."

He pushed up from the floor. "Which was your designated pee corner?"

"Huh?"

She saw his smile for the first time. It was an interesting mix of innocent and cheeky. "You know." He chuckled. "The joke about being stuck in an elevator and assigning corners for the bathroom."

"Oh." She emitted an awkward snigger but she sounded like a strangled hyena. "Ummm . . . the front right-hand side."

"The joke doesn't seem so funny now, does it?"

"No. Not funny at all." Replacing his position at the back, she squatted down. She heard his zipper and as she scanned the elevator shaft, she tried to block out any further sounds.

Moments later, he lay on his stomach beside her again.

"Are you sure about this, Madeline?"

"Absolutely." She hoped he didn't notice the uncertainty in her voice.

The height didn't worry her and although she knew she could do it, there was a little niggling voice in the back of her brain telling her she'd fail. The childlike tone was nearly always there, instigating crippling self-doubt that often had her giving up before she'd even tried.

Not this time, though. Not when her only other choice was to return to the stifling cube and simply wait to be rescued. She couldn't do that a moment more. Pushing through the negative vibes, she capitalized on the adrenalin pumping through her veins instead. It was the same sensation she had before every show. It'd helped her succeed hundreds of times before. "I'll lean in through the hole, headfirst. You just need to hang onto my feet."

"Okay."

She couldn't read his voice and wished she could see him properly. To see if he truly was committed. After all, he was literally about to have her life in his hands. "And, Sterling?"

"Yeah?"

"Don't let go."

"I won't. I promise." His hand touched her arm and slid up to her shoulder. "You're so brave."

Madeline huffed. After she'd been rescued from that dungeon, she'd been told a thousand times over that she was brave. But it never made any sense. Brave people took risks, sometimes deadly risks, for the sake of others. When she was held captive, she hadn't taken any risks to try to escape.

It was very different now though.

She *was* taking a risk. In fact, she was risking her life to save them both. A warm glow filtered through her, tingling out to her extremities, boosting her resolve. Sterling was right. What she was about to do really was brave.

Riding that triumphant notion, she lay on her stomach on the floor. "Okay, here we go." She curled her head, shoulders and upper body into the hole face-first, bending at the hips.

Sterling squeezed her ankles and she winced at the pain. She'd forgotten all about her bruising. Clenching her jaw to block it out, she focused on the horizontal grill she was aiming for. The thumping pulse in her neck was twice as forceful now that she was upside-down. She stretched her fingers toward the grill, but was still a good foot or so away.

"Sterling, I need to flip over."

"Okay."

Gripping onto the edge of the trap door, she curled over so only from her knees to her toes were still in the elevator. "Okay, hang on."

"I've got you." His voice boomed with authority. She imagined it was a tone he used often around the schoolyard.

She released her hands and curled backward into the shaft.

The ship groaned as if casting a warning. *Oh God.*

The hairs on her neck bristled. *What the hell am I doing?*

Chapter Twenty-One

MADELINE

Madeline reached out again. *Yes!* Her fingers hooked into the metal. "I got it. Okay, lower me down."

Sterling squeezed her bruised ankle, and gritting her teeth, she blocked the agony as she was lowered into the shaft. The grill was the perfect design for hanging onto and with each inch she sank, the more purchase she had. Once she had the length of her forearm across the grill, she said, "Okay, let me go."

"What? Are you sure?"

"Yes, let me go."

He released her right ankle, but squeezed tighter on her left. "Sterling, let go!"

He did, and using her core strength, she lowered her body until her Vans were safely on the flat lower grill. "Okay, I did it."

"Oh my God. You're amazing."

The ship tilted sideways. The elevator screeched against the walls. Madeline ducked, pressed her palms to her ears, and prayed the thing didn't come plummeting down. The sound was excruciating. Like metal being shredded by a chainsaw. Her heart pounded out every second.

When peace returned, a renewed sense of urgency blazed through her. "Sterling, get down here."

"What?" His voice was shrill, like he was being smothered.

"It's your turn. I'm not climbing down this thing alone. Lower yourself feet first. You're taller than me so I'll be able to swing you over to the ledge with me."

"Shit! Shit! I don't know about this. Shit! Shit!"

"You can do it."

"Just let me think, okay?"

His footsteps pounded in the elevator as he paced back and forth. The sound had her tumbling back sixteen years, pitching her into that dungeon where she'd paced the dark space, over and over. And over. Nine big strides, or thirteen normal ones. *Nine. Thirteen. Nine. Thirteen.* She'd crossed that room at least a thousand times. She hoped Sterling wouldn't take too long.

The ship groaned again, deep and menacing.

"Sterling, I can't hang around here all day."

"Okay. Okay."

"You can do this." *You can do this.* That, too, was a mantra she'd repeated over and over in her life. At eleven, she'd taken up dancing as a form of therapy, and her high pain threshold had proved to be an asset when it came to grueling dance routines. Her body was the pillar of strength, however, her mind was a battleground between striving to succeed and giving up. Honing in on positivity was something she'd had to learn.

She was going to need it now.

"Sterling. Listen to me. You're strong; you can do this."

"I'm not! The only exercise I do is surfing." His voice quivered.

"Lower your legs through the hole. Do it." She changed her voice from encouraging to commanding. Some people needed that. Maybe Sterling did too. "I'm not moving without you."

"Okay. Okay."

Shuffling noises sounded above her, then his legs appeared in the gap. Madeline hooked her fingers into the grill and leaned out to grab his foot. "I've got you. Keep coming."

He lowered farther and she wriggled her hand to his ankle, then calf muscle, then the back of his knee. "Good, you're doing good. A little bit more—you're nearly there."

Another three inches and the tips of his Converse sneakers touched the same grill she was standing on. "That's it, you're here." But his shoulders and head were still in the elevator. The last part was going to be the hardest.

Madeline wrapped her hand around his belt. If this all went to pieces, she wasn't sure she could actually hold him. An image of him tumbling into the void below, arms flailing, mouth wide with a scream, slammed into her mind.

Jesus Christ! Focus, Maddy.

With her fingers clutching the grill, she tightened her grip on his belt and pulled him toward her. "You can do this, Sterling."

"Okay, get ready."

"I'm ready."

He huffed out a forceful breath and a second later, his weight shifted.

Sterling swung below the elevator. He screamed as his hands slipped free.

She screamed and reached out. Desperate. Panic-driven.

He clawed at the air. His fingers snatched around her outstretched hand, nearly ripping her fingers off. Gritting her teeth, she roared an almighty growl and used every ounce of her strength to pull him in. But she couldn't do it. She wasn't strong enough.

Her heart hit sledgehammer mode as each terrifying second passed with brutal clarity.

Terror in the whites of his eyes.

Veins bulging in his neck.

Agony as her fingers clutched the grill.

Their united screams were amplified a thousand times in the chamber of hell.

"Grab on!" she yelled.

His breaths shot in and out. His eyes shot from her to the shaft below.

"Sterling!" Madeline forced calm into her voice. "Look at me."

His darting eyes found hers.

"You can do this! Grab onto me and pull yourself in."

"Okay. Yes. Okay." Inch by inch, with the tendons in his neck bulging, he dragged his body toward her.

The instant Sterling's feet were firmly planted on the grill beside her, he clutched his arm around her neck, pinning her to his chest. "Thank you. Thank you."

Madeline sucked in the smoke-filled air, fighting for oxygen. "Are you okay?" Her voice wobbled with frazzled emotion.

"I am now. Thank you."

United, their vigorous breathing echoed about the hollow shaft. When the elevator screeched with another collision, they jolted out of their embrace.

Despite her trembling legs, they had to keep moving. "Are you ready to climb down?"

"Yeah, but let's see if we can open that door first." He nodded at the bottom half of the doorway opposite them.

"Okay. Good idea." She shuffled along the grill, inching toward the front of the elevator shaft. But it was pointless. The doors wouldn't budge. She banged on them instead. "Help! Help!"

Sterling shouted with her. In the empty shaft, their voices were deafening.

If anybody *was* on the other side, they'd have to hear them. A prickle raced up her spine as the unwelcome words *ghost ship* crept into her brain again.

When they stopped yelling, the silence was creepy.

Something was seriously wrong.

After accepting that shouting was pointless, she studied the shaft, assessing the route downward. It looked easy. "Shall we climb down?"

"Sure." He actually sounded chirpy. He flashed a grin, the terror of moments ago completely gone from his eyes. "Got nothing else to do."

She chuckled. "That's true."

They moved together, taking the rungs one at a time, keeping in pace.

At a point she'd determined was about halfway, she paused to glance down.

But something weird caught her eye. The light below was flickering.

Her heart slammed into her chest.

That's not emergency lighting below. Or the glow from the engine room.

It's fire.

Chapter Twenty-Two

GUNNER

By the time Gunner had doused all the fires in the engine room and returned to the bridge, the moon was high in the sky, the ship's sway had become more pronounced and a mob of passengers had crowded into the restricted area inside the bridge.

Many were wearing life vests.

Many had cell phone screens lit up.

All seemed angry. Clenching his jaw and his fists with equal intensity, Gunner charged through the unruly mob.

Every step was hindered by people clutching at his arms and barking questions.

"Is the ship sinking?"

"Are we going to be rescued?"

"Who killed the Captain?"

"Do we need to abandon ship?"

Ignoring them all, he headed for Officer Sykes who was at the front windows, scanning the ocean with the binoculars glued to his eyes. Captain Nelson was still on the floor with Gunner's jacket over him, and four passengers were practically standing over his body like he was nothing but a roll of carpet. He fought the urge to yell at them to get back.

Considering the bedlam around him, Sykes appeared very calm, but when he turned to Gunner, his wide eyes and angry scowl confirmed his distress.

"Captain McCrae, am I pleased to see you." His lips drew to a thin line.

Gunner touched Sykes' shoulder. "What's our status?"

He shook his head. "Nothing to report, sir."

After a curt nod, Gunner turned to the crowd who were still barking questions at him and raised his hands. "Attention! Attention, please!"

"Do we need to abandon ship?" A man of line-backer proportions was at the front of the mob. The straps securing his life vest were under serious duress.

Ignoring his question, Gunner waved his hands, seeking silence. "Please, I need your attention." The din continued. "Quiet!" Gunner bellowed.

Their shouts continued.

"Please! Quiet down." It took four more attempts before they adequately hushed. "Thank you. My name is Captain Gunner McCrae."

"What happened to the real Captain?"

"Ladies and gentlemen." Gunner forged on. "I will make a major announcement very soon on the Lido deck. That's the top deck where the main pool is."

He turned to Cloe and Quinn who'd managed to make their way to his side. "Would you two like to direct them?"

"Of course, Captain." They spoke in unison, and just the way they looked at each other, with love in their eyes, had his heart aching for his wife. Adelle was his everything. Gunner would be nothing if it wasn't for her. *Oh God.* He'd do anything to find out if she was okay. But he couldn't allow his anguish to drag him down that rabbit hole.

The passengers needed him. His crew needed him.

"Ladies and gentlemen, Cloe and Quinn will guide you." He indicated to the couple and they put their hands up. "Follow them.

Please also help us by telling anyone you see to go to the Lido deck. Okay? Go! Now!"

Cloe nodded at Gunner and wriggled her eyebrows. "See you at the other end."

Gunner nodded. "Yes. You will. Thank you."

With her hand raised, Cloe began pushing through the crowd. "All right, everyone follow me. Let's go."

Gunner was impressed with her booming voice. For a small woman, she sure could command attention.

The passengers did a collective pause as if undecided over what to do, and then gradually, they turned and shuffled out of the bridge. A hand wrapped around his wrist, and Gunner glanced down to a frail elderly woman who was clutching an illuminated cell phone like it was a life source. Her smoky-gray eyes were riddled with so many spider veins they looked to be bleeding. "Captain, are we sinking?"

He touched her shoulder and felt the bones beneath. "No, ma'am, we are not. What's your name?"

"Bronwyn. Bronwyn Applegate."

"Okay, Bronwyn, please keep with the crowd. I will make an announcement very soon at the Lido deck."

She held his gaze for a couple of beats, then nodded and shuffled out of the bridge.

Finally, with some breathing space, Gunner huffed out a sigh.

Sykes' shoulders sagged like he was deflating. "What took you so long, Captain, sir?" His eyes were fused with both anger and fear. "I thought they were going to kill me."

"I'm sorry. It's a mess down there."

"Are we sinking?"

"That's the only good news. The plane impacted a huge area. At least six decks. There was a flash fire in the engine room." He squeezed his temples. "Everybody's dead."

"Oh jeez."

"We've got no chance of getting power."

"She's starting to roll, sir, and drifting dead in the water without stabilizers it's going to get worse. Based on the increasing swell and that lightning ahead, I predict we are heading into that storm we were tracking before the power failed."

Pain boomed behind Gunner's eyes and he pinched the bridge of his nose. "What time is it?"

"Twenty-three forty-seven, sir."

Nearly midnight. He'd been awake nineteen hours.

He opened his eyes and met Sykes' glare. "We've just got to get through tonight. Come daylight, we'll be able to assess the situation better."

Sykes placed the binoculars on the table. "Are we abandoning ship, sir?"

"Have you seen any other ships?" He dodged the question.

"Not one, sir. Prior to the strike there were three we were tracking. It's like they've all vanished."

"If they are without power like us, then they'll be impossible to see. Where's the rest of the crew?"

"I don't know. You're the first to return."

"The doc?"

"No, sir."

Gunner frowned. The medical clinic was at the rear of deck four. He hadn't gone near that section of the ship. He made a mental note to add it to his list of priorities. "Sykes, hear me out."

Sykes stepped his boots shoulder-width apart, clenched his hands at his hips and drew a scowl on his face that was typical Sykes. "Sir."

"We have nine hundred and twenty-two passengers on board. Plus two hundred and fifteen crew members. Our first priority is to keep them safe."

Sykes nodded.

"Rose of the Sea would be much easier to spot in the ocean than a clutch of life rafts. At this stage, remaining onboard with food and facilities makes more sense than abandoning to life rafts where we will have limited supplies. Especially as we have zero confirmation of a rescue. Do you agree?"

"Sir?"

"Sykes, I'm asking for your opinion."

"Sir, it's not—"

"Cameron," Gunner interrupted. "We've only known each other for twelve days, but you are the right man to help me. What we are going through is unprecedented. And if Captain Nelson was right about it being an EMP strike, and I believe he was, then that plane hitting us was the least of our worries. The entire continent could be in trouble and we may be stranded at sea for a very long time without any hope of a rescue. So, First Officer Cameron Sykes, do you concur with remaining onboard Rose of the Sea?"

Sykes' body deflated even more, as if yielding to the pressure of such a decision. After an excruciating pause, he nodded. "Yes, Captain, I agree."

Gunner touched his shoulder. "Thank you." He huffed out a sigh. "Keep up the good work."

"Yes, sir. Thank you." A frown drilled his dark eyebrows together. "Sir . . . please, don't forget about me."

Gunner paused at that. He was the second crew member to make that statement. Maybe it was because they didn't really know him. If they did, they'd know they wouldn't need to ask.

"I promise you this, First Officer Cameron Sykes. If I think we need to abandon ship, I will consult you first."

He nodded, then sat down and positioned the microphone to his mouth. "Mayday. Mayday. Mayday. This is . . ."

As Gunner strode from the bridge, he silently prayed for an answer to that desperate call for help.

But his gut told him it was never going to come.

Chapter Twenty-Three

GUNNER

Using the phone for light, Gunner made his way toward the stairs. His eyes snagged on the elevators and his brain shuddered to a halt. Those poor people would no doubt still be stuck.

Even if they had managed to find the escape hatch in the roof, they'd never get out that way. Blue Earth Cruise Lines had learned the hard way that the space above the elevator was an ideal stowaway spot. Lord knew how many times it'd been utilized before one unfortunate nineteen-year-old Venezuelan man had been crushed to death while attempting to flee to America. After that, all elevator service doors had been padlocked on the outside and only a select few crew members knew the combination.

I will rescue them.

But it would have to wait. There could be more than a thousand people waiting for him on the Lido deck. *Oh god, I hope it's at least a thousand.* But with the amount of dead people he'd already seen, he dreaded it was much less. Regardless, every last soul was his priority.

He strode past the blackened-out day spa, the fitness center, and the coffee shop that was usually brimming with people, both day and night. When he pushed through a set of double doors, the sharp pain behind his eyes hit icepick intensity at the size and noise of the crowd. Hundreds of people were crammed into the area. Above the Lido deck, on the walking track level, hundreds more people were leaning against the remaining portion of the railing and looking down.

The weight of their survival was an anchor on his shoulders.

Every single one of them counted on him to know what he was doing. Anxiety barreled through him like a tsunami.

No amount of training could've prepared him for this.

The damage to the deck was shocking. Overhead, one of the railings dangled down like it was a flimsy cable tie and not high-tensile steel. The boat swayed to port side and the pool water sloshed onto shrieking passengers who scrambled from the soaking. Crunching on broken glass and trying but failing to ignore the grisly row of bodies lined up like felled dominoes, he aimed for the bar.

If the need arose for passengers to be corralled into one place, it was usually done in the grand theater. But without power and lighting, the theater was impractical. Out here on the open deck, where moonlight and working phones were their sources of illumination, was the only option.

As he squeezed through the crowd, people turned to him. Fear riddled their faces. Tears streaked their cheeks. Blood and wounds stood out like beacons.

Forcing himself to breathe, he pushed past a couple who were each holding a small child in their arms. Normally, he'd acknowledge every possible passenger with a confident smile, and a handshake when appropriate. Not this time. Instead, he lowered his eyes and forced himself to keep on walking before his trembling knees crumbled him to the deck.

Of the two hundred or so crew on the ship, the bulk of them were in back-of-house services such as laundry, housekeeping, passenger entertainment, and food and beverage duties. Then there were those involved in running the ship—electrical, technical, engineering, and carpentry. Now though, only a fraction of the crew was gathered around the bar. The number of absentees had Gunner's mind reeling.

Jesus! Were they all dead? Horror scraped through his veins.

Maybe they're just scared and are hiding amongst the crowd. *Yes, please let that be it.* As he clung to that glimmer of hope, he vowed to flush them out. He needed all the manpower he could get.

The crew at the bar were wearing either all white uniforms or white and blue. Except for Cloe and Quinn, who were still in civilian clothes. Between them, they only had about ten phone lights.

All eyes turned to him as he approached. The distress in their eyes matched that of the passengers. They were scared. Hell, he was scared. Acid coiled in his stomach over the pressure to lead. To do the right thing. To keep everyone safe.

But he had no choice. He was in charge. *How the hell did this happen?*

Shoving the shit aside, Gunner eyeballed Head of Security on approach and swallowed back a giant lump of fear. "Mr. McMaster, we've got our work cut out for us. I trust you are prepared."

The security guard puffed out his chest. "Yes, sir."

"Good, okay. Listen up." They encircled him and the surrounding passengers crowded in. Ignoring them, he tried to meet the gaze of each and every one of his crew as he spoke. He hoped they didn't see the anguish in his eyes. He hoped they didn't see through his façade. "We have a very serious situation. We have no power, no communications, and no engines. And it's impossible to know how long it'll take to get any or all of them working again."

"But . . . but we have to," a young crew member blurted. "I have to get home. My engagement party is in three days." Cindy was bar staff. She'd served him a mocktail on his second night on the cruise and had waited with a dazzling grin for his approval of her drink. She wasn't grinning now.

Dragging his eyes from the glitter and blood on her cheeks, he trudged on. "To get through this, we need to work together as a team. We need to make some very difficult decisions. Our first priority is safety. Do we know how many fatalities we have?"

They shook their heads.

"Okay, with our systems down we need to create manual lists of all the remaining passengers and identify the deceased." Gunner turned to the head of security again. "Willis, I want the passengers to form eight lines. Eight of you are to record passenger details. I want names, ages, cabin numbers, and contact phone numbers." That last detail may be pointless if communications never returned.

"Sir, may I also suggest we detail their skills?" Willis said. "There may be doctors or mechanics amongst them."

"Good idea, Willis."

Gunner twisted his wedding ring around his finger. The circle of gold didn't instil the reassurance it usually did. "I need eight volunteers to record passenger names."

Ten put up their hands. "Good. Grab pens and paper from behind the bar. We've got to do this old school. I want you set up in each of the four corners on both levels." Gunner pointed out the positions. "Willis and you two." He chose two crew members at random. "You'll be instructing people where to go. And if you find any more crew, send them to me. Understand?"

They all nodded.

"If anyone is missing a member of their family or traveling party, direct them to Cloe. Pop your hand up, Cloe." She did. "Hopefully, you'll be able to reunite some people."

His brain scrambled with a thousand necessities and he tried to prioritize them into a workable order. "We need to take care of the deceased. Do I have any volunteers for that?" Three men put up their hands. "Thank you. We have set up a temporary morgue in Petals at the stern and have started to list the deceased. Please carry all the bodies there and do what you can to identify them." He scanned the group. "Quinn, where are you, Quinn?"

Quinn stepped forward. "Here, sir."

"As each body is identified, tag them, and add their name to the list." He huffed out a wobbly breath. "It will make Cloe's job easier."

Quinn nodded with a glance at Cloe. "Yes, sir."

Gunner squeezed his temples, trying to relieve the pressure brewing behind his eyes. "Who hasn't got a job yet?"

About a dozen crew members put up their hands. "Water and

food are about to become a major priority. But without manpower, the kitchen will be impossible to secure."

"How about the fitness center, Captain?" Willis said. "It has one entrance. Easier to guard."

"Good idea, Willis. You four." He pointed at Cindy, two other bartenders, and another crewman who were standing together. "Grab every can and bottle. Fresh food, canned food. Anything that isn't already open or cooked. Use the dish trolleys to move them. Willis, where's the rest of your crew?"

The security guard shook his head. "I haven't seen them."

"Okay, you and you." He pointed to the two tallest men who hadn't been allocated jobs. "You're in charge of guarding the fitness center."

The crowd were becoming restless, escalating in volume and voicing questions loaded with anger. "Okay, anyone who hasn't got a job, stick with me. We'll do this on the fly."

He glanced around the crew. "Are we all good?"

"Yes, sir." Their collective response was a mixture of brisk affirmations and reluctant ones.

"Right." Gunner hauled himself onto the bar top and waved his arms over his head, seeking the crowd's attention. "Ladies and gentlemen."

The boat rolled to starboard side, and he clutched at a pole to prevent himself from toppling off the bar.

Rose of the Sea was moving too much.

Way too much.

Things were about to get a hell of a lot worse.

Chapter Twenty-Four

GUNNER

A collection of cell lights shifted Gunner's way, placing him in the spotlight. The moon's reflection in the water looked picture perfect, offering a setting that appeared deceptively serene.

Nothing about this night was serene.

Not for him, nor the agitated passengers assembled before him.

"Ladies and gentlemen, please quiet down." Gunner tried to project his voice but it was near impossible with the large crowd and the outdoor setting. He looked down at the crew members and was surprised to see Brandi at his side. The beautiful blonde had bloodshot eyes, confirming she'd been crying. She no longer looked the defiant young twenty-year-old he'd met earlier.

"Brandi, stick with me, please. I need you to help me remember things. Somebody get her a pen and paper. First thing on the list, Brandi, is find a megaphone. And someone needs to go to the shops and grab candles and matches before all these phones run out of batteries. Got it?"

"Yes. Okay. I can do that." She wiped a green fingernail over her cheek.

Gunner returned his attention to the crowd and felt every pair of eyes glaring at him. Expecting him to know what he was doing. Expecting pearls of wisdom. Expecting him to keep them all safe.

A blaze of panic shot through him. All at once he was both boiling hot and frigid cold. Pain surged behind his eyes and his legs teetered beneath him. Gunner swallowed, tasting a bitterness reminiscent of the charred bodies in the engine room. The urge to jump down from the spotlight and pretend it was all just a terrible nightmare was overwhelming.

The boat groaned beneath his feet and when she heeled to port side, the bulk of the crowd shuffled sideways like a massive line-dancing ensemble. Trouble was, she was just getting started. Now that Rose of the Sea had begun rolling, the momentum was destined to heighten. Especially if that storm hit.

A foul guttural sound confirmed somebody was vomiting, and by the way a group in the crowd shifted, Gunner assumed he or she was near the remaining spa. Then another person threw up. Vomiting had a cascading affect. It always did. Within seconds, people were hurling at their feet or running to the railings and throwing up over the side.

The best antidote for sickness was to find land or to dose with medication. Option A was going to need a miracle. "Brandi, add to the list that we need to get all the seasickness medication up here asap."

The next best remedy for seasickness was distraction. "Ladies and gentlemen, please, can I have your attention."

The crowd's agitation steamrolled; eyes darted left and right. Boisterous passengers fired questions at him.

"What's going on?"

"Where's the Captain?"

"Yeah. Who the fuck is running this ship?"

A vision of Captain Nelson lying dead in the bridge flashed in his mind. Acid turned in his stomach. Bile rose up his throat, flooded his tongue. He wasn't ready for this. Clutching the pole, he fought a wave of terror crawling through him like a million bull ants.

His eyes snagged on the little old lady who he'd met in the

bridge. Bronwyn. She was still clutching her phone and staring up at him. Waiting for him. Expecting him to take control.

He mentally slapped himself. She needed him. They all did.

He swallowed hard, forcing down his weakness. He had to be strong. Assertive. He had to do it for them. For himself. He had to make his wife proud.

"Ladies and gentlemen, I have a lot to tell you. Please listen and hold back your questions for now. Please. Please." A wave of stillness rippled through the crowd and when the silence was complete, the crowd seemed to bristle with static, poised in nervous anticipation.

Gunner cleared his throat. "A few hours ago, Captain Stewart Nelson passed away from a suspected heart attack." Gunner ignored the spread of unintelligible mutterings and carried on. "My name is Gunner McCrae. I am your new Captain."

A baby started screaming somewhere beyond the pool. Another person threw up. The sounds seemed amplified, cutting through the silence like sonic booms.

"As many of you know, a plane crashed into the stern of the ship. I have personally assessed the impacted areas and can assure you that the ship is safe. We are not sinking. I repeat, we are not sinking."

The cell lights moved from him to each other, and the murmur that rolled through the crowd was a fraction more positive than the last.

"That's the good news," he bellowed and braced for his next announcement. "Now for the bad news."

Except for the crying baby, the crowd plunged into silence. The air prickled.

"At seventeen, forty-eight this afternoon, we lost power to a large portion of the ship. Eighteen minutes later, that plane crashed. These incidents are related."

Several people gasped and a chubby man in a Hawaiian shirt shot his hand up and spoke at the same time. "It's an EMP strike, Captain McCrae. Isn't it? Am I right?"

His booming voice must've carried a long way because a woman in the back shrieked.

"Quiet, please."

The passengers did the opposite. Their collaborative voices escalated and grew rowdy again. They fired questions at him, one after another.

"What's an EMP?"

"Are we going to die?"

"Please, I need your attention," he yelled.

The crowd divided between growing quiet and antagonized shouts at him.

"Sir." Gunner spoke to the man in the Hawaiian shirt. "What's your name?"

He pointed at his own chest and Gunner nodded. "Albert. Albert Schaeffer."

"Step forward, Mr. Schaeffer." The man glanced to his right and Gunner assumed the similarly dressed people near him were his friends.

He shuffled forward and stopped two feet from the bar, and when he looked up, Gunner crouched down. "Mr. Schaeffer, what do you know about EMPs?"

He turned to glance over his shoulder again, then looked back at Gunner. "I . . . did some research a while back and I . . . I don't know, we just, we talk about stuff like that. You know, end-of-world stuff. Apocalypse. Armageddon. Movies and shows. The debate has been raging for years. But it was never about *if* it was going to happen—more *when* it would happen, and who would do it to whom. What's happened to the ship and that plane? Well, it makes sense that it was an EMP. I mean, look at our phones. It also means we're screwed. But not just us. All of America."

The man spoke in one rambling statement and only stopped when he seemed to be out of breath. Albert's EMP knowledge could possibly come in handy. But Gunner needed to get the passengers sorted first. Then he intended to find out just how much Albert knew.

Gunner met Albert's wide-eyed glare. "I believe you are correct, Albert, and I'll talk to you in more detail very soon. But first, do you think you can use that voice of yours to settle the crowd?"

Albert wiped his hands over his rotund belly, then put two fingers in his mouth and emitted a whistle that had stillness gripping the crowd.

"Thank you." Gunner stood again. "Okay everyone. We have been unable to relay messages from the ship, so we have no idea what's happening beyond Rose of the Sea. What we *do* know is that we are safe."

The crowd started murmuring and he carried on before they got away from him again. "Our goal is to get through tonight. Come morning, we'll have a greater understanding of this unprecedented situation." He hoped he wasn't lying. "Right now, though, I need your help." Gunner detailed his plan regarding obtaining passenger names and gave instructions. The crowd began moving before he'd even finished, and while some seemed to be following his instructions, a good portion were not.

It wasn't surprising. Rarely did crowds follow orders correctly.

He was about to reiterate the plan when every single mobile phone that'd been in flashlight mode died.

Two seconds later, someone screamed.

Chapter Twenty-Five

GABBY

Gabby glared at Max, biting back the fury she wanted to blast him with.

He was bending over, his hands on his knees, and gasping for breath in a manner equivalent to his heaving after he'd run the full marathon last year. She gripped his bicep, urging his attention. "Max, will you stop? Please."

"I can do this." Again, he braced against the opposite wall and charged shoulder-first into their cabin door. Again, he failed. Again, she winced.

"Stop it!" she hissed. "You'll hurt yourself."

"I can't get any momentum."

"I don't care. I'm fine now. I don't need the medication." He'd managed to crack their cabin door open two inches, but whatever was blocking it on the other side was impossible to budge. They'd wasted too much time trying to break in and she was not going to watch his futile attempts any longer. "If you don't stop this foolishness right now, I'm going to look for the kids without you."

"You need your tablets."

"No. I need to find the kids. I'm *fine*!" The words snapped off her tongue like bitter lemon. "Now!"

His face sagged with the weight of apparent failure. It was a look she'd seen every time he was unsuccessful at one of his stupid self-imposed fitness goals. But this wasn't a chest-beating moment. This was life or death. *Oh God!* Comprehending the enormity of that was like swallowing barbed wire. It cut her to the core. But it was true.

"Okay." He squeezed her hand. "But the second we find them, we're getting your meds."

"Okay. Okay!" Her world had changed the moment she'd been diagnosed with epilepsy. When people learned of her condition it was like she'd mutated to a weaker version of herself. Suddenly, she needed help. Needed to be careful. Like they expected her to pass out at any moment.

To say it was infuriating was an understatement.

As a consequence, she fiercely guarded the knowledge of her genetic disorder. Especially with her employers and co-workers. If word got out that Gabrielle Kinsella had epilepsy, she'd be relegated to mail room duties faster than a producer could say 'cut'. No more racing through traffic with horns blaring, or frantic helicopter rides to be first on the scene. Lord no! If she ever had an episode at work, her co-workers would step over her shuddering body to fight for her position in front of the camera.

Just the thought of that injustice had her clenching her teeth. Gabby wasn't weak. She was the opposite. In fact, her condition had made her stronger. More determined. More focused. More ruthless. Taking a daily tablet was the only drawback. She loathed relying on medication. But she did take it, religiously. Most of the time she forgot she even had the stupid condition.

Until a seizure took hold.

But with each and every one of those sordid events, she rose up and forced herself to be stronger.

Strength was what she needed now. Mentally and physically. Riding that affirmation, she snatched Max's candle from the floor and glared at him. "Let's go."

He nodded, and when he reached for the candle, she shoved it at him, spun on her heel and strode on ahead. It was a couple of beats before Max's feet pounded behind her.

With the minimal candlelight, it seemed to take forever to reverse the route they'd taken to reach their cabins. Each ticking minute had dread oozing through Gabby like a doomed spirit. Her overactive mind bounced from one rotten thought to the next. The ship seemed to be alive, rolling and swaying and groaning like it had a painful tumor.

Gabrielle's creative thoughts were in overdrive. Normally, she'd embrace them. Now, though, it was adding additional strain to her splintered nerves. Her only savior was in the momentum of moving. Pushing forward. Searching. Searching. "Sally! Adam!"

They took turns calling the kids' names, scouring the never-ending corridors. The darkness was complete. Scary. It gave the illusion that the already lengthy passages were even longer. Every step was frantic. Every roll of the ship was notable. Every sound was amplified. Every doorway was met with newfound hope. But the unsuccessful conclusion at the end of each passageway produced another layer of gut-wrenching hopelessness.

Time became their enemy.

When one deck had been searched, they pushed up to the next. Deck four. Five. Six. All were empty. Smoke stung her eyes . . . burned her throat. The swaying ship had her hips and elbows slamming into walls.

The ache in her heart was a giant fist. Clenching. Crushing. Throbbing.

Her throat tightened against the smoke-filled air and she emitted a grating wheeze.

Max spun to her—he'd heard it too.

His hands rubber-banded to her, reaching out, and her world wobbled. "Hey, babe, let's take a rest here."

"No! We have to find the kids."

"And we will."

A sob burst from her throat as he forced her to sit on the carpet. "What if we can't find them? What if they're . . ." She couldn't finish her sentence. Wouldn't. She would never believe they were gone.

Max wrapped his arms around her and in the narrow, swaying passage she cried onto his shoulder.

But tears were pointless. A weakness. One she didn't want to show. They were wasting precious time. She sucked in a shaky breath, pushed back from Max, and wiped her eyes. "I'm fine. Okay? I just need to find the kids."

Maybe the candlelight showed the conviction in her eyes, because for once he didn't argue. Instead, he helped her to her feet, and with his hand sheltering the flickering flame, he led the way up the stairs to deck seven.

They'd learned from the previous two decks that the left-hand side of the ship had suffered the most damage from the plane crash. So, keeping to the right, they pushed through double fire doors. Rather than entering more narrow passages housing endless cabins, they stumbled upon the nightclub. Floor-to-ceiling windows lined the far side, allowing moonlight to filter in, and Gabby raced across the dance floor. "Sally! Adam!" She searched the other side of the room, checking the curved booths, behind the bar, and in the 'crew only' areas.

Nobody was around. The whole damn ship seemed deserted.

Chapter Twenty-Six

GABBY

"Sally. Adam." Max searched the bathrooms but raced back to Gabby within seconds.

"Where could they be?" The ship swayed, and Gabby stumbled sideways.

Max clutched her shoulders. "Hey, let's take a rest."

"No, Max! Stop it. I'm fine."

"No. You're not."

She lashed out, slapping his cheek. "Stop it."

The candle flame made his bulging eyes look hideously huge.

"The ship swayed; that's all. Now let's go." She strode from the nightclub, through a door that led to an outer deck.

The ocean breeze was swift and so very welcome. Clutching the railing, she sucked in the fresh air hoping to cleanse the smoke from her airways. The moon was a third of the way off the horizon and allowed sufficient light to see the boiling sea. The waves were at least nine or ten feet high and topped with white froth. Her mind snapped to all those poor people who'd gone overboard after the plane engine had skidded across the deck, and she imagined a field of people floating face-down. It was a brutal image.

She'd done enough cruises to know that waves of this scope

shouldn't have any impact on a ship the size of Rose of the Sea. But it was a different story when the ship's engines and electronics weren't working. They were essentially on a cork, bobbing on the water.

At the mercy of the sea.

Max reached the railing beside her and a heartbeat later, a blaze of lightning forked the sky, emitting a violent crack that made her jump.

"Sally's scared of lightning." Max's voice was loaded with sorrow.

Gabby was a second off rebuffing his statement when she glimpsed the trouble in his eyes. It confirmed it was true. A piece of her heart cracked at her not knowing that about her own daughter.

"She'll be hiding somewhere inside then." Gabby stormed away. Clenching her teeth, she charged back through the doors. Barely any moonlight penetrated the space and the blackness was so complete, it left her no choice but to wait for Max and his candle.

His candlelight allowed her to get her bearings, and she saw two posters beside a set of elevator doors. "This is where we first boarded the ship."

"Oh yeah. You're right.

One of the posters had a woman wearing a skimpy silver costume and dangling upside down from a red sash. The other poster had a picture of three chargrilled prawns sitting atop a colorful salad. Her stomach rumbled as if it smelled the food. It was impossible to remember how long ago she'd eaten. The kids had been going to join them for dinner at the Chinese buffet.

"The kids missed dinner." Max must've read her mind. "They must be starving."

"Pfft." She chuckled, trying to make light of the moment. "Adam probably filled up on every flavor of ice cream."

"He's lactose intolerant." Max looked at her, deadpan.

A blaze of heat raced up her neck.

She knew that. Of course she did.

Max's expression morphed from bewilderment to disappointment. But there was something else there she couldn't pinpoint, almost like he'd had a reality check. Fearful he was about to say something she didn't want to hear, she turned toward the right-hand doorway. "Let's go."

Striding across the flattened carpet, she passed the abandoned shore excursion desk and the photo gallery where a week ago they'd laughed themselves silly at the ridiculous family portrait the overzealous photographer had pressured them into taking. It'd seemed a good idea at the time, particularly as all four of them were together *and* because they were dressed for the evening show. But the resulting photo had been amateurishly photoshopped to adjust their skin tones and cropped to position them in front of a photo of Rose of the Sea.

Oh God. That ghastly photo could be the last family portrait they'd ever take.

No. *It will not.* Fear stabbed at her stomach. Stabbed at her brain.

We will take many more family photos. Proper ones, with a real photographer.

She spun on her heel and stormed back to the wall of photos. It took her two seconds to find it. She snatched it off the wall and ripped it to shreds. With that done, she turned back to Max. His jaw was ajar and eyebrows raised, posing a silent question.

"Don't ask." She pushed past him again, and the sound of voices had her heart jumping. "Do you hear that? Sally? Adam?"

Casting caution aside, she strode onward. "Sally. Adam."

But her thumping excitement nosedived when she found the source of the voices. "What are you doing?" she yelled at the group of men inside the duty-free cellar door.

One of the men jumped. "Jesus, lady, you scared the crap out of me."

"What the hell are you doing?"

"We're drinking. What does it look like?"

"You know the ship's sinking, don't you?" She tried the same tactic she'd used on the kids looting the store.

"Huh. Where'd you hear that? The Captain said it's definitely not sinking."

"He did? When?"

"We overheard him talking to some of the crew when they were heading toward the pool deck. As soon as he said that, we came down here. . . figured we can't do anything else, so we might as well drink."

While it was a relief to hear the ship wasn't sinking, it was what she hadn't heard that was the worry. "What else did he say?"

The young man offered an open bottle of bourbon to her and although it was very tempting, she declined. "The Captain said something about not being able to communicate back home. Oh, and he mentioned that it was an EMP, but we've got no idea what that is."

Gabby nodded. She'd been right. And that meant they were in real trouble. Not just her family. But every single person on this ship. She clutched the man's wrist. "Have you seen a couple of teenagers, a boy and girl, about this high? We've lost our kids."

He tried to snatch his arm away. "Calm your farm, lady. Let go of me."

"Have you seen them?"

"No." He yanked himself free.

A young woman stepped forward. Her blond hair curled about her face with a youthful bounce. "Listen . . . everyone was told to go up to the pool deck. Your kids are probably up there trying to find you."

"She's right, Gabby. Come on." Max reached for her hand, dragging her away.

As they departed, the group burst into laughter.

Come tomorrow though, they wouldn't be laughing. Everything was about to go to hell.

Hell . . . they were probably already there.

Chapter Twenty-Seven

GABBY

Gabby raced after Max, and when they passed a couple of shops which had a dozen or so people looting the shelves, Gabby joined them and replaced the candle she'd lost with another one. And once again, she filled her pockets with chocolate bars.

At the cocktail bar, several people were helping themselves to drinks. They had candles lit and were chatting and laughing like it was all a big joke.

She shook her head at the absurdity of it all.

Sadly, it was exactly the type of behavior that would make headline news. She could picture it now . . . *Sipping cocktails while the ship went down—what a way to go.*

It was all so surreal.

At the atrium, they stopped and called out the kids' names again. The large open space spanned four decks and their voices echoed into the dark void. It was like a scene from a post-apocalyptic movie.

"Sally! Adam!" Gabby screamed until her already suffering throat burned. When she pulled back, she rubbed her weary eyes. She didn't want to admit it, but she was tired. And hungry. But most of all, she was scared for her children. "Where could they be?"

"Maybe we *should* go up to the pool deck and see if they're there."

She rolled the thought around her brain. It just didn't feel right.

"Gabby." Max touched her shoulder. "Come on."

After walking through a carpeted area with cushioned seating set in various configurations, they entered a section that looked like an enormous wrecking ball had smashed through it. But it wasn't a wrecking ball. Gabby knew exactly what it would've been. The plane engine. The giant projectile, about the size of a cement truck, had carved a trail of destruction through the middle of the ship.

The entire elevator shaft was obliterated. Doors gone. Walls gone. Elevator gone.

The size and extent of the damage was consistent with when the engine had smashed through the upper deck, taking out everyone like they were bowling pins.

The only thing left of the elevator was a shredded foursome of two-inch cables that had once held it in place.

A whistling noise came up through the hollow shaft and her brain forked in opposing directions when she pictured the demise of the elevator itself. The first was utter horror for anybody who may've been inside when it dropped to the bottom in about three seconds flat.

The second was a potential headline: *Dozens killed in elevator plummet*.

Headlines like that attracted attention.

The eerie quiet had her artistic license already working the silent creepiness into an engrossing news story when she heard something. "Shhh! Max, listen."

"What?"

"Do you hear that?"

The boat groaned and she clutched the handrail as she pitched to the right.

"Help." It was a child's voice. Barely audible.

"Oh my God." Her heart launched to her throat. "Did you hear that? Hello. We're here. We can hear you."

"Help!" The voice was distant, a mile away.

"We're coming. Where are you?" Gabby bounced off the walls, left and right as she raced to keep up with Max.

"Help!" It was a girl's voice. *Was it Sally? Please let it be Sally.*

Gabby's brain froze on a mental picture of her beautiful daughter, covered in blood and screaming for help.

"We're on our way. Where are you?" Max's voice boomed in the enclosed passageway.

"In here. In the theater."

Max shot ahead, and Gabby dashed after him. They burst through the double entrance doors to the theater and she gasped at the disaster zone. The giant engine that had crippled the elevator had demolished several rows of chairs and destroyed the upper theater stalls before it had smashed a gaping hole in the side of the ship.

Faint light streamed in through the hole, and it took Gabby a couple of thumping heartbeats to realize it was the moon.

"Sally! Adam!" Max screamed into the near-black room.

"Dad."

Gabby just about crumbled to the ground. "Adam!" Her throat was choked with emotion; she could barely breathe.

"Adam! Adam!" Max's screams were shrill with terror as he clambered over chairs. "Where are you?"

"We're up here."

"Oh my God." Gabby flicked away tears as she tried to keep up with Max. The moon provided enough light to see through the smoky haze. What she saw had her crying for both joy and fear. Her son was looking down from the only remaining portion of the upper theater stall.

"Adam. Where's Sally?" Gabby yelled up to him.

He shook his head. "I don't know. What's happening?" Despite the dimmed light, she saw tears streaming down Adam's blackened face. Beside him were two boys and a girl. All were crying.

"Are you hurt?" Max stood on a chair and looked up at the balcony.

Barely ten feet of the stall was remaining. Gabby's legs buckled beneath her as she realized with utter horror that their son . . . their thirteen-year-old boy, Adam, had been inches from death.

The boat shifted and Gabby clawed at chairs as she toppled. She missed them all and landed heavily on the floor. Blinking back her shock, she turned and came face to face with a young girl whose long dark hair covered her face. But her head was twisted at a hideous angle.

Gabby squealed and jerked back. Tears stung her eyes. Her chin quivered.

"Sally? Oh God, Sally?" A sob burst from her throat. "No. No. No. No. No."

Gabby couldn't breathe. She couldn't think. With trembling fingers, she reached forward and scooped the hair back from the girl's face.

"Oh, thank God." Relief liquified her bones as she gasped at the young girl's eyes, staring blankly into the distance. Shivers rained up Gabby's neck. She scrambled to push away from the tiny child, riding a painful wave of both guilt and relief. Then she saw a pair of bloodied legs in the aisle.

A terrified shriek tumbled from her throat as she scrambled over chairs to get to the body. It too was a young girl, barely eight years old. Gabby rode another violent wave of guilt as she thanked God the body wasn't her daughter's.

Standing again, she turned her gaze toward Adam, whose howling strangled her heart, but her eyes snagged on yet another body. Then another. Three. Six. Ten. All of them were young kids. All sprawled at awkward angles. All dead.

Her heart thumped in her neck. Her breathing rushed in and out in short, painful gasps. Dragging her eyes away from a bloody corpse, she looked up to her son. Tears streamed down his dirty cheeks. His mouth was wide open with terrified screams.

"Adam." Her chin quivered. "Where's Sally?"

He shook his head. "I don't know." His wailing carved a brutal hole in Gabby's heart.

"When did you last see her?"

"She was going to our cabin to change her shoes."

"When?" Gabby shrieked. "When?"

"It was . . ." he howled, ". . . it was right before that happened."

Gabby's mind snapped to the shredded cables where the elevator had been.

She fell to her knees. Her world swam. In the distance, lightning blazed across a thick black cloud and her brain struggled to comprehend how that could be. A stench as pungent as it was sickening invaded her nostrils. She gasped for air, sucking back the rancid odor. She tilted sideways. Her cheek hit the rough carpet.

Her arms and legs were lead weights. Impossible to lift.

Everything swirled around her like she was caught in a tornado.

Her body melted into the carpet.

Her world went blank.

Chapter Twenty-Eight

MADELINE

"What're we going to do, Sterling?" Madeline's voice was hoarse from screaming. Her fists were sore from banging on the closed elevator doors and her eyes stung from the smoke that was growing thicker by the second.

"I don't know. We've run out of options."

They'd stopped halfway down the elevator shaft. According to the number on the back of the metal doors beside her, they'd reached deck four. Above them was their elevator, stuck somewhere between the sixth and seventh decks. Below them was an elevator shaft, at least four decks deep, filled with smoke. And at the very bottom was a fire.

They couldn't go up. They couldn't go down. They had no way out.

Madeline knew exactly what it was like to have no way out, yet at the same time cling to ludicrous hope that a solution would miraculously appear. The crazy cycle of hope and disappointment could spin around with fierce and soul-crushing repetition for days.

Every time Professor Flint had opened the door to the dungeon, her hopes had soared. Sometimes she'd actually looked forward to his visits. Begged for them even. And then the horror would happen.

Afterward, he'd turn off the light and shut the door, plunging her into absolute darkness.

Absolute darkness.

It was still her greatest fear.

With the flames flickering below, at least she could see.

She turned her gaze to Sterling. He scanned the elevator shaft. Down to the fire. Up to the stranded elevator. To the doors that were impossible to open. To the four solid walls that were impenetrable.

She should be petrified too. Out of her mind.

But she wasn't.

Maybe after surviving the very worst a human could suffer, nothing could be as terrifying. Even dying.

She'd thought about killing herself many times in that dungeon. After she was rescued, she'd thought about killing herself too. She'd felt like a freak. Nobody knew how to talk to her, how to look at her without getting all weird. The media were relentless, hounding her for sordid details. Snapping pictures like she was a monster. Sneaky reporters would pretend to be her friend only to ruin that trust in the most soul-crushing of ways.

Her therapist had diagnosed her with Post Traumatic Stress Disorder. PTSD. The acronym had been rolling around her brain for sixteen years. During her entrapment, she'd taken to humming and picturing herself dancing to music. Free as a bird in the beautiful blue sky. Her therapist had honed in on that. It had turned out to be the only good thing to surface from that therapy . . . the suggestion that Madeline take up dancing.

She didn't just take it up. She'd become obsessed and it had consumed her life.

Dancing made her free.

It made her glad she hadn't killed herself. She was glad to be alive.

I am glad to be alive.

Anger boiled in her belly. Heat blazed up her neck. Her pulse thumped in her ears. The idea that she was going to die in this smoke-filled shaft seeped into her brain like ink, staining her sanity, and cell by cell, sending her just a little bit mad.

Her rage formed a volcano. Flaming-hot fury swelled from deep inside her, inching up her backbone like a slithering cobra. Unable to contain it a moment more, she stood on the grill and screamed into the void.

"What? What?" Sterling's eyes were huge. His expression confirmed he was petrified.

"Sorry." She'd been so caught up in her own demise that she hadn't thought about Sterling. "I'm so sorry, I just—I can't believe this is happening again."

His eyes bulged further. "You've been stuck in an elevator before."

"No. Not specifically."

"But you've been trapped before?"

She nodded, but didn't elaborate.

"Okay." He paused, maybe waiting for clarification. An awkward beat passed between them. "How did you get out last time then?"

She liked that he didn't pry; it demonstrated the type of man he was—compassionate. Not many people she met fit that criteria.

She gazed down at the fire.

She'd survived a fire last time. She was determined to survive this.

The flames seemed to be subsiding, yet it had the opposite effect on the smoke. It was becoming thicker, more caustic. Covering her hand over her mouth, she blinked through the haze and spied the second lift. It was right down at the bottom. But there was something weird about it. It was out of shape. "Sterling. Look at that other elevator."

He craned his head to look downward.

"See it? It's all buckled. Maybe that's what that huge bang was. The elevator falling."

His jaw dropped and his eyes bulged. "Oh God, do you think there were people in it?"

"I don't know." She shook her head, frowning. "But we need to find out. Maybe they're alive."

But the elevator was mangled. Almost beyond recognition.

It would be impossible for anyone to have survived.

The last time Madeline had seen a dead body, it'd been a sight that'd plagued her nightmares ever since.

If someone had been in that elevator, then they would have some horrific injuries.

Madeline wasn't sure she could cope seeing something like that.

Chapter Twenty-Nine

ZON

Zon had struggled to keep his trap shut during the Captain's speech. After all, the dude had only been promoted to Captain because the real Captain was dead. He was probably feelin' like he was king shit. Being a new boss an' all. And he was treatin' 'em all like idiots.

Then when everyone's phone went out like that, Captain Dickhead had crouched down to talk to the fat dude in the Hawaiian shirt. It was Zon's mate, one of the ones he'd met at the Chinese buffet. And whatever they were talking about, it had the Captain lookin' like he'd shat his pants. So, whatever it was, it affected Zon.

And every other fucker on the ship.

There was so much going on around him. People spewing. Women screaming. Babies crying. Hell, even grown men crying. The shit was totally hittin' the fan. And that meant Zon could get around like he was invisible.

He strode to the chick with the hoop earrings. "Hey."

"Oh, hey." She looked up at him and tucked her hair behind her ear. The way she did it was kinda erotic, and Zon had a feelin' she liked what she saw.

"Whadaya think's goin' on now?"

"Phase two."

"Huh?" He tugged on his beard. "Phase two?"

She glanced at the Captain and the dude talkin' to the Captain, and then turned back to him with a confused look on her face. *Was she scared to tell me?* Like it was some kinda secret pact all them Hawaiian shirts were in on, and Zon wasn't invited.

The Captain stood again. The fat dude whistled again. But the crowd didn't shut up so much this time.

"Please, everybody. You need to remain calm," the Captain hollered.

Zon scanned the faces around him. Calm was not what he was seeing. Nope. Calm weren't playin' no part in it.

"Ladies and gentlemen, please. I need your attention."

Zon offered earring chick his sexiest smile. "It's going a bit crazy, huh?"

"This is just the beginning."

"Really? So, ahhh, what's this phase two?"

She did a little head-dip thing and, thinkin' she wanted to be discreet, he leaned in.

"Phase one was the first EMP strike. Takes out any electrical components within line of sight of the initial detonation. People think everything has gone to shit. But anybody who's smart would've had a backup plan. They'd have a bug-out bag. But phase two is a second EMP, timed to trigger several hours later. And it's delayed like that on purpose to take out the bug-out gear."

"Bug-out gear?"

"Yeah, you know—grab bag, battle box, INCH bag . . . whatever you want to call it. It's where you stash your necessities to get you through a disaster."

"You mean like survival gear—guns and food and stuff."

"Exactly. So anyone who'd opened their bug-out bag and was using their phone or two-way or sat phone just got them fried in the second EMP."

"Shit, huh?"

"Yeah. Oh shit, is right. If the Captain thought anyone was coming for us before . . . they're not coming now. You think this is hell? Come morning, reality is really going to sink in. You noticed the engines have stopped, right?"

He nodded.

"That's the least of it. Water's stopped pumping. The toilets stopped working. No power. No air-con. People can't get into their cabins. Everyone will be thirsty and starving come sunrise. Parents will do anything to feed their kids. And the number of fatalities we have now are going to multiply quickly."

Zon shot her a glance.

"I mean it. Some of the people who are already dead died because their pacemaker got fried. The diabetics who need refrigerated insulin? Well, in this heat?" She waved her hand like she was trying to catch the heat waves or somethin'. "They've got no chance."

"You know a lot about this stuff, huh?"

"Not me. My dad." She nodded at the fat dude in the Hawaiian shirt.

Zon shot a glance at him, and then back to her. "He's your dad?"

"Yep." She rolled her eyes and Zon had to agree with her. It was hard to believe those two were from the same planet, let alone related.

"Please, everyone, line up in an orderly fashion." The Captain was still trying to command attention and sexy chick's dad was still whistlin' to help him.

There wasn't no way Zon was givin' his name to no one. Especially if it meant linin' up. He don't line up for nothin', or nobody. The crowd had gone crazy. Half of 'em were cryin'. People were spewing. Some did as they were told. But some were lookin' around like they couldn't make a decision.

Not him. Zon knew exactly what he was gonna do. He had no intention of spending the night on that deck with no lights and people spewing their guts up everywhere. He was gonna go down to his cabin and sleep in his own bed. Didn't matter that his key didn't work; he'd bash down the door. He didn't even have to sneak away.

He'd just follow the big crowd of people who seemed to have the same idea as him.

But when he glanced down at sexy chick, he was suddenly torn. For the first time in forever he was enjoyin' someone else's company. And a chick too. "Hey, I'm Zon, by the way."

"Zon. Cool name."

She shook his hand, and that right there confirmed she really did like him.

But she didn't tell him her name, and he waited for a bit, expectin' her to say it. She didn't. And it got to feeling so awkward he couldn't ask no more. He shoved his hands in his pockets and felt all that cash he'd stashed in there. It reminded him of all them other valuables he'd scored. He should go and stash them proper. But on account of there being no lights, he figured he'd wait till tomorrow. He glanced down at the sexy chick. "So, what's your plan?"

She nodded at her daddy. "I'm sticking with him."

"Ahhh. You got your bug-out bags, huh?"

She shook her head. "Nope. Dad's real angry at himself about that. He's got a heap of them set up at home, ready to go. Lot of good that's going to do us now."

One of them Hawaiian shirt dudes came up next to them. He looked at Zon, then back at the earring chick. "Hey, Jessie, we're going to line up over there." He pointed to a front corner.

"Okay, I'll meet you when Dad's finished."

"Okay, but don't wait too long." The dude shot Zon another look, then strode away.

At least now Zon knew her name.

She was lookin' at her dad, but seemed okay with hangin' with Zon. Nobody ever wanted to hang with him so he figured he might as well try and learn somethin' while she was here. "How come your dad knows so much?"

"Dad's a researcher for Paramount Pictures. You know, the movie-makers."

"Oh, really?" Zon glanced over to the fat dude with a new level of respect. "That's cool."

"Yeah, it is."

"Has he worked on anythin' famous?"

"Sure. Ever seen *War of the Worlds*?" She tugged on one of her earrings.

He studied the five silver loops threading up her ear as he searched his brain for an answer. "Ummm."

"You know . . . aliens invade the world and start harvesting humans. Remember it now?"

"Oh yeah." He lied. Zon ain't seen a movie in a long time.

"Remember . . . the aliens used an EMP attack to destroy all electronics."

He nodded but at the same time, he was wonderin' why the fuck anyone would watch somethin' so stupid.

"Anyway, Dad was the factual researcher for that movie. He learned a lot of stuff about what would happen if the entire country lost power. It was fascinating. Fun, even, to think of all the things that wouldn't work and the consequences if such a thing happened. Dad became obsessed with it. But that was just a movie. This is real."

Zon glanced at her daddy. The fat fucker didn't know it yet, but he'd just made his-self Zon's new best friend. He turned his gaze back to the sexy chick.

She glanced up at him with one eyebrow raised. "It's not going to be fun anymore."

Chapter Thirty

GUNNER

Gunner jumped down and pulled Albert aside. He had a million questions, and every one of them was slamming into his brain like carriages on a runaway train. He blurted out the first one that came to mind. "Albert, why did some phones work after the EMP?"

Albert simultaneously shrugged and rolled his eyes. "An EMP can penetrate via a front door or back door. Examples of front doors are the antennas, couplers, or transmission lines. Back door access is paths of entry through doors, windows, vents, power cables, control lines." His eyes bulged. "Look around—your ship was practically begging to be attacked. Many items below deck could've been protected. The reason for the second EMP strike is to take out the electrical components they missed in the first strike. A two-phase attack. So, any phones that survived the first attack, if they were mobilized into a front door or back door position, and that plane . . . well, it's essentially gave the second EMP a massive back door."

Albert's explanation of phase two did two things for Gunner. First, it confirmed that the United States of America was at war. An

EMP strike could be the result of a solar flare. Two EMP strikes, though, confirmed they were man-made.

Second thing it did was scare the hell out of him. If America really was at war, he should be home with his wife and daughter. He should be protecting them, not trying to save hundreds of strangers.

Maybe Adelle would go to her father. Gunner's father-in-law was ex-Navy. Hank was also overweight, drank way too much, and spent more time restoring vintage cars than visiting his granddaughter but Hank would look after them. Hell, he would die for them.

Gunner's mind flashed to his mother and his galloping heart set a different beat, faster, harder. Who would look after her? Would they release her from prison? Oh God . . . if they did, where would she go?

The unanswerable questions kept coming, stinging with random brutality, like a wasps' nest had exploded in his brain.

The second EMP strike meant there was zero chance they would be rescued. Not when the government had an entire nation in trouble.

Gunner's gut twisted.

Rose of the Sea was officially dead in the water and more than eleven hundred people were trapped. They were about to become thirsty. And hungry. And scared and desperate.

And angry.

More than a thousand people were expecting him to have answers. Answers that he absolutely did not have.

But the passengers didn't need to know his grizzly assumptions about the EMP strike. They'd already been through enough. Adding the real story behind their troubles would do nothing other than incite elevated panic.

With Willis' help and Albert's ear-piercing whistle, Gunner had managed to get the crowd's attention again and finally, with just the moonlight guiding their way, most of the passengers were following orders and lining up to give their information at the eight designated stations. He was damn lucky it wasn't a cloudy night.

Gunner jumped down from the bar top. Brandi was still at his side with her pen poised over the paper. He didn't need her hearing what he was about to say, so he reached for the paper. "Thank you for your help. Now, go find your brothers and get in line. Okay?"

She nodded, her bottom lip quivering. Clearly, she had something to say, but either she couldn't shape the words, or she didn't want to do it in front of Albert. Either way, she offered a lopsided smile, turned and disappeared into the restless throng.

Gunner pulled Albert aside. "Please don't tell anyone about the possibility that this was a terrorist attack. We don't need to scare them any more than they already are."

Albert snuck a glance at his friends, who were now waiting in one of the lines and looking at Albert with greedy expressions. Like they were hungry for gossip. "Okay. I understand."

Gunner shared his gaze between Albert and the agitated crowd moving about the deck. The crew were directing the passengers to the various areas. It was organized chaos. But at least they were doing something. He touched Albert's shoulder. "Thank you for your help. At my first available moment, I'd like to pick your brain on the implications of these EMP strikes."

Albert's eyes drooped. "Yeah, sure. I feel like an idiot."

"What? Why?" A couple with four crying children shuffled past, and when the woman's sunken eyes met his, Gunner's fear rose like a demon. They were so young. So innocent. And they were about to go through hell. Everyone was.

He shifted his gaze back to Albert, who was rambling.

"We'd always talked about this happening and I thought I was prepared. But I don't have my bug-out bags with me, and even worse, I should have predicted the second strike. I should have kept my phone in my cabin where it was protected." He thumped his phone into his hand, which was now nothing but a useless lump of plastic. "That's why they do it. I should have known better. I can't believe they got me." Shaking his head had his second chin wobbling. "I thought I was prepared."

"Don't beat yourself up. This is unprecedented. The United States has never suffered anything like this before. Look, I need to sort some things out. I'll come and find you soon. Now join your friends in that line."

"Yeah, sure. Will do."

Judging by the animated reunion Albert received when he rejoined his friends, Gunner wasn't a hundred percent certain his new advisor would keep their secret to himself. Albert and his friends looked way too wired to keep things under wraps. Hopefully they'd contain it within their group.

Yet he doubted that miracle would happen.

A bolt of lightning fractured the night sky, illuminating a cloud like it was an enormous floodlight. The moon's visibility was crisp and clear, yet the swirling black cloud beneath it was a fat roll, tumbling over, and about to consume their only light source.

Without warning, wind hit them like a sonic boom. A collective force blew bits of debris and small children over. Gunner looked skyward and frowned.

Another fork of lightning razed the sky with a heart-thumping crack that had hundreds of people screaming and ducking for cover.

Gunner's brain hit panic mode. He'd missed the warning signs.

A thousand people were about to be hit with nature's fury.

Chapter Thirty-One

GUNNER

Gunner charged toward the crowd. "Albert! Get inside. Now!"

Albert's eyes bulged. His jaw dropped. But he must've seen Gunner's panic, because he reacted by grabbing the wrist of a dark-haired girl and pulling her toward the exit doors.

Gunner was furious at himself but there was no time for that.

If he'd had radar, navigation equipment, and electronic charting systems, he would've seen the storm coming.

If he'd had sirens, a PA system, and his full complement of crew, he could've warned the passengers to get inside.

With engines, he could've turned the ship to face the waves rather than tackle them broadside.

But he had nothing.

Rose of the Sea was positioned at the worst possible angle to combat the swell that was about to hit them. A blaze of lightning forked the sky and at exactly the same moment, fat raindrops spewed from the clouds, heavy and hard.

People began screaming. And running.

"Everybody. Get inside." He clutched passengers' arms, dragging them toward the two doorways either side of the bar. "Inside. Quick."

The ship reared up, steady and silent. Port side first, a good twenty-foot lurch, and slammed down with a bone-jarring clash that knocked dozens of passengers off their feet.

Gunner wanted to help them. But a thousand things were happening at once.

Screaming intensified. Any semblance of order was lost and *every man for himself* became the mantra as they all ran for cover.

Passengers were trampled in the rush. A young girl slipped over and her mother was frantically trying to drag her upright. People trampled her small legs. The girl screamed. An elderly man tumbled sideways, taking out the elderly woman at his side. Both crashed over a deck chair.

Gunner fought the ship's imbalance as it bucked like a rearing bronco. Grasping at a pole, he dragged people forward. Clutching Cindy's outstretched hand, he pulled her toward the bar and shoved her in the direction of the crowded doorway.

Lightning pierced the heaving clouds, highlighting the chaos, and the passengers' terrified screams intensified. A thunderclap exploded like a supersonic boom.

The ship rolled. Twenty feet. And again. Twenty-four feet. Up and down. Over and over. People clung to deck chairs and both them and the furniture were tossed sideways. The deck became slippery. An Asian woman in pink stilettos grasped a man at her side and both of them were knocked off their feet and swept toward the damaged railing. The woman's mouth was wide open, but Gunner didn't hear her scream as they were tossed off the deck and disappeared into the black beyond.

The ship rolled again, twenty-six feet this time, and the pool water rose like a liquid hand and swept over the crowd. Together, men, women, and children screamed as they barrel-rolled toward the wrecked railing. They clawed the deck. They clawed at each other. But they were powerless against the force of the water.

Gunner snapped his gaze to where the life-jacket storage box should've been in the corner. But it was gone. Obliterated in the plane crash.

There was nothing he could do to save them.

A blaze of lightning lit the sky, giving Gunner a perfect view as another two dozen or so people vanished over the side. Despair stabbed at him like thousands of ice picks.

The wrath of the storm was bad enough. But the twin doorways on either side of the bar were bottlenecks. As the terrified passengers rushed forward, people were crushed in the stampede. The pile of trampled bodies grew as others stomped over the top of them in their rush to exit the maelstrom.

A sense of utter uselessness swept through him. His mind exploded with caged terror.

His gut twisted. The pain behind his eyes stung like a million bull ants.

A bolt of lightning blazed through the blackened cloud like a billion fluorescent lights. He snapped his eyes to the ocean. His heart was set to explode.

An enormous wave, forty or fifty feet high, was headed right for them.

"Hang on!" he yelled. "Hang on!"

He screamed over their terrified cries. But getting their attention was impossible.

Cloe and Quinn appeared through the tangled bodies. Cloe's eyes were wide, terrified.

"Cloe! Quinn! Fucking hang on," he yelled.

Pauline and Jae-Ellen were running toward him, dodging people and deck chairs, slipping on the steeply angled deck. He shot a glance at the wall of water.

Ten seconds.

Shoving off from the bar, he ran with his hands wide, hoping to scoop up both Pauline and Jae-Ellen.

Eight seconds.

Rose of the Sea slammed down, knocking Pauline off her feet. She screamed as she tumbled over and over, gaining momentum.

Six seconds.

Port side was rising. But it was too slow. Time seemed to stop, and he saw things with perfect clarity. A small child standing with her hands at her sides, screaming. A woman on the ground by the door with a man in board-shorts stomping across her back. Cloe and Quinn peering over the bar at the enormous wave. The whites of Jae-Ellen's fear-riddled eyes. And a giant wall of water, dozens of feet high, barreling right at them.

Three seconds.

He dove at Jae-Ellen, tackling her to the ground, and used the momentum to collect Pauline. As port side heaved upward, ready to take on the wave, he slid with the two women to the starboard side. He was counting on the railing to save them from going overboard.

One second.

They hit the railing in a tangle of limbs.

"Hang on!" He wrapped his arms and legs around the metal, flattened his body to the deck as much as possible and turned to face the rogue wave. One of the women screamed as the wave barreled over the deck. Rose of the Sea was nearly at the pinnacle of her rise when the wall of water slammed into them.

Gunner snapped his face away, sucked in a huge breath and squeezed his eyes shut.

The sound was a freight train crashing into solid concrete. Glass smashed. Metal squealed as it buckled and sheared off. People screamed.

It hit with the intensity of a Mack truck. The railing bit into his cheek. The water crushed his back, pinning him down. He couldn't move.

Rose of the Sea bucked beneath him and released an almighty groan as if furious over the attack.

The wave was gone as quickly as it came and gasping for fresh air, he peeled his body off the railing.

Lightning blazed through a cloud, giving him enough light to scan the deck behind him. It'd been wiped clean. Passengers. Crew. Deck chairs. The spa. Every single thing that hadn't been bolted down was gone. Even things that had been bolted down were gone. His heart was in his throat as he glanced at the bar where Cloe and Quinn had been hiding. It was still there. *Thank God.*

"Are you okay?" He touched Jae-Ellen's shoulder.

Her chin quivered as she shoved wet hair from her eyes. "I think so."

"Pauline! Pauline!" He crawled to her. Her arms and legs were tangled around the railing. Her eyes were clamped shut.

"Hey, it's over. But quick, you need to get inside." He pushed to stand, and glared at the ocean as the ship dipped again to port side. The timing of the ship's roll had been their saving grace. If they'd been port side down when that wave had hit, they would've been slammed with the full force of that water.

It would've been a thousand times worse.

His heart thudded to a halt. *I'm lucky to be alive.*

Gunner twirled his wedding band around his finger. *Please God. Please give us more of that luck.*

Lightning lit the sky and the flash provided enough light for Gunner to confirm that the wave that'd hit them was indeed a rogue one. For now.

He turned to Jae-Ellen and Pauline. "Go inside. Quick."

Gunner left them and moved to attend to a limp body farther along the railing. The woman was wedged between the rails; her hips had been what'd stopped her from disappearing forever. "Are you okay?"

The woman didn't move. He eased her back and flinched at the hideous wound on her face. Gunner felt for a pulse. "Yes. Okay, I've got you." He weaved her body free and hoisted her into his arms. Clutching her to his chest, he strode to the doorway. "You're okay. You're going to be just fine."

Quinn ran forward, his arms outstretched.

"She's alive." Gunner handed the unconscious woman to Quinn and raced back out to the deck, searching for more survivors.

He rode the ship's momentum in the twenty-foot swell. Lightning flickered on and off like strobe lighting, brightening the nightmare around him in one-second grabs.

Bodies dangling from railings.

Sheets of metal wrapped around poles like they were merely ribbon.

The kettle drum impaled on a post.

The entire rear section of the running track . . . gone. Nothing but jagged pieces of metal remained.

Twenty minutes ago, hundreds of people had been looking down at him from that very section of the boat. The loss of life had already been huge after the plane crash.

Now it would be staggering.

No matter what happened from then on, Rose of the Sea would be permanently etched into the history books. And not for the right reasons. His name would be alongside her . . . Gunner McCrae, the cruise ship Captain who lost half his passengers at sea.

Scraping his thoughts together, he silently prayed there weren't that many fatalities. Yet as he glanced around, hoping to see someone alive, he conceded it was too late for prayer.

In the bolts of light before the wave hit, there had been at least three hundred people within his line of sight.

Now every one of them was gone.

Chapter Thirty-Two

GABBY

Gabby smacked her lips together, trying to produce moisture on her tongue. The taste in her mouth was both familiar and revolting. Suddenly, she pitched sideways on the carpet and although her brain urged her arms to save her, they didn't. She slammed face-first into a mangled pile of twisted metal and plush burgundy cloth.

Searing pain shot up the left side of her face and pounded behind her temple. Rolling to her side, she flicked her jaw from side to side, testing her movement.

Blinking with confusion, she sat and the bitter taste in her mouth confirmed she'd had another seizure. It'd been more than a year since her last one. Two in one day was simply contemptible. Fighting a bout of self-loathing, she pushed up onto her hands and knees. Bolts of memory came flooding back.

Fighting with Max. The plane crash. Bloody gashes up her legs.

"Adam, can you get down?" Max's panic-filled voice cracked through the eerie silence.

Gabby suddenly remembered where Adam was. And what had happened.

"Look around," Max hollered. "Is there a rope or something?"

"No! I can't find anything." Adam's voice was shrill, verging on hysterical.

Max had been so engrossed in their son that he'd missed her seizure. Relief washed through her. She didn't need him fussing over her like she was an invalid. Not when their son was trapped twenty feet above them.

Clutching a distorted chair, she begged her legs to hold her upright. She paused, praying the dizziness swirling across her eyes would subside. Her panic needed to subside too or she was likely to tumble into yet another blackout.

The ship started tilting sideways again and she planted her feet, ready to ride out the imbalance. But this wasn't a gentle roll like the others had been. It went farther. Much farther. "What's happening?"

Max turned to her; the terror in his eyes confirmed her worst fears.

They were capsizing.

Loose chairs flew across the room. Debris and chunks of mangled wreckage and lifeless bodies did too. The curtains on the stage swung in a wild arc and a large box on wheels zipped across the dance floor like it was possessed.

Gabby didn't have time to scream when a wall of water charged through the hole in the ship's side like a billion-gallon spout. She was swept up, jammed into a row of chairs and pinned in position by the liquid battering ram.

She couldn't breathe. She couldn't move.

Her face was driven into the rough fabric.

The giant spout abruptly stopped and she toppled to the carpet. Gasping for breath and shoving her hair from her eyes, she dragged herself upright.

But when the ship rolled back the other way, the water now trapped inside, came with it. It hit her dead center, tossing her around like she was entombed in a giant washing machine. She slammed into another chair, powerless to escape.

Screams penetrated her brain, and they weren't her own.

Adam!

She clawed at the water, at the seat, at her hair, desperate to see. A flash of lightning blazed through a cloud and it was a couple of thumping heartbeats before she realized she was looking outside through an enormous hole in the ship.

Now she understood what the water was. A wave. A giant wave.

Shoving her hair from her eyes, she clutched a padded seat, trying to steady herself as the ship leaned heavily sideways again. It paused at that angle, like it was steadying itself, then rolled back the other way. The trapped water went with it, barreling over everything in its path like a tsunami. She used a flash of blinding lightning to scan the wreckage for her family. "Adam! Max!"

The upper balcony was empty. "Adam!"

Her heart speared her throat. *"Adam!"*

The ship groaned as if it were crying. Ignoring the eerie sound, she scrambled over mangled chairs, trying to get closer to where she'd last seen Max. "Adam! Max! Talk to me."

She couldn't see. But a roar confirmed the wall of water was coming again. Screaming, she ducked below a row of chairs and hung on as the wave crashed over her. The timing of its departure matched a lightning flash and she studied the upper balcony.

Water poured through a giant gash in the landing. "Adam!" Flicking away tears, she screamed his name until her throat burned. "Adam! Max!"

"Here. I'm here." Max's deep voice was muffled, distraught.

Gabby spun around and the angle of the ship and another wave joined forces to rip her feet out from under her. She hit chairs as she fell and a metal bar slammed into her ribs, punching the wind out of her. Gasping at the pain, she pushed up from the floor and scanned the blackness. "Max. Where are you?"

Gabby scrambled over the chairs, aiming for where she'd heard his voice. "Max! I can't see you?"

He groaned. The agonizing sound was like nothing she'd ever heard from him before. Lightning flashed a blaze of light across the room and the extent of the damage made it impossible to recall just how grand the theater had been. "Max, I can't find you."

"Here. I'm over here." Another flash highlighted his raised hand on the other side of the theater. The force of the water had shot him right across the room.

"I'm coming. I'm coming."

She scrambled over twisted rows of chairs blocking her way, and the boat continued to roll from side to side. Thankfully the quantity of water in the internal wave had diminished, and it no longer knocked her flying.

As she clawed her way across the room, Gabby did something she'd never done before . . . she prayed. For both Max and her baby boy. Adam's silence was a clamp squeezing the life out of her heart.

Finally, she saw Max in a theater aisle, pinned beneath a row of upturned chairs. "Oh God, Max. I'm here, babe." She fell to her knees and clamped his hand in her own.

"Are you okay?" It was so typical of Max to be thinking of others.

"I'm fine."

He was beneath a row of chairs. The large metal bar that secured them together was pinned across his chest.

"Are you hurt?"

"I'm just stuck." His voice was brittle, damaged, lacking his usual confidence. "Can you get this thing off me?"

With another blaze of light, she studied his position. He was in an aisle. His back was against a row of stairs. Gabby clutched the bar that secured the chairs together and groaned as she lifted. To her surprise, it moved a fraction.

"That's good." Max wriggled around so he could put his right hand beneath the bar. "Let's do this together."

"Okay. Ready?"

He nodded.

"One. Two. Three." Gabby clenched her jaw and pulled.

Max shoved upward.

Her arms and legs quivered with the strain. The chair stack scraped against metal, emitting a sharp, grating noise as they lifted. Flashes of lightning strobed across the theater giving Gabby millisecond images of their progress. It was slow, too slow. *We need to find our boy. Now.* "Come on!"

"I think I can get out. Can you hold it there?"

"Yes!" Gabby bellowed her response, desperate to keep her pledge. Her back buckled. Her fingers burned. Her knees wobbled. She wasn't sure she could do it. "Hurry! It's slipping!"

Max's face contorted as he squirmed beneath the bar. Inch by inch, he wriggled, and when he released an agonized howl, Gabby realized he was hurt.

Her knees burned and trembled. Her fingers did too. But she was determined to do it. To prove how strong she was. "Hurry, Max! Hurry."

"Okay, nearly there." He twisted his head and neck at an awkward angle and suddenly, he was free.

Gabby dropped the bar, and ignoring the new aches and pains accosting her already battered body, she dropped to Max's side. He was sucking air through his teeth. She'd seen that involuntary reaction in many crash victims. Max fought agony.

When a crack of lightning flashed across the theater, Gabby gasped.

That split second was all she needed to confirm he was in serious trouble.

Chapter Thirty-Three

MADELINE

Madeline clutched the elevator shaft grill as the ship rolled to her left. But instead of a slight pause before it swung back the other way, it kept going. Tipping farther and farther.

"What's happening?" Sterling's terrified voice echoed from his position a few feet below her.

The ship shuddered. The metal screeched.

Her heart thundered in her chest. "Oh my God, the boat's tipping."

An explosion boomed somewhere far away and the shaft trembled as if it'd been hit with a million-watt Taser.

"Jesus!" Sterling hollered. "We're capsizing!"

Madeline screamed as her legs were wrenched out from under her and dangled across the void like an act in one of her high-ropes shows.

"Hang on. Hang on!" Her fingers clutching the metal grill were the only things stopping her from plunging to her death.

"Ohhh, shit!" Sterling's terrified cry ricocheted about the metal walls.

Madeline snatched a glimpse downward, and in the dark, fragmented light, Sterling's legs were also suspended across the shaft. But he was gripping by just one hand.

"Jesus, Sterling, hang on!"

"It's tipping over!" His voice was shrill. "I'm slipping!" His free arm flailed. His legs swung wildly.

Gritting her teeth, Madeline fought gravity and dragged her legs back to the grill. Dangling upside down, she glanced at Sterling. "Hang on! I'm coming." But the second she moved, her feet slipped out again. Realizing it was pointless, she hooked her fingers into the grills and scrambled down the wall like she was climbing giant monkey bars.

"Jesus Christ!" Sterling bellowed.

His panic carved another layer of terror through her. "I'm nearly there. Hang on!"

He was just five feet away, but it might as well have been twenty.

Her heart thundered in her chest as visions of him tumbling into the flaming cavity invaded her mind.

Finally, she reached his grill. Clinging on with just her fingers, she stretched out with her legs and wrapped them around his torso. Just as his free arm clutched her thigh, the ship jolted back the other way like a released pendulum.

Together, they slammed face-first into the grills. Madeline squealed as an explosion of pain erupted behind her eyes.

In a tangle of arms and legs, they gripped each other and the grills as they rode another roll of the ship. Thankfully it wasn't anywhere near as bad as the last one. She used the reprieve to settle her frazzled breathing.

After two more rolls of the ship that didn't have either of them screaming for their lives, she eased back from Sterling. "You okay?"

"Yeah. Thanks to you." He rested his hand on her leg and the warmth and comfort it provided was so unexpected that her heart seemed to dance. It was like nothing she'd ever experienced before. Even with Aiden. Her ex-fiancé hadn't been a very affectionate man, which had suited her just fine.

Maybe their near-death experience had her emotions going haywire. She shook her head at his comment. "It was nothing."

"It wasn't nothing. I'd be dead if it wasn't for you." Sterling eased his fingers behind her neck, pulled her to his chest and squeezed. "Thank you."

"Oh." Words completely escaped her, but as her veins pulsed out a therapeutic beat, she lost herself to the moment by weaving her arms around him. He smelt so lovely, and clutched in his embrace, she felt so right. It was such a strange thing to admit. Especially when she'd spent most of her life resisting human touch.

All too soon, Sterling eased back and when he looked at her, even in the dim light, he seemed to be really, truly looking at her. The intensity of his gaze had her skin prickling. She glanced away and cleared her throat. "We need to get out of here."

Clinging to a grill, he climbed to his feet and offered her his hand. "I agree. I am so hungry I could eat my left arm."

"Me too." She huffed. "The hungry bit, that is—not the arm bit."

He offered her a lopsided grin, and once again she was grateful she wasn't alone.

The ship was still swaying and just the thought of repeating what they'd already been through had a sense of urgency shooting through her like adrenalin.

Madeline studied the shaft, and the second she'd identified the best route, she started climbing down. This time, though, she didn't wait for Sterling. She just hoped he'd keep up.

Four feet down, she reached the writing on the back of the next elevator door.

Deck three.

She glanced below. The flickering flames caught her eye. What could be fueling them? The firemen who'd rescued her from Flint's home had said she was lucky the timber house had been crammed full. It had been stacked to the ceiling with old newspapers, egg cartons, boxes of bulk items he'd never opened, and loads and loads of rubbish. It had meant there wasn't enough oxygen to cause an inferno.

Frowning at that memory, she studied the flames again. The elevator was all metal. No wood or combustibles. The smoke, however, was growing thicker, caking her tongue with a bitter tang. She flicked her hair from her eyes and upon seeing her black hands, she recalled the thick grease that was slathered over the cables at the back of the elevator. Maybe that was fueling the fire.

Or maybe it was a ruptured fuel tank spewing highly flammable diesel that was about to explode in a giant fireball.

That horrifying thought blasted from nowhere. She scrambled down faster.

Deck two.

The lower she went, the more visible the other elevator became. It had exploded outward. The external walls were buckled, yet the back corner was crumbled in, like it'd been stomped on.

That elevator had fallen a very long way.

Shuddering at the thought, she silently prayed that nobody had been inside. She also thanked her lucky gods that she hadn't been. For the briefest of moments, she clutched the tree-of-life pendant around her neck. She'd had the gold medallion made for her twenty-first birthday. The tree had five colorful crystals on each of its limbs that represented the five months she'd been held captive. Not that she needed reminding of those horrific months—Lord no. However, she did need reminding that she'd survived. And not just survived—she'd moved on.

Gritting her teeth, she vowed she was going to do both again. She was not ready for her life to be over.

A deep roar rumbled from somewhere outside the shaft.

"What the hell was that?" she yelled up to Sterling.

"I don't know." The fear in his voice was terrifying.

Next second, water poured in from above them. Like someone was blasting them with a fire hose. "Shit. Shit. Shit!" She squealed. "Are we sinking?"

"I don't know. Quick! Move!"

Cold water pounded onto her head and splashed in her eyes. Squinting through the waterfall and smoky haze, she scrambled down the last ten or so feet. Three rungs to go. Two.

The water doused the flames making them hiss and flare and produce more smoke.

Coughing the caustic air, she finally climbed through to the second shaft and stood atop the buckled metal of the other elevator. Sterling joined her a few seconds later.

Coughing stung her throat. Smoke stung her eyes.

Desperate to see an escape from their hell, she crouched down and peered through a gap in the roof of the battered cube.

Dim light speared the crack in the door, like a distant flashlight was being aimed through it, and Madeline glimpsed a bright pink fabric. She leaned farther over for a better look. "Oh, Jesus. Hello? Are you okay? Hello?"

A small girl lay on her side on the bottom. She wasn't moving.

"Sterling, there's a girl in there." Water poured into the elevator, splashing up onto the girl. She still didn't move. "Oh God! I think . . . I think she's dead."

"Let me see."

She eased aside and as she swept her wet hair from her eyes, he lowered down onto his stomach and poked his head through the gap.

"Hello. Are you okay?" After a pause, he pulled back. "I can't tell if she's alive or not. But those doors are slightly open. If we can get in there, maybe we can get out." His voice was loaded with hope.

It was the energy boost she needed. "Okay. Okay."

Blocking out the image of the girl's lifeless body, she searched the dimness for the access point to the elevator. Her heart sank at what she saw. It was another combination lock with a shank as thick as her little finger. "Shit! Not again. How are we going to break this?"

Sterling squatted at her side and she inhaled his delightful cologne. It made the situation so bizarre. Water tumbling onto her head and splashing up into her face. Smoke stinging her eyes and burning her throat. A lifeless girl in the ruined elevator below. And a handsome man who smelled lovely at her side. She was in a warped dream.

"Stand back." He reached across her chest and guided her away from the access panel. "I have an idea. Get up on that." He pointed to one of the beams that crossed the top of the elevator.

Sterling stomped onto a panel between two thick metal beams. He did it again and again. Each time, the sound changed a fraction, like it was somehow becoming more hollow. Madeline joined in, using her good leg, concentrating on stomping her sneaker in the same place near the access door.

They hit it in unison and it bowed inward. He grinned at her. "It's working. Keep going."

Three more kicks and the side came away, buckling into the space below. "Yes!"

The waterfall above them had petered down to a trickle. *Hopefully that's the last of it.*

Finally, the entire panel fell inside the elevator, barely missing the girl. Yet she still didn't move.

"We did it." Sterling's grin was a mixture of triumph and grim reality. He held his hand toward her. "Ladies first."

Madeline reached for him, and squeezing his palm to hers, she sat with her feet dangling into the elevator, held onto a metal crossbeam, and jumped down. Pain shot up her leg and she winced at her ankle injury. It seemed like days ago since she'd done that. She hoped like hell it wasn't.

Sterling joined her, and they had to wriggle away the panel they'd broken to reach the girl. He knelt down and touched two fingers to the girl's neck. Madeline dragged her eyes away from the limp body to study their planned exit instead.

The right-hand door was tilted at a twenty-degree angle. But the gap wasn't big enough for their escape.

"She's alive!" Sterling blurted.

A wave of relief wobbled through Madeline. "Thank God."

Sterling squeezed the girl's arm. "Hey, are you okay?" She didn't move.

Madeline guessed she was thirteen or fourteen years old. She was on her side and had no obvious injuries. At least none involving blood.

But then she spied the soot around the girl's nostrils. "Smoke.

She's suffering from smoke inhalation. See the black smudges around her nose and her puffy skin?"

"Are you sure?"

"Trust me. I know." Madeline's mind flashed to the first time she'd looked into a mirror after she'd been rescued from that house fire. She hadn't seen herself for more than five months. That reflection had been horrifying. She'd barely recognized herself. Yet it wasn't because of the black soot around her nose and mouth. Nor the fresh cigarette burn on her neck. Or her greasy matted hair. It was her eyes. They were sunken, withdrawn, vacant, and her irises had been much darker than she'd remembered.

Madeline shuddered the recollection free as she watched Sterling try to awaken the poor girl. "We need to get her out of here."

The ship's sway had become more pronounced. Maybe it was because they were in the enclosed space. She hoped that was it. But the ship shuddered and tilted again, rattling the metal around her. Something was catastrophically wrong.

Clutching the railing along the back of the elevator, she braced for the ship to roll back the other way.

A roar as loud and as terrifying as the one they'd heard earlier rumbled around them.

Sterling shot to his feet. His wide eyes darted from her to the doors. "What the hell--"

Water burst through the gap in the door, spearing them in a powerful spray.

Chapter Thirty-Four

MADELINE

"What's happening?" Madeline yelled, turning away from the torrential water and scrambling to a corner.

"I don't know." Sterling slammed to the back wall with her.

Within seconds, the water was over her Vans. "We have to get out of here."

Sterling dropped to his hands and knees, crawled to the girl, lifted her face from the water and rolled her onto her back.

But the girl was the least of their worries. If they didn't get out of there, they would all drown. With her hand guarding her face, Madeline stepped through the waterspout and used the door as a shield. "Sterling. Help me! We have to pull them apart."

He sloshed to her side and together they wrapped their fingers around the broken door. "Ready?"

"Go!" Clenching her teeth, every muscle strained as she pulled on the door.

"Keep trying." The vein on Sterling's temple bulged. "We can do it."

Madeline heard a choking noise and spun toward the sound. It was the girl. Her face was in the water. Madeline jumped through the spray and lifted her head onto her lap. "Hey, it's okay." It was too dark to see if her eyes were open. "Can you talk?"

"Madeline!" Sterling yelled. "We have to get out of here now."

The decision to leave the girl was brutal. She could drown. Then again, if they didn't open that door, they'd all die. She rolled the girl onto her back. The girl's head bobbed in the water to just over her ears. The teenager actually looked peaceful.

Madeline stood again and gasped. The water was already above her knees. The whites of Sterling's eyes were enormous. He was terrified too.

"Madeline." Sterling yelled over the gushing water.

She bulged her eyes at him. "Yes."

"I'll push from this side; you pull. Okay?"

"Okay." She huffed out a huge breath.

"Ready."

She gulped air and held her hands forward.

"Set. Go!"

Squeezing her eyes shut, she plunged through the waterspout. Her hands connected with the edge of the door, and bracing her feet against the other door, she blocked out her throbbing ankle and pushed.

Nothing happened.

She pushed harder.

Her back bones crunched together. Pain shot down her legs.

Water rammed into her left ear, and she pictured her eardrum bursting.

Her brain careened from 'we're nearly there' to 'we're going to die.'

Yet the door didn't budge.

Just as she began fighting a mental debate over giving in, it jolted sideways and she lost her footing. She splashed into the water, plunging right under. When she scrambled to her feet, the water was up to her hips. Shoving wet hair from her eyes, she glared at the gap between the doors. It was barely twelve inches. It would be a tight squeeze for her, let alone Sterling. "Is it enough?"

"It'll have to be." He waved her forward. "Come on. Come on. Hurry." His clipped voice was machine-gun staccato.

Using her hands, she shoved through the water to reach him.

He grabbed her arm, dragging her forward. "You go through first, then I'll push the girl through and you grab her."

Madeline glanced at the girl. She was floating on the water, thankfully face-up. She was so still. Madeline's heart clenched like a fist. Maybe she'd passed away.

The boat began tipping sideways again. Water crawled up her body. "What's happening?" It reached her waist, her breasts, her shoulders, her neck. She was forced to swim to keep her head above the water.

"We have to get out of here." Sterling clutched her wrist and pulled her toward the door. "Go, Maddy. Go through." The triangular-shaped gap they'd created was now beneath the waterline and light filtered through the green water like a weird alien eye.

She glared at him. "I'm not going without you."

"I'll be right behind you."

She shook her head and clenched her jaw. There was no way she was leaving him. Madeline knew what it was like to be abandoned. It was the most soul-crushing experience in the world. "I'm not leaving you."

Sterling palmed her cheeks, drawing her eyes to his. "Listen to me. You first, then the girl. Then me."

She shook her head. "We can do this together."

"No, we can't." He clutched her shoulders. "But we have to move now. Or we'll all drown."

Her mind battled with indecision. Her gaze shot from Sterling's wide eyes, to the floating girl, to the green alien light.

"Madeline!" He shook her. "Go! Now!"

"Okay, but if you don't come out, I'm coming back in."

"You crazy woman." His hands clutched her cheeks and without warning, he kissed her.

It was so sudden, so spontaneous, so perfect, she couldn't help but grin. "You don't know the half of it."

"Go. Go!"

Madeline turned to the spouting water, sucked in a few breaths, then, with a huge lungful, she plunged beneath the water and dove toward the gap. She was through and out so quickly she was taken by surprise.

Swimming in neck-deep water, she glanced around. There was enough green light to see boxes and crates everywhere. Some of them were floating. The bigger ones were toppled like they'd been merely Lego blocks and not the size of washing machines.

She banged on the door. "Sterling. I'm out."

A beat of silence was followed by a long groan from the ship. It was deep and loud, like she was trapped inside a monster with an ulcer. That thought had shivers racing up her spine. "Sterling. I'm out. Do you hear me?"

"Sterling!" She slammed her fist on the door.

"Okay, get ready. Here comes the girl."

Her rising panic evaporated at the sound of his voice. She stood next to the crippled door with her mouth barely inches above the waterline. She pushed her hands through the gap in the door. "Ready!"

A heartbeat later, she felt a small hand. Clutching the girl's wrist, Madeline pulled and the girl came through as a lifeless body. The second Madeline lifted her head above the water, she started sputtering. "Okay. You're okay." The girl's eyes remained shut but at least she was gasping for air.

But Madeline had to ignore her for now. Sterling needed her help.

She dragged the girl to an upturned pallet, and using all her strength, she half rolled, half shoved her limp body on top. The second the teen was secure with her face free from the water, Madeline swam back to the elevator.

"Sterling. She's safe now. Your turn."

He banged twice on the door. "Okay."

She repeated her earlier move, bracing herself against the door and pushing her hands into the gap. But the water was higher this time and to reach him she had to hold her breath and dive under. When his hand clutched hers, she gripped on and pulled. His arm came through far enough that she could raise her head above the water. The top of his head appeared.

But then he stopped.

She pulled harder, but he didn't move.

His hair floated about as his head snapped from side to side.

Screaming in frustration, she pulled harder.

But it was useless. Sterling was stuck.

Twenty seconds.

She braced her feet on the door and pulled with everything she had. He thrashed from side to side. But his head remained submerged.

Forty seconds.

His hand squeezed around hers. She clenched tighter. "Come on!"

One minute.

A sob burst from her throat. "I'm not leaving you."

The boat groaned as if defying her. "Come on, Sterling!"

The water began to flow in the reverse direction. In the space of a few seconds, the height dropped five inches. It was a miracle.

He tried to pull back, but she kept him there. Every inch . . . every second, was a mental battle between keeping him there and letting him go.

"Hang on. The water's moving." She screamed through the door, but she had no idea if he heard her.

The top of his head emerged from the water and she wedged her hands beneath his chin. His eyes opened and she kept his gaze as the water crept down his face with excruciating slowness.

The second his nose came free, his nostrils flared, sucking in oxygen. His mouth was next and Sterling gasped for air with great heaving breaths.

"Oh thank God, thank God." She brushed a curl of hair from his eyes. "Are you okay?"

"Yeah." He panted. "I'm fabulous."

Ignoring his sarcasm, she repositioned her hand beneath his chin. "The ship's going to roll back again, so we don't have much time. Where are you stuck?"

His fingers bit into her wrist. "My hips."

"Okay, try going one hip at a time. Curve your back."

He released her grip, and dropped his hand into the water. The agony on his face had her cringing in sympathy. He clenched his jaw and a growl roared from his throat. The angle of the boat began to shift. It was rolling back again.

"Oh shit, Sterling. Quick! Come on."

"I'm trying," he screamed at her, fury in his eyes.

"That's it. Use that anger."

The water was inching up the elevator wall again, covering his chin. He sucked in a huge breath. Water covered his nose. His eyes. His forehead.

He was completely submerged. His head thrashed. Bubbles swirled around him.

Her heart slammed in her chest as she crawled into the water beside him. "I'm here. I'm not leaving you."

Madeline put her hands on the elevator doors and put her foot up on the lip of the wall. Using every ounce of her strength, she tried to pull them apart.

Tears streamed down her face. A sob burst from her throat.

His hand reached up and she clutched it. Leaning forward, she kissed his hand. "Come on, Sterling. You can do this."

The water was still rising.

He yanked his hand from her grasp and splashed her with his thrashing.

"No!" she screamed at the heavens.

Suddenly there was an eruption of water and Sterling appeared, gasping for air.

She dove forward and hugged him to her chest. "Oh my God, I thought you were gone."

He wrapped his arms around her. "Me too." He was coughing and choking, but also laughing at the same time. "Shit, that was close."

They held each other until her heartbeat and his breathing returned to normal. When they pulled back, he looked into her eyes. "Thank you."

"I didn't do anything."

"You didn't leave me."

She shook her head. "I'd never do that. I know what it feels like."

He reached up and touched his palm to her cheek, and although he didn't ask her to elaborate, she had a strange feeling he already knew.

Chapter Thirty-Five

GUNNER

"Captain?"

Gunner heard the distant voice but couldn't find its origin. His mind was scrambled with pictures of bloodied bodies and calls of people reaching out to him, begging for help.

"Captain." A hand touched his shoulder, and he snapped his eyes open. Jolting upright, he knocked something over and it fell to the floor with a thud. He blinked at his surroundings, trying to piece them together.

"Captain. Sir?"

He was in the bridge, seated in front of the blank consoles. Turning, he looked up at the woman. "Jae-Ellen?"

"Sir. You fell asleep, sir." She picked up the binoculars he'd knocked over and placed them beside him.

His eyes were like sandpaper as he tried to blink them awake. Last thing he remembered was returning to the bridge to see if First Officer Sykes was okay after that wave. He had been, but only just. Sykes had seen the wave coming, but there was absolutely nothing he could do about it. So, he'd hidden in the men's room and prayed that the last moments of his life weren't going to be spent looking at the back of a bathroom door.

He'd still looked terrified when Gunner had found him several hours after the wave. The bridge had been a mess. Several windshields had shattered into a million glass shards that littered every surface. Nearly all the chairs were gone and a whole row of computer monitors had been ripped from their footings, never to be seen again.

Captain Nelson's body was gone too.

Gunner reached for the binoculars. "What time is it, Jae-Ellen?"

"It's sunrise, sir."

Gunner grunted. Sykes' watch, which had been a gift from his grandfather, had been shattered and was now missing both hands. Their only time device now was the sun.

Gunner stood and groaned. Nearly every muscle in his body protested against the movement. Using the binoculars, he scanned the horizon. The rays of sunshine bursting up from the ocean were a minor relief after their night in forced darkness. It must be about 06:00 hours.

His first goal had been making it through the night. Thanks to a miracle, he'd done that. Many had not been so lucky. After confirming there was nothing out on the ocean other than mild waves and a lone albatross, he put the binoculars down and turned to Jae-Ellen. "Is everything okay?"

"Is that a trick question?" She cocked her head. Her right eye was severely bloodshot, and the swollen bruise surrounding it was a hideous purple. If she'd hit her head a fraction to the left, she could've had permanent eye damage.

He squeezed his temples. "Sorry. Stupid question. Are you okay?"

"Yes. And no."

He knew exactly what she meant.

He reached for the binoculars again and scanned the ocean. But what was the point? If he did see another boat, he had no way to communicate with those onboard. And worse still, pirates could come storming at them right now, and there'd be absolutely nothing he could do about it. Then again, if there was a boat out there,

First Fate

pirate or otherwise, chances were they too were in just as much trouble as Rose of the Sea.

His insides twisted with angst and hunger pains, and a full bladder.

"Sir. I want to thank you for saving my life." A tear teetered on Jae-Ellen's lower eyelashes.

He shook his head. "There's no—"

"Sir," she interrupted. "What you did to save Pauline and I was the most selfless act I've ever seen. We would've been washed out to sea if it wasn't for you."

He placed his hand on her shoulder. "I was lucky."

"No, sir. You were thinking. *We* were lucky." She flicked a tear away and sucked her lip into her mouth as if trying to stop it from quivering.

A groan tumbled from his throat and he shook his head. "I should've seen the signs. That storm—"

"Don't do that to yourself. The situation was crazy. You saved as many as you could."

"We shouldn't have been on that deck."

"We had no choice. Without lighting, it was our only option."

He glanced at the remaining computer screens that were all blank and then back at Jae-Ellen. "Nothing's changed?"

She lowered her eyes and groaned. "It's worse."

He squeezed his temples but it didn't alleviate the pressure pulsing behind his eyes. Giving up, he lowered his hands and nodded toward the bathroom. "Okay, give me a minute, then walk with me."

"That's the 'worse' I was talking about, sir. The sewerage has backed up."

He groaned. Moving sewage around a ship required water and power. They had neither. "It's going to be an interesting day." Deciding he had no choice, he crunched across shattered glass as he strode toward the men's room. "Wait here."

Thankfully, his restroom was clean and tidy. He could only imagine what was happening at the other end of the ship. Raw sewage created disease. His heart clenched. So did dead bodies. There was so much to think about his brain already hurt.

Without the ability to flush, he simply closed the lid and strode to the sink. The mirror replicated how he felt—shattered. At best guess, he'd had two hours of sleep. He was hungry and thirsty. But that wasn't even the worst of it. Hundreds of passengers were relying on him to know what to do. But images of the deck before and after that wave hit flashed through his mind.

Hundreds of scared people, scrambling to get off the deck.
Just a handful of bloodied and battered bodies.

So many dead already, and it'd only been about twelve hours since the first EMP.

How many more deaths would today bring?

That pressure was like a ten-ton weight, crushing the life out of him. Although he'd been striving toward a Captain's role for years, he'd never truly appreciated the responsibility that position held.

Until now.

Did anyone in charge of passengers fully understand the true meaning of it? Pilots? Train drivers? Bus drivers? Every person onboard a vessel expected the respective authority to know what to do in an emergency. But it was a skill that was never truly tested until it was too late.

He turned on the tap to wash his hands and face but after an initial splutter, it stopped. Clenching his teeth, he shook his head at his own stupidity.

Sanitation was about to become a huge issue. A Petri dish of diseases could spread through the remaining passengers like wildfire. He rubbed soap into the small ration of water on his hands and wiped it off with a paper towel.

He pushed back through the door to the bridge and caught Jae-Ellen yawning. "Have you had any sleep?"

She shook her head.

It was a miracle she was even standing. "Walk with me to the other end. Then go rest."

"But, sir—"

"That's an order."

"Sir." She bowed her head. "Thank you, sir."

He turned and crunched across the glass to the exit, and Jae-Ellen fell in beside him. "Talk to me."

"Most of the passengers are still in Petals. That's where the bulk of them slept. We have no power. No water. The toilets aren't working. During the early hours, some people tried to fight their way into the kitchen to raid the food we hadn't yet moved to the gym. We've managed to hold them off for now, but once everyone is awake, I'm not sure how long we can last. We are well and truly outnumbered."

"How many crew do we have?"

She looked up at him, and the anguish in her eyes cut a swathe through his heart. "Only thirty-seven have stepped forward, sir."

"Thirty-seven!" He did the math. Ten percent. "Where . . . what's happened?" His brain couldn't formulate the right question.

"Cloe and I have been discussing it. Many were lost in the plane crash, including the entire engine room crew. Many also were swept overboard in the storm. Those on the top deck who were helping to corral passengers were all lost. A lot of the service crew simply don't want to step forward. Most of them don't speak very good English and won't take on responsibility." She sighed. "That leaves thirty-seven."

He ran his hands down his face, feeling the sharpness of his stubble. "Best guess on how many passengers are in the restaurant?"

She swallowed so loud he heard it. "Best guess . . . two hundred and twenty or so."

Gasping, he shunted to a stop. "No!" He blinked at her. "That can't be true. Nine hundred missing?"

She lowered her eyes. "Missing or dead."

His eyes drifted to the calm ocean. It was a stunning day. Crystal-clear sky. Vivid white altocumulus clouds that looked like floating marshmallows. Breeze, so subtle it barely registered. The setting was as peaceful as a sleeping baby.

It did little to improve his mood.

The rogue wave that hit them had only been about forty feet high. It should never have had such decimating affects to the seventy-thousand-ton Rose of the Sea. But at the time when the wave hit, the ship had been facing broadside. She'd been low in the trough and had had zero propulsion.

He squeezed his eyes shut, and a tsunami of sickening emotions blazed through him. Grief. Inadequacy. Disbelief. At the very top was anger. *How could this happen?*

He snapped his eyes open. It wasn't time for reflection. It was time for action. "Right then. We need to make sure every single passenger that's still alive remains that way."

She did a curt nod. "Yes, sir."

"Has anyone done a search of the cabins?"

"No. We needed daylight for that. Also, without power, we can't open the doors."

"Jesus. Of course." He clamped his jaw shut at his foolishness. "Have we given out any more food or water since last night?"

"Not yet. I'm sorry, but without light, it was all impossible."

"No need to be sorry. I'm grappling with what needs to be done myself."

"May I make a suggestion?"

"Of course."

"You'll need to make a decision on what to do with the deceased."

His gut twisted. It was another aspect he hadn't even considered.

"Not just because it's deadly, but it's also not good for everyone's spirits. In this heat, the bodies are starting to smell, and we have the deceased in the same room as the survivors."

"I agree. How is Doctor Merkley going with the number of injuries?"

When she didn't respond, he glanced her way and noted twisted confusion in her expression. "I . . . I haven't seen him."

Oh shit! The doctor's still missing. "What? Not at all?"

"No. Come to think of it, I haven't seen Miguel or Hastings either. Remember, you sent them both to find the doc when the Captain had his heart attack? I haven't seen Reynolds, either, for that matter; he went to get the chief engineer."

"Christ!" His shoulders sagged with a new layer of burden. *Had he sent them to their deaths?* "I'll head to the medical clinic as soon as I can."

They went up the internal stairs to the pool deck. He paused at the fitness center to greet a burly man who was leaning against a wall with his arms folded, a jagged blue vein zig-zagged across his temple adding to his expression of animosity. The man looked ready for a fight. But when he eyeballed Gunner, his demeanor completely shifted and he nodded.

Gunner stepped forward and offered his hand. "Hello. I'm Gunner McCrae."

"Captain, sir, I'm Dane Tanner, casino supervisor."

"I wish we'd met under better circumstances."

"Me too, sir."

"Have you had any trouble?"

"There was an incident in the early hours with a big bald guy. I remembered him from the casino; the security guard had already dealt with him once."

"Did he hurt you?"

"No, sir, nothing like that. He was just demanding more than his ration of food and water."

Last night, Gunner had made the decision to ration the water prior to going to the bridge. Once each passenger had detailed their name and cabin number, they were allocated one bottle of water. Their instructions were to make it last one day and to retain the bottle.

The passengers had seemed ready to comply.

But he wasn't sure how long that civil attitude would last.

He'd seen enough news broadcasts of disasters to know that wild brawls and looting were inevitable. It was only a matter of time before Rose of the Sea had her own desperate gangs to deal with. "I'll send some additional help very soon." He shook Dane's hand again. "You're doing a great job."

"Thank you, sir."

He left the fitness center and walked past the salon and the café. The lingering aromas of coffee had his hunger pains biting like rabid dogs. Forcing the cramps to the back of his brain, he stepped through a set of doors onto the pool deck.

When he'd first seen that enormous wave, he hadn't worried about the boat capsizing. That sort of thing only happened in Hollywood. Rose of the Sea was equipped to take a battering from waves like that one.

But he wasn't prepared for the sight before him now.

The devastation was extensive. Four-inch-thick poles were buckled and twisted like cable ties. Blood stained the wood-lined deck, as did a dozen or so bodies. In the cold light of dawn, the extent of the damage to the upper running track was brutal. Nothing but a series of mangled metal spikes remained.

It looked like a war zone.

Several people were wandering around. Their stunned expressions were justified. He felt the same. Even though he'd lived through it, it was impossible to comprehend what had happened. It was a miracle anyone survived.

Jae-Ellen was silent at his side as they passed the section of the railing that had literally saved their lives. Based on the damage to some of the other framework, it was surprising the railing *had* remained intact. Thank God it had, or he'd have been lost at sea forever, just like all those other poor people.

Squeezing the rotten image from his brain, he made his way past the section of the deck that should have had two spas. One was gone altogether, and the other looked like it'd lost a battle with a steamroller.

A foul stench drifted his way and when he scanned for the source, he nearly gagged at what he saw. Raw sewage. An inch-high river of human waste spewed from the restrooms at the back of the pool, crossed the deck, and spilled overboard.

Jae-Ellen covered her mouth. "Sorry, sir. We haven't found anyone willing to clean it up. And I haven't had time."

He huffed. "I'm not surprised about the cleaner. And I don't expect you to do it. But there's no point anyway if we don't stem the source. Do we have a plan B in place for the toilets?"

"The men are using the back railings, and now that we have

some light, the women are venturing to other bathrooms. But it's only a matter of time before they back up too."

Gunner nodded. He tugged the to-do list from his pocket and added solve toilets to the next line. The list was already out of control, and he'd only been awake fifteen minutes.

The second he stepped into Petals, the items needing attention multiplied threefold.

As he strode around the restaurant, the weight of the weary eyes of passengers followed his progress He couldn't help but stare at those that didn't stir, searching for signs of life.

The number of fatalities and missing people was shocking.

But, no matter what he did, it was going to be near impossible to stop that mortality landslide.

Chapter Thirty-Six

GABBY

Light speared across the destroyed theater hall and Gabby blinked at it for several seconds. Her jaw dropped. *It's the first rays of dawn.* Her brain scrambled to calculate that it had been about twelve hours since the EMP strike. An overwhelming blanket of sorrow engulfed her and she fought both tears and a huge lump in her throat.

She hated that she wanted to break down into a blubbering tearful mess. She hated that her tangled emotions were messing with her rational thoughts. Now was not the time for weakness. Not when her daughter was still missing, her son was no longer visible, and Max's hand was severely injured. *How was he even conscious?*

Max pushed up from the floor with a brutal groan. "Adam. Where's Adam?" His usually healthy, glowing skin looked terribly pallid. Max had been drifting in and out of consciousness since he'd scrambled out from beneath the broken chairs. Each time he'd drifted away, she'd been torn between searching for Adam and searching for help. She'd done both, but had succeeded in neither.

She shook her head. "I don't know." Last time she saw him he was up on the balcony. Now most of the balcony was gone, and she couldn't find Adam anywhere, and he wasn't answering her cries.

"I've been trying to find him. But . . . but . . ." It was impossible to speak with the lump blocking her airway.

Max clutched at the back of a seat with his good hand, and scrambled down the stairs. "Adam! Adam!"

Following him as he dragged his body over a mountain of debris, they aimed for the location where they'd last seen their son. Max's usual strong posture was gone. Instead he was hunched over as if his insides were buckled, and nearly every step was met with a groan of pain. As Gabby trundled after him, it was clear that his crippled hand wasn't the only injury Max had suffered.

He had at least two broken fingers, possibly four. His middle finger was bent at a horrific angle. He would need surgery. His hand was already swollen to nearly double in size, and the rapidly spreading bruise over his fingers, hand and wrist was as dark as the ocean outside.

She'd seen dozens of horrific injuries in her early ambulance-chasing days, mostly broken bones and hideous gashes, sometimes full amputations, and it had always surprised her when she'd encountered seriously wounded people who remained conscious, let alone made viable conversation.

Either Max was ignoring the extent of his wounds or he had a very high pain threshold. It was probably both.

"Adam!" Max stood on a row of chairs lined up below the balcony where they'd seen Adam just before the wave hit. "Come on, buddy, where are you?" His voice was forlorn, broken. Just like his body.

Water dripped from the damaged landing, giving a pitiful heartbeat to the eerie silence around them. The ship continued to sway from side to side, slow and steady, like it was rocking a baby to sleep. Sunlight beamed in through the hole in the ship—a giant beacon spotlighting the extent of the damage. Her eyes snagged on a small body. It was the little girl she'd seen during the night. She was curled up on her side and looked peaceful, like she was having a beautiful dream.

Gabby already knew she wasn't sleeping.

That image could be one of those headlining photos that Gabby lived for. She hated that her mind went there. Whose little child was this? Were they searching for her too? Gabby knelt down and gripped the girl's tiny hand in her own.

Was someone holding Sally's hand like this?

How could I have ever thought an image like this was gold?

I am soulless. A monster.

Some poor parent had lost their daughter and her focus would have been on a news caption that would potentially feature for about an hour. The girl's parents, however, would suffer for a lifetime.

A shocking thought blazed across her mind. *Am I being punished because I cared more about the story than the people in it?* She could picture her headline now: *Heartless mother receives brutal reality check.*

Gabby placed the tiny hand upon the girl's chest, and with her heart as heavy as a brick, she climbed over a few chairs to Max's side. Bracing herself against the back of the chair for balance, she cupped her hands around her mouth. "Adam!"

She screamed his name until her throat hurt. But her frantic calls were met with nothing but silence.

Glancing at her husband, she saw a man crushed with sorrow. Her chin quivered and the lump in her throat made it impossible to breathe. "Oh God, Max, you don't think he was washed out . . . out?" Unable to finish her question, she stared through the gaping hole in the side of the ship. It was enormous. Big enough to wash a dump truck out to sea, let alone a small boy.

"Don't say it, Gabby. Just don't." Max's insipid face paled even further. "Look around. He's probably stuck under some of this crap like I was." He sucked air in through his teeth as he climbed down from the chairs, then, with his crippled hand tucked in close to his chest, he started tossing mangled pieces of furniture aside like they were mere toys. "Adam! Adam!"

Gabby did the same, working in the opposite direction to Max. Her wet skirt clung to her body, making it difficult to climb over chairs and rubbish, and each time she glanced down she spied the hideous gouges disfiguring her legs. The extent of the mutilation should have horrified her. But it didn't. It didn't matter anymore. Nothing mattered. Nothing but finding her children. "Adam!"

They took it in turns calling for their son, and with every piece of furniture she checked beneath, another layer of dread stacked onto her already battered emotions. Tears flowed and she flicked them away, furious that she couldn't pull herself together. She'd seen miracles before. Many, many miracles. She was going to see one today. No! Not one. She would find both her children. Alive . . . they would both be alive.

Adam and Sally will be alive.

Repeating the mantra over and over, she trudged across and around mangled wreckage. The sunlight grew stronger by the minute creating as many shadows as it did pockets of light. Each time she spied another dead child she rode out her guilt, cursed the light and prayed the image would eventually fade from her memory just like all the stories she'd covered in her career.

But this wasn't a story. This was her family. This was . . . she stopped still. Her eyes darted around the room. There . . . a voice. "Adam!" she yelled. "Max! I think I heard him. Adam!"

"Adam!" Max scrambled onto the stage and screamed his name.

"Dad."

Her eyes darted back to the balcony. His voice was barely a whisper, yet it spoke volumes.

"Oh, thank God." Her heart pounded in her chest as she flicked tears from her cheeks.

"Where are you?" Max bellowed.

"Up here."

Gabby's knees barely kept her vertical as she shoved debris aside to return to the chairs below the upper tier.

Somehow, Max beat her there. "Adam. Adam. Are you okay?"

"No."

Gabby climbed up onto the chair next to Max. "Are you hurt?"

Adam's hands appeared on the railing, then his face. A gray tinge had washed over his flesh and his wet hair was a scrambled mess. He was crying.

"I feel sick." Adam barely got the words out before he turned and vomited.

The boat's momentum was more pronounced now that Gabby had stopped racing around. It was no wonder Adam was probably seasick. Yet if he'd been unconscious all this time, then he may be seriously injured.

"It's okay, buddy. We're going to get you down."

Max scanned the room. Wincing in pain, he climbed off the chair and hobbled toward the stage. "Gabby, help me."

She raced after him, careful not to step on the little girl's body curled up in the aisle.

Max wrapped his good hand around a fistful of curtain and dropped his weight onto it. "We need to get these down." But the fabric didn't budge. "Help me."

She copied his move and together they pulled on the heavy fabric, but after a good minute or so of straining it was obvious it wasn't going to release. Shaking her head, she let go. "It's not working."

"Shit!" Max tossed the curtain aside and it swung back and hit him in the chest.

He stumbled backward and crashed to the stage with a howl that burst from his throat.

Chapter Thirty-Seven

GABBY

"Jesus, Max. You're really hurt." Gabby reached for him, but he avoided her grip and pushed to stand again.

"I'm fine," he snapped. His blazing eyes dared her to defy him. "We need these curtains to get Adam down." He slapped the wet fabric with his good hand and it sounded like he was slapping wet toast.

"Hang on." She reached for the curtain. "There's two layers here. Maybe the thinner one will come down easier."

"Good idea."

She separated the sheer curtain from the heavy velvet one. "Okay, here we go. Ready? Pull!" Clenching her teeth, she dropped her full weight downward. When Max did the same, she tried not to look at the agony on his face. It wasn't an expression she'd ever seen on him before. Max was usually full of life, the epitome of strength and vitality. The man in front of her was on the verge of giving up, and that wasn't the Max she knew.

With a sudden jolt, the fabric came away. She tumbled to the dance floor, and Max fell to his hands and knees and screamed in agony. Gasping, he toppled sideways. Tears filled his eyes and the torture on his face was brutal.

She crawled to him. "Oh, Max."

"Dad!" Adam yelled from the balcony.

"I'm okay." Max shifted so he could see his son. "I'm okay, buddy. Just fell over—that's all." His voice wobbled and he sniffed in a shaky breath. He was barely holding it together. He glared at Gabby. "I'm okay." He spoke through clenched teeth.

"I know." Sucking her lips into her mouth, fighting her own emotions, Gabby placed her hand on his cheek. "I know you're okay."

A crooked smile snaked across his mouth. "Okay." He winced. "Let's get our boy down."

Gabby clawed the sodden curtain into her arms and when they scrambled their way back to the chairs beneath the balcony, Max was a couple of beats behind her.

She dropped the curtain and glanced upward. The distress on Adam's face was agonizing. "Hey, little man. How are you feeling?"

"Terrible." Adam sniveled and shook his head. "I feel so sick." He sobbed.

"I know, I know. We'll get you—"

"You don't know! What took you so long?" he screamed at her, and the venom in his voice caught her by surprise.

"It's okay, buddy. We're here now, and we'll get you down." Max slipped into caretaker mode. His voice was calm and in control.

Using his teeth, Max tried to rip a section of the curtain away, but with only one hand, his movements became more frantic by the second.

She clutched his bicep. "I'll do it."

"No, I've got this."

"Jesus! Stop arguing with me. Look at your hand, for Christ's sake. You can't do it."

His eyes didn't leave hers. It was like he was refusing to see his hand and thereby refusing to admit he was injured. He clenched his jaw, and worried that he was set on continuing the argument, Gabby pushed in front of him and snatched the curtain. "What are you trying to do?"

His shoulders sagged. "I was trying to tear off a long, narrow strip."

"Okay then." Gabby put the disgusting fabric in her teeth and pulled. To her surprise, it tore like it was merely paper. Once it started, she was able to use her hands to rip it the rest of the way down.

"We're coming," Max called up to Adam.

Their son vomited again.

Adam sobbed and Gabby's heart ached. She hadn't heard him cry like that in years.

"Poor little man." Max squatted down and undid his shoelace. "Hopefully it's just seasickness." Max's eyes drifted to the dead little girl. "He's very lucky."

"So are we."

Max stood with his shoe in his hand. "Yes." He nodded. "Yes, we are."

Gabby tore the final strip of fabric free and he handed her his shoe. "Tie the strip to the shoelaces. And make it tight; we don't want it coming free."

Frowning at the absurdity of his request, she resisted asking for reasoning and followed his instructions.

Once she'd done it, Max clutched the shoe and turned to look up at the balcony. "Adam. Buddy. Get ready to catch this."

Her son appeared at the edge of the landing, wiping the back of his hand across his mouth. "Okay."

Max stepped away a fraction and when he rolled his arm, ready to throw, a gasp burst from his throat.

"Jesus, Max." Gabby snatched the shoe from his hands. "Give it to me."

"But you can't throw."

"Watch me." Clenching her jaw, she stepped back a few paces, raised the shoe up over her head and, harnessing every ounce of her determination, she released a guttural growl of purpose and threw it.

The shoe sailed about fifteen feet sideways and didn't even touch the upper tier.

"Shit!" she cried.

Max clutched his hand over his mouth. Humor danced in his eyes.

She glared at him and pointed her finger. "Don't you dare."

He shook his head. "I wasn't going to say anything."

"Yeah, well don't." She fetched the shoe and readied herself again.

"Stop!" he blurted. "At least let me help."

She rolled her eyes. When the kids were little, Max had tried many times to involve her in sporting activities. But exercise and Gabrielle Kinsella were words that should never be together. Her hand-to-eye co-ordination was obsolete, and her reflexes were too slow. Many times, she'd been hit in the face with a football . . . much to the delight of her husband and children.

But this was different. If she didn't get this shoe up to Adam, he would never get down. Her son depended on her. She huffed out a forceful sigh. "All right then. Show me."

As Max showed her the finer points of the skill of throwing, she tried to block out the heartbreaking sounds of her son throwing up.

But she couldn't stand it a moment more. "Okay! I got it. Let me do this."

She wriggled her head and shoulders. It was a technique she'd used dozens of times to eradicate the tension before a news broadcast. She inhaled a calming breath, stepped back, and braced her feet like Max had shown her. She raised the shoe over her right shoulder.

"Come on, Mom. You can do it!"

Riding on her son's words of encouragement, she aimed her left hand at him and in one swift movement, she snapped her right arm forward and released the shoe at the perfect moment. It sailed through the air and Adam caught it.

Gabby squealed with delight.

Max's eyes bulged. "Holy shit! You did it."

"I told you I could."

Max placed his hand on her shoulder. "I'm so proud of you."

Then he stepped forward and looked upward. "Good boy. Pull the curtain up."

Inch by inch, the fabric slithered up to the balcony. "That's it. You're doing good." Max's encouragement continued until the last of the curtain disappeared over the edge. "Good. Now tie the end of the curtain to something. Nice and tight."

Adam disappeared from view and vomited again. He was still crying too. Her heart clenched. His discomfort was her agony too. "It's okay, little man. You'll be down soon."

He appeared on the balcony. "I did it, Dad. It's on."

"Okay, now listen to me. You need to climb over the balcony and slide down the curtain."

"I hope you're right about this," Gabby whispered as she shot her gaze from her husband to her son.

"He's strong. He can do it. I know he can."

Gabby couldn't watch. Instead, she glanced out the hole that had been punched in the side of the ship. With each dip in the swell, the view changed from the distant watery horizon to the cloud-dotted sky where a single bird swooped in the morning breeze. It looked lonely. Yet there was something else it seemed to symbolize . . . was it strength? Independence?

No. She realized what it was—the lone bird looked at peace.

Gabby couldn't remember the last time she'd felt peace.

And based on the last twelve hours, it was going to be a very, very long time before she could even consider peace again.

She turned her gaze back to her son, and her heart lurched to her throat. Her baby was over the balcony. After twelve hours of searching she was finally about to touch him. To hold him. He slid down the fabric like it was something he did every day and she ran to him, arms outstretched, but he dashed around her and burst into tears as he clutched his father.

"Thank God you're okay." Max kissed the top of his son's head, but his eyes were on Gabby.

A viper curled in her stomach at the look in her husband's eyes. He didn't need to say a thing, because the sting of her son's actions screamed it all loud and clear.

Her heart crumbled to a million pieces and drifted away in the ocean breeze.

Max had been right. She hadn't been there for her children.

Ignoring the savage awakening, she stepped forward and knelt down, and when she wrapped her arms around her husband and son, she cried.

Chapter Thirty-Eight

MADELINE

When Madeline stood, the water was nearly over her shoulders. Half-walking, half-swimming, she headed toward the young girl who was still draped across the upturned pallet.

The girl hadn't moved and as Sterling checked her pulse, Madeline half expected him to say she was no longer with them.

He huffed out a breath. "Thank God. She's still alive. We need to get her to the doctor." Sterling pressed his hand to the girl's forehead. "She's burning up."

The girl's skin was deathly pale. Her eyes were shut. But she didn't look like she was just sleeping; it was much deeper than that. Like she was in a hypnotic state, or worse, in a coma.

Madeline met Sterling's gaze. "Do you want me to help carry her?"

"No, I've got this." He leaned forward and wove his arms beneath the girl's knees and behind her back. He lifted her as though she barely weighed anything. The girl didn't stir and when Sterling readjusted her position, Madeline gasped at the massive bruise on the girl's thigh.

"Oh God." Wincing, she eased the girl's clothing upward. "Jesus. Do you think her leg is broken?"

"Shit!" His jaw dropped. "That's not good."

The girl's mouth was open and her chest rose up and down with a shallow breath. The wheeze in her throat sounded painful.

"Come on. Let's move." Sterling nodded at Madeline to lead the way.

Madeline turned to scan the area beyond the lifts. It was dotted with boxes and crates and was about the size of a dance floor. At the other end was a blank wall and either side of that were two passages. A slight breeze wafted a slip of hair across her face as she tucked it behind her ear. The direction the breeze was coming from seemed as good a choice as any. Using her hands as paddles, she forced her body through the water toward the left-hand passage.

Shoving boxes aside as she went, she entered the corridor, and Sterling splashed through the water behind her. He was taller than she was, so unlike her, he didn't need to swim to move forward.

The passage was short compared to many of the corridors she'd walked along since boarding the ship, and within a couple of minutes, they pushed through a set of double doors and entered one giant room. It was an enormous warehouse. Light was coming from somewhere, but it was impossible to work out where. It was like the water had been permeated with some kind of green incandescent fluorescence.

Against the far wall, spanning the gap between the waterline and the ceiling, was a series of giant pipes. But they were buckled out of shape and oozing black liquid. Maybe that was what had been fueling that fire.

The ship rolled to her left. Her feet left the ground. And she was caught up in the swell. Boxes and all sorts of other crap came at her. She fended them off, punching them away. Kicking like crazy, she fought to keep her head above the water. She slammed into a wall. Her side snagged on something sharp. Pain ripped across her flesh. A scream burst from her throat.

"Madeline!"

She touched her waist just above her hip and felt both torn fabric and jagged flesh. Flinching, she raised her hand above the water. Blood covered her fingers. "Shit! Shit. Shit."

"Madeline!" Sterling's panicked cries pierced her brain, and she searched the green haze for him.

"I'm here."

"Madeline."

"I'm here," she screamed louder. "Where are you?"

His hand appeared above a field of boxes. "Over here. Can you swim back?"

"Okay." Forcing her brain to forget her new injury, she put her feet on the wall and kicked off. But just as she did, the wave began to curl back the other way. All of a sudden, she was barreling toward the other side of the room. Boxes, plastic bottles and scraps of debris came with her.

"Sterling!" she cried out. "Help—"

She squeezed her eyes shut. The wave crashed over her, trapping her in a garbage soup. She clawed at the water, searching for air. It was impossible to know which way was up.

The back of her head smashed into something and stars danced across her eyes. Her lungs screamed for oxygen. Her head screamed with pain. She needed a breath. Needed it now. The throbbing in her lungs was excruciating, and without thinking, she opened her mouth and sucked in the foul water. She bucked against the onslaught. Her eyes snapped open and in the green swamp, she saw a miracle.

Sterling's hand.

It snatched at her wrist, and she was dragged sideways.

She burst through the surface and sucked in a huge gulp of air. Her lungs burned as she spewed the foul sludge over and over. As she treaded water, her tears started, spilling down her cheeks in relentless rivers.

Sterling's arm draped over her shoulder. "Hey, you're okay now. I've got you."

"Where's the girl?"

"She's okay. She's safe."

Any hope of speaking was swallowed by the swell of emotion racing through her. Maybe he saw her turmoil because he wrapped his arms around her and tugged her into his chest. Embracing him seemed so natural . . . like they'd done it a thousand times before. She wove her arms around his back and melted into his body.

"We're going to get out of this. I promise," he said.

She nodded and as she listened to the therapeutic beat of his heart, she couldn't remember a time when she'd felt so safe. Considering their situation, it was a very strange admission.

He glided his hands over her hair. "Now . . . if you've stopped messing around, I've found some stairs."

Chuckling, she pulled back, and when she saw the cheeky grin on his face, she playfully slapped his arm. "Really?"

"Yeah, really. The two of us were waiting for you. So come on, hop on my back." Before she had a chance to protest, he turned around.

A swell of childish joy spread through her as she eased her chest up to his back, wrapped her arms around his neck and peered over his shoulder.

"Hang on."

She did.

Sterling leaned forward, and using his hands to push through the water, he aimed for the opposite corridor they'd come from. The boat continued to sway from side to side, but Sterling battled through the swell like it was nothing. He shoved through a doorway and entered a dim stairwell. When he turned around, she eased off his back.

Sterling pointed up the stairs. "The girl's outside the door at the next level."

Gripping the railing to combat the boat's movement, she climbed the stairs. The first curve in the stairwell was completely dry. At the next landing, she pushed through a door labeled deck two and found the girl on her back on the floor. Her chest was rising and falling as if she were still in a peaceful sleep.

A wave of exhaustion flooded through Madeline. She crumbled to the carpet, tugged a band from her hair and ran her fingers through her wet tresses. Shivers trembled through her, but it wasn't from being cold. She was thirsty, starving, exhausted, and terrified. But not cold. In fact, it was very warm. Too warm. Zero air-conditioning made the area as stifling as an oven. And what little air they did have was still tainted with smoke and fumes.

A strip of green lighting lined the edge of the walls. It was why the water had a green tinge. Add to it the smoke in the air and the area had a strange, spooky feeling. Like a technique movie directors would use to make a graveyard appear more ominous. It didn't help that the place was empty and deathly quiet. She'd been on the ship for nearly two weeks and not once had she heard silence like this.

The horrifying notion that they were the only three people left on the ship crept into her mind, but when Sterling crawled in beside her and she inhaled his lovely tropical scent, the brutal thought evaporated from her mind.

He turned to her. "You okay?"

"Yeah, I guess." She nodded. "Thank you."

"My pleasure. Happy to be your trusty steed any day."

"Careful." She attempted to grin, but it was probably more like a grimace. "I may have to hold you to that offer." Wincing, she rolled to her side and peeled up her shredded cotton shirt. The jagged gash in the side of her waist was about four inches long, and the dark blood in the middle confirmed it was deep. Blood and water mingled together and flowed down her hip in morbid rivers.

"Oh Jesus." Sterling eased closer. "That's bad."

She lowered her eyes, not wanting to see the worry in his gaze. "This?" She shrugged. "This's nothing."

A crooked smile wobbled across his face and he placed his hand over hers. His gaze flitted from her to the teenager, still unmoving at their side. "Now, we need to get both of you to the doctor. Do you think you can walk?"

The warmth of his palm and the concern in his voice were so lovely that her heart seemed to melt. "Of course."

Sterling climbed to his feet and offered his hand to help her stand. The ship wobbled beneath them and the second she put her foot down, pain shot up from her leg like a poisonous barb. She yelped. The blue stain bulging over her ankle bone was bigger and darker than the last time she'd checked. When she'd woken with that yesterday morning, she'd thought it was the worst thing in the world.

Karma was playing tricks on her again.

Sterling cupped her elbow. "I forgot about your ankle."

"Yeah, me too. I'm a mess, aren't I?"

"Actually, no." His expression softened with a tantalizing pause. "You look perfect to me."

She curled her lip in through her teeth as her mind pirouetted with a delicious mix of excitement and curiosity.

He reached over and when he curled a slip of hair behind her ear, butterflies danced across her heart. "You're the bravest and strongest person I've ever met."

No words could ever explain how she was feeling. All she could do was grin. She didn't even care that she'd look like a crazy woman. Nothing could ruin this moment.

An awkward pause crossed between them before Sterling bent over to collect the girl into his arms. Once he shuffled her into position, he turned to Madeline. "Let me know if you need to rest. Okay?"

She saluted him. "Yes, Captain."

He chuckled. "Very funny. For that, you get to lead the way." He nodded at the door they'd come through. "Let's keep going up those stairs."

She turned to the door and the ship's sway had her landing heavily on her bruised foot again. Clamping her jaw, and fighting the urge to cry out, she pushed through the door and held it ajar for Sterling. A sharp, metallic scraping had the hairs on her neck prickling. She leaned over the railing and tried to see up the stairwell, but it was too dark.

"Hello?" Her voice bounced off the walls. "Hello, is anyone there?"

"What was that?" Sterling stepped to her side and glanced upward.

"Don't know." The metallic scraping happened again. It was like nothing she'd ever heard before. Whatever it was, it couldn't be good.

Leaning heavily on the railing, she hobbled upward.

Dealing with pain was one of the most powerful skills she'd ever learned. It had been out of sheer necessity when Flint had burned her with his cigarettes. But the initial pain was nothing compared to the sting that came afterward. Skin had interesting pain receptors. A flesh wound could hurt just as much as a swift amputation. Apparently.

Bruises, however, were a different story. Madeline had received her share of those in her life, and not just from her kidnapper. Learning to dance was a delicate balance between pleasure and pain. She lived for them both.

Ahead of her was the door for deck four. She glanced over the railing up at the next set of stairs.

"Oh no!" A giant concrete cylinder, as wide as her body, had demolished the next section of stairwell. An entire row of stairs had been obliterated.

Twisted and buckled metal was all that remained.

Chapter Thirty-Nine

MADELINE

The boat shifted and the metallic scraping sound became deafening. Madeline covered her ears and glanced at Sterling. Even in the dim light, fear flashed in his eyes.

"Jesus." He shook his head. "Go through the door."

She pushed through and stared wide-eyed at the destruction. The entire left-hand side of the hallway was demolished. The giant pipe had taken out everything in its path. Rooms were crushed in. Wires dangled everywhere.

"Holy shit!" Sterling's jaw dropped. "What the hell happened?"

"I don't know." She shook her head. "What're we going to do? We're trapped."

"There." He nodded toward the opposite corridor. "Go that way."

With her heart pounding in her chest, she entered the dim corridor. It stretched ahead of her for what seemed like miles. Closed cabin doors lined each side of it. The breeze she was walking into came with strange scents: the ocean, smoke, fumes, and something else, something pungent and feral, something that had her empty stomach curdling.

They checked each door they passed. All were locked shut.

Finally, they reached a door that was open, and she stepped in. "Hello?"

It had four bunks, but the mattresses had shifted and the pillows were on the floor. Cupboard doors swung back and forward with the ship's sway, as did the curtain over the window.

Madeline shoved a mattress back into place and Sterling placed the girl onto the lower bunk. He raised her head, and as Madeline placed a pillow beneath it, he brushed her hair away from the girl's eyes. He gave a gentle squeeze to the girl's arm, but she still didn't stir. "Hang in there. We'll get you help soon."

Madeline forced back the lump in her throat. "Mind if I use the bathroom?"

"Go for it."

Stepping into the cubicle, she flicked the switch, but the light didn't turn on. It was too dark to shut the door, so she left it ajar.

She shouldn't have glanced in the mirror. Her skin was pale, her eyes were red, and dark smudges lined her cheeks, neck, and down her chest. She tried to wipe them away, but it was grease from the elevator cables. It'd be impossible to remove without a long, hot shower. Hopefully, she'd get one very soon.

After using the toilet, she flushed. At the sink, she turned on the tap and held a face washer beneath the faucet. After an initial burst, it spluttered, then stopped. Scowling, she used what little water she had to dampen a cloth. She lifted her ripped shirt and studied the cut on her waist. The blood had coagulated and slowed, but that didn't make it look any better. Wincing, she dabbed the wet cloth to the wound's outer edge, attempting to clean it. But it was pointless. Aware that she was going to need a lot more than a trickle of water, she gave up and tossed the bloodied cloth into the waste bin.

She stepped from the bathroom and found Sterling standing at an open cupboard.

His grin was photo-worthy. "Look what I found."

Her eyes lit up. "Food."

He offered her a packet of nuts, and opened a second one for himself.

"But they're not ours."

"We'll pay them back."

She hesitated barely a second before she tore open the packet. They were the tastiest nuts she'd ever eaten.

"Excuse me for a sec." Sterling disappeared into the bathroom.

She returned to the bunk beds and sat opposite the unconscious girl. Her top had ridden up a fraction and Madeline gasped at a dark stain on the girl's stomach. She put the nuts aside to raise the girl's shirt.

An enormous black bruise spread from her hip and covered a third of her torso. It was a horrifying mix of purple and red. Madeline had received her share of injuries in her life, but nothing had ever looked as bad as this.

It wasn't hard to picture how she'd received this bruise. When the elevator had hit the bottom, the poor girl would've slammed down with the full force of gravity.

"Oh shit, that's not good."

She hadn't heard Sterling's approach. "No. Do you think she has broken ribs?"

"Possibly. I don't think we should move her anymore."

"I agree."

"How about I go and see if I can find a doctor?"

She snapped her gaze to Sterling. "Oh no you don't. You're not going anywhere without me. We stick together, remember?" She clenched her jaw.

"Okay." Sterling must've seen her determination. "Okay."

He tugged a sheet off the opposite top bunk and draped it over the girl. "Come on. Let's go get some help."

At the cabin door, Sterling paused. "Four one four nine. Remember that cabin number."

"Got it. Four one four nine."

Back in the narrow corridor, Sterling led the way. The sway was worse than before and the strange-smelling breeze was stronger. Ahead of them, a light filtered in from somewhere and Madeline allowed her hopes to rise.

But barely thirty steps later, Sterling halted. "Oh, shit."

Her brittle moment of optimism was crushed to a million pieces as she stared, openmouthed, at an enormous hole in the ship. The light she'd seen was the sun, and the breeze was from the ocean.

"What the . . .?" Sterling didn't finish his sentence.

She turned from the gaping hole to look at what was left of deck four. The devastation was massive. Walls, floors, and ceilings were charred and demolished. Lights dangled from flimsy cables. Strips of metal had been shredded to pieces. Wires spewed from every angle. Rubbish was everywhere.

"What the hell happened?" Sterling crunched over bits of glass and plasterboard, heading farther into the wreckage.

She followed him, grappling with what she saw. Almost everything was charred, and huge chunks had broken away into a massive smoldering pile. It explained the smoke. It explained the weird fumes.

She looked up and her jaw dropped. "Is that—" She pointed to a large white object embedded in a wall on the other side of the area. "Is that the wing of a plane?"

"Oh my God! I . . . I think it is."

Madeline's heart slammed against her chest as her eyes darted from one unbelievable aspect to another. "Do you think it was a suicide bomber?"

He huffed out a breath. "I have no idea." Sterling stepped over a pile of rubble, crouched down, and came up with a dinged can of cola. He held it toward her. "Here."

"Oh, it's okay. You have it."

"We'll share." He pulled the ring and black liquid spewed from the rim. "Shit." He poured the cola into his mouth and once it stopped, he offered it to her again. "Sorry."

She chuckled. "It's fine." She sipped the sweet fizz that was both warm and hardly enough.

"Hey, look at that." Sterling climbed over more rubble, and pulled a small trolley upright. A food cart. "Hope there's some left for us." He tugged open the top drawer. "Yes." Grinning, he tossed a packet of cookies toward her.

As she munched on the oatmeal cookies, she scanned the wreckage. Her eyes snagged on a blackened object in the corner. She stopped chewing. Bile crawled up her throat. "Oh my God." Her hand snapped over her mouth. "Is that . . . is that--"

Sterling followed her gaze. He took a few steps toward it, then spun around. The horrified look on his face confirmed her fear. It was a body. A charred, mangled body.

Madeline scrambled to a corner and threw up what little food she had in her stomach.

It was a long time before she was able to turn back around.

Thankfully, Sterling had found a large sheet of what looked like aluminum foil to cover the body.

He walked back to her with another packet of cookies. "You need to eat."

She nodded. He was right. She knew only too well what crazy things starvation did to her mind. Reluctantly, she opened the packet and bit into another cookie.

Complete silence seemed to grip her. There should be people everywhere. But they hadn't seen nor heard a single soul for what seemed like days. The thought that'd lurked in the dark recesses of her mind took shape again, dark and ominous, like a sadistic demon. "Oh my God . . . you don't think . . . have they abandoned ship and left us behind?"

His face morphed into a deep scowl, but he shook his head. "No. They would've sounded the alarms if they were evacuating."

A wave of dizziness washed through her. "But where is everyone?"

"I don't know. But they wouldn't leave us. They have checks for things like that. They wouldn't leave anyone behind." Although he said it calmly, his eyes blazed with fear. He snatched four more packets of biscuits from the dinner cart and handed two to her.

She was no longer hungry. Not after that terrifying thought. But she forced herself to eat. She turned her gaze to the wreckage around them and spied a sign on the far side of the disaster zone. "Look—the medical clinic . . . It's over that way."

But between them and that doorway was a mountain of charred bits and giant chunks of debris.

The passageway was completely blocked off. It was going to take forever to get through that mess.

They were still in trouble.

Chapter Forty

GABBY

Each time Gabby tried to hug her son, he pushed her away. But he was in shock. He'd just witnessed the death of several new friends and nearly died himself.

She had come so close to losing him.

But they couldn't dwell on it a moment more. "Max, we have to find Sally."

"Yep. Let's go to the top deck. She'll be up there, I'm sure."

For some inexplicable reason, Gabby didn't share that confidence.

They exited the theater and when she walked past the demolished elevator shaft, icy serpents slithered up her back at her second sighting of the severed cables.

What if Sally . . .?

No! She couldn't think like that.

She managed to put a full stop to that thought.

Sally was still alive. She had to be. There was no reason to think any other way.

Max would say she was being ludicrous for worrying that she might be dead.

She'd get that look from him too . . . like she was an irrational fool.

It was a look men often flashed at her. Maybe it was her natural blonde hair that instigated such hostility. After all, despite the ridiculous all-encompassing generalization of the term dumb blonde, it was still widely and infuriatingly purported.

Gabby forced the burning anguish from her chest and turned her gaze to Adam. She was surprised at how tall he was. At just thirteen years old, his brown hair was already in line with her husband's shoulders. He was broad too. Max had said Adam was strong. She'd had no idea that Max had begun training him.

A flash of jealousy streaked through her. Max knew their children better than she did. But she'd made sacrifices for them. Important sacrifices. For all three of them. And their lives were enriched because of those sacrifices. She hadn't regretted the decision to focus on her career once since her children were born. Until now.

Adam's hand remained clutched in his father's good one as they made their way up the dim stairwell and every question her son had was directed at Max. Not one was sent her way.

At the ninth deck, they were forced to return back into the dark passages that had barely any sunlight penetration and the sway of the boat had all three of them bouncing off the never-ending cabin doors.

Halfway along, Max dropped Adam's hand and sprinted ahead.

She and Adam raced forward. Max fell to his knees, and when Gabby finally caught up, Max was holding the hand of an elderly woman. The toppled wheelchair at her side was the likely answer for her awkward position on the floor. She was opposite an open cabin door, which thankfully provided enough light for them to see. Her body was tilted sideways, with her back against the wall and her legs, as thin as those often seen on malnourished prisoners of war, were at graceless angles beside her.

"Are you okay?" Max patted her arm.

The woman nodded and tried to push up.

"It's okay; stay where you are. Are you hurt?"

She shook her head.

"What's your name, love?"

"Gladys. Gladys Fairway."

"Okay, Gladys. My name is Max. This's my son, Adam, and my wife, Gabrielle." He glared at Gabby, and she had a feeling he was trying to say something with his eyes, but she had no idea what.

"Hello." Gladys' brittle voice was barely audible.

Max winced as he adjusted his mangled hand across his chest.

"Oh my goodness, you're injured." Gladys reached out with knobby, arthritic fingers to touch the bruising that had spread to his forearm.

Max shook his head and chuckled. "It's nothing."

"I can tell you now, son, that it is not nothing." Gladys seemed to have found her voice. "You have multiple fractures, and I'm sure every movement is giving you immense pain."

Max actually smiled as he cupped her elbow. "Can you stand?"

"No." She shook her head. "Sorry."

"No need to be sorry."

"My legs have been useless for years."

Gabby studied the woman's physique. Her legs may have been as thin as kindling, but the upper half of her body was plump and round, and she probably weighed at least two hundred pounds. Even if Max had the use of both his hands, he couldn't possibly think he'd be able to lift her.

"Okay, Gladys." He squeezed her shoulder, then stood and using just his good hand, he returned the wheelchair to its upright position. "We'll have you back into your chair in no time."

"It's stopped working."

"That's okay; don't worry about that. I'm going to get some help. Gabby and Adam will stay with you, and I'll be right back." Max turned without even glancing at Gabby and looked set to run off.

"Max!" Gabby blurted.

He spun to her, his jaw clenched, ready for a fight. Gabby stepped over Gladys' legs, latched onto his arm and leaned in. "What're you doing?"

His glare was evil. "I'm going to get help."

"What about Sally? Our daughter. Remember?" It took all her might to keep her voice as a whisper.

"I can't leave her like this. The poor woman's probably been stuck in that position since yesterday."

"I can't believe you'd do this."

"Don't be so callous, Gabby."

"Callous! This isn't callous. This is putting the life of our daughter ahead of a complete stranger."

"No, Gabby," he hissed in her ear. "This is me putting the care of a crippled, elderly woman, who is directly within our reach, into perspective."

Gabby groaned and clenched her fists until her long nails dug into her flesh.

She had no retort, nor did she have time to think of one, before Max turned and sprinted away.

"I'm going to look for Sally," she yelled after him. But he neither replied, nor looked back.

Biting down her fury, she turned to her son. Adam's face was ashen, his lips drawn into a thin line. He shook his head at her, like he despised what she'd done. She went to speak, to tell him his father's priorities were so very wrong, but before she'd decided on an appropriate way to say it, he looked away.

Gabby huffed out a sigh and looked down at the crippled woman.

Gladys met her gaze. "I'm sorry to be a burden." Her red eyes had become even more red, and fearing she was about to cry, Gabby looked away too.

It was a long moment in which the only noise was the groaning of the ship before Gabby decided what she had to do. She cleared her throat and squatted so she was level with the elderly woman. "I'm really sorry. But my daughter is missing, and I can't . . . I can't just stay here when I don't know where she is."

"There's no need to explain. Please go find her; she's more important than I am."

Gabby touched her arm and the elderly woman's clammy skin quivered. "Thank you." Gabby stood. "Come on, Adam."

He shook his head and backed away. "Dad will be back soon."

"Adam, you're coming with me."

"No! I'm not."

She cocked her head. He'd never defied her before. "Adam. I'm your mother; you do as—"

"I don't care!" He folded his arms across his chest. "Dad said he'd be back, and I'm waiting for him."

"Adam!" The gaze of the elderly woman had heat flashing up Gabby's neck.

"I'm not moving."

The pressure to take charge was equal to the embarrassment blazing through her.

When did I lose control of my kids?

It didn't matter. There wasn't time to think about that. Sally needed her.

Now it was Gabby who had to choose between her own children. With her eyes locked on Adam, she decided to use the same strategy Max had done. Adam was fine; it was Sally who needed her. She pointed at her son. "You stay right here with Gladys. Do not move until your father returns. Got it?"

He nodded and his shoulders lowered as if unburdened. "Yes, Mom. I will. I promise."

"When your father returns, tell him I'm upstairs searching for Sally. Tell him to meet me by the bar on the Lido deck. Okay?"

"Okay. I will."

Gabby strode to her son, pulled him to her chest and kissed the top of his head. But even as she clutched him there, she felt his stiffness . . . his utter reluctance to hug her. She told herself it was a normal reaction for a thirteen-year-old boy, but at the same time, she fought the other rotten truth—he didn't love her anymore.

She turned, and as she followed the direction Max had taken, her vision wobbled through the tears pooling in her eyes.

After climbing two sets of stairs, in which she didn't encounter a single soul, she arrived at the Lido deck. It'd been the party zone for the first twelve days of the cruise. Drinking, dancing, swimming, and socializing had been the themes for the large open expanse both day and night.

Now, though, with the sun a huge fireball high in the sky, not even a whisper of breeze drifting off the ocean, *and* bodies strewn everywhere, it truly was the definition of hell.

Hundreds of people stood around. Or sat on deck chairs in the stinking heat. Everyone looked to be in a trance and nobody seemed to be doing anything. Nothing constructive at least.

The stench was horrific. In this seventy-degree swelter, no bathing was exacerbating the problem. But it wasn't simple body odor that invaded her nostrils. No. It was worse. Much worse. Vomit. Sewage. And death. Gabby had been to many crash scenes where people had lost control of their bodily functions, but this was beyond anything she'd encountered before.

As she scouted everywhere for her daughter, it was impossible to comprehend how these people could just sit here. *Were they just waiting for their pitiful end?*

She still had no idea who was in charge.

And, more importantly, why weren't they doing anything?

Gabby paused in the middle of the field of bodies and did a slow scan of the deck. Each time her eyes snagged on a young angelic profile, her heart would sink and almost simultaneously leap at the confirmation it wasn't Sally.

"Sally," she called across the crowd. People turned her way. Their grubby faces were devoid of emotion. Their lethargic bodies lacked in urgency. It was like they'd all given in.

"Sally!" She cupped her hands around her mouth in the hope of projecting her voice.

More people turned toward her. Gabby was accustomed to being the center of attention but it was usually met with admiration. The glares she received now bordered on hostility.

She didn't care. "Sally! Sally! Sally, where are you?"

A woman in a white uniform touched her shoulder. "Ma'am. Ma'am . . . can I help you?"

"I can't find my daughter." Gabby's chest squeezed. The lump in her throat made it impossible to breathe. Gasping for air, she leaned forward, put her hands on her knees, and stared at the bloody scars running down her legs.

The woman rubbed her back. "It's okay. Take it easy. Nice deep breaths."

Okay? Nothing was okay.

Gabby didn't make scenes. At least, not in front of strangers. She could imagine the headlines: *Gabrielle Kinsella crumbles into a blubbering mess.*

That nasty epiphany had her sniffing back her grief. She inhaled a shaky breath and let it out in a huge huff. Clenching her jaw, she flicked away teetering tears. She straightened her shoulders and faced the woman in uniform. "As I was saying, I can't find my daughter."

"Okay. If you come with me, we have a list over there of people who can't locate loved ones. Maybe she's looking for you." The woman indicated for Gabby to lead the way and as she stepped through the crowd toward the bar that had lost its mirror in that explosion, she saw Max and two other men with a deck chair in their arms, running out the doorway.

He didn't so much as glance in her direction.

Shaking her head over Max's warped priorities, she waited at the counter as the woman scrolled down the immense list of names. "Sally Kinsella? Is that right?"

"Yes. She's fifteen years old. She's about this high, with long dark hair."

The woman flicked back to the first page and started at the top again. As she turned over the pages, scanning with her finger, a dagger of despair stabbed at Gabby's sanity.

When the woman reached the end of the list for a second time, she paused without shifting her gaze from the page. She stiffened too and was struggling to look into Gabby's eyes.

"No." Gabby's voice was barely audible. "No. No. No!" She shook her head. "This isn't happening. It's not happening."

The woman finally looked up. Her pupils were enormous. Gabby knew the sign well. *Distress.* "I'm sorry, Gabrielle."

"But where can she be? It's a ship, for goodness sake. It's not like she can—" Gabby stopped mid-sentence. Her heart gripped in a vise. She took a step sideways and turned so her view included the damaged railing that'd been eradicated by the enormous plane engine when it had skidded across the deck and gone overboard.

Gabby fell to her knees. She clutched her hands over her face.

And for the first time in her life, she didn't care who was watching as she burst into inconsolable sobs.

Chapter Forty-One

ZON

Zon couldn't stand the pain shooting through his gut no more. He had to eat. This rationing crap was bullshit. He was bigger than every fucker still alive on the ship. That meant he needed to eat more than they did.

Everybody was just sitting there, waiting for handouts like good little children. A can of beans or corn. A stale bread roll. Sticks of carrot or celery. Or worse, an apple. Where the fuck were the T-bones? With all this broken shit lyin' around, they could whip up some kinda griddle quick smart and cook up some steak. And what about the beer? They had bucket loads of beer. Fuckers were probably keeping 'em for themselves.

That new Captain thought he was king shit, deciding who got what, and who did what. And for some fuckin' reason, everyone did it. McCrae and his bitches had rooms set up with food and water stores, and dumb fuckers guarding it like it was gold or somethin'. They were constantly counting it and sorting it. They'd count the passengers too, and Zon was pretty sure that each time they did, there were less mouths to feed.

Rationing to one bottle of water a day was fine. When the food ran out, people would get weak. But it was the shitting situation that was gonna get 'em all dead.

Once when he was a kid, his daddy had started shittin' so bad he'd done it in his pants. Zon got smacked over the head for laughin' about it, but his mama, when she got riled up, ya didn't go messin' with her. She'd whacked the crap outta his daddy with a frying pan, cussing and carryin' on until he got his-self sorted. Thing was, though, by nightfall, all of 'em —his daddy, his mama, Bitchface, and him—coulda all shat through the eye of a needle. Went on like that for days. And they was so weak nobody could clean up the mess.

In the end, Zon had slept in the chicken pen. The chickens were more accommodating than his fucked-up folks anyways.

It was several days before his mama came looking for him. Which was good, 'cause he was so sick of sneaking into the kitchen and stealing food that he was considerin' eating one of them chickens. But that wouldn't a been a grand idea. He'd learned the hard way that eating chicken that wasn't cooked right woulda done much worse than whatever disease his daddy had brought home from the abattoir.

But it wasn't just the shitting problem that was causing him grief now. It was all this sitting around waitin'. Waitin' for food. Waitin' for water. Waitin' for Captain Dickhead to make a plan about abandoning ship. Zon didn't wait for no one. Deciding he'd start hunting for his own rations was easy, but waiting until darkness settled in? That was the tough part.

It came swift though. One minute the sun was changing everyone's skin to shades of red; next second, it was sinking into the ocean. There was even a spray of colors to mark its plummet. He wouldn't normally notice that shit. But today, as he'd spent a few hours hovering around Jessie, he'd heard her talk about it with her father. They'd made some crack about there being pink in the sky bein' a good thing. He had no idea what they were jabberin' on about, but he'd laughed along all the same.

Although he was mega fat, Jessie's dad was kinda cool. Albert included Zon in the conversation like he'd been officially invited into some group. That shit never happened to him. Maybe when a huge crowd faced death together, it made people go all weird.

He didn't know. He didn't care for no reason neither. He just liked it.

But it did make it harder to sneak away.

The first two times he'd stood, they'd asked him what he was doin'. Each time he'd pretended to stretch and ended up sitting right back down again. The third time though, he'd made up his mind that he had to get goin' before the pains in his stomach had him punchin' someone in the face.

He stood, rubbing his stomach.

Jessie looked up at him and tilted her head in that cute way he was gettin' to like. "Where're you going?"

Zon was certain she was thinkin' of going with him. As much as he liked the idea, he didn't need no baggage slowin' him down.

"Need to do a shit," he said it all matter-of-fact like.

"Oh." Jessie giggled, and it sure was the sweetest sound he'd ever heard. It nearly had him sitting right back down next to her. He fought the urge though, and with a nod in her direction, he began striding through the field of barely-movin' bodies.

Zon glanced at several of them as he walked. Based on what he was seeing, he wouldn't be surprised if half of 'em were dead by morning.

Zon looked at one old woman as he stepped over her legs. Her gaping mouth and bulging tongue were sure signs she was a goner. But the people around her either didn't care, hadn't noticed, or were too weak to do anything about it.

Things were going to shit. And it was coming down to the fact that the last man standing was gonna be the sole survivor. Zon was adamant that was gonna be him.

Maybe he could save Jessie too. That'd be nice.

Checking nobody was followin', he headed straight for his life raft. He had a nice little stash in there now. In addition to the booze, the money, and the bar snacks, he also had matches, candles, his cigarettes, and even some of his clothing. He climbed up the ladder, slipped beneath the orange canvas cover and climbed inside. After a quick check along the deck, makin' sure nobody had seen him, he put the cover back in place. In full darkness, he felt around for the matches he'd stashed to one side.

He struck a flame and lit one of the candles he'd nicked from the stupid souvenir shop. The flickerin' light reminded him of the endless campfires he'd sat around out on the swamps. There was somethin' comforting about the endless noises of the Louisiana bog. The bugs that never stopped chirping. The fish that jumped and the gators that teased Zon with the snap of their jaws.

After lighting a cigarette, he closed his eyes and inhaled the smoke, long and deep. But he only had six more left in his packet. That meant he'd be raiding the duty-free shop later.

The temptation to count his money and make sure nobody was stealing it was strong, but his hunger pains were hurtin' like hell. So, he settled for a long slug of his XO Cognac.

The golden liquid burned his throat and warmed his belly.

It was like taking his time with his grandmama's apple pie. He sure did miss her pie since she'd gone an' died. Had him wonderin' if Jessie could cook. He smiled at that. Maybe she could learn to bake apple pie just like his grandmama. Playing house with a chick wasn't somethin he was accustomed to thinkin' about, and he huffed. Maybe this starvation thing was sending him looney.

After another long swig of the Cognac, he chomped through a packet of cashews. But even once he was done, his gut kept right on rumbling. He needed meat. And lots of it. That wasn't gonna happen anytime soon though. Maybe he'd find something real decent in one of them cabins. So far, it'd been nothin' but fuckin' granola bars, and they barely touched the sides. And they tasted like cardboard.

He thought about bringin' the axe he'd found in the raft's kit of goodies, but if anyone saw him with it, he'd have some explainin' to do. Besides, he'd been able to break into the cabins all by his-self so far, so it shouldn't be no different tonight. With the snuffed-out candle and the box of matches in his pockets, he climbed back out of the life raft.

He'd already done the rounds of the ship a few times, so he knew where he was going. Yesterday, he'd seen the staff raiding them shops and the kitchens for food and water, but he was pretty sure they hadn't raided *all* the cabins. They'd done some, found a couple of things worthy of keepin', but mostly they'd just come back with more bodies.

He didn't reckon they'd even started on the lowest decks.

Zon made his way to the atrium, paused again to check he was alone, and climbed down the stairs to the bottom level. He waited a minute before he lit his candle. The glow was about as useless as his fuckin' mother. But it was all he got.

With his hand cupping the flame, he walked along a corridor, strode between the section that connected one side of the ship to the other, and entered another corridor.

He didn't need to waste no more time. Zon put his candle on the floor, took two strides back, and, with his shoulder down, charged at the door. It burst from its hinges and slammed backward with a *bang* that sounded like shotgun pellets hitting an empty forty-four-gallon drum.

First cabin, and within seconds he'd scored two chocolate bars and a bottle of that green girly booze. He didn't care; he'd drink the Midori when the rest of his stash ran out. Chomping on a Snickers bar, he searched the bathroom and spied some of that fancy men's cologne shit. His thoughts were on Jessie as he splashed it onto his cheeks. A whiff of his armpits had him rummaging for deodorant. He rolled that on too. Hopefully the new scents would get Jessie's attention. Maybe he could find her some jewelry. A ring or something. That'd be nice.

Figuring that cabin was done, he hit the next one.

It was like hunting for lost treasure, only no map was required. The most he'd ever earned in his life was from a fourteen-foot gator he'd caught and sold last year. But that was merely pocket change compared to what he already had stashed up in his life raft.

By the time they hit dry land again, Zon was gonna be richer than every other fucker on this boat.

He was gonna be in charge too.

He'd do a better job than fuckin' Gunner McCrae, that's for sure. *Captain, my ass.*

Stupid bastard don't even look like he wanna be top dog anyways.

Chapter Forty-Two

GUNNER

Gunner's heart was as heavy as a cannon ball as he surveyed the hundreds of sheet-wrapped bodies lining the deck. And these were only the bodies they could find. In the two days following the rogue wave, he and the crew had searched everywhere in an attempt to find all the deceased. A huge number of people had gone overboard and would be forever lost at sea. Although he hadn't seen any, images of bodies floating face-down in a churning ocean were ingrained in his brain like a hideous dark stain.

He'd had two truly gut-wrenching moments in his life. This was the second one. He would never be the same knowing that he had a hand in all these deaths. He was thirty-eight years old, and he'd never been to a funeral. Not attending his father's burial had been an easy choice. He had no idea if his father's parents were still living; he'd never met them. His grandparents on his mother's side were still alive, although they rarely caught up. He'd never even buried a pet.

But that was about to change in the most horrific of ways.

Nausea churned through his stomach at the sheer number of bodies before him. Yet they still hadn't finished carrying all the deceased outside.

When Rose of the Sea had left Los Angeles fifteen days ago, there had been just over eleven hundred people on board.

Only one hundred and seventeen survivors were counted as still alive two hours ago.

However, there were only three hundred and sixty-four bodies prepared for burial.

That meant six-hundred and fifty-six people had vanished, presumably lost at sea.

Or they were still somewhere on the ship, yet to be found.

The enormity of those numbers threatened to engulf him. He'd failed hundreds of people. He shouldn't be in charge. It should have been Captain Nelson. It should have been *anyone* but him. But what would Captain Nelson have done differently? The answer was probably nothing. There was no precedent for this. There was no instruction manual guiding the way. There was nobody he could call for directions.

He wanted to close his eyes . . . to pretend he was at home with his wife and daughter. To laugh at Bella's adorable giggle when he tickled her tummy. To hear his wife's voice when she whispered she loved him as she turned out the bedside lamp. He wanted to crawl into a corner, to hide away from the ongoing horror, to block it all out.

The stench had him ratcheting back to reality.

As did the sorrowful cries of the bedraggled mourners.

He had deliberately delayed actioning these funerals. His hope had been that they'd be rescued by now, thereby extricating Gunner from the harrowing decision of whether to rid the ship of the bodies, or not. But after three days drifting at sea, the onset of flies had made the bodies too lethal to ignore. Disease was now their deadliest enemy and with each passing hour, it seemed to claim another life.

Gunner had no choice. The deceased needed to be tossed overboard.

The survivors standing around the macabre scene were looking at him. The weight of needing to offer something profound was a mountain on his shoulders. He wasn't a religious man. He'd been to church only twice in his life . . . his marriage and his daughter's christening.

He scanned the forlorn faces and his eyes fell on the blonde woman at the front. There was something about her that caught his attention, yet he couldn't pinpoint what. Beside her was Max, who, despite his horrific injuries, was continually offering assistance to Gunner and his crew.

When the blonde raised her gaze to meet his, a beat passed between them and she frowned. When she cocked her head and a lock of hair fell forward across her face, he left his position at the front of the bodies and walked toward her. The curiosity on her face multiplied as he approached.

Gunner held his hand forward. "Hello, I'm Captain Gunner McCrae. I'm sorry I didn't introduce myself under better circumstances, but have we met before?"

She did a little chuckle and swept her hair aside. "I'm Gabrielle Kinsella. You may have seen me on television? I'm the anchor woman for *America Today*."

He clicked his fingers. "That's right. I saw your report on America's food crisis. It was very interesting."

"Thank you." She grinned at Max, and Gunner had the impression she was giving him some kind of an I-told-you-so look.

Max, however, seemed unfazed and offered his good hand. "Hello, Captain. How are you holding up?"

"I've been better, Max—that's for sure."

"Oh, you know my husband?" Gabrielle's frowning eyes bounced between them.

"Sure do. Max has been more than helpful, especially considering his injury. How is your hand?"

"Getting there but, man, I tell you what, Gladys has a brutal bedside manner."

Gunner chuckled. Gladys had fooled everyone. She may be an elderly cripple who'd just lost her husband and had hands riddled with arthritis, but her mind was still as quick as a whip. And although she hadn't practiced medicine for a dozen years, she'd proven to be invaluable with helping Gunner handle the mounting casualties. "I hope you followed her instructions?"

Max grinned however Gunner didn't miss the pain in his expression. "Are you kidding? Of course. She scares the hell out of me."

Gunner huffed; he knew exactly what he meant. He'd seen Gladys in action. "Did she manage to ahhh . . ." He paused, glancing at Max's hand, trying to piece his question together.

Max shook his head. "She could only reposition the dislocated fingers. The two broken ones will require surgery." His arm was in a sling, but it wasn't enough.

He needed a hospital and pain medication and a plaster cast.

A silent beat passed between them. Both men knew the likelihood of Max receiving the attention he needed anytime soon was negligible.

Gunner touched Max's shoulder. "Right, well don't go overextending yourself, okay?"

"Yes, Captain."

Gunner turned his attention to Gabrielle. Her cheeks were smudged black with soot and her hair was a tangled mess. He imagined she would never have looked so disheveled in her life. "Gabrielle, can you help me?"

She palmed her chest. "Me?" She scanned the field of bodies, and the crowd of mourners standing around them. She turned her gaze back to Gunner and the confusion had her brilliant blue eyes darkening. "How can *I* help?"

"As a recognizable figure, I wonder if you'd be able to help me and all these mourners by saying a prayer, or at the very least saying something in honor of the deceased."

Her eyes bounced from Gunner to Max, who nodded in what Gunner hoped was encouragement. Then she gazed at the elderly woman beside her. Gunner followed her gaze to Muriel . . . the elderly woman whose husband had been one of the first to die. His pacemaker hadn't stood a chance against the EMP. Yet, despite her loss, Muriel had told Gunner that her husband of forty-seven years would've been happy with how his life had ended. Not only had he experienced the holiday of a lifetime, but he'd been playing the slot machines with her at his side, and a whiskey in his hand when he'd passed.

Muriel placed her frail hand on Gabrielle's arm. "Go on, dear. We'd like to hear something nice."

Gabrielle nodded. "It will be my pleasure."

"Thank you." Gunner indicated for Gabrielle to walk ahead of him and as she did, she tucked her hair behind her ears and ran her hands down her crinkled skirt, as if trying to straighten it.

Once positioned at the front of the crowd, Gunner cleared his throat. "Ladies and gentlemen, I would like to introduce you to Gabrielle Kinsella. Some of you may already recognize her from *America Today*." A murmur rumbled through the crowd and people gave knowing nods. "Mrs. Kinsella--"

"Oh, please call me Gabby," she interrupted.

"Gabby has kindly offered to say something on behalf of our loved ones."

She nodded and when she stepped forward, he eased back, away from the attention, and spied the hideous gashes running down her legs. The pain she would be suffering would be excruciating. He made a mental note to make sure she sought medical attention for those wounds.

"Hello everyone. It's with a heavy heart that I've been asked to do this today." Gabby's voice wobbled and her bottom lip quivered. But just when Gunner thought she was going to crumble, she cleared her throat and did a little head shake, like trying to rattle her emotion free.

"Every one of us has been touched with this unspeakable horror. Our cruise on Rose of the Sea was meant to take us on a journey of fun, excitement, and discovery. But this disaster is beyond anything we've ever experienced or even could have imagined. The fact that we . . ." She swept her hand toward the crowd. ". . . you . . . us . . . all of us are standing here is a miracle. But sometimes miracles come at the result of unspeakable loss. Every one of us has lost on this cruise. It may be a loved one, or a friend or an acquaintance. At the very least, we've lost our happiness."

She paused to let that sink in. Gabby was good. She had the

crowd hanging off every word. Gunner was relieved he'd at least made that decision right.

"Now we have no choice but to send the bodies of those who have left us into the ocean. Yes, this is incredibly sad, however. . ." she half turned, "look at this spectacular sunset. Look at the view. This is probably one of the most beautiful sights you will ever see. From this day forward, every time you see a sunset shimmering orange, yellow, and gold, you will think of this moment with the knowledge that you did the very best possible for your loved one."

Again, she paused. Her eyes fell on Gunner and he nodded his approval.

"So, I encourage you all to say your last goodbyes."

Twenty feet away, a woman with a swollen black eye and a bandage on her arm stepped forward, and with her head bowed, she placed her hand on a shrouded body. Muriel followed suit, hunching over to touch a covered body that Gunner assumed must be her husband.

Others copied and soon nearly every single person in the crowd was saying goodbye to someone beneath a sheet. Gabby waited several moments before she too stepped forward, leaned over, and placed her hand on the cloth-covered head of a body that nobody else was touching. It was a couple of beats before Gabby looked up, and when she did and gazed Max's way, Gunner had the feeling something truly special had crossed between them.

Gabrielle stood again and when she straightened her skirt, Gunner noticed one of the cuts on her legs was now bleeding. That wasn't good. Why hasn't she had her injuries seen to? He and his crew had made every effort to ensure the injured were looked after as much as possible. Their medicinal supplies were minimal, but despite their numerous attempts, they'd been unsuccessful in breaking through that damaged section of deck four to access the medical center.

His heart clenched. Was Doctor Merkley still alive?

Or Safety Officer Hastings, who Gunner had sent to find the doc?

Gabrielle cleared her throat, dragging Gunner from his impossible questions.

"Thank you, ladies and gentlemen. And now, if you care to join us, please help in sending these people on their final journey." She looked at Gunner, and using her eyes, she indicated to the body she'd touched.

Gunner and Sykes stepped forward, and with both of them grasping the electrical wiring tied around the deceased person's body, they tugged the cadaver forward and tipped it into the ocean. Seconds later it splashed, dipped below the water and then bobbed back to the surface. As body after body joined the first, the crowd became a collective of harrowing cries. Some were just sniffles; some were gut-wrenching howls of despair.

Somebody started the Lord's Prayer and as Gabby added her voice to the mourners', Gunner and Sykes stepped up to the remaining bodies, and as gently as possible committed them to the ocean.

Once it was done. Gunner stood back to watch the field of white bodies, bobbing like corks on the water as they gradually drifted away. Gabrielle was right; despite the horror of what they were doing, it truly was a beautiful scene.

Next second, a giant splash coincided with a body disappearing beneath the water.

Then another.

Someone screamed.

Gunner stepped forward. His eyes darted from one cadaver to the next. His heart launched to his throat. A fin cut through the water like a knife. "Get the children back," he yelled over the screaming. "Get them back!"

People ran. People screamed.

Bodies disappeared beneath the water and returned in a burst of crimson with chunks missing.

One fin became four. Four fins became twenty.

In the space of minutes, the beautiful ceremony became a gruesome bloodbath. Gunner couldn't drag his eyes away.

I was already the worst cruise Captain in the world.

Now I'm also the Captain who tossed the bodies to the sharks.

Chapter Forty-Three

GABBY

Gabby stared wide-eyed and openmouthed at the bloodbath and a truly rotten thought blazed across her mind. If she'd had the means to record this, she would've won the exclusive Pulitzer Prize.

She hated that her mind went there. Hated it.

But after two decades of chasing a good story it was ingrained into her being.

Sensationalism was what the viewers wanted.

Controversy was the key.

Sharks feeding on bodies that had already suffered . . . now that was controversy.

Her next thought had her clutching the railing as a dry heave wrenched up her throat.

Was Sally taken by a shark?

No. She clamped her jaw and fought back frightful images. Sally did not go overboard. She didn't. Sally was still somewhere on the ship. Alive and waiting to be found. Gabby refused to believe otherwise.

She dragged her eyes away from the bloody ocean to glance at Max. He was holding Adam to his side. Her boy's shoulders heaved with obvious distress. Max bulged his eyes at her, then clamped his jaw in a look that she'd come to recognize as his seething fury.

She mouthed, *'What?'*

He just shook his head.

She scowled right back at him and returned her gaze to the ocean.

She had no idea what his problem was; it wasn't like she'd planned for this to happen. Her eyes caught a flash of orange to the rear of the boat and she did a double take.

"There's a boat!" she yelled. "Captain! Captain! There's a boat." She pointed toward it. "Captain!"

The chaos around them stilled. People turned to her with their gaze aiming in the direction of her outstretched arm.

Gunner pushed through the crowd, raced to her side. "Where?" Sykes joined him and they shielded their eyes from the setting sun.

Leaning over the railing, she pointed. "At the back, there. See it?"

"Shit! Sykes," Gunner blurted. "Is that our tender?"

"Those idiots," Sykes hissed.

"Quick, get my binoculars."

Sykes spun around and sprinted away like he had a bullseye on his back.

"Who is it? Where'd they get the boat?" Gabby shared her gaze between the slow-moving boat and the bulging-eyed Captain. His look of fury was as potent as Max's had been moments ago.

"It's our tender. The boat we use to take people to shore."

"You have another boat? Why haven't we used it to save us?"

He shook his head. "It's designed to take passengers from ship to shore, not for the open ocean. And it's not just that; unless they found fuel somewhere, they'll be lucky to get twenty nautical miles. Oh God, those stupid people. They're going to die on that thing."

"But how come the engine works?"

He shook his head, and a frown rippled his forehead. "It obviously doesn't have any electrical components."

"Sir." Sykes shoved the binoculars at the Captain.

Gunner snatched them and peered at the departing boat. "Jesus Christ! It's Dane Tanner and Riley Cohen."

"Who are they?" She asked.

"The men who were guarding our water and food." Sykes clenched his jaw.

"Son of a bitch!" Gunner spoke with the binoculars to his eyes. "There's about thirty people on that thing. Oh God, those idiots."

"Sir." The muscles bulged along Sykes' rigid jaw. "They probably took supplies!"

The Captain lowered the binoculars. Blood drained from his face.

Without a word, the two of them took off, running along the deck toward the rear of the ship.

Gabby couldn't help herself. She raced after them.

The Captain and Sykes were much faster than her, and she lost sight of them once they dashed through a set of double swinging doors. But Gabby knew where they were going . . . the gymnasium.

All their food and water had been stored and secured in there, and over the last three days, the Captain and crew had been carefully rationing their servings to ensure longevity of the supplies. With a hundred or so mouths to feed, it was an activity in diligence, planning, and continual monitoring.

But if their supplies had been depleted by a group of selfish thieves, then the remaining people on Rose of the Sea could be in serious trouble.

Gabby could barely breathe by the time she reached the gym.

"Fuck!" Gunner clenched his fists and banged them onto a counter top. He glanced at her and held his hand up. "Sorry."

She shook her head. "No need to apologize. How bad is it?"

He heaved a heavy sigh. "They've taken over half our water, all the remaining fruit and vegetables and at least a third of the canned goods."

"They must've been planning this for a while." Sykes kicked a huge bag of flour that was yet to be opened.

The Captain nodded. "I can't believe they used the funeral as a decoy."

"Gutless bastards." Sykes' eyes darted about the room as he drove his fingers through his buzzcut hair.

"Yeah, well." Gunner shook his head. "They've probably just signed their own death notices."

"Why do you say that, Captain?" Gabby wished she had her recording stick. "With all the food and water they've taken, they should be fine. Shouldn't they?"

He shook his head. "We'd already checked the devices on the tender and all the life rafts. The GPS's are all dead, and even if they were working, there are no damn satellites anyway." He slapped his hand on a wall. "Those idiots have no idea where they're going. It's only a matter of time before they run out of fuel and then they'll be floating around out there in that stupid little boat. God!" He threw his hands in the air. "I should've seen this coming."

"Don't beat yourself up, sir." Sykes gripped the Captains shoulder. "This was unpredictable."

"No." His steely gaze radiated anger. "This was inevitable. Hungry people get desperate."

"What do we do now?" Gabby asked.

The Captain rubbed his hand over his rough beard and when he squeezed his eyes shut, they flickered beneath his eyelids like he was trying to eradicate horrific images. Between bloody shark attacks and burned bodies and amputations, and people dying by the minute, he had plenty to choose from.

Gunner huffed out a forceful breath and straightened his shoulders. "Okay, first let's count how many souls we have remaining on board, then we'll count the rations. Sykes, you guard this stuff like your life depends on it."

"Yes, sir." He saluted the Captain. "I think it does."

He nodded. "Sadly, you're right." He turned to her. "Mrs. Kinsella, can you help me please?"

"Of course. But only if you call me Gabby." She offered Sykes what she hoped was a reassuring smile and then she fell into stride with Gunner.

Her brain was like question soup, and they'd reached the beauty salon before she scooped out one to ask. "Captain, how many days' worth of food do you think we have left?"

"Please, call me Gunner."

"Gunner." She nodded. It would be a great name for a headline. *Gunner McCrae, a Captain made with mettle.*

"It's not the food I'm worried about; it's the water." His tight lips made the grim statement even more so.

"But we can't run out of water."

He looked at her, deadpan. "I'm afraid we can."

Her stomach twisted. "But I don't understand. This ship is built for up to fifteen hundred passengers; there are only about a hundred or so of us left. There should be an ample supply remaining."

He stopped and faced her. The dread dominating his expression had her heart skipping a beat. "Gabrielle, when we left Los Angeles, we were stocked for a fourteen-day cruise. Because of space constraints and spoilage issues, we only carry the minimum, plus an additional five percent for contingencies. We are now at day fifteen. Our desalination plant was destroyed and the storage tank that supplied clean water throughout the ship was ruptured in the explosion. We only have bottled drinks remaining. And as we are also using bottled water to clean wounds et cetera, they are diminishing fast."

Gabby's hand went to her mouth. Her heart launched to her throat.

The grim fear the Captain emanated was every bit real.

The possibility that they may not actually get off the ship alive blazed through her like a firestorm. Blood pumped faster through her veins. Her head began to swim. An odor as potent as it was evil invaded her nostrils.

Gabby's knees buckled. Her world toppled. Everything went black.

Chapter Forty-Four

MADELINE

Madeline sucked air through her teeth, forcing her brain to ignore the agony in her side as she dragged a lump of plasterboard away from the never-ending pile of rubble. Although the blood flow had slowed, the stinging was becoming worse.

For the umpteenth time, she examined the wound while in the restroom. It needed stitches. Her only hope was there'd be a doctor in the medical center when they finally got through the mountain of wreckage.

Moving the rubbish was the distraction she needed.

But they'd already been at it for more than a day, and there was still so much more.

With each scrap she moved, the creep of dread crawling through her stomach grew that little bit more. The niggling feeling that they'd been abandoned wouldn't budge. She knew that horror all too well. Dozens of times during her kidnapping, Flint had left her for so long that she'd thought she'd been abandoned.

Her and Sterling hadn't seen or heard anyone since those stupid people were giggling in the dark on the other side of the elevator. At least, not anybody alive.

Sterling groaned as he hauled a twisted strip of metal aside and turned to her with an overwhelmed expression on his face.

Maybe he's thinking the same thing.

He wiped sweat from his forehead, leaving black smudges above his brows. "Let's stop for a break, huh?"

"Sure."

Sterling fetched a couple more packets of food from the food trolley while Madeline checked on the girl. She was resting on a mattress they'd tugged from one of the cabins. Madeline knelt at her side and brushed away a wisp of hair that was curling across the girl's cheek. That alone should have had her stirring, but the girl's breathing was the only indication she was alive.

"She okay?" Sterling asked.

It was an impossible question. "She's still breathing."

"Then she's okay."

Madeline sat with her back against a wall and Sterling slid in beside her and handed her the snacks—nuts and pretzels this time—and a bottle of water. As she nibbled on the pretzels, she gazed out the hole in the ship and inhaled the ocean breeze. It was a refreshing tonic after the smoke they'd inhaled a few days ago. The sun was no longer visible but thankfully there was enough light bouncing off the clouds and ocean for them to still see. They were about to spend another night in the dark and there was nothing they could do about it.

After the snacks, Sterling dusted his hands on his shorts and stood. He heaved a sigh and rolled his head and shoulders. "Ready to keep going?"

A pang of sorrow squeezed her chest at the gloom in his eyes. Hopelessness was creeping in like a poisonous weed. She'd been there before and if they didn't curb it, it would take over every thought. It was up to her to turn on the positive vibes. Slapping away her tangled emotions, she smiled up at him and offered her hand. "Sure am. I'm excited."

"Liar." His chuckle had the dimple in his left cheek deepening, transforming his forlorn expression into a stunning smile.

Her breath caught at how handsome he was, even with the black smudges and sweat-soaked hair. He gripped her hand, helping her to stand, and when he touched the small of her back, butterflies did lovely pirouettes in her stomach. The sensation caught her off-guard and for the briefest of moments she forgot that they were trapped in a disaster zone with a burnt body barely forty feet away, and an unconscious girl at their side.

But her brief reprieve was obliterated when her gaze shifted to the huge pile of debris still blocking their access to the medical clinic.

How long have we been at it?
And how much longer will we have to work?
And why haven't we heard or seen anybody else?

With each passing hour, their precious light diminished. Shadows dominated their work area. Each step became more precarious. And a hive of bees buzzed in her belly at the horrendous notion that they truly had been abandoned.

"That's nice."

His comment made her jump and she blinked at him. "Pardon?"

"Your humming . . . It's, it's nice."

"Oh." She hadn't realized she'd been doing it. "Sorry."

"No. Don't stop. I like it."

The bees in her stomach morphed into butterflies and her heart skipped a beat. For the first time in her adult life she was gripped with the temptation to voluntarily tell someone about her childhood. But the instant she contemplated it, she reeled in the idea.

She wanted him to think she was normal.

They'd discussed stopping twice. But both times they'd agreed to carry on for just a little bit more.

Madeline scrambled up the pile that didn't seem to be diminishing. At the top, she grabbed onto an unrecognizable chunk of debris and tossed it aside. She turned back to the pile and her eyes snagged on a small hole, barely bigger than her big toe. Yet it was enough to emit the now familiar green-hued lighting. She pumped her fist. "Sterling! Quick. Look."

He crawled over wreckage toward her, his eyes following her outstretched finger. "Yes! We did it."

Finally, a miracle.

"Thank God!" Sterling's face lit with a curious mix of relief and elation. He pulled her in for a hug. She wrapped her arms around him and for the briefest of moments, closed her eyes and imagined they were somewhere else. Somewhere sunny and fresh. Somewhere that didn't have bodies and giant chunks of wreckage. But then another thought crawled through her that was as silly as it was harrowing.

Once they were out of this hellhole, would Sterling want to see her again?

Suddenly, she wasn't sure she wanted to go any further.

Sterling slapped his grubby palm to her shoulder. "Come on, let's keep going."

Wrestling her ragged emotions, she joined Sterling's side and they attacked the rubbish with renewed energy. The hole gradually increased and a wind whistled into the passageway.

They pulled aside a mangled door, enlarging the hole a fraction more, and were blasted with a rotten stench that enveloped her like a sewer pit.

Gagging, she recoiled. "Oh God, what's that?" Slapping her hand over her mouth, she eased away from the breeze.

Sterling did the same. It was a long moment before he stepped forward again and dragged another large mangled sheet of plasterboard away. With it gone, they were able to see the source of the smell. Madeline gasped.

The corridor was lined with bodies and the green light made the ghastly scene even more horrific.

Sterling crawled through the hole first, reached for Madeline's hand and helped her through.

A woman lay on her side with one hand stretched out and one hand beneath her cheek. She looked to be sleeping. She wouldn't be.

Sterling knelt at the woman's side. "Are you okay?" He nudged her shoulder and the woman's head wobbled.

Sterling pressed his fingers to her neck and then, after a few heartbeats, he shook his head and stood.

"Sterling, look at her hands." The woman's fingers and palms were covered in blood.

Madeline shot her gaze from one body to the next. All of them had bloody hands. "What do you think happened?"

"They were trying to claw themselves out."

"Oh jeez. Why are they all dead?"

"No idea." Shaking his head, he reached for her hand. "Come on."

Sterling led the way along the green-lit corridor. Madeline kept her hand over her mouth as she followed. At the first open cabin door, Sterling looked inside and with a guttural groan, his shoulders slumped. Madeline didn't want to see, but unable to help herself, she peered around Sterling's side.

A man was on the floor near the entrance. On the double bed were three other bodies: a woman and two children, a boy and a girl. They were all dead.

Their brief glimmer of hope of a rescue shattered to a million pieces. A sob burst from her throat, and when Sterling turned to her, his skin was bathed in a ghastly green tinge. He tugged her to his chest. Madeline wrapped her arms around him and she felt his need for the hug as much as she did. She inhaled a shaky breath. "What's going on, Sterling?"

He glided his hand down her back. "I think it's some kind of poisoning."

"What?" She gasped and stepped back. "We should get out of here."

He glanced back at the people, but otherwise didn't move.

"Sterling, we have to get out of here."

"I think we'll be okay."

"What? How can you be so sure?"

"That pile of rubble we moved. Did you notice the breeze after we did that?"

"Yes, but—"

"I think this was carbon monoxide poisoning. It's deadly in confined spaces."

"Are you sure?"

He shrugged. "I think so. We had some training on it at the school last year. And a couple of us teachers bought those detectors. It's the only way to confirm if there's a carbon monoxide leak. It's odorless and tasteless."

"So, these people had no idea . . ."

"No. It's like when someone commits suicide in their car by using the exhaust pipe. They simply go to sleep and never wake up."

"Oh my God." She glanced at the mother who lay with her two children in her arms. "These poor people."

Sterling clutched her hand in his. "Come on. Let's keep going."

Squeezing his palm to hers she knew in her heart that Sterling would do anything to protect her. It was a powerful, delightful yet peculiar sensation, especially considering they'd only known each other for a few days.

Along the passage, they found many more bodies. Men, women, young and elderly. And children. When they finally reached the medical clinic, Madeline wasn't sure she could enter.

Sterling squeezed her hand. "You okay?"

He must've sensed her hesitation. "No."

When he swallowed, his Adam's apple bobbed up and down, as if he were forcing back nausea. "You can stay here if you want."

"No." She shook her head. "We stick together, remember?"

With a small nod and a heavy sigh, he crossed the threshold.

A shiver ran up Madeline's spine at the sight before them. Each seat in the waiting room was occupied. But every single person had their eyes closed and mouths open . . . a morbid homage to those creepy clowns at the penny arcades. Sterling didn't bother to check if anyone was alive. There was no need.

Clutching his hand again, she stepped with him through the waiting area to another room where there were ten patient beds. Each one had a patient. Each patient was dead.

In the doctor's office, they found three nurses and the doctor.

First Fate

They were seated side by side, and the three nurses were holding hands.

Sterling reached for a note on the table and cleared his throat. The paper quivered in his trembling fingers as he read aloud.

I'm Doctor Phillip Merkley, lead physician on Rose of the Sea, of Blue Earth cruise lines. Rose of the Sea has experienced a massive explosion and is critically damaged.

Sterling glanced at her and cocked his head. "Maybe he didn't know it was from the plane."

"No. Maybe not."

He continued reading.

We have no power and no running water. All communications are down and we've been unable to connect with the bridge.

One hundred and sixteen souls, including myself, have been trapped in a section of the fourth deck since the explosion. Within minutes, several people started falling asleep and couldn't be aroused. I have diagnosed this to be carbon monoxide poisoning. Based on the speed with which people succumbed, I estimate the concentration to be extremely high—at least 1000 part per million. Without an avenue for escape or immediate ventilation, we will all die. If you have this letter, it means my prediction is true.

I hope the remaining passengers onboard Rose of The Sea survived.

Please tell my wife and children that my last thoughts were with them.

Dr Phillip Merkley
3 Hudson Parade
Palm Harbor, Florida

"Oh, that poor man." Madeline looked at the doctor. He had a kind face and a half smile was etched on his lips, like he was about to say something cheeky. He looked peaceful despite the gut-wrenching truth in his letter. "He knew what was happening, but could do nothing about it."

Sterling shook his head, and when his eyes met with Madeline's, they'd taken on a darker, fearful shade.

"What?" Dread crawled up her neck. He seemed frozen, unable to speak. "Sterling. What?"

He drove his fingers through his hair and placed his hand over his mouth.

"Sterling, talk to me."

When he removed his hand, his pale lips quivered. "What if everyone was poisoned and we're the only ones still alive on the ship?"

Chapter Forty-Five

GUNNER

Gunner snapped his eyes open. He sat bolt upright, wiping sleep away. His stomach groaned. His back hurt. His brain was a clouded fog. Thankful for the pre-dawn glow filtering in through the giant windows, he glanced at the people sleeping nearby. Something had woken him, yet everyone else appeared to be still asleep.

Rubbing his eyes, he scanned Blossoms. After the disastrous funeral yesterday, he'd kept as many people as possible busy with setting up the lounge bar as a communal encampment. There was plenty of seating for people to rest, and each of them had dragged their own mattress up to the area too. And an additional bonus was that they could open the doors on either side to keep fresh breeze flowing through. Their precious supplies were now stored in the duty-free shop with a door they were able to secure with a padlock and key.

While many had taken to sleeping in cabins in the deck below, just as many people wanted to stay near him and the crew. He scanned a couple resting nearby. They looked peaceful. But it was a cruel illusion. Sleep was a necessity. Everyone was exhausted.

Starvation was another factor exacerbating their fatigue. More than half of them had been suffering sea sickness for days.

A shudder rumbled through Rose of the Sea, low and deep, like she was a giant trembling dog. Sykes sat up this time and when he blinked at Gunner, Gunner placed his finger over his lips. *Keep quiet.*

Stifling a yawn, Sykes frowned at him and Gunner shrugged.

Rose shuddered again. This time it was significant enough to have a portion of the crowd stirring. Gunner jumped to his feet, and careful not to step on anyone, he strode to the outside deck. Sykes and Quinn joined him. The nearly full moon added additional light to the pre-dawn sky, providing a decent visual over the ocean. Eight-foot waves were big enough to be visible, but not too big to be trouble.

Clutching the railing, he rode the ship's dip to port side. Without ballast, once she'd started the perpetual rolling it was likely never to stop. Size didn't matter when it came to competing against the ocean.

Rose began her steady rise upward and the railing beneath his fingers quivered like it was high-tensile wire that'd been flicked.

Sykes' eyes bulged. "What the hell's that?"

Shaking his head, Gunner leaned far over the railing, peering up the length of the ship toward the front, but in the dim light, he saw nothing out of the ordinary—except for the tail of the plane and a mighty big hole in the side of the ship, that was.

The ship slumped into the next swell, but when it shuddered this time, it came with a horrific noise, like a demonic scream. Gunner shot a glance at the two men at his sides. Their fear-riddled eyes confirmed their dread.

He turned and sprinted through Blossoms, no longer caring who saw. At the starboard-side deck, clutching the railing, he peered over the side and up the length of the ship.

Air punched from his lungs. "Jesus Christ!"

A huge container ship was wedged against Rose of the Sea.

Gunner ran along the railing and shot in through an open set of doors, and as he raced past dozens of mattresses lined up on the floor, passengers popped up, jolted from their slumber. His dash across the room would alarm them, but he couldn't help it. His thumping feet were matched with the pounding boots of Sykes and Quinn behind him. He raced down a set of stairs, then another, and when he sprinted onto the promenade deck, he just about choked on his tongue.

Rows and rows of shipping containers were lined up alongside Rose of the Sea. It was as if they'd pulled into port, except they were moving up and down in opposing directions. As Rose went up, the other ship lumbered down, each countering the swell of the other.

"Fucking hell!" Sykes' hollered as he clutched the railing.

When Rose lowered into the trough, she released an almighty squeal as her sides scraped against the container ship.

"Why isn't it being pushed away?" Quinn asked.

"By the list on that ship," Gunner shouted, "my guess is she's wedged up against something. Maybe another ship, or worse, a reef."

"Why's that worse?"

"If it's a reef, her hull will be shredding to pieces and without power, we've got no chance of getting separated."

The crowd doubled in a matter of minutes. Alarm flared across all their faces.

Gunner peered over the shuddering railing again as the Gannila clashed into Rose of the Sea. The point of impact affected about three decks. His ship was taking another battering. How much more could she take? She was twenty-five years old, but she was sturdy. This old girl could've gone for another fifty years. Before she'd become a total write-off, that was.

Rose did another bone-rattling shudder and emitted a deafening screech like she was experiencing an exorcism. Bolts of dread shot up Gunner's spine.

He turned to Sykes. "We need to get onto that ship. I doubt there's anyone alive. If there was, they'd be looking at us right now. But we need to check. And, as dishonorable as it is, we need to raid their ship for supplies. We're desperate enough. Who knows? Maybe they have a Morse code machine."

First Officer Sykes was a big man, bigger than Gunner by a good four inches. He was built like a fridge too. Normally he looked like he could handle anything. This was not normal, and for the first time since everything went to shit, Sykes' troubled eyes showed signs of him cracking. "Agreed. How?"

"Don't know yet. Follow me." Gunner pushed through the crowd, ignoring questions the terrified passengers fired at him.

"Is it damaging our ship?"

"Where did it come from?"

"Should we abandon ship?"

He couldn't answer any of them anyway.

By the time Gunner had sprinted down to deck six, the sun was a golden haze on the horizon, and the additional light made the cargo ship look even more ominous. As the two boats came together again, he leaned over the railing to assess the impact.

Thanks to the minor swell, the two ships were barely kissing. But when the tide turned and the wind and swell started ramming them into that cargo ship, it was going to be a different story.

He turned to Sykes. Cloe, Quinn, Jae-Ellen, and Pauline stepped up to form a huddle around him. "We need to get over there. Any thoughts on how we do it?"

"Just jump over." Gunner turned to the voice. The bald man with a red beard standing behind Jae-Ellen had a weird grin on his face, like he was actually enjoying himself. He'd seen the man around a few times, but for the most part, the passenger had kept his distance. Gunner forced back a retort. "Any other thoughts?"

"Actually, I'm with this guy." Sykes thumbed at the bearded man.

"Zon." The man offered his name and stepped up to their huddle.

"I'm with Zon." Sykes nodded at him. "Jumping over there is the only way."

Gunner eyeballed the towers of shipping containers as they swayed with the roll of the Korean ship. They were stacked five containers high, like giant Lego blocks. Only these had the potential to be lethal. A coil of dread twisted in his gut at what Sykes was proposing.

Sykes unclenched his jaw. "We'll need to—"

"Just—" Gunner held up his hands, cutting Sykes off. "Just, let me think this through." The boats collided again and Gunner looked over the railing and timed the connection. Seventeen seconds from initial impact to parting. It was sufficient time to jump over to it, but it could be a different story when it came to returning to Rose.

"Captain, I'll look for the best place to make the jump." Sykes' voice was assertive, and without waiting for Gunner's response, he strode toward a section where two life rafts had been ripped from their brackets by the colliding ship.

Everyone, including Gunner, followed him.

If they'd had a full contingent of passengers, the loss of the two life rafts would've been a problem. But now that they were down to just eighty-two survivors, they had more than enough.

Eighty-two souls. The death toll was sickening.

Gunner gripped the railing and as he leaned out to watch yet another collision, he hoped like hell that, come lunchtime, there wouldn't be more bodies to add to his morbid list.

As Rose's starboard dipped into the swell, the Gannila shunted upward. At the pinnacle, the stacks of shipping containers towered several decks above them, but the cargo ship's main deck was barely a few feet away. As the boats shifted, he glanced through a row of containers at the sunrise glistening off the water on the other side.

He studied the dual movements six times, analyzing the situation and counting the seconds of contact. A plan firmed in his mind and he turned to the crew. "Okay, this does look like the best place to jump. If I time it right, it'll be easy."

"Whoa . . . Captain. Sir. You are not going anywhere." Sykes dropped a bombshell on Gunner's plans. "You cannot leave this ship."

"I will not be asking any of you to do—"

"You didn't ask, sir." Sykes thrust his chin forward. "I volunteer."

"Yo, me too." Zon's weird grin had Gunner wondering if the man was missing a few brain cells.

"Thank you, Zon. But you're a passenger; I can't ask you to do that."

"You didn't."

Gunner shook his head. "It should be me."

"No, sir." Sykes shifted his feet apart as if preparing to wrestle. "Rose of the Sea is your responsibility. The Captain stays on the ship."

The decision was taken out of Gunner's hands and the effect was like a grenade being lobbed at his feet. His thoughts shattered to a million pieces and a thousand unanswerable questions whizzed across his brain.

But as Gunner watched the preparations unfold with crippling distress, one question slammed into his conscious over and over.

Were Sykes and Zon about to be added to his unacceptable tally of deceased?

Chapter Forty-Six

ZON

Zon knew every one of 'em fuckers was watchin' him. They was probably hoping he missed the jump and face-planted into the hull. Or, for a real show . . . that he missed everything and splashed into the ocean below.

It was time to prove 'em all wrong.

Sykes was already over there, and he'd done it just fine. Zon wasn't worried he wouldn't make it. But he didn't wanna make no fool of his-self either. Not with Jessie standing at the front of that railing, watchin' him.

The other ship dropped lower and lower and the second it started to rise again, he aimed for the gap between a row of shipping containers and jumped. The change in direction from one ship to the next caught him unawares and even though he landed on his feet, he went ass over tit and rolled headfirst into a forty-foot container. Didn't hurt none, but after rubbing his skull, he blinked in surprise at the blood on his fingers.

"Shit, Zon, are you okay?" Sykes tapped him on the shoulder.

"Yeah, it's nothing."

"You sure?"

He wiped the blood on his pants. "Yep. I've had worse."

"Okay then, let's get this done." Sykes took off, running ahead without waiting for him.

Zon glanced up at the row of containers and between the moving clouds and rocking ship. It looked like the fuckin' things were swaying.

He tried to keep up with Sykes, but with his missing toe, runnin' just about killed him. He was dizzy too. Probably 'cause them fuckers were starving him with their rationing crap. He'd barely eaten in the last twenty-four hours. It was a wonder he could move at all.

Most of the cargo ship's top deck was covered in shipping containers but at the back, about a football field away, was the wheelhouse. That was where they was headed.

He couldn't believe Captain Dickhead was hoping someone was alive. The last thing they needed were more fuckin' mouths to feed. Zon was happy that people were still dropping like flies. Each morning, there'd been more dead bodies. So long as it wasn't him kickin' it, or Jessie, he was mighty fine with that.

Up ahead, Sykes reached the door to the tower. He turned and nodded at Zon, like he was checking he was still followin', then he went on inside. The door was shut by the time Zon got there, and it pissed him off that Sykes hadn't waited. But the second he opened the door, a rotten stench hit him like one of his daddy's sucker punches. Death.

He inhaled fresh air, then stepped through the doorway.

The room was about the size of one of 'em shipping containers. The walls were mostly windows and some of 'em were open. It had a few tables and chairs, and Sykes was just standin' there with his hand over his mouth and eyes that were as big as Zon's mama's cakehole, which she never shut. Zon searched for a body or bodies, or whatever was making the stink. He didn't need to look far. An arm was visible near the corner of the room, hidden behind an overturned table.

Suddenly, the arm moved. Zon glanced from the arm to Sykes. He mustn't a seen it 'cause he didn't move. "Hey, he's alive."

"Shit." Sykes dashed toward it, and when a pile of birds burst into the air all squawking and shit, Zon was grateful it hadn't been him checkin' it out.

Sykes reeled backward, lookin' like he was gonna chuck his guts up. "Son of a bitch!"

Zon gawked at the body. It was a bloody mess. Eyes gone. Lips gone. Flesh mangled. Zon had never seen anything so disgusting. And he'd seen his share of rotten, half-eaten animals out in the swamps.

"Fucking hell." Sykes strode away and paused at an exit leading deeper into the ship. "You coming?"

This time, he waited for Zon before he opened the door.

They entered a corridor and the stench was worse than anything Zon had ever smelled. And that was sayin' somethin'. His granddaddy's body, after they'd dragged him off the crawfish griddle, had been the worst stink up until now.

"Fuck me, this's bad." Sykes pulled his shirt up and covered his mouth with it and his hand.

Zon did the same.

They had three ways they could go: up, down, and straight ahead. Zon waited for Sykes to decide, then followed him up the metal rungs. The boat's angle shifted and when the whole fuckin' thing rattled and a roar bellowed up the stairwell, Sykes gripped the walls like he was gonna shit his pants.

When it stopped, Sykes bolted up the stairs like he had a firecracker up his ass. He paused at the top for Zon. Zon gulped a breath and nodded that he was ready.

But when they pushed inside, the stink wasn't that bad. The open windows woulda helped.

"Hello? Is anyone here?" Sykes strode to a pile of computer monitors. They were blank and a microphone that dangled on a spiral cord bounced from side to side with the sway of the ship.

Zon spied a stack of soda and beer cans in the corner and walked toward them. He was two feet away when he found the reason behind the stink. The body slumped on the floor didn't look no good, and there weren't no way Zon was gonna check he was alive. He turned to Sykes. "Hey, there's a body here."

Sykes strode over. There was no need to check for a pulse. The dude's grey face was enough to know he was a goner.

"What do ya think happened?" Zon asked.

Sykes shrugged. "Same as us. Without fresh water, disease is rife. It could have been any number of things."

"Shit, huh." Zon shook his head, pretending he was sad. "How long they been dead, you reckon?"

Sykes frowned. "Days, probably." He returned to the computers and as he jabbed a few keys, the boat did its rumble thing again. "Their system's fried too. Come on. Let's keep moving."

Zon glanced out the window. A crowd of people were lined up on the cruise ship, looking their way. "Hey, they can see us." He waved and a heap of people waved back.

Sykes looked at him all weird, but Zon just shrugged and waved again. When he turned away from the window, the cans caught his attention and he picked up a beer. It was empty. "Think they'll have more beer stashed?"

Sykes nodded at the can. "Hopefully they have some food or drink." He opened the door and disappeared into the stairwell.

Zon followed Sykes out the door and back down the stairs. This time, he went along the narrow corridor and the metallic squeals were even louder.

"Hello?" As he walked along, Sykes yelled between the screechin'. "Hello, is anyone here?"

The doors along the passage that weren't shut opened and slammed over and over. With that goin' on, and the boat creaking and groaning like it was alive or somethin', it was creepy. And Zon didn't do creepy.

With each step, the passage grew darker. They checked out two rooms and found three more bodies. Sykes didn't even bother confirming they were dead. One look was enough.

The next room they went into, though, the guy looked like he musta just died. Like minutes ago. His skin was normal and he was sitting in a chair with a book in his lap. The whole time Sykes had his fingers beneath the dude's chin, Zon expected the body to wake up and start swinging.

But he didn't. Pity. Zon woulda liked to have seen that.

Sykes stood, and when he looked over Zon's shoulder his eyes snapped even wider, like he was shittin' bullets.

Zon spun around and looked right into the eyes of the fuckin' walking dead. "Fuck me." He stumbled backward.

A scrawny white dude was in the doorway, and the stupid fucker was naked. Blood covered his lips and chin, and his squinty eyes were so fuckin' red that he doubted he could even see. The color of his skin was like his granddaddy's was, not after they'd pulled him off the flaming griddle, but just before that, when it was gray, like the underside of a fish that'd spent its life scavenging in the mud.

The man took a step forward and some kinda weird noise came outta his mouth. Like he'd lost his tongue or somethin'. Maybe that was what all the blood was about. The dude had eaten his tongue. As Zon pondered whether that was even possible, Sykes pushed past him and stepped up to the walking stiff.

"Hey, buddy, it's okay. We're here to save you."

"Help me." His voice was straight outta a crappy ghost movie, all wobbly and cursed.

"We will. We're here to help." Sykes led the man into the room and sat him down on a chair next to the other dead dude. The weirdo either didn't know he was naked or didn't give a fuck. Sykes solved the issue by snatching a pillow off the bed and placing it across the man's lap.

A bloody bald patch on his scalp made it look like he'd pulled out a fistful of his own hair. His mouth stayed open and his breath came out in a creepy wheeze, like he'd been punched in the throat.

"See if you can find water." Sykes eyeballed Zon.

"Yeah, all right." Zon stepped back through the door and bounced off the walls as he strode up the narrow passage. It was hot and dark, and the squealing was fuckin' noisy. Unlike Sykes, he didn't bother knocking on the doors. He just shoved them open, scanned inside, and kept on goin'.

In one room, he found three bodies. He didn't bother checking if they was alive. Just like when his grandmama died, these guys had checked out with their mouths open and their tongues stickin' out, like they'd been strangled to death. Maybe they had.

That thought hit him like a punch in the nose.

Maybe they had been strangled to death. Runnin' out of water woulda made 'em do crazy things. Last man standing got whatever was left.

Last man standin' looked to be the zombie Sykes was tending to.

Now that'd be interestin'.

Chapter Forty-Seven

ZON

Zon pushed open another door and stepped into a kitchen. He strode toward the fridge. Two steps later he jumped back.

"Ahhh fuck." Two bodies were on the floor.

But that wasn't the problem. Rats were crawling all over 'em.

Rats! Why did it have to be rats? He could handle any other critter . . . snakes, spiders, roaches. But not them filthy bastards. It was his mama's fault. She'd told him the half-moon shaped scar on his arm was from rats. According to her, they'd feasted on him while he was still in his cot. Over the years, he'd got to thinkin' about that story. And if he had been eaten by rats, then it was her fuckin' fault. Whether it was true or not, he hated her for that. Hell, he hated her for a whole lotta stuff.

Fuckin' vermin. He'd take a gator any day. At least that beast had some pride.

Rats . . . they ate their own.

He grabbed a chair and flung it at the feasting swarm and they darted all over the place. Which was way fucking worse. He shoulda left 'em where they were. Some, though, kept right on chewing, either oblivious or fearless. He grabbed another chair, ready to chuck it at 'em if needed, and with one eye on the corner of the room and one eye covering the rats, he strode toward the fridge. He was halfway there, when he realized it was propped open, so his hope that there'd be somethin' worth eating quickly evaporated.

Stepping around another dining table, he tugged the fridge door wide and jumped back. "Fuck. Fuck. Fuck!" A crap-load of rats spilled from the shelving. Whatever had been wrapped in the tin foil was long gone. Hell, even the foil was half-eaten.

He slammed the fridge shut. The fuckers still inside would probably eat themselves to death.

Using a broom handle, he tugged open the cupboards and except for a pile of rusty old tools, they were all empty.

He turned on the kitchen tap and wasn't surprised when it didn't work.

Zon spun back to the door. A dark patch on the floor caught his eye.

His heart skipped a beat.

A gun.

It was sitting right there in the middle of the kitchen . . . in full view, like it'd just been used.

He collected the Glock and checked the magazine. Three bullets. One whiff of the barrel was enough to figure it'd recently been used. He turned to the bodies, searching for bullet holes in their foreheads. But with the rats feasting on their faces, it was impossible to decide if it had been the cause of their deaths.

Zon shrugged. He'd had his share of lucky days lately. Today was another. He pushed the gun into the back of his jocks, pulled up his jeans, covered it with his shirt, and ramped his search up to triple time. Now he was less focused on food and water, and more on weapons and bullets. He found a bolt-cutter and chain, but both were too heavy to keep as weapons.

The heat in that kitchen became more unbearable with each cupboard door he opened. And he couldn't ignore the fuckin' rats . . . their smell . . . their gnawing teeth . . . fucking darting about the place. Deciding to settle with his lucky find, he headed back toward Sykes and the zombie. The gun metal touching his lower back already had him feeling stronger.

Sykes looked up as Zon re-entered the room. "How'd you go?"

Zon shook his head. "Found more dead people. Nine I think." He hadn't thought to count 'em. Not that it mattered. "No food or water."

"Yeah, he told me as much."

"He's talking, huh?" Zon assessed Zombie, checking out his bloodshot eyes, and wonderin' if the scrawny fucker woulda had it in him to kill the others.

"Yeah, his English is minimal and he's really weak. Delirious too. He can't tell me if it's been three or four days since he last had water and food. He told me the Captain took their only life raft along with all their supplies. He's the only survivor."

"Shit, huh? What an asshole. The Captain, I mean. Not him." Although . . . Zombie could be an asshole. They just didn't know yet.

"Give me a hand. We have to get him out of here." Sykes raised Zombie to his feet and when the pillow dropped to the floor, Zon couldn't believe he was still fuckin' naked. Zombie wobbled and Sykes wrapped his arm around his waist and hooked his bony arm up over his shoulder. Zombie's eyes were open but it was like he couldn't move them or something 'cause all he did was stare at the wall.

"Come on." Sykes hissed at Zon. "Help me."

Zon raised his hands and backed away. "Ain't no way I'm touching that."

"You'll do as I say, and that's an order."

"Fuck off. I don't take no orders from no one."

"Ahhh, for fuck's sake." Sykes shuffled forward and Zombie half-stepped, half-dragged his feet.

Zon held the door open and as the pair shuffled past, Sykes glared at Zon, but if it was meant to be a death stare, Zon had seen better on his bitchface sister.

Zon was stuck behind 'em, and the whole time, as they bounced off the walls, all he could look at was Zombie's white ass. The dude sure could use a bit of sun. "You shoulda dressed him, ya dickhead."

Sykes groaned. "Well, go find some clothes."

The way Sykes said it confirmed Zon was right.

"And make it snappy. This rocking is getting worse."

Zon strode back down the passage, pushed into the first room he reached and stepped over a body to open the cupboard. He plucked a pair of pants from the shelf and a shirt off a hanger. But before he returned to Sykes, he searched the room. He wasn't looking for no food or water, though that'd be nice. He was lookin' for guns and ammo.

He rifled through two more rooms, but figuring his delay wouldn't look so good, he strode back to Sykes.

The ship shuddered up and down, makin' more damn noise than his mama did in the shitter.

Sykes was waiting for him at the intersection of the three doors. "We have to get out of here, Zon, so fucking help me."

Maybe it was the feel of the cold metal of the gun at his back that made Zon feel all generous, 'cause he let Sykes shove Zombie into his arms to hold him upright. Zon wanted to get this shit over with. He had a gun he needed to stash.

Gritting his teeth, and trying to block out the rotten stench coming from Zombie's breath, Zon held the scrawny asshole upright while Sykes pulled the duds on. The second he was dressed, Zon shoved Zombie back at Sykes, shuffled around 'em and opened the door to the outer deck. His nose whistled as he sucked in the fresh air, but the wind howling through the containers, like it was possessed or something, blocked it out.

When they'd first got on the cargo ship it had rolled from side to side. Now it was up, down, side to side, and bucking like a gator with a bullet in its jaw. It was makin' it damn near impossible to stay upright. Especially once they got in amongst the shipping containers. Zon kept watchin' 'em, wonderin' if the damn things could actually keel over. He'd like to see that. There'd be all sorts of shit inside 'em. Computers. TVs. Hell, there could even be cars. He could be standing amongst a gold mine. A soon-to-be-deserted gold mine.

And the whole damn lot was gonna end up on the bottom of the ocean.

With an ear-splitting screech, the ship bucked sideways, and both him and Sykes tumbled over. Zombie hit the deck like a dead man and as Zon scrambled upright again, he watched the scrawny dude for a bit, hopin' he really was a dead man.

But no, no such luck.

Zon eyeballed Sykes. His eyes were as big as beer cans. Zon had felt fear before . . . known it like it was injected into his veins. He wasn't even close to that now. Sykes, though . . . he looked like he'd seen the devil his-self. "What?" Zon bellowed over the bedlam.

Sykes ran in the opposite direction of the cruise ship. Zon chased after him.

Without warning, the whole damn place scuttled sideways, knocking him off his feet. Zon's head slammed into a shipping container, givin' him another whack that hurt way worse than the last one. Ignorin' it, though, he scrambled his-self upright and chased after Sykes.

He reached Sykes' side and the damn deck dropped out beneath him. Zon gripped the railing as they fell a good ten feet. Lucky he'd hung on or he'd a gone ass over tit into the ocean.

"Fucking hell." Sykes was leaning over, looking down. "She *is* stuck on a reef."

Zon peered over the railing. Waves crashed onto a crap-load of jagged rocks that covered an area about the size of his bayou back home.

"Jesus Christ." Sykes pulled away from the railing and looked at Zon like he had a hook in his eye. "There's no way we're getting this ship off that reef. She'll start breaking up in no time."

As if it were agreein', the boat screeched like a fucking psycho and slammed down again.

"We need to get Rose off this thing, or we'll go down with her."

"How?"

"No idea. Come on. Let's tell the Captain."

Sykes took off and Zon tried to keep up. He was halfway back to Zombie when the ship crashed down again. A massive groan roared around him. He shot his gaze upward and the air punched from his lungs.

"Fuck!" Zon dived backward, scrambling on his hands and knees, as an entire row of shipping containers tipped sideways and slammed into another tower. It was the loudest fuckin' thing he'd ever heard.

"Fuck, Zon, get out of there!" Sykes waved him forward.

Zon clambered to his feet and with one eye on the wobbling padlocked towers and one eye on Sykes, he ran faster than he'd done in years. With each crippled step, he expected the toppled containers to make him into mincemeat. The towers swayed. Sykes' eyes grew bigger. The groaning got louder. Zon's heart set to explode as he dove out of the row of containers, skidded across the deck and landed at Sykes' feet.

Sykes clapped him on the back and offered his hand to help him up. "Jesus, man, you've got some balls."

Zon grinned, barely noticing his nose was whistlin'.

"Let's get out of here." Sykes bent over to pick up Zombie, whose head had rolled back and mouth had fallen open.

"You sure he's alive?"

A frown messed up Sykes' forehead as he put two fingers beneath Zombie's chin. "Yeah, he's alive, but barely."

The cargo ship jolted sideways, takin' the legs out from under 'em. Zon slammed to the ground ass-first, but Sykes and Zombie weren't so lucky. Sykes came up with blood on his chin, and the other guy now had a cut across his cheek that made the Zombie name suit even better.

Zon dusted his hands and eyeballed Sykes. "So, genius . . . any ideas on how you're gonna get Zombie over to our ship?"

When Sykes pulled a face, confirmin' he had no fuckin' clue, Zon shook his head. "Well . . . while you're thinking that shit through, I'm gonna check out what's in these containers."

Zon didn't bother waitin' for no response.

Instead, he trotted toward the wheelhouse, and in particular, the kitchen cupboard where he'd seen that large bolt cutter.

Chapter Forty-Eight

GUNNER

Gunner's heart had just about stopped as he'd watched Sykes and Zon jump over to the Korean ship, and it didn't get any better when they landed safely or when they disappeared into the wheelhouse.

But he had things to do, and he had to believe that Sykes and Zon would make it back safely.

His eyes shot to the rising sun. Clouds were brewing on the horizon, but not enough to warrant concern. Thankfully, the breeze was minimal . . . it'd barely register on the anemometer. *If* they had a working one, that was. It made him realize just how technology dependent they'd become. He'd always been obsessed with weather watching; now it was even more important.

Rose bucked beneath his feet and screamed her objection at the collision with the other vessel. The swell was driving them into the giant rust bucket, but high tide was protecting them somewhat. When the wind picked up, as it always did in the afternoon, they'd be in serious trouble.

What they were experiencing now was nothing compared to what was coming.

They were positioned to take a battering. And he wasn't sure Rose of the Sea could take much more.

Forcing his gaze from the cargo ship, he turned to his remaining crew. They all looked like he felt: completely shattered. They were also looking to him for answers. He wiped sweat from his brow. "We have about five hours before the swell decreases. Do you agree, Pauline?"

Pauline's diminutive frame seemed to have shrunk in the recent days. Her eyes were sunken too, no longer offering the intelligent spark they'd had when he'd first met her and she'd talked about her new fiancé. She blinked up at him as if trying to formulate a response. "Yes, sir. I concur."

"And the wind. How long is it going to remain like this?"

Again she blinked, then she turned her gaze to the sun, and something shifted in her eyes. Maybe she was contemplating if it would be the last sunrise she'd ever see.

Clenching his jaw, he slapped that thought away. "Pauline?"

She jumped. "Sorry, sir. Yes, it will begin to ramp up within two hours."

"Right." He fought simultaneous urges to question her certainty and hit the major panic button. If she was right, they had one hell of a tight time schedule on their hands. "We need to get away from that ship. ASAP." As his peers looked at him with wide, fearful eyes, the enormity of the situation truly hit home.

For his entire career, he'd contemplated being the Captain of his own ship. He'd idolized the idea. Romanticized it. Even pretended it was *the* most important goal in his life. He'd been so wrong. Nothing was more important than the passengers and crew around him. But even more so, his wife and daughter. His family, who were counting on him to get home.

Precious lives were in his hands.

It didn't matter how he got the captaincy role. He had a job to do.

Command this ship.

A powerful sense of honor blazed through him. The headache that'd started the second he opened his eyes that morning hit a whole new level, but he forced it away. Unclenching his jaw, he tried to ignore the crowd gathering around them and looked at each of his crew in turn. "In about five hours, we'll have both the tide and the wind against us. Our best opportunity to get us off that monstrosity is right now. I'm open to any ideas on how we move our seventy—thousand-ton ship without power."

Quinn cleared his throat. "Could we try to catch the wind somehow? Like a giant sail?"

Gunner tried to picture how to construct such a contraption. "Good idea, but I think the time involved in doing that would outweigh the possible outcome."

"What about decreasing the weight of the ship? We could toss things overboard to lighten our weight," Jae-Ellen offered.

Gunner shook his head. "The heaviest items are the ones that will be impossible to move, and the time involved with tossing hundreds of small items will be a waste. But good suggestion."

"Could we put the anchor into a life raft and somehow haul it out over there." Quinn pointed to port side. "Drop it into the ocean and then just winch us away."

Gunner didn't need to think about this one. "Each link in the anchor chain weighs three hundred and fifty pounds. Put them together, and there's no way any of us can lift the chain, let alone the anchor."

Rose emitted another high-pitched squeal. Gunner clutched onto the railing and glanced at the water between the two ships. An idea began to form. He turned back to the group and felt the weight of a decision in their eyes.

"Here's what we're going to do. We'll toss anything that floats over this side. With a bit of luck, it'll provide a buffer between us." The crew began nodding. "Anything that cushions us from getting pummeled is a good thing. The more we toss into the gap, the greater the distance will grow."

Another horrific crunch reverberated through Rose. Gunner silently prayed it wasn't her hull shredding apart. So far, the damage looked superficial. But it was only a matter of time before that changed.

Time they didn't have.

"Okay." Gunner stepped back and turned to the crowd that were hovering around. "Listen up, people. We need everyone's help. We have to toss anything that floats, like mattresses, plastic chairs or foam, over this side to create a cushion between the two ships. First, I need two people to stay here and relay any messages from Sykes and Zon. Cloe, that's you and Brandi." The young girl did a double take, and he recalled her defiant expression the first time he'd met her. The poor girl had aged ten years in the last four days. The prospect of imminent death did that. "Yes? You got it?"

"Yes, sir." Cloe nodded.

"Okay, anyone who is able, follow me." Gunner strode along the deck and entered through the single fire door at the end. The bulk of deck six was cabins—exactly what he needed. These cabins had already been raided for food, water, and medication, so every door had been smashed open. He strode into the first cabin, yanked a mattress from the top bunk and tossed it toward Quinn, who hooked it and a second mattress under his arms and disappeared out the door.

Cindy was next. The young bartender still had glitter on her cheeks. Her smile was gone though.

Lindsay, one of the passengers who was always quick to offer his help, stepped forward next. The retired train driver was in his seventies, yet he had more vitality than some of the younger crew. His wife, however, was the opposite and the poor thing had been suffering terribly with sea sickness.

The ragtag team of crew and willing passengers took turns transporting the mattresses from Gunner to the outer deck, where they tossed them overboard.

Cabin after cabin, they repeated the process. Sweat dripped down his back and under his arms, and caked in his hair. The rooms were stifling hot, and without water and little food in his belly, with each new cabin came increasing dizziness. But Gunner didn't stop.

The pressure to have this plan succeed was like having crosshairs on his back. Only the shooter was a massive rust bucket set on dragging their ship and everybody onboard her down with it. The agony over the debate to abandon ship grew with each mattress he tugged free.

There were still only two options.

Stay on the ship and hope for a rescue.

Or scramble to the life rafts and hope to find land.

Stay and fight, or jump and pray?

It was like teetering on the edge of a giant cliff with a starving tiger eyeballing them for dinner.

Neither option was good.

Chapter Forty-Nine

GUNNER

"Sir. Captain." Cloe's voice lurched Gunner's brain from the tumbling abyss.

He searched for the voice, and the room and everyone in it wobbled like apparitions. He struggled to focus. Stars darted across his vision, and blinking them away, he saw her standing at the door. "Cloe? Is everything okay?"

"Yes, sir. Zon found a container full of baby products, and we thought that you might be interested in the baby formula."

"Baby formula!" He huffed. "That's like finding gold."

"That's what we thought, sir. Sykes and Zon can toss the tins over, but we'll need you all to help us catch them."

Gunner nodded, straightened, and blinked back his dizziness. The idea of returning to fresh air sounded almost as good as a cold beer. Almost. "Come on. Let's take a break and go help."

Gunner followed the small group of men and women who'd been proving themselves time and time again since everything went to hell. They looked like they'd just finished playing a football grand final which they'd lost, badly.

"I can't believe I'm saying this . . ." Quinn chuckled, ". . . but I'm pretty darn keen to eat some of that baby food."

"As long as you don't start crying like a baby." Cloe slapped her husband on his shoulder. "Or shitting like one."

"Num, num, num, get me some baby food in ma belly." Quinn rubbed his stomach, and as he and everyone else laughed along, Gunner wished he'd met them all under better circumstances.

The instant they arrived at the railing, two-pound tins of baby formula started flying across the gap. Gunner's energy returned almost immediately with the excitement of those around him. Just the thought of having food, even though it was baby food, was a dose of elixir for everyone.

But with each tin Gunner caught, images of his baby girl, Bella, flashed across his mind. Her laughing. Her dancing. Her brilliant smile that lit up the room. A blaze of guilt rocketed through him. He should be with his wife and daughter. They needed him. How much had the EMP affected them? Had Adelle rallied with their neighbors, Phil and Roxanne, who helped her so much when Gunner was away and during Adelle's cancer treatment. Was her father helping? Or was he downing the whiskey instead?

Their marriage was perfect. It was so exciting when they'd decided to start a family. But it wasn't easy. Adelle had two miscarriages before their beautiful daughter was born. Bella was six weeks premature and things were a little touch-and-go for a while. But she was now seven years old. . . going on thirteen. Every time he returned home, Bella was just that little bit bigger and much cheekier.

Rose of the Sea pitched sideways, jolting Gunner back to reality.

A dozen passengers, who'd been standing back, tumbled over like they'd been hit with an invisible wrecking ball. Screaming, they were a mass of uncontrollable limbs as they hit the railing full on.

Five of them went right over the top.

Gunner dashed forward, but he was too late. He leaned over the side, desperate to see them. Their screams stopped when they hit the water. He tried to spot them amongst the masses of mattresses. But it was impossible. They were gone.

"No!" A man bolted to the railing. It was Lindsay, who until moments ago, had been helping Gunner with the mattresses.

First Fate

"Cheryl! Cheryl. Oh God. No." He burst into wracking sobs and fell to his knees. "No. No. No."

It happened so quickly. Nobody'd had time to think.

Five more people dead. Just like that. Never to see their families again.

Will I ever see my wife and daughter again?

Shoving the thought aside, he dashed to help the eight lucky people who'd been on the brink of death. As he pulled them back, he declared that no matter what, he would make it home to his wife and daughter. Even if it took years.

Years!

Could it really take that long?

God, he hoped not.

There was no time to mourn the new losses of life, and maybe the crew arrived at the same conclusion because they quickly lined up at the railing with him again and resumed catching the tins.

Thankfully, most of the curious onlookers had retreated inside, and Gunner didn't have to worry about any of them tumbling overboard. Max curled his arm around Lindsay's shoulder and led the inconsolable man away. Gunner made a mental note to offer his condolences to Lindsay as soon as he was free.

When Rose shuddered beneath him and parted from the cargo ship, Gunner glanced between them. There had to be at least three hundred mattresses down there and yet the two ships were still slamming into each other.

He'd been certain his mattress idea would work.

Now, though? He wasn't so sure.

It seemed like hours before Sykes and Zon tossed the last of the tins, and when half the guys crumbled to the ground with absolute exhaustion, Gunner stepped forward, gripping the rail. "Anything else worth saving?" he yelled across the void.

Sykes cupped his mouth. "No, sir. Just fancy cars. Fridges and freezers. Televisions. Nothing of value."

The irony in his response was almost laughable.

Would he ever know a normal day again?

Gunner glanced to the heavens. He wasn't one to resort to praying, but this seemed like as good a time as any to start. As a lone albatross dipped and swooped nearby, he silently prayed that all the remaining souls on Rose of the Sea made it home to safety.

His ship bucked and groaned beneath him, as if she'd heard his prayers, but she had a completely different plan.

Chapter Fifty

ZON

Zon was fucking tired of tossing them damn tins. There were thousands of 'em. The first shipping container he'd broken into, he'd thought he'd hit the big time. It had just two cars: a Jaguar I-Pace and a Porsche 911 turbo. Sweet rides. He'd a done anythin' to take one of 'em for a spin.

The next container was loaded to the max with fancy TVs and stereos. He'd never had anything like it, and it was a damn shame they was gonna end up on the bottom of the ocean. The fridges and freezers were boring and he was shitty that he'd wasted time breakin' into that container. But when he'd found the fuckin' baby food and crap, Sykes had carried on like he'd dug up treasure or somethin'.

Zon felt totally ripped off. All that fancy stuff within reach and not a damn thing he could do about it.

By the time they'd finished tossing the tins over to the others, he'd decided that if Captain Dickhead didn't reward him with much more than the scabby rations he'd been getting so far, then the new weapon in his jocks was gonna make a show very soon.

Rolling his shoulders, he turned to Sykes. He was bending over

Zombie who was still sprawled on his back, lookin' deader than ever.

Zon had forgotten all about the freak. "You got a plan for him yet?"

Sykes wiped his hand across his forehead and rubbed the sweat onto his pants. "Not yet." He hooked his arm around Zombie and dragged him toward where they'd jumped onto the ship. Each time the deck dropped out from below them, Sykes and Zombie slammed into a shipping container. Zon nearly tumbled over twice his-self. Things were getting out of control.

"He ain't gonna make it, you know," Zon said.

Sykes didn't respond.

"Just leave him here."

Sykes didn't respond to that neither, but he did attempt one of his pathetic death stares.

"What?" Zon shrugged. "Sometimes it's best to let nature do its thing. Besides, we don't have enough food for everyone already." It was only a matter of time before they'd be tossing Zombie overboard like all the other dead people. Zon was looking forward to that moment. It wasn't very often he got to say *I told you so.* Especially not to a man like Sykes, who thought his shit didn't stink.

When they finally got to the spot where they'd jumped across ships, Captain Dickhead and about twenty other people were all standing at the railing, looking over at them.

Sykes lowered Zombie to the deck, all careful like, then he picked up the rope they'd tossed across earlier, strode toward the nearest shipping container tower, and climbed up them like he was some kind a monkey. At the fourth one up, he looped the rope around the ladder and tied it off. The rope was on an angle that sloped from the shipping container down to the cruise ship.

Sykes climbed back down and squared off at Zon. "I'll need your help with the next bit."

"Yeah . . . what for?"

The boat slammed down again and Sykes fell flat on his ass. Zon thought it was kinda funny that the man who practically lived on boats couldn't keep his-self upright.

Sykes stood again, and this time when he looked at Zon, he scowled like he'd eaten a rotten shrimp. "I need your help."

"So you keep sayin'." Zon glanced from Zombie to Sykes and saw two things: one was a guy who was settin' to die any minute. The other was a guy who was desperate.

He saw one more thing. An opportunity.

"Okay," he said. "I'll help. But I want extra rations. Food and water."

"Fucking hell, you're a piece of work. You know that, don't you?"

Zon shrugged. "I'm telling you, he ain't gonna make it. And if you're makin' me risk my life to save a dead one, then I wanna get somethin' for it."

Sykes had his jaw clenched so tight, he was gonna snap a tooth for sure. Instead of answerin' Zon, he just picked up Zombie, flopped him over his shoulder and strode back to the container stack he'd tied the rope to. "Get over here, Zon."

Zon swaggered that way. "Do I get my extra rations?"

"I'll make sure you do," Sykes said it all calm, and Zon liked that Sykes had finally figured out who was in charge.

While Sykes climbed, Zon had to stop Zombie's sorry ass from fallin' off his shoulder. It wasn't easy, 'cause the freak's stupid feet kept getting caught. They were lucky Zombie only weighed a hundred and twenty pounds, or maybe less.

At the top, Zon had to hold Zombie while Sykes climbed onto the rope, which was flopping about all over the place. Sykes moved so he was hanging upside down with his hands and feet crossed over the rope.

"Feed him through, onto my stomach," Sykes yelled over the screeching boats.

Sykes' plan wasn't gonna work. But he did it anyways.

Hanging onto the container, he tried to hand over Zombie, but between the two of 'em hanging on, and the ship bucking all over the place, and zero help from the dead man, they were fucked.

Zombie toppled sideways and Zon only just managed to grab his scrawny ankle. He had no idea why he'd done that . . .

shoulda let Zombie go. Then they wouldn't a had the problem no more.

But when he heard a cheer from the cruise ship and glanced over to see the crowd waving and cheering, he got a warm an' fuzzy feelin' like when he drank too much tequila.

Damn, it felt fine.

Ten minutes after Sykes began his fucked-up idea, they were right back where they started . . . on the cargo ship's deck with Zombie flat on his back at their feet.

After Sykes stopped leaning over his knees and huffing and puffing like he'd run from a smash-an'-grab or somethin', he turned to the crowd, cupped his hands over his mouth and yelled, "I can't do it. I need more help."

"Okay," Captain Dickhead yelled back, and then him and his buddies huddled together.

Zon searched the crowd, hoping to see Jessie. The cargo ship bucked, catching him unawares. His feet whipped out from beneath him and he slammed into the corner of a container. Pain burst through his mangled foot and a howl burst from his throat. "Fuck!"

Stars darted across his eyes. Stabbing pain shot through his remaining toes.

He stood. He'd had enough of this shit. With fury driving him on, he picked up Zombie and tossed him over his shoulder like he'd done with dozens of animals.

"What're you doing?"

"Getting this shit over with so I can eat. I'm fucking starving."

At the front of the container, he shifted Zombie's body for better balance, then began climbing. Each time he reached for another grip hold, Zombie's head whacked the middle of Zon's back, and all he kept thinking about was Zombie's blood gettin' onto his Louisiana Ragin' Cajuns football jersey. It was his favorite. He'd even lined up to get his favorite player, Tillman, to sign it. And he didn't do lineups.

Sykes was with Zon when he reached the rope, and at exactly that moment, the two ships collided. A huge fuckin' boom followed. Zon figured that another tower of containers had lost it. Knowing his luck, the one he was on would be next. Then again, his luck was gettin' good these days.

The gun in the back of his jocks was proof a that.

Zon had no intention of hanging around to see if he was right though. He reached for the rope and secured Zombie's head between his arm and his neck. Then, as he dragged Zombie across his body, he countered his balance by putting his opposite foot onto the rope. Sykes helped him hook his other boot.

Hanging upside down, Zon dropped his head back so he could see where he was going, and hand over hand, he dragged his-self and Zombie's lifeless body toward the cruise ship.

People began cheering, and Zon couldn't help the smile bursting onto his face. Nobody had ever cheered for him, not even in his footy days.

The rope swung like crazy, and next second, the guts fell outta the cargo ship and the cruise ship went the other way. Now he was climbin' uphill. But it didn't stay like that long before it slammed back down again.

Another sonic boom confirmed more containers were goners.

The cheering got louder.

"You can do it."

"You're amazing."

"Go, Zon." The fact that they knew his name had him feeling a sensation he'd never had before. *Respect.*

"Don't look down."

Of course, that made him look down. He just about died at what he saw. He was right over the gap between the two ships. The ocean below was covered with mattresses, but also boiling with whitewater. If he lost it now, he'd be shark meat.

"Come on, Zon." A chick's voice drifted to him and when he tilted his head back again, he saw Jessie.

"Go, Zon."

His heart skipped a beat. A girl . . . no, not just any girl, a fuckin' hot chick was actually calling for him. Zon felt like he was the champion quarterback sprinting toward the goal line. The crowd was cheering. Every single muscle burned. His hands hurt. His ankles hurt.

And Zombie stunk like shit.

Three feet from the railing, the rope suddenly dropped.

Zon clung for his life.

He clenched his jaw.

The cargo ship halved in size. The cruise ship doubled. The angles were all wrong. With his eyes clamped shut, he could do nothing but cling on.

One second. Two. It took an eternity for them to change positions. *Six. Fifteen.*

It was like waiting for a mountain to move.

His body trembled. His arms quivered like a stray mutt who'd survived torrential rain.

His grip began to slip.

"Zon. You're nearly here."

"Don't let go."

"Go, Zon."

"Go, Zon!"

The crowd's chanting got louder.

"Go, Zon." Jessie's voice stood out from all of 'em, and he pictured her waiting for him completely naked.

That was a vision worth hanging on for.

Way too slowly, the rope's angle changed, then, as if a monster had picked up the cargo ship, the rope shifted back the other way.

Zon uncurled his fingers. Every one of them ached and his knuckles felt like they'd tripled in size. He clawed forward. Inch by inch.

Hands were thrust at him. Reaching for Zombie. Reaching for him. Clapping him on his back like he was a real hero. They lifted him off the rope and lowered him to the deck.

And then Jessie was there, right above him. Her long, dark hair tickled his chin. "You're amazing. You're a hero." Her grin was spectacular.

And in that perfect moment, Zon knew what it was like to feel special.

Chapter Fifty-One

GUNNER

It took the rest of the afternoon to finish raiding the cabins and once they'd exhausted the supply of mattresses, Gunner met with Sykes at the railing overlooking the cargo ship.

Gunner waited until Sykes had drunk his allocated share of water and caught his breath before he spoke. "I didn't get a chance to say it before, but well done with that guy. I'm not sure he's going to make it, but you did the right thing. Hard to believe the Captain abandoned them and took their supplies."

"Yeah." Sykes rolled his eyes. "It wasn't me who saved him though; it was Zon."

"Yes, I must thank him."

Sykes scanned the deck, possibly looking for the big bald guy, but they'd all disappeared inside. After the day they'd had, he wouldn't be surprised if everyone was already passed out asleep.

"He's a bit of an oddball, that one."

"Oh." Gunner frowned at his First Officer. "What do you mean?"

"He's strange. He told me to leave that guy to die on the cargo ship."

"Really?"

"Yep. He was going on about the natural order of things, and how not everyone should be saved."

Gunner frowned and scanned the deck again, but he and Sykes were the only ones out there.

"I'd be watching out for him if I were you." Sykes' tone turned severe.

What did he mean? Gunner studied the man he'd come to know much better than he'd imagined he would at the start of the fourteen-day cruise. Was he implying Zon might have had something to do with the deaths of those few passengers who had died without an obvious cause? There weren't many of them—a few each night. But still.

"Sir, there's something else."

The dire look in Sykes' eyes had Gunner inhaling a deep breath and mentally preparing for the new hell Sykes was about to unleash.

"That ship's wedged onto a reef. The way she's bucking up and down like that, she'll be ripped to shreds in no time. Unless the incoming tide is big enough for her to break free, she'll soon be sitting on top of the reef like a giant black dildo." Sykes offered an awkward laugh, then swallowed. "Once that happens . . ."

He didn't need to finish the sentence. Gunner could already picture the damage. Hardened steel was no match for jagged coral. It was a long pause before he turned his gaze away from the swaying cargo and back to Sykes. "We need to get away before those containers start flinging about."

"You read my mind."

"Any thoughts on what else we can do?"

"Not one."

Gunner turned toward the Gannila again. The Korean cargo ship was shorter than Rose of the Sea by about thirty feet. Just like Rose, she was without power but now unmanned and completely at the mercy of the elements. Six of the container stacks had already toppled, like giant sets of killer dominoes. Once the towers were off-balance, they'd be stripped from their attachments.

Once the boat started to break up, they'd be tossed into the ocean.

Gunner had seen firsthand the damage suffered by a ship running into a rogue shipping container floating on the surface. It wasn't pretty.

He guessed there were about a thousand mattresses still wedged between the two ships. But the wind direction wasn't behaving and despite their efforts, Rose was still pinned right up alongside the Gannila. With each movement, more and more mattresses popped out the back, and behind the ships were a field of beds that stretched as far as he could see in the diminishing sunlight.

He took his gaze skyward. It had been a stunning day with a perfect blue sky, but with the onset of dusk, the change from the stillness they'd had earlier that morning was significant. Wind speed had picked up to about forty knots and the swell was now at ten to fifteen feet. Waves crashing port side had white caps and wind spray.

Out to the horizon, thick cumulous clouds formed in long, gray-topped barrels. The thunderheads were at least fifty miles away, but if the winds kept at it, they'd be upon them in no time. "Any chance this wind will change direction?"

Sykes followed his gaze out to the horizon. "If it's like the last three days, it's possible, yes. But it won't be for several more hours."

"Coinciding with high tide." Gunner did the math. "That's our best chance." A thunderous roar had him looking over at the cargo ship in time to see a tower of containers topple and slam into the Gannila's wheelhouse. Glass exploded and a spray of shards glimmered in the diminishing sunlight like tiny fireworks. "Well . . . we've done everything we can. Now we'll just have to wait and see."

"Either that . . ." Sykes' usual controlled voice unhinged, ". . . or it's time to abandon ship."

Nodding, Gunner stewed over the statement. He'd deliberately delayed abandoning ship for as long as possible, hoping for a miracle. But it hadn't eventuated. They were now four days overdue and had no idea whether anyone was looking for them.

On the ship, there was a chance of being spotted.

In the life rafts, without power and comms, they were at the mercy of the gods. And the weather.

And that didn't always cooperate.

They could be stuck in the bright orange capsules for a very long time.

Playing the what-ifs through his mind convinced him that staying with his ship for as long as possible was still the best option.

He just hoped that when they were finally located, their rescuers would have someone to save.

Chapter Fifty-Two

MADELINE

The adrenalin that'd been pumping through Madeline's veins that morning was long gone, replaced instead with utter exhaustion. Every muscle ached. Her hands hurt from scratching through debris. Her eyes stung with grit from the never-ending dust. Her brain hurt from her thoughts slamming between 'we're going to make it' to 'we're going to die right here next to charred and poisoned bodies, and mutilated wreckage, and in a disaster zone that rattles and squeals like it's the devil.'

As the sun disappeared somewhere over the ship creating a brilliant orange glow, her thoughts fixated more on the latter.

For nearly every day-lit hour, she and Sterling had scoured the section of fourth deck they were trapped in, searching for a way out. But it was impossible. The elevator they'd escaped from wasn't an option; nor was the stairwell that now consisted of mangled chunks of concrete and twisted railings. And there was no way she was returning to that water-filled hull below. Not with the ship rolling about like it was. The cut on her hip stung as if reliving that debris-peppered wave that'd smashed her into a wall over and over.

With each hour that'd passed and each dead end they had encountered, Madeline's need to escape became palpable. And with the diminishing daylight, the idea of spending another night in the dark, with a groaning ship that shifted beneath her feet non-stop, had her desperation hitting tipping point.

Searching for a possible climbing route, she studied the devastation, focusing on the area where the plane's wing had carved a gash through two decks. Squinting into the darkness, she peered up to the highest point of the demolished area and spied an angular corner that looked like the top of a passageway door. It could be a way out. Climbing up that wreckage wasn't going to be easy. But climbing was her thing. If anyone could do it, she could.

She strode toward the base of the rubble.

"Madeline, what're you up to?" The pleading tone in Sterling's voice indicated he knew exactly what she was doing.

Using that top corner as a target, she examined the twisted pipes and mangled wreckage, assessing a potential climbing route. Once she'd identified a direction, she rehearsed the route in her mind twice, just like when she visualized her choreography before a dance, and by the third time through the sequence, she was convinced she could do it. "Don't worry." Ignoring Sterling's objections, she stepped up to a toppled pipe with a circumference greater than her waist. "I'll be careful."

"But we stick together, remember?"

"I know, but climbing is what I do for a living, not you. Don't worry; the second I get to the top, I'll find help."

"I'm not worried about that, Madeline."

She turned from the pipe and met his gaze. The intensity in his expression took her breath away.

"I'm worried about you."

A delightful flutter threaded through her, and in that brief, invigorating moment as she gazed into Sterling's stunning blue eyes, she felt both warmth and peace at how much he cared for her. She also felt invincible. It was her job to save them. And with the absolute notion that she would not fail, she smiled at him. "I'll be fine. I promise." Flicking her ponytail over her shoulder, she turned back to the rubble and reached up, wrapped her hand around a twisted piece of metal, and hauled herself onto the giant pipe.

But with the boat's unpredictable swaying and unstable rubble becoming dislodged with every foot she climbed, the invincible feeling dwindled away. The boat shook like a timid dog and deafening groans came from deep down in its bowels. The sound of tearing metal shrieking across every wall had Madeline torn between scrambling upward as quickly as possible and climbing down to the deceiving safety by Sterling's side.

Gritting her teeth as she held onto a shattered piece of wall, she reached up with her foot and an entire section caved in. She screamed as her feet fell out from beneath her.

The cut in her side, that was only just beginning to heal, split open again.

She dangled by just one hand. A cloud of dust billowed around her.

"Madeline! Madeline!" Sterling's panicked cries reached her.

"I'm okay." Gasping at the chalky air burning her throat, she clawed with her other hand and prodded with her feet, desperate to find a foothold. "I'm okay."

"Jesus, Madeline, please stop."

As the cloud of dust settled, she spied a shattered plumbing pipe sticking out of the wall, and reaching forward, she was able to place the toe of her sneaker onto it for support. When she was finally able to see upward, her heart sank. The climbing route she'd been following had been obliterated. Every foot and handhold she'd identified were gone.

When she looked down, a chill raced over her spine. She had come very close to being buried beneath a mountain of rubble.

Conceding that she'd failed didn't come easily. For more than a decade, Madeline had dedicated her life to proving herself. But now she'd not only failed herself, she'd failed Sterling as well.

The ship jolted sideways. A groan emanating through the walls was much louder and more violent than the previous ones. Everything around her shifted and moved, like they were living through an earthquake. The tremors were getting worse.

"Madeline, are you okay?" The distress in Sterling's voice pierced her tumbling thoughts.

"Yes. I'm coming down."

"Thank God."

When she finally lowered her feet to the deck, Sterling pulled her to his chest. "Please don't do that again."

As they wrapped their arms around each other, she melted into his embrace and listened to his thumping heart. Despite the ship convulsing beneath them, and chunks of concrete and splintered wood tumbling all over the place, and the terrifying sounds becoming so loud she could barely think, Madeline felt their brutal reality melt away. It was just her and Sterling sharing a united need to hold each other.

After a long moment, they parted. She looked into his eyes. They'd crossed an invisible boundary. They were no longer strangers sharing a life-threatening situation; they were a couple on the verge of a new relationship. A relationship that offered the promise of love like she'd never had before. Her heart swelled. Sterling offered her a knowing smile that lit his eyes, and she knew he felt exactly the same.

A deafening screech shuddered through the walls.

"Jesus, what's happening?" Her eyes darted from one corner of the area to the next.

"I don't know."

The violent tremor lasted a long time, a good ten or so seconds, and had a new level of fear inching into her belly. When it finally stopped, the silence was just as scary. Like the ship was getting ready for the next onslaught.

It came just moments later, equally as loud, and just as terrifying.

Chapter Fifty-Three

MADELINE

"I think the ship hit something," Madeline yelled with her hands over her ears. "Do you think it's a reef?"

Sterling shook his head. "No idea. But it's not good." Deep concern rippled his handsome features. He reached for her hand, but halted, gasping. "Madeline, you're bleeding."

"Oh." She groaned; she'd forgotten about her wound. A stream of blood dribbled down her leg. "It's nothing."

"That's not nothing." He clasped her hand in his. "Come on. Let's go see if the doctor is available."

"Very funny."

Back in the medical center, Sterling lowered a deceased middle-aged woman off a bed and onto a chair with great care, then helped Madeline onto the mattress. He disappeared into the doctor's office and returned with two bottles of water. They'd discovered the crate of water bottles in the staff room yesterday, along with a supply of muesli bars and crackers, peanut butter and Nutella.

She took a full swig of water and swilled it around her mouth, hoping to get rid of the dust she'd been tasting all day.

"Now, let's take a look at this, shall we?" Sterling's mock British accent had her giggling.

He peeled back a section of her bloody, shredded jumpsuit and winced. "Why didn't you tell me this was so bad?"

She shrugged. "It's nothing."

He cocked his head, pouting, and she imagined it was a look he gave to many naughty students in his class. "Don't move."

She saluted. "Yes, boss."

He returned to the doctor's office and as he rummaged around, she glanced down at the jagged gash. It wasn't the most painful wound she'd ever had, but it was the most gruesome-looking. She shifted her gaze to outside the porthole. The sky had morphed into a stunning array of citrus colors that fanned up from the dark blue ocean like a rooster tail. The beautiful scene was picture perfect and a dramatic contrast to everything else around her.

Sterling returned with a tray of bits and pieces and a medical mask over his face.

"Ha ha, very funny."

The delicate wrinkles beside his eyes deepened and his eyes sparkled. Even with half his face covered, his smile was spectacular.

He removed the mask, and when he returned his gaze to her hip, his expression grew serious. "I'll have to cut away some of your clothing."

"That's okay." Gritting her teeth against the pain, she shifted over to raise her hip higher.

With painstaking care, Sterling cut a rectangular section away from her jumpsuit, and each time the ship vibrated he stopped and asked her if she was okay. His fingers trembled as he opened a packet of medical gauze, folded it over, and wet it with a fresh water bottle.

He paused with the wet gauze in his hand. "Sorry, but this will hurt." The distress in Sterling's voice matched the concern in his eyes.

"It's okay. Just do it."

He placed his hand on her bare hip and inhaled a deep breath. "Okay, ready?"

"Yes. Stop mucking around, Doctor." She tried to make light of the situation, but Sterling either didn't hear or didn't find it funny.

His fabulous blue eyes grew darker and after huffing out a sigh, he dabbed the medical gauze across her bloody flesh, gradually getting closer to the wound. When he touched the jagged scar, tears stung her eyes. She fought the agony by watching Sterling. Everything rattled around them. The ship shuddered and swayed. Yet his concentration remained unyielding.

He huffed out a long breath as he patted a fresh gauze to the clean wound. "This isn't good. You need stitches."

She nodded. She'd already assumed as much. "You'll have to do it."

"What?" His brows shot up, and he backed away. "No way."

"Ummm." She glanced at the bodies around them. "Shall we ask the doctor to do it?" Her attempt at a joke didn't simmer Sterling's distress.

His beautiful eyes grew wider. "But . . . but—"

"If I could do it myself, I would."

"Far out. You're serious, aren't you?"

"Yes." She reached for his hand. "It's okay. I've had worse."

His Adam's apple bobbed up and down. "One day, I'm going to ask you why you keep saying these things."

"Careful. I may hold you to that promise." She chuckled and was surprised at how comfortable she was with the notion of sharing her childhood nightmare with this man.

A vibration ripped through the ship. She clung to the bed, as did Sterling. A pile of items pitched off a row of shelving. A glass-framed certificate catapulted from the wall and shattered to pieces.

When the vibration stopped, Sterling clutched her hand. "I'm not going to do it while all this is going on."

"But—"

He placed his finger on her lips, hushing her. "Come morning, when we have better light, and if these crazy movements have settled, I promise to sew up your sexy butt. Okay?" A smirk crawled across his lips.

Madeline burst out laughing. "Okay."

"Good, but before you move, let me cover that for you."

Sterling dabbed Savlon onto the wound, covered it with fresh gauze and secured it in place with adhesive strapping.

He helped her down and they each grabbed three bottles of water. Crunching over glass, they returned back to where they'd left the young girl sleeping on the mattress.

The teenager hadn't moved since the first day they'd rescued her. Every time they'd checked on her, Madeline prayed that she'd give some indication she'd be okay. Madeline knelt at her side, tilted her head, and tipped water onto her tongue again. Her eyes shot open, and she spluttered the liquid. "She's awake!"

Sterling knelt at her side. "That's it. Have a drink."

"You're safe now," Madeline said. But when the ship emitted an almighty groan and shuddered so hard an avalanche of rubble tumbled down the mountain pile, her comment seemed ludicrous. They were far from safe.

They took turns speaking to her, but after she'd swallowed some water, she closed her eyes again and went right back to sleeping.

"I think she's going to be okay," Sterling said, once they'd shifted away.

Madeline nodded. "Yeah, I hope so." But even as she said it, she didn't believe it. The girl needed urgent medical attention. Not just a sip of water.

The sunlight vanished with surprising swiftness, and together they sat with their backs against a cabin door and gazed out the giant hole in the ship. The moon rose up out of the ocean. The ship's movements became seismic shifts. Hideous noises raked shivers up her back. Yet it wasn't long before sleep well and truly beckoned.

After they'd shared a few crackers with peanut butter and washed it down with a bottle of beer, she reached for Sterling's hand. With their fingers woven together, a sense of contentment washed over her. She shuffled closer and rested her head on his shoulder. "Thank you."

"What for?" He squeezed her warm palm within his.

She paused. What for? There were so many things. "For being here."

He curled his arm around her shoulder, and she lifted her head onto his chest. "I wouldn't be anywhere else in the world."

Her heart swelled.

The extent of the boat's rise and fall meant their horizon line kept changing. One minute they were looking at the magnificent night sky, complete with a giant moon and millions of stars. Next minute they were looking at the black ocean reflecting the beautiful astronomical display above.

Madeline closed her eyes and listened to Sterling's steady heartbeat.

If this was to be her last night on earth, then she'd be happy with how her life had ended.

Chapter Fifty-Four

GABBY

Gabby snapped her eyes open and blinked through the grittiness. It was completely dark outside. She wiped her hand across her dry lips and as she pushed up from the mattress, every single muscle groaned. Yesterday, other than when they'd stopped to watch the commotion over the baby formula, her and Max had continued their never-ending search for Sally.

They'd crawled over and through mountains of wreckage, climbed up and down hundreds of stairs and traversed from one end of the ship to the other dozens of times. On top of all that, the scabs were beginning to set on her legs and just about every movement split them open again.

Her body was living through its very own battleground.

But it was her heart that was taking the biggest battering. And it would stay that way until she wrapped her arms around her beautiful daughter again.

She didn't want to stop searching. Not until Sally was in her arms.

It had been six days since they'd seen her, yet Gabby knew her baby girl was alive. She would never believe otherwise until she saw it for herself. Gabby had to trust she was somewhere with food and water. And hopefully other people. Just the thought of her being all alone took a brutal chunk out of Gabby's heart.

In the end, once the sun had disappeared, they'd had no choice but to return to the lounge area where everyone else had been resting. Adam had run to them when they'd arrived. He'd clutched his arms around Max and squeezed so hard Max's breath had caught. Her poor boy had been to hell and back and she'd tried to hug him, to take away his pain, but he'd shoved her away.

That, too, had taken another chunk from her heart.

A dozen or so candles, secured in glass jars, were dotted about the place, and slumbering, grubby bodies were lined up on mattresses like a scene from a bad medical drama. Many were snoring.

Including Max. He was on his back, his mouth open, his chest rising and falling with steady breaths. His damaged hand was in a sling across his belly, but despite the bandage that Gladys had applied, the ghastly blue tinge made his swollen fingers look utterly hideous. His black beard had gone beyond the three-day growth that he sometimes courted and the dimple in his chin was now hidden beneath the scraggly mess. His hair was just as bad. The rest of his face was smeared black with grime. She couldn't remember ever seeing him look so unkempt.

With no shower for days and dirt, filth and soot covering every inch of her flesh, she imagined she looked just as ghastly. Her hair was as dry as a bird's nest and she'd been crying so much the skin around her eyes was puffy and dry.

She wriggled sideways. Her breath caught. Her heart stopped still, but a beat later she realized the tiny body sleeping beside Max was Jennifer, the little girl who'd lost her entire family in that rogue wave. She was wearing one of Sally's favorite dresses. The yellow frock was way too big, but the only outfit Jennifer had was the polka-dotted bathers she'd been wearing when the plane engine had wiped out her family.

That already seemed like weeks ago.

Preparing to get up, Gabby shuffled over on the mattress, and Max touched her arm. "Hey, where're you going?"

Max's soothing tone was one of the things about him that she truly loved. It was his voice that had kept her sane when she'd had that car accident all those years ago. Max had squeezed her palm to his and talked in that delightful soothing melody until her car had been dragged back onto the safety of the bridge and her body had been cut from the wreckage.

She'd fallen in love with him that day.

Gabby lay back down and rolled on her side to face him. Despite the dim light, his bloodshot eyes were still visible. They looked as bad as hers felt. He'd also been crying. She tried to swallow past the huge lump in her throat. "Sally . . . is . . . is she—" Her chin quivered and the lump in her throat burned and burned.

Max tugged her to his chest and as he glided his hand down her back, and spoke in his soothing tone that had diffused many situations, tears spilled from her eyes.

But his words failed to register. Her mind swirled. A pungent smell invaded her nostrils, and she clamped her teeth so hard, pain shot to her temples. Yet she couldn't release them.

Sounds drifted in from miles away, impossible to comprehend.

Her world wobbled; nothing made sense.

A blanket of dread enveloped her and when she slumped forward, all the pretty candlelights vanished.

～

"Hey, there you are." A voice, deep and soothing, reached out to her. "Come back, babe. It's safe here."

Her eyes opened in painful flutters, and she squeezed them shut again.

A warm hand touched her cheek. "Hey, Gabby. Adam and I are here."

She smacked her lips together, rolled her tongue around her mouth, and, opening her eyes, she squinted against the glare of the flickering candles. "Sally." She cleared her throat. "What about Sally?"

There was no reply.

Gabby wanted to go back to sleep. To be taken away from the pain crushing her heart. She squeezed her eyes shut and tucked her knees to her chest, and when her throat thickened, breathing became unbearable.

"Mom, it's Adam. I love you, Mom. Please be okay."

The pleading in her son's voice cut through her pain. In the back of her mind, she registered that he'd never seen her like this before. He didn't even know about her condition. But her secret was out now.

He'd never look at her the same again.

"Mom?" Adam crawled in beside her and she nuzzled against the warmth of his body. Smelt the sweat in his hair. His knees eased into her belly and he curled his arm over hers. "I love you, Mom."

Tears spilled from her eyes, and when one trickled down her cheek someone flicked it away.

She forced her eyes open and both Adam and Max were looking at her. Tears teetered in their eyelashes and her already broken heart tore open even further. "I'm sorry." A sob burst from her throat.

"Hey, don't be silly. Come on." Max inched in closer.

She shook her head. "I am truly sorry. I've been a terrible mother. A terrible wife."

"Come on." Max placed his hand beneath her elbow. "Let's get you up."

Adam wriggled backward and then both he and Max helped her to sit.

She wiped her nose and smeared it onto her blood-stained skirt. She felt disgusting. Dirty. Smelly. Rotten. Her gaze shifted from her crumpled clothing to her son.

He offered a lopsided grin, shuffled forward, wrapped his arms around her and buried his face in her neck. The lump in her throat swelled again, and she squeezed him to her chest and breathed through the painful knot. She couldn't remember the last time they'd hugged, let alone experienced one that meant so much. Gathering strength from her son's embrace, she looked at Max. He nodded, and his tear-laden eyes were filled with a sense of knowing that had her hurting even more.

"Ladies and gentlemen." She jumped at the voice booming across the room.

"Ladies and gentlemen, please, I need your attention," Captain McCrae hollered.

Brandi sat up. As did one of her bothers. Bronwyn rubbed her eyes. Jessie yawned.

"I have a critical announcement."

The crowd wrestled themselves awake, and as if some kind of switch had been flicked, the ship's movements became more violent.

Gabby shot her gaze to the Captain. Distress riddled his face.

Their situation was dire.

As if in confirmation, the ship released a brutal, penetrating groan.

Chapter Fifty-Five

GABBY

"Ladies and gentlemen." Gabby couldn't take her eyes off the way the Captain twisted his fingers. "I have not made this decision lightly."

A distressing murmur emanated through the crowd. They'd already been through so much, but the horror on their leader's face proved the worst was yet to come.

"Please do not panic." The Captain paused but despite his pleading, panic raged through her blood. "It is time to prepare to abandon ship."

Pandemonium broke out. People burst into spontaneous sobbing. People jumped to their feet. People shouted questions across the room. Some remained still, stunned beyond thinking, or too exhausted to care.

Max reached for her hand and squeezed. "We'll be okay."

"Please. Please," Captain McCrae yelled.

Albert made an ear-splitting whistle that had the crowd hushing.

"There are seventy-seven of us remaining on the ship. We will all fit into two life rafts. We'll also take two additional rafts for supplies and equipment. We'll make all the preparations now so as soon as sunrise provides enough light, we can load you into the rafts safely."

"Why now?" somebody yelled from the crowd.

"Yeah. I thought we were free from the cargo ship."

"I thought all those mattresses were going to help."

McCrae held up his hands, attempting to hush the questions. "We did break free. However, the wind is moving us back onto the reef. It's only a matter of time before we hit it and we don't want to be around when the hull starts tearing apart."

As if on cue, the ship emitted a tremendous groan, louder than any of the previous ones. Max stood. The boat bucked violently beneath them. A few people screamed.

"Please. Please remain calm. We have plenty of time."

Gabby stood too and reached for Max's hand. "Max, I'm not getting off this ship."

He spun to her, shaking his head, his eyes bulging. "Gabby—"

"Not without Sally."

His shoulders softened but his chin quivered. "Gabby." He shook his head, glanced quickly at Adam and back at her again. The sadness in his eyes was fierce. "Gabrielle. Sally has gone."

"No!" She snatched her hand free.

"We've looked everywhere."

"We haven't, and you know it. There's still that section of the fourth deck. We can get in there; we just have to—"

"Gabby!"

She flinched. Max never yelled at her. Ever. The sadness in his eyes was gone, replaced instead with anger.

But seconds later, his fury vanished. "Gabby . . ." He pleaded her name. "Think about Adam."

She looked down at their son. Her poor boy was trembling. His wide eyes darted about the room. When she followed his gaze, she saw what he was seeing. Every corner of the room had another distressing scene, each one as shocking as the next. People crying. People yelling at the Captain. People praying.

Gladys, the elderly ex-nurse in the wheelchair, dabbed tears from her eyes.

Lindsay, the man whose wife had gone overboard yesterday, fell to his knees and let out a gut-wrenching howl.

Jennifer clutched her arms around Max's leg. She wasn't crying, but her bloodshot eyes were wide. Her cracked lips were drawn into a thin line. But the little orphan morphed into the most heart-breaking image Gabby had ever seen. She was no longer seeing Jennifer. She was seeing Sally. Covered in blood. With blue lips. Her stunning almond eyes wide open, unmoving.

Sally was gone. She was never going to see her baby girl again.

A strangled cry burst from her throat. Tears pooled in her eyes.

Adam clutched his body to hers. Deep, wracking sobs burst from her chest as she squeezed him to her. Through her wobbling vision, she met Max's pooling eyes.

He was right. Adam needed her.

It didn't make the decision any easier.

Albert whistled again, and her attention shot to his Hawaiian shirt.

"Please, everyone." The Captain's tone was more assertive, yet there was no missing the fear in his voice. "Rose of the Sea will not stand a chance. Once she runs aground on the coral, she'll break apart. It may take months, but it may only take hours. She's already suffered a battering, so we don't know how stable her frame is. I don't want to wait until it's too late to get everyone safely onto the life rafts."

"Have you had any contact with back home?" Brandi yelled across the room.

"No." McCrae didn't elaborate.

"But how long will we be in the life rafts?" the boy with the enormous afro asked.

The Captain shook his head. "It's impossible to answer that question."

"Fucking hell. We could be floating out there forever," Zon bellowed over the crowd.

McCrae scowled at him, but didn't respond.

Gabby's over-imaginative mind skipped to them drifting at sea for days on end in a tiny life raft, without any hope of survival. At least on the ship they could move around, sleep on mattresses, have some privacy. She turned to Max. "Do you think this is a good idea?"

He nodded. "Yes. This is the only idea. The Captain is adamant that the ship will not remain stable once it hits the reef."

"But we could be in the life raft for weeks. Months."

"Yes. But it could be just a day." The vein across his temple pulsed, proving that his calm façade was just on the surface. Turmoil was brimming beneath.

He turned from her, scanning the bedlam around them.

It was just like Max to put a positive spin on a dire situation. He'd done the same when she'd been trapped in that car. Her heart squeezed at how much they'd loved each other. Her heart squeezed even more over how she'd let it all go.

"Ladies and gentlemen, please listen. We have plenty to do before we get into the life rafts. I need those of you who are capable to step forward."

Max spun to her and when their eyes locked, her breath was taken away by the love in his chocolate irises. For the first time, she fully understood his need to help others. She offered what she hoped was an understanding smile. "Go on. Go help them."

Relief flashed in his return grin. He cupped her cheek, leaned in, and kissed her. It was a brief kiss. Gentle on her lips, but utterly brutal to her heart.

Max knelt in front of their son. "Adam, you stay with your mother. No matter what happens, do not leave her side. If you need to go to the bathroom, you tell her. Do you hear me?"

Adam's eyes were huge. "Yes, Dad."

Gabby reached for Adam's hand. "We'll look after each other, won't we, Adam?"

He looked up at her. His distress made him look much younger, more frail . . . more vulnerable. He sucked his quivering lip into his mouth, and she pulled his head to her chest and squeezed.

Fighting back the knot in her throat, she eyed Max. "You come back to us as soon as you can."

"I will. I promise." He nodded, and knelt in front of Jennifer.

"Hey, Jen, you do the same, okay, honey? Stay with Gabby." Max guided Jennifer's tiny hand into Gabby's, and Gabby squeezed it.

As Max strode through the crowd toward the Captain, she hugged Adam's and Jennifer's bodies to hers and surveyed the chaos around her. The scene was the newsworthy despair she'd lived for. She was getting exactly what she'd always wanted—heartbreaking headlines. Was this her punishment for her lopsided priorities?

As her pulse pounded out a painful beat, Gabby made a promise to herself.

Nothing would take precedence over her family again.

If they survived.

Chapter Fifty-Six

GUNNER

Gunner strangled the railing as Rose of the Sea bucked wildly beneath his feet. Unclenching his jaw, he shot his gaze along the sea of stricken faces. The survivors were lined up along the deck, all clad in bulky lifejackets, all terrified. "Sit down! For Christ's sake." Over and over he'd been yelling at them to sit, and they would for a minute or two, then when one of them stood, they all did.

The deck jolted, shifting a good two feet beneath them. The crowd tumbled forward like a pile of drunkards. Most managed to find their feet, but Maude and Frank, an elderly couple, kept going.

"Hang on," Gunner yelled out to them.

He was too far away. Age, agility, and gravity were against them. They hit the railing with a bone-jarring crack and tumbled overboard.

They didn't even have time to scream.

"Son of a bitch!" Gunner bellowed. He wanted to race forward. To peer over the railing and see if they were alive. But it was pointless. Their lifejackets may have saved them, but until the life rafts were deployed into the water, there was nothing else he could do.

"Sit down! Please! You're going to get yourselves killed."

As the night sky faded, Rose of the Sea's violent shuddering became more deadly. She'd hit the reef. With each wave that barreled into her, it was impossible to predict what reaction the ship would have. The outgoing tide . . . the thirty-knot winds . . . her broadside position to the reef . . . it was all stacked against her. She had no hope. The entire starboard side was taking the full brunt of the jagged rocks and coral. Each time she rose up and crashed down again, another chunk of her underbelly would be ripped to shreds.

Each time, Gunner willed her to hang in there just a little bit longer.

Gunner, Sykes, and fifteen dedicated helpers had checked every foot of the ship, searching for any survivors. They didn't find one. And the section of deck four that'd been decimated by the plane, remained impenetrable. As much as Gunner prayed that there were people still alive in that section, he also hoped that there wasn't, as they were about to be left behind and there was nothing anyone could do for them now.

After that search was complete, they'd loaded two life rafts with as many supplies as possible: the baby formula, all drinking fluids, and all packaged and canned food. Medication, first-aid kits, mobile phones, blankets, towels, bowls and knives.

The gut-wrenching list with the names of the known deceased.

Each family were allowed one small backpack of belongings. He hoped they'd chosen wisely.

The rafts were equipped with an insulated canopy to protect them against heat and cold and contained a pre-packed set of survival gear. They'd previously removed the tinned food and water. But they'd spent all night moving all the additional gear on those rafts onto the four rafts they were about to deploy.

Each life raft had a repair kit, a non-folding knife with a buoyant handle, an axe, a tin opener, a pocket knife with twenty built-in gadgets, a pair of scissors, a first-aid kit, a whistle, six flares, an anchor, ropes, fishing tackle, and, of course, a survival manual. They had a means to collect rainwater. Paddles. Bailing buckets and signaling mirrors.

The solar-powered lamps were useless after the EMP, as were

the waterproof flashlights. And the chances of the EPIRB finding a working satellite signal were negligible. But Gunner still resisted throwing those items from the rafts.

Gunner wasn't just preparing to vacate the ship.

He was preparing to be at sea for an unforeseeable length of time.

With the stocks secured, and sunlight mushrooming on the horizon, it was time to release their first supply raft. Usually, dual electronic winches would lower the rafts with steady precision. Gunner had performed this life-saving task dozens of times in his career, but never under duress, and never without the use of functioning electronic winches. Not once had his training covered life-raft deployment in the event of power failure. The brutal reality of that now glaringly obvious safety breach was that neither he nor Sykes were confident in what they were doing. He was just grateful that they'd had surplus rafts to practice with. They'd already tried two with disastrous results. Thank God he hadn't had people or supplies in either of them. It took two more attempts before they'd established a workable deployment.

The rise and fall of the ship was dramatic, a good fifty-foot shift in each direction. To minimize impact on the raft, they needed to release it when it was positioned nearest the water.

Timing would be everything.

Calling out to each other over the screams of shredding metal, he and Sykes released the life raft from the clasps that secured it to the deck and it rocked wildly with Rose's unpredictable movements. The only thing stopping the pod from tumbling into the ocean were two ropes secured at either end by the pulley systems on the winches.

Gunner studied the waves, trying to assess a pattern.

The pressure to get it right was like pulling the pin on a grenade and knowing when to toss it for maximum result.

After four waves, approximately eight to ten feet high, Gunner yelled to his First Officer. "We'll do it after this one, Sykes. You ready?"

"Yes, sir." Sykes' commitment to his duty was unwavering. The man deserved a medal.

The ship rose with a crippling shudder that had glass exploding somewhere inside the deck behind him. She listed dramatically to starboard side and the supply-filled raft bounced against the side of the hull like a giant orange football.

The wave crashed toward them. The eyes of the terrified survivors watched him.

Rose of the Sea was about to reach its pinnacle and if Gunner was right, seconds later, she'd slam back the other way.

The screeching grew louder, more critical.

The boat bucked beneath them, whipping left and right.

The raft slammed backward and forward like a toy boat in a hurricane.

He held his breath, counting out every painstaking second. *One. Two. . . Five. . . Nine.*

"Ready!"

The boat fell out from beneath them.

"Go!"

At exactly the same moment, they released the ropes and as Rose slammed back into the water, creating a massive wave, the unmanned life raft plummeted.

Gunner's heart stopped. The orange pod hit the water. It rolled to its extreme right, but righted itself within seconds. The crowd behind cheered and the swell of relief that washed through him had his knees buckling. He turned to Sykes and they nodded at each other. A touch of hope coursed through his veins. But it wasn't over.

It was a long way from over.

His reality check was met with another deafening roar from the ship's hull. This one was different. Deeper. Longer. An agonizing cry for help from a seventy-thousand-ton vessel in peril.

He and Sykes raced to the next pod, and within minutes it too was released into the water and quickly began drifting away. Thanks to Sykes' clever thinking, they'd tied the rafts together, otherwise each surge Rose created when she plunged back into the water would've pushed them farther from reach.

The moment he'd been dreading since Captain Nelson had declared the ship dead in the water had arrived. It was time to abandon ship. Nausea wobbled in his throat. Bile burned in his stomach. Biting it back, Gunner turned to the survivors. They'd been pre-arranged into two groups, sharing those who needed assistance and those who didn't between the two rafts.

Their eyes were wide. Their silent screams were terrifying.

They were counting on him. He was their leader; he needed to lead.

Chapter Fifty-Seven

GUNNER

Gunner nodded at Pauline and Jae-Ellen, and the two women jumped up. Gunner had an immediate swell of pride as they pushed through what would no doubt be immense fear to start shuffling the elderly and injured passengers forward.

Gladys was first. As Pauline wheeled her forward, Gunner tried to offer the petrified woman what he hoped was a look of confidence. He stepped up to her, and she clutched her fingers around his wrist. "Please, forget about me. Take the others."

He peeled her fingers off his wrist and as she repeated her protests, Sykes, Quinn, and the twins, Col and Ken, manhandled the massive woman through the narrow entrance of the life raft. There was no graceful way to do it, and with the unpredictable movements of the ship and Gladys' crippled legs unable to help, she tumbled into the escape pod like a soggy cadaver. The process to secure her in the raft took much longer than he'd anticipated. It was time they didn't have.

Tossing the wheelchair aside, he reached for Jennifer. The little girl was screaming hysterically by the time they shoved her into the raft. Max followed quickly behind, and despite his damaged hand being strapped to his chest, he still helped his wife and son into the raft with him.

The sun was a blazing beacon on the horizon by the time they had the thirty-four passengers and five crew into the third life raft, ready to deploy. It was Quinn's turn to operate the second winch, and Sykes had given him detailed instructions on how to manage it.

Sykes strode to Gunner and offered his hand. "Sir, it's been an honor working with you, sir."

Gunner nodded. "Likewise, First Officer Sykes. I'll meet you at the bottom."

"I'll be waiting for you, sir."

Sykes saluted, then climbed into the life raft, and after giving Gunner one last look, loaded with understandable apprehension, he flipped the cover closed on the life raft's hatch and disappeared inside.

"Okay, Quinn," Gunner yelled over the thunderous noise. "On my call, okay?"

"Okay, sir."

"Ready. Set. Release the locks." Once unshackled, the life raft rocked wildly. The screams from inside it were terrifying. Forty people were in that raft, being held by just two ropes. Their lives were in his hands. His brain shattered. Would anybody die in the fall? Would he see them again? His body flashed hot and cold. Acid burned up his throat, almost choking him. A panic attack took hold.

What if every single person died?

He shot his gaze from the rocking pod to the churning ocean to Quinn. His eyes were huge, his jaw clenched, his fear obvious. He was waiting for him . . . trusting him to make the right decision.

Just like every one of the seventy-five survivors.

"Ready, sir." Quinn blinked at Gunner.

Gunner's movements became robotic. He was no longer a man; he was a machine.

Doing the improbable.

Making impossible decisions.

Hoping for a miracle.

"Quinn. Ready. Set. Go!"

The raft released with a sharp zipping sound from the ropes and wild screams from the people inside the pod. An enormous splash from the ship engulfed the pod and for three heart-stopping beats, she vanished beneath a million gallons of white water.

It popped to the surface, wobbled wildly from side to side, then righted itself. Seconds later, the hatch opened. Sykes stood and when he gave Gunner the thumbs up, all the remaining survivors onboard the ship cheered.

"Good work, Captain." Quinn smiled.

Gunner chuckled and returned his smile to a man who'd barely left his side since the shit had hit the fan. "Good work, Quinn."

While Gunner, Cloe, and Quinn coordinated the loading of the remaining passengers and crew into the last pod, Sykes pulled the already deployed supply rafts together and secured them closer to each other.

It took way too long to get everyone inside the final pod. It was time they didn't have. Every ticking minute, Rose reared with another spine-jarring jolt that confirmed she was suffering. If they didn't get off this thing soon, then they were going to suffer too.

After Quinn climbed in, Gunner leaned into the capsule's hatch. That tiny space was destined to be their home for the unforeseen future. God help them all. Thirty-four people looked at him with wide-eyed fear. "Listen up. When I release the clips, the raft will start rocking. As soon as I can I'll release the ropes. Just hang onto those handles and it'll be over before you know it."

His gaze fell on Zon. The big man's eyes were wide, fearful. Zon had insisted on being in this specific life raft. He had assumed it was because Zon had packed the supplies into this one. But maybe Zon wanted to stay with Gunner.

"It's okay, Zon. You'll be safe in no time." Gunner hoped his words didn't sound as hollow as they did in his own brain.

Zon's scowl implied he had no idea why Gunner had singled him out.

"Good luck, everyone. I'll join you soon." Gunner flipped the sheeting back over the entry hatch and clipped it into place. He turned his attention to the two ropes still keeping the pod in position. Sykes had rigged it so Gunner only had to release one tether to set the pod free. It was as simple as it was brilliant.

The catch was, someone had to stay back to do it. Him.

He was the Captain. It was his job to be the last man to leave the ship.

Gunner wouldn't have it any other way.

Once everyone else was safe, all he had to do was jump off and swim out to the raft.

Easy.

Provided he judged his timing of the waves right.

His heart banged against his ribs, nearly crippling him when he considered the enormity of his plan.

But he had to get through deploying the raft first.

The ship emitted a long groan. It was deep. It was loud. It was catastrophic.

She was on her last legs. Any minute now, Rose of the Sea would break into pieces. It was time to do this.

"Okay, hang on," he shouted. "I'm releasing the clasps."

He unhooked the fasteners. The raft flopped out with the roll of the ship. Terrified screams bellowed from inside the raft. The squeals around him were like those of strangled demons.

Timing was everything. He studied the roll of the ocean for a good couple of minutes, searching for a pattern to the waves. "Okay, get ready." He counted them down. "Five. Four. Three. Two. One."

He flicked the latch. The rope whipped up, released from the other side, but it snapped around his wrist. His arm jolted upward and the clipping mechanism crunched down on his hand.

A spray of blood shot across his face.

Gunner howled. His feet slipped out from beneath him. The only thing stopping him from toppling overboard was his trapped hand.

The ship bucked violently, slamming his loose legs onto the railing.

Bile shot up his throat. Every breath was caustic. He couldn't think.

Screams bellowed from the pod. Gasping through the pain, he

First Fate

looked down. The raft was still there, banging into the ship. Its angle was all wrong, perilous.

Rose thrust upward. Higher this time. Committed. An almighty roar confirmed she was taking her final beating. Glass shattered. Metal squealed.

Gunner couldn't do a thing.

Pain ripped up his arm. He saw stars. He saw blood. He saw mangled fingers.

His scream was a strangled cry. Of mortal terror. Unworldly.

His throat burned. His eyes stung. His legs banged against the railing, shooting barbs along his shins.

The raft slammed onto the ship's hull. Terrified screams burst from the pod and in that one bracing instant, Gunner knew he'd failed them.

He was trapped, and all the people in the life raft were trapped with him.

Zon's head appeared through the hatch. His mouth was moving, apparently yelling up to him. Gunner heard nothing but his own terrifying moans.

The ship bucked beneath him, and he slammed against the life raft's holding bracket. His temple smacked into a giant bolt. Pain darted to his brain and for a brief second, he forgot about his hand.

The crippled life raft swung about. Screams of caged horror ate at his soul.

Panting against the pain, Gunner looked up at his hand. Blood drained from his body. Two crushed fingers were protruding from beneath the metal clasp. Two were missing altogether.

His world became a series of devastating snapshots.

The trapped raft slamming against the ship.

Blood dribbling down his wrist.

Rose shuddering beneath him.

Mangled and bloodied fingers.

A lone albatross ducking and swooping across the brilliant blue sky. It looked impossibly serene, like an angel.

Maybe it was an angel.

Zon appeared out of nowhere. He must've climbed up the rope.

"Fuck me. You're fucked." He had a weird smirk on his face, like he was enjoying himself. Gunner wanted to punch that grin right off the cocky asshole's mouth.

But he couldn't move. "Cut the rope." Gunner hissed through clenched teeth. "You need to cut the rope."

"I figured that." Zon held up an axe. Its highly polished blade glinted in the morning sun.

"Cut it."

Zon cocked his head. "But the raft's gonna go and you're gonna die on this fuckin' ship."

"I know. I know. Just do it. You have to save them. Do it. Now!"

Zon nodded. But he didn't do anything. The bald man looked down at the raft, looked up at Gunner's hand, and then the smirk on his face grew wider. "I got another idea." The glint in his eyes had *madman* written all over them. Zon raised the axe. "You might wanna look away."

"What're you doing?" Gunner screamed.

Zon wrapped his arm around Gunner's waist, clutching their bodies together. Then, with a flash of steel, the axe slammed down.

Gunner howled as he slumped free. A spray of blood spurted across Zon's face.

Fighting through the agony, Gunner looked at his hand.

Everything below his wrist was gone.

Chapter Fifty-Eight

GABBY

Gabby had screamed as the life raft plummeted. It was barely a four-second free fall, yet it had been the most terrifying moment of her life. It'd hit the water with a shattering jolt that had shot right up her backbone. When the raft had flung sideways, her cheekbone had hit the side wall. The pain was like a dozen wasps simultaneously stinging her left eye.

The raft had flipped from one side to the next in rapid succession, then, as if a giant had steadied it, it stopped.

Max was trying to placate Jennifer. The poor girl was utterly sobbing. Rubbing her cheek, Gabby reached over to Adam. "Hey, you okay?"

His lips were drawn into a thin line. His chin quivered. "I hit my head." He rubbed behind his skull.

Gabby strained against her belt to check his head. Thankfully, there was no blood. She wanted to wrap her arms around her son, to tell him everything would be okay.

But without Sally, nothing was okay. Their family was forever shattered.

She would never sleep soundly again not knowing what happened to her baby girl.

Max's eyes were riddled with pain, yet he held it together. Probably for the sake of Jennifer, who was clutching Max's good hand with both of hers.

The other passengers' reactions were a mixture of relief and shock. Gabby had seen scenes like this many, many times. How people coped during extreme life-threatening situations could never be predicted. A big, burly man with a buzz cut could crumble to a foetal position, while a feeble grandmother could look fear right in the face.

Through the circular window beside her, she spied the other life raft. She lurched forward. "Shit!" The raft was dangling at a precarious angle by just one rope. Her stomach writhed as she imagined what those poor people inside the raft were going through.

The ship rolled into the water and she saw both the Captain and Zon. What was Zon doing up there? *That wasn't the plan.* Her stomach dropped. Captain McCrae was holding his arm. Blood squirted from his wrist. His hand was missing.

She wanted to pull her eyes away, but couldn't.

A week ago, she would've cursed herself for not having her camera. The gruesome scene would've been a gripping newsflash.

She could picture the headline: *Ship's Captain makes bloody sacrifice.*

But the concept of sharing his agony with complete strangers made her blood curdle. Too many times, she'd captured people at their lowest point, in extreme conditions. She'd relished in their vulnerability. Guilt and revulsion threaded through her. She was a monster. An evil, soul-sucking monster.

And for what?

For her own selfish reasons.

A vile cascade of self-loathing oozed through her.

Her chin quivered. It was a wicked twist of irony that she too had reached the lowest point in her life. She was worthless. Nothing she did was valuable to anyone, unlike nearly everyone around her. Her husband. The Captain. The crew. Gladys, the elderly woman in the wheelchair, who'd stopped nursing over a decade ago—even she was more valuable than Gabby. All of them were worthy of every accolade possible.

At great peril to themselves, they were helping others.

Especially the Captain. She peered at him through the porthole. Zon was holding him up. The Captain writhed and cried in agony.

His evacuation strategy had careened irreversibly off-course.

Their situation was growing more deadly by the second.

Sykes stood through the hatch and yelled toward the ship. His bellows got louder. But the ship's shrieking upped a crescendo too.

Movement on a lower deck, to the far right of the dangling life raft, caught her eye.

A flash of red. A waving hand.

Her heart lurched to her throat. Her eyes bulged. With trembling fingers, she scrambled to unclip her belt. She shoved forward and stood in the hatch next to Sykes.

Gabby squealed. "Look!"

Hope surged through her veins.

Sally was there. Her fuchsia shorts stood out like an oasis to her nightmare. But her elation exploded in a heartbeat.

Sally was in a man's arms. Her body was limp. "No!"

Icy shards shot up Gabby's back. "No. No. No!" Horror gripped her heart in a vise and strangled it.

"Sally!" Her daughter's name was clawed from Gabby's throat. "Sally!" She screamed louder than she'd done in the thousand times over the last four days. But there was so much noise, it was impossible to know if they'd heard her.

Max squeezed up next to her, and she pointed. "Over there. With those people. It's Sally. Oh God, Max, is she alive? Tell me she's alive."

"She must be. Why else would they be holding her?"

"Yes! Exactly. Sally! She's alive. Max. I told you. I knew it. She's alive!" Gabby waved her hands and the woman waved back.

"We have to get her!" Gabby dug her fingernails into Sykes' forearm. "We have to get my daughter."

Sykes yanked his arm free. "We will. Just hold on." He turned his gaze back to the Captain and the dangling life raft.

"No. I won't hold on." Gabby climbed onto the small ladder.

Max clutched her wrist; his eyes were enormous. "What're you doing?"

"I'm saving my daughter."

With one last glance at Sally's lifeless body, she dove into the turbulent water.

Chapter Fifty-Nine

ZON

Zon felt the moment Gunner lost his shit. One second, Captain Dickhead was staring at the bloody stump at the end of his arm. Next second, he slumped forward, nearly dragging the both of 'em overboard. Lucky Zon was hanging onto a pole at the time.

Zon hauled the Captain backward and he flopped onto the deck like a dead man. His chest was still moving though, so he wasn't a goner just yet.

The boat suddenly dropped out from beneath him and he crashed to his hands and knees. The whole fuckin' place was buckin' and movin'. It was like diving onto a wild boar and trying to figure out which way it was gonna go.

Projectiles were shootin' everywhere. Smoke was so thick it burned his throat. And the damn noise, it was disturbing.

He stepped toward the edge of the deck. Down below, the raft was still dangling about like bait on the end of a line, and the screaming from inside was louder than his bitchface sister. Zon raised the bloody axe and chopped the rope. The raft plunged like a brick, hit the water and nearly upended itself.

That was when he remembered all his booze inside.

"Fuck!"

Scowling, he pictured his bottle of fancy brandy smashing and the liquid gold spilling out all over the place. He shoulda thought of that. Stupid! If they saw that brandy, they'd find his other stuff.

There was no chance anyone would find the gun though; he'd found the perfect spot for it. But the rest of his loot—the poker chips, the money, his booze, his snacks—all of that took up space, which was why he'd volunteered to pack the raft. He weren't stupid.

He just hoped like hell they was still tucked in beneath all them seats.

His lucky streak had been treatin' him good lately. Maybe it was still going.

Down below, Sykes had moved his raft closer. He was lookin' up at Zon with his mouth wide open and eyes bulging. Given that Zon was still holdin' the bloody axe, it was kinda justified. Not too many people woulda done what he'd done to Captain Dickhead. But he'd just saved the Captain's life. Stupid fucker was gonna go down with the ship. That was a guaranteed way to get dead. Now, as long as he didn't lose too much blood, he'd live.

Provided Zon could figure out how to get 'em both down to them rafts.

The ship was still joltin' all over the place, slamming up and down non-stop. Going up was kinda smooth but the down was like dropping into a canyon. Each time the ship hit the water, it wobbled for a couple of seconds before it rose again. That pause, just before it started upward—that'd be when to jump.

If he got it wrong, he and Dickhead were dead.

Zon had no intention of face-plantin' into the hull. Not when his booze, poker chips, and all that money was stashed on the life raft below, waitin' for him. And Jessie. She was worth more than all that other stuff.

That thought came outta nowhere.

He'd never put a chick in front of anythin' before, especially money. All this bullshit was makin' him mental. Just like his grand-daddy. By the end, the stupid bastard had been crazier than a raccoon in a spring trap, sayin' all kinda weird shit that had his grandmama whackin' him over the head all the time.

First Fate

That blonde TV bitch was next to Sykes, wavin' and carryin' on. But next second, she dove off the raft. Maybe she was coming to help him. He'd a thought Sykes would a done that. But her arms and legs were all over the place, and the stupid bitch was going in the wrong direction. She weren't doin' no rescue. He had no idea what the fuck she was doin'.

"I'm over here, ya stupid bitch," Zon hollered at her and waved, but she swam right on past them. He shook his head. "I'm surrounded by dickheads."

Speaking of dickheads . . . He turned to the Captain. He was still dead to the world. Zon was gonna have to do everything for him. He waited for the slow rise of the ship upward before he hauled Gunner's body from the ground and tossed him over his shoulder.

It was just like he'd done with Zombie, who like he'd kept tellin' everyone, ended up dead anyways. Zon smiled at the memory of tellin' Sykes 'I told ya so.' Stupid fucker shoulda listened to him. Woulda saved 'em a whole lotta time.

Captain Dickhead's blood was drippin' onto Zon's favorite shirt as he stepped toward the edge of the deck. Sykes had moved his raft closer, but he was still a good fifty or so feet out. Probably too scared 'bout the ship slammin' down on top of him or something.

A rumble, like the thunder in a good ol' Louisiana storm, roared from within the ship. Zon glanced sideways. His jaw dropped. A giant split was carvin' its way through the deck. Plank after plank snapped in half like they was just kindling. The gap got bigger, and within seconds, it was so big it coulda swallowed his prized gator catch whole.

The whole fuckin' ship was 'bout to split in two.

Time to get the fuck outta there. He adjusted Captain Dickhead on his shoulder and rode the ship's rise and fall twice more. Each time, the gap openin' at his side grew bigger. The ship was no longer smooth on the way up neither; it jolted more than his mama did when she started dancin' after a bottle of tequila.

Decidin' that the next one was gonna be it, he waited out the ship's rise and when it slammed back down, creatin' a wave that charged into Sykes' raft, Zon gripped onto Gunner's legs and jumped.

Zon didn't scream or nothin'; that was for pussies. He hit the water feet-first. Captain Dickhead slammed face-first into the ocean. If that slap in the cheek didn't wake the Captain, nothin' would. Zon aimed for the churning surface. The second he sucked in fresh air, Sykes was swimmin' toward him. Treading water, Zon turned Gunner over and the Captain spluttered.

"Jesus, Zon. You're fucking crazy." But despite his words, Sykes was smiling. "Help me get him up."

Together, Sykes and Zon dragged Gunner, who Zon was pretty sure was crying, toward the closest life raft. Once there, a man and a woman dragged his ass up.

Zon reached for the ladder, ready to climb, but Sykes grabbed his shoulder. "Hang on, bud. We got a few more to rescue." He pointed over his shoulder to two people standing in the giant hole in the ship. The guy had what looked like a dead girl in his arms. Sykes began swimming toward 'em.

Zon had already seen firsthand just how useless Sykes was when it came to rescuin' people, so he figured he'd better go help or they'd never get outta there.

TV bitch was splashing up a storm just out from the ship. The stupid cow was always stickin' her nose up at Zon like she was better than him or somethin'. If she wanted savin' too, then he just might accidentally-on-purpose dunk her under a few times first. She fucking deserved it.

"You have to jump." Sykes was at TV bitch's side, yellin' up to the people still on the boat.

Zon swam to them and when TV bitch smiled at him it was like he was lookin' at a different person. The stick up her ass musta been pulled out or somethin', 'cause she touched his shoulder like they was long-lost buddies.

The boat reared up again, but this time when it reached the top, a huge explosion detonated somewhere inside the ship. Fireworks sprung out of every crack and next second, the entire ass-end dropped away. When it hit the water, the woman fell from the ship, her arms and legs flapping like she could fly.

The wave it created barreled over him and the others, spinning him around like he was in a fuckin' washing machine. When he came up again, Sykes was swimmin' toward the woman. Zon followed.

She was still screaming for help when Sykes grabbed her arm and dragged her away from the ship. "Look after her." Sykes shoved the woman at Zon.

Before Zon could do nothin' she wrapped her arms around his neck, pushing him under. He clawed her hands off his head and kicked up to the surface. "Fuckin' hell, you're gonna drown me."

"Sorry." She put her hand on his shoulder. "Jump, Sterling! Jump!" She squealed in his ear, just 'bout sending him deaf.

The guy holding the girl jumped and they hit the water together. Sykes swam in to get 'em. TV bitch did too.

Figurin' he weren't needed no more, Zon swam back toward the rafts.

He needed to make sure no one was touching his stuff.

Especially his gun.

Chapter Sixty

MADELINE

Madeline dove off the raft, plunging into the tiny ocean pool created by the four pods roped together. She popped up to the surface and waved at Sykes who was overseeing the swimmers.

It had taken three long days in the raft before Sykes had agreed to let people swim in that area if they wanted. Every day since then, everyone except the severely injured, and poor Gladys with her crippled legs, had taken a dip. It helped to reduce the body odor that was festering in the life pods. And it allowed them to go to the bathroom.

They were lost at sea with the remaining seventy-two survivors and nearly every day since they'd crawled into the rafts, they lost another person. Yet Madeline wasn't as scared as some of the others were. Fresh water and canned food were being rationed, but they were fed enough. And the fish . . . the fish were abundant. Every line they tossed out came up with a decent-size trevally or cod. Eating them raw, though . . . she wasn't sure she could ever get used to that. She and Sterling had spent the morning fishing and Sterling had made it fun. They'd both laughed so much. Maybe too much, given their situation.

The cool ocean was invigorating, and Madeline scrubbed the

salty water onto her arms and legs, ridding herself of the sweat and grime that came with living inside a humid, unventilated pod with forty other people. Gladys had sewn up the wound on her hip, and Madeline barely noticed the occasional sting when she leaned over too far.

Breast-stroking across the tiny pool, she felt revitalized. It was great to stretch her legs and with a contented sigh, she floated onto her back. Brilliant blue sky filled her vision. Turning her head sideways, she admired Sterling bathing. When he ran his hands through his wavy hair, the sun caught on the blond tips, making them look like they were gilded in gold.

There had been moments on the ship when she and Sterling had lost all hope of a rescue, and there were several times when she'd thought the ship was going to implode with both her and Sterling inside it.

During those moments, she'd tried to stay focused on all the good things she'd done in her life and what precious aspects of it she appreciated. It was a little trick she'd learned during her kidnapping. She'd been grateful that she had the stinky rubber mattress rather than just the bare concrete floor. She'd felt blessed that little Peanut had chosen her hovel as his home. She'd also always known in her heart that her parents would never stop looking for her.

It seemed she only truly appreciated the important things when she thought she'd never live to see another day. There had been many times in her life when she *didn't* want to live another day.

Not now though.

Despite everything they'd been through, and as hopeless as their situation still seemed, not once had she wanted her life to end. She wanted to live for many, many more years. Decades even. And she wanted to share every one of them with Sterling.

Even once they'd been rescued off the ship, and despite eight rough days in the cramped confinement of the life raft, their new, blossoming relationship had continued to grow. Their connection was so powerful, she was certain it'd been destiny that had trapped them together in that elevator.

Sterling must've felt her watching because he met her gaze and smiled. With his shirt off, and the beads of water glistening on his toned chest, he could easily have graced the cover of any women's magazine.

"What?" He frowned, but his spectacular grin was clearly visible through his blond beard. He swam up to her and curled his hand behind her neck; the gentle touch of his fingers had delicious shudders threading through her body.

He leaned forward, closing his eyes. She did too. Anticipation sizzled between them. When his lips met hers, fire and passion mingled together. Her heart fluttered and her mind melted into everything that was heavenly about him. About them.

Their kisses, though way too brief given that Sykes was watching them, had her trembling both inside and out.

When their lips parted, Sterling pulled her to his chest, and they remained in that embrace, treading water until Sykes hollered that their time was up.

Until now, she'd been living as a robot, going through the motions of life and yet never feeling. Finally, Madeline was truly alive.

She was looking forward to what their future held.

But she still hadn't told Sterling everything about her past. It wasn't because she didn't want to tell him. It wasn't because he didn't deserve to know. She just didn't want him to change the way he treated her. People always did when they learned what her kidnapper had done. Her own mother was testament to that.

When the time was right, she'd tell him everything. She just hoped that when she did, Sterling wouldn't look at her like she was a victim. She hoped he'd look at her like she was a survivor.

And once they were rescued, both of them would have incredible survival stories to tell.

Chapter Sixty-One

GUNNER

Gunner drifted in and out of consciousness. Every time he opened his eyes, the light inside the raft was different. Completely dark from the blackness of night. Bright with piercing light from the break of a new dawn. Or like now—the sepia hue from the afternoon sun.

Yet the raft carried on, bobbing in the water. Floating the ragged survivors in a never-ending nightmare to an unknown destination.

He lost track of the days and nights in the raft. Was it three? Was it ten? Fifty? Whenever he woke, Max and Gladys were there, fussing over him, checking the bandage on his wrist, giving him water and the sickly baby formula.

It seemed like forever before Gunner could sit without throwing up. It was even longer before he could recall everything that'd happened. It was as if his brain had deliberately fogged over the gory details, allowing him to forget while he healed. But he'd never forget.

Not the pain. Nor the look in Zon's eyes when the psycho had brought down that axe.

His hand throbbed and stung. Well, not his hand. That was gone.

It was weird though; he could still feel his fingers. He could still feel the blinding agony from when they'd been trapped in the winching bracket.

Gunner stared at the bandage. Bile shot to his throat as he recalled Gladys sewing up his bloody stump. Max had been there too, holding his arm for her while Sykes had pinned him down. Although he'd faded in and out of oblivion, he'd felt every sting of that needle and worse, the thread pulling though his skin.

And the blood . . . there'd been so much blood.

His blood.

The bandage he had on now wasn't as bloody as the one he'd seen last time he'd roused; obviously Gladys had replaced it recently. Or maybe the bleeding had stemmed somewhat. He hoped it was the latter.

He went to twist his wedding ring and his heart nearly stopped. It was gone. Of course it was gone. His whole fucking hand was gone.

His heart shattered to a million pieces as his thoughts shot to Adelle and Bella. His beautiful wife and daughter. He'd never clasp their faces in his hands again. Or hold his mother's hand in his when he next visited her in jail.

Tears flooded his vision. A lump in his throat burned and swelled. He couldn't breathe.

He wished Zon had left him there on the ship.

He was the Captain; he should've gone down with Rose of the Sea.

He should be dead.

A flood of heat blazed through his veins. The urge to throw up gripped him.

He had to get out of there. Dragging himself upright, he clutched onto the handrail above him and squeezed past people's knees, aiming for the open hatch.

It was the first time he'd stood since he'd been thrown into the pod. Everything spun in long, lazy circles as he inhaled the fresh, salty air, breathing life into his limbs. Waiting for the dizziness to subside, he clutched the ladder and scanned his surroundings.

Their four pods were strung together. Sykes had done an elaborate job with the ropes. The rafts were close, but not so much that they bumped into each other non-stop. But close enough that they could easily reach more supplies as they needed them.

The afternoon sky was magnificent shades of orange and pink. A scattering of clouds was visible and a few stars already dotted the darkening backdrop. A seagull caught his eye. Another one joined it. The pair ducked and swooped on an invisible updraft, gliding through the air with all the time in the world. They did it again, up and up, and then turning in a long, lazy loop as they swooped toward the ocean.

Gunner's heart skipped a beat. His brain kicked into gear.

Holy shit!

He jolted upright. Seagulls usually remained near land.

Shielding his eyes from the sun with his hand, his only hand, he scanned the horizon in a slow circle. The ocean was a giant indigo blanket that stretched on forever.

There!

Something. A slight shadow. A variation to the never-ending horizon.

"Quick! Someone give me the binoculars." He waved in the pod but didn't shift his eyes from the anomaly. Binoculars were shoved into his hand.

Max popped up beside him. "What is it?"

"Not sure yet." Out of habit, Gunner went to use both hands to hold the binoculars. It was a brutal jolt of reality. His insides churned. He would never be able to do that again.

Casting that bullshit aside, he clutched the binoculars, scanning for the variance that'd caught his eye in the distance.

There! Yes!

Holy shit! It's an island.

It was a fair distance away, but it was the best thing he'd seen in a very long time.

"Sykes!" he yelled across to the other three life rafts, unsure which one Sykes would stand up in.

Seconds later, Sykes appeared in the raft to his right. "Gunner, you're awake."

"Get your glasses."

Sykes didn't even question him; he just bobbed below, and reappeared with Quinn and Cloe at his side.

"Good to see you, Captain," Quinn said.

Gunner didn't respond; he didn't want to lose sight of the island. "Over there." He pointed without lowering his glasses.

"I see it!" Sykes' voice elevated with excitement. "I see it! It's an island! Compass—someone get me the fucking compass."

Gunner lowered the binoculars. Both relief and misery shared the same space in his mind.

They'd made it. He didn't want to say it was a miracle. Not when there were only seventy two souls remaining. A miracle would've been saving every single passenger.

The survivors broke into spontaneous cheering.

Yet, as much as Gunner wanted to celebrate with them, he couldn't.

He peered through the binoculars again. The island looked small.

Way too small. He searched for signs of civilization. Boats. Smoke. Hell, even a bottle on the beach would have done it. But as they moved closer, and details became firmer, there was still nothing. Not a damn thing.

Despair crashed through him like a tsunami.

They were still a very long way from a rescue.

He lowered the binoculars and stared at the brutal stitching at the end of his arm.

Just like his hand, they were cut off from the rest of the world. "God help us all."

TO BE CONTINUED . . .

THANK YOU FOR FOLLOWING GUNNER, GABBY, MADELINE AND Zon's journey in this crazy survival story. But their nightmare is far from over. Continue the series with FERAL FATE

By the way, if you enjoyed First Fate, would you consider placing a review on Amazon or Goodreads? They really do help other readers discover my books.

Cheers to you,
Kendall Talbot

Turn the page for more thrilling books by Kendall Talbot.

But before you go, would you like a FREE ebook? I'd love to share my crime thriller Double Take with you. Double Take is set in my home town of Brisbane, Australia and it will have you guessing to the very end. And if you sign up to my newsletter, you get it for FREE.

Here's the link to receive your FREE book: https://kendalltalbot.com.au/doubletakefree.html

Feral Fate

The nightmare is far from over.

After surviving the EMP blast that crippled their cruise ship, the exhausted passengers from *Rose of the Sea* finally reach dry land. But the deserted island has a sinister history, and one wrong step on its sandy shores can mean the difference between life and death.

Gunner. When Gunner loses his position as leader, he fears the threadbare semblance of order will fray into lawlessness—and nothing will be left to stand in the way of desperate humans.

Gabby. Now also caring for an orphaned child, Gabby is determined to see herself and her tortured family to safety on the mainland. But without her epilepsy medication, her condition is a ticking time bomb.

Zon. Hungry for power, Zon appoints himself as leader of the fracturing group. When a reckless decision leads to a deadly accident, he finds himself at the mercy of the island and those he tried to control.

Tempers are high. Supplies are low. Will the group shatter into chaos? Or will the island's deadly secrets destroy all they have left?

Find out in this gripping survival thriller.

FERAL FATE is the second book in the Waves of Fate series.

Jagged Edge

A grieving detective with nothing to lose.
A dying town with everything to hide.

After the shocking death of his daughter, suspended detective Edge Malone who seeks oblivion in a bottle and plans to photograph a rare blood moon in isolated Whispering Hills, California. But his night takes a deadly turn when a high-tech drone is shot from the sky—and a ruthless gunman murders an innocent bystander who dares to visit the crash site. Driven by instinct, Edge seizes the drone and escapes into the woods.

Now being hunted, Edge unwittingly thrusts Nina Hamilton into the chase—a street-smart beauty who is no stranger to men with dangerous motives. But when the drone data leads them to a shocking discovery, they quickly learn that no one in Whispering Hills can be trusted. The truth of the small town is anything but quiet, and the price of secrets runs six-feet deep…

Jagged Edge is a full-length, stand-alone thriller that will have you turning the pages all night long.

Lost In Kakadu

Together, they survived the plane crash. Now the real danger begins.

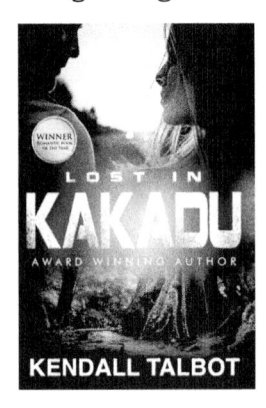

Socialite, Abigail Mulholland, has spent a lifetime surrounded in luxury… until her scenic flight plummets into the remote Australian wilderness. When rescue doesn't come, she finds herself thrust into a world of deadly snakes and primitive conditions in a landscape that is both brutal and beautiful. But trekking the wilds of Kakadu means fighting two wars—one against the elements, and the other against the magnetic pull she feels toward fellow survivor Mackenzie, a much younger man.

Mackenzie Steel had finally achieved his dreams of becoming a five-star chef when his much-anticipated joy flight turned each day into a waking nightmare. But years of pain and grief have left Mackenzie no stranger to a harsh life. As he battles his demons in the wild, he finds he has a new struggle on his hands: his growing feelings for Abigail, a woman who is as frustratingly naïve as she is funny.

Fate brought them together. Nature may tear them apart. But one thing is certain—love is as unpredictable as Kakadu, and survival is just the beginning…

Lost in Kakadu is a gripping action-adventure novel set deep in Australia's rugged Kakadu National Park. Winner of the Romantic Book of the Year in 2014, this full-length,

stand-alone novel is an extraordinary story of endurance, grief, survival and undying love.

Extreme Limit

Two lovers frozen in ice. One dangerous expedition.

Holly Parmenter doesn't remember the helicopter crash that claimed the life of her fiancé and left her in a coma. The only details she does remember from that fateful day haunt her—two mysterious bodies sealed within the ice, dressed for dinner rather than a dangerous hike up the Canadian Rockies.

No one believes Holly's story about the couple encased deep in the icy crevasse. Instead, she's wrongly accused of murdering her fiancé for his million-dollar estate. Desperate to uncover the truth about the bodies and to prove her innocence, Holly resolves to climb the treacherous mountain and return to the crash site. But to do that she'll need the help of Oliver, a handsome rock-climbing specialist who has his own questions about Holly's motives.

When a documentary about an unsolved kidnapping offers clues as to the identity of the frozen bodies, it's no longer just Oliver and Holly heading to the dangerous mountaintop . . . there's also a killer, who'll stop at nothing to keep the case cold.

Will a harrowing trip to the icy crevasse bring Holly and Oliver the answers they seek? Or will disaster strike twice, claiming all Holly has left?

***Extreme Limit* is a thrilling, stand-alone, action-adventure novel with a dash of romance set high in the Canadian Rockies.**

Deadly Twist

An ancient Mayan Temple. A dark family secret. A desperate fight for survival.

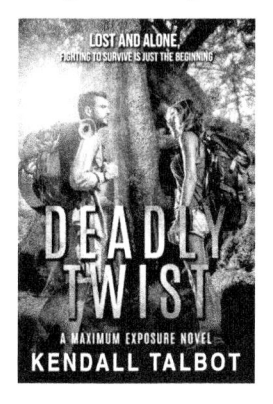

When a mysterious ancient Mayan temple is discovered by a team of explorers deep in the Yucatan jungle, the world is entranced. But Liliana Bennett is shocked by the images sweeping the headlines. She's seen the temple before, drawn in detail, in her late father's secret journal.

Now, the explorers at Agulinta aren't the only ones digging up secrets. Liliana is consumed by the mysteries surrounding her father's sketches and, refusing to believe she's out of her depth, she heads to Mexico, determined to see the temple for herself.

To reach the heart of the jungle, she'll have to join forces with Carter Logan, a nature photographer with a restless heart and secrets of his own. But a journey to Agulinta means battling crocodiles, lethal drug runners, and an unforgiving Mother Nature.

Lost and alone, they stumble upon something they should never have seen. Liliana's quest for answers becomes a desperate race to stay alive. Will Agulinta be the key to their survival? Or will Carter and Liliana become victims to the cruel relentless jungle and the evil men lurking within?

***Deadly Twist* is a gripping, stand-alone, action-adventure novel with a dash of romance, set deep in Mexico's Yucatan Jungle.**

Zero Escape

To survive, Charlene must accept that her whole life was a lie.

For twenty years, Charlene Bailey has been living by the same mantra: pay in cash, keep only what you can carry, trust no one and always be ready to run. That is until her father is brutally murdered in New Orleans by a woman screaming a language Charlene doesn't understand. When police reveal the man she'd known all her life was not her biological father, Charlene is swept up in a riptide of dark secrets and deadly crimes.

The key to her true identity lies in a dangerous Cuban compound run by a lethal kingpin, but Charlene can't reach it alone. After a life of relying on herself, she'll have to trust Marshall Crow, a tough-as-nails ex-Navy man, to smuggle her into Havana.

The answers to Charlene's past are as dark as the waters she and Marshall must navigate, but a killer in the shadows will stop at nothing to drown the truth.

Zero Escape is a heart-pounding, stand-alone, action-adventure novel with a dash of romance that crosses from New Orleans to the back streets of Havana, Cuba.

Treasured Secrets

Sunken treasures. Dangerous enemies. Action-packed romantic suspense.

When Italian chef Rosalina Calucci finds a clue to an ancient treasure, she makes the mistake of bringing it to rogue treasure hunter Archer Mahoney, a dangerously sexy, frustratingly irresponsible, Australian millionaire. Something she knows all too well since he's also her ex-fiancé, and it was his secrets that tore them apart.

Archer Mahoney, will do anything to drown out his painful past; breaking up with the irresistible, smokey-eyed, woman of his dreams is proof of that. But his talent for finding lost treasure is almost as good as his talent for finding trouble and his feisty ex is just the beginning.

Rosalina's clue could be the key to locating an ancient treasure that's haunted Archer for years. But some treasures are buried in blood, and a deadly enemy will stop at nothing to keep a sinful secret contained. Can they mend the ocean between them, or will Rosalina's quest for answers be just the beginning to Archer's nightmare?

Get ready for the adventure of a lifetime, with a happily ever after guaranteed. Treasured secrets is book one in a steamy romantic suspense Treasure Hunters series, full of drama, danger, and passion. It features a strong heroine and the rugged-yet-mischievous millionaire who steals her heart.

Printed in Great Britain
by Amazon